Foul Trouble

ALSO BY JOHN FEINSTEIN

Last Shot: A Final Four Mystery
Vanishing Act: Mystery at the U.S. Open
Cover-Up: Mystery at the Super Bowl
Change-Up: Mystery at the World Series
The Rivalry: Mystery at the Army-Navy Game
Rush for the Gold: Mystery at the Olympics

John Feinstein
Foul Trouble

Alfred A. Knopf
New York

THIS IS A BORZOI BOOK PUBLISHED BY ALFRED A. KNOPF

All rights reserved. Published in the United States by Alfred A. Knopf, an imprint of Random House Children's Books, a division of Random House, Inc., New York.

Knopf, Borzoi Books, and the colophon are registered trademarks of Random House, Inc.

Visit us on the Web! randomhouse.com/teens

Educators and librarians, for a variety of teaching tools, visit us at RHTeachersLibrarians.com

Library of Congress Cataloging-in-Publication Data
Feinstein, John
Foul trouble / John Feinstein.
p. cm
Summary: "College recruiters are clambering to sign up Terrell Jamerson, the #1 high school basketball player in the country. But not all of these recruiters are straight shooters, and Terrell will have to think fast if he wants to stay in the game."—Provided by publisher
ISBN 978-0-375-86964-8 (trade) — ISBN 978-0-375-98246-0 (lib. bdg.) —
ISBN 978-0-375-98454-9 (ebook) — ISBN 978-0-375-87169-6 (pbk.)
[1. Basketball—Fiction. 2. African Americans—Fiction.] I. Title.
PZ7.F3343Fo 2013
[Fic]—dc23
2012042982

The text of this book is set in 12-point Goudy.

Printed in the United States of America

November 2013

10 9 8 7 6 5 4 3 2 1

First Edition

This is for Tom Konchalski and Frank Sullivan—
the two best men in any gym.

PART I

ONE

Sitting in the backseat of his father's jeep, Danny Wilcox was fantasizing about the moves he was going to make going head to head against the top high school basketball players in the country at a showcase summer camp.

Of course, it helped that the best high school player in the country was sitting in the front seat and would be Danny's teammate while he was facing all those *other* top players.

Terrell Jamerson was basketball perfection. Lean, wiry-strong, six foot seven. His jumping ability had been described by one scouting service in a few words: "There's not a high school gym in America that can hold him. Maybe—*maybe*—the Dean Dome or Rupp Arena can hold him." Terrell could dunk with either hand, sucked up rebounds like a vacuum cleaner, and was deadly from the outside—making 47 percent of his three-point attempts.

Danny, by comparison, was six feet tall and could jump reasonably well—"for a white boy," as Terrell liked to put it. He made about 35 percent of his three-point attempts—mostly wide-open shots because Terrell was being double-teamed.

Maybe his most telling stat was that he shot 92 percent from the free throw line. Danny's game was about practice, determination, and smarts. A coach's kid, he'd been around the game all his life. He knew the history, the X's and O's, the options. Which made him a terrific point guard, running the offense for his team. He knew each of his teammates' abilities, knew where the ball should go—usually to Terrell.

Where Danny spent the game analyzing, Terrell just played. He had the kind of raw ability that made his game look effortless.

Danny was fully aware that he was attending this camp because of Terrell. His dad too, really. Andy Wilcox had been the coach at Lexington High School for twelve years and had always produced solid, competitive teams. But everything had changed when Melinda Jamerson had decided to move her son from Hartford, Connecticut, to Lexington, Massachusetts, because she didn't like the environment he was going to school in. As luck would have it, Melinda's decision to move her family had coincided with her son's six-inch growth spurt the previous summer. Suddenly, Terrell Jamerson was unstoppable.

The year before Jamerson arrived, the Lexington Minutemen had gone 17–10. A year later, with Terrell in the lineup, they went 27–3, won a prestigious Christmas tournament in Myrtle Beach, and just missed out on the state title. And that was only because Terrell had fouled out of the championship game.

People had noticed.

By midwinter, Lexington's gym had begun to fill up—not just with fans but with coaches. The college coaches were easy to pick out because they almost always wore a shirt or a sweater in their school colors with the school's name or logo on it. But they weren't the only newcomers. No one from Lexington ever came to see the Minutemen play wearing a suit, but suddenly there were very expensive suits seen in the stands.

"Agents, shoe company reps, bird dogs for agents—you name it, they're there," Danny's dad told him one night at dinner. "None of this is good."

"It isn't?" Danny asked. "Isn't it good that all these people think Terrell can be a star?"

"It doesn't take any kind of genius to see that Terrell can be a star," Andy Wilcox answered. "What he needs is to pick a college and a coach who will care about *him* and not about promoting his own career."

Following that breakout season, Danny knew that Terrell was being bombarded with letters from coaches and with phone calls, emails, texts, tweets, and Facebook messages. Even though the NCAA had all sorts of rules about how much contact coaches could have with high school recruits, it seemed like a flood to him.

It had even spilled over into Danny's life. Realistically, Danny figured his best bet to play in college was at a Division III school. His dad kept pushing him to keep up his grades so he could have a shot at Williams or Amherst, which had high-quality D-3 teams. And there had been some interest from academic-minded Division I schools like nearby Holy Cross and even Harvard. When Danny showed his father the introductory letter from Harvard's coach, Tommy Amaker, his eyes had gone wide. Harvard, like the Division III schools, didn't give athletic scholarships, but his father didn't care. "You find a way to get in there, and I'll find a way to pay for it."

But as Terrell's national profile had broadened, so had Danny's. All of a sudden, he had letters from Kentucky, Indiana, North Carolina, Maryland, and UCLA. Which was weird. Danny knew his game had improved greatly since he started playing with Terrell. But he also knew he wouldn't play very much, if at all, at any of *those* schools.

"It's called a package deal," his father told him. "They know you're Terrell's best friend. If they think that taking you will entice him to come, then they'll give you a scholarship. They always have one or two extra, because there are thirteen scholarships allowed and no one plays more than ten guys."

"So I'd be on the team to help during practice," Danny said.

"You'd be on the team as long as Terrell is on the team," his father answered. "Don't feel bad. You're not the only one. Suddenly, a lot of schools think I have potential as an assistant coach."

It was all so dizzying. In order to try to protect Terrell from the outsiders, as he had started to call them, Andy Wilcox decided to start his own summer league team so he could keep a close eye on Terrell during the summer camps and tournaments where the recruiting process would begin in earnest. At first, the AAU—which ran most of the tournaments—balked, claiming there was no time to certify the new team for the summer. When Andy Wilcox informed the AAU that the only team Terrell Jamerson would play for that summer was the newly formed Rebels, the team was miraculously certified within a couple of weeks.

Coach Wilcox had explained to Terrell that he wanted to coach him because he didn't trust a lot of the AAU coaches who were in charge of summer league teams to watch out for him. Terrell had agreed but then showed up at the house one night appearing upset. "Coach, you've been great to me and to my mom . . . ," he said.

"But?" Andy Wilcox said.

"Some people are sayin' you want to coach me this summer so you can make a name for yourself—maybe get a college job out of it."

"Stay right here," Coach Wilcox said. He stood up and left the room. A moment later he was back, a clutch of papers in his hands. "Read these," he said, handing the papers to Terrell.

Terrell read them, his eyes widening as he did. "All these guys are practically offering you jobs," he said. "Big-time schools too. Whoa."

Coach Wilcox nodded. "So your friends are right—being your coach *does* open up opportunities for me. But I don't want some college job. Terrell, there are a lot of people out there who are trying to get to you. Either directly or through a back door like me. They see you as someone who can help make them rich and maybe even famous someday. I don't want to give you a big head, but when someone like you comes along, people want to get on for the ride. Look at the posse LeBron James has. Those guys are all living on his money and his fame."

"But, Coach, I'm not LeBron. . . ."

"I know you're not, Terrell, and I'm very glad you know you're not. But you have *lots* of potential. No one knows who is going to be the next LeBron James and who is going to be the next Lenny Cooke."

"Who's Lenny Cooke?" Terrell and Danny asked at the same time.

"He was a kid people thought might be as good as LeBron when they were both in high school. I guarantee you, he had as many people hanging on him as LeBron did, and as you do now. I can also guarantee you they're long gone. All these new friends, Terrell—you think if you tear up your knee tomorrow, they're still going to be hanging around? The coaches? The shoe company reps?"

Terrell was quiet for a moment, still staring at the letters. "I get it, Coach."

"You've got a million options, but you have to be careful, Terrell," Coach Wilcox said. He looked at Danny. "We all have to be careful."

* * *

They'd had no problem filling out their new team. Players from all over New England and New York wanted to play with Terrell—they knew they'd get to travel all summer and get plenty of exposure. Sure enough, the Rebels had been invited to start their summer at the Brickley Shoes "School Comes First" Camp in Teaneck, New Jersey.

The name was laughable, but the competition, Danny knew, would not be. Most of the elite players in the country would be there. For sure, Terrell belonged in that class. But did he?

Time to find out, Danny thought as they pulled into the parking lot by the gym.

TWO

Danny knew this camp was a big deal, but he still wasn't prepared for the gaggle of reporters and TV cameras that engulfed them as they parked in front of the Rothman Center, on the campus of Fairleigh Dickinson University. And judging from the look on Terrell's face, he wasn't ready, either.

"Coach, can we just get Terrell for a quick moment?" asked someone who was wearing a suit (and yet somehow not pouring sweat in the summer heat).

"I need a moment too, if that's okay," said a very attractive dark-haired woman, who had a cameraman right behind her.

Coach Wilcox held up a hand. "Hang on, hang on," he said. "First, we need to get inside and get registered. Second, I believe there are specific rules on media contact with the players during the camp."

"Camp hasn't started yet, Coach," said someone dressed a lot more casually. He held a notebook in his right hand. "You can say no if you want, but you can't hide behind any rules to do it."

Danny saw a flash of anger in his dad's eyes. "Who are you?" he asked, turning toward the notebook toter.

"Bobby Kelleher," the guy replied. "I'm with the *Washington Herald*. I really don't need to talk to Terrell. I just want to see how you're going to handle everyone *else* who wants to talk to him."

Danny saw the angry look in his dad's eyes fade just a bit. "I know who you are," he said to Kelleher. "You and Bob Ryan are friends, right?"

That got Danny's attention. Bob Ryan had been a columnist at the *Boston Globe* forever. For as long as Danny could remember, a lot of his mornings had started with his dad shoving the paper across the kitchen table at him and saying, "Read Ryan." When Bob Ryan had come to one of the playoff games to write about Terrell, Coach Wilcox had spent a long time talking to him after the game.

"I've known Bob for years," Kelleher said. "He's one of my role models in life."

"As he should be." Andy Wilcox nodded.

"Coach, what about talking to Terrell?" the guy in the suit said, breaking in.

Danny's dad shook his head. "Not now. We really *do* have to register, and we're arriving later than I'd planned. But he'll talk after we play our first game today. At least, that's what the guys running the camp told me yesterday."

That seemed to satisfy everyone for the moment—except for Kelleher, who fell into stride with Coach Wilcox. "Andy, can I grab your cell number?" he said quietly.

"Mine? Why would you want my number?" Danny heard his dad say.

"Because I'd rather have it and not need it than not have it and need it," Kelleher answered.

That was apparently a good enough response. Danny was still smiling about Kelleher's line when they reached the next barricade. Standing outside the back door to the gym was the group of five young men whom Danny had taken to calling the dudes. These guys were like Terrell's fan club, or something, coming to every game, hanging with him all the time.

"Yo, dude, we thought maybe you weren't coming," Maurice, the unofficial dude leader, said as Terrell, Danny, and Coach Wilcox approached. He gave Terrell a hug and one of those silly soul shakes that had gone out of style about twenty years ago.

"I can't believe you guys *did* come," Terrell said, but Danny thought he looked pleased.

The dudes were an interesting mix, almost out of the "hoops hangers-on" catalog. There were two white guys, two African Americans, and an Asian American who always seemed to be wearing a T-shirt that said "Yao Rules," with a photo of Yao Ming, the seven-foot six-inch retired Houston Rockets center, on it.

Maurice politely shook hands with Coach Wilcox and pointedly ignored Danny.

"Hey, Mo, you remember Danny, right?" Terrell said.

"Yeah," Maurice said sullenly, somehow managing to

put his hand out. When Danny shook it, he got a cold fish. He knew he should just shut up and keep moving, but he couldn't resist. "Dude, no hug, no soul shake for me?" he asked.

Maurice said nothing. The other dudes glared at Danny—who glared right back.

"Okay, let's get going," Danny's dad said. "We need to register. Maurice . . . guys . . . nice to see you, as always."

There were nods back and forth, and the other dudes gave Terrell quick hugs as he, Danny, and Danny's father made their way—finally—to the gym. Once inside, Danny breathed a sigh of relief. For one thing, the air-conditioning felt great.

There was a man in a Brickley Shoes sweat suit standing just inside the door. "Coach Wilcox, welcome," he said. "Over there, to the right, you guys can sign in and get your schedules and all your gear."

That sounded good to Danny. If he got nothing else out of this camp, he knew he would get a lot of Brickley gear. Except they weren't quite finished running the pre-registration gauntlet. Standing between the three of them and the registration desk was another man in a Brickley outfit and a middle-aged man who looked completely out of place in a pinstriped suit.

"Andy, Terrell, Danny . . . you guys made it," the Brickley guy said, shaking hands with Danny's dad. "We were getting worried about you."

"Little bit of traffic on the Tappan Zee," Coach Wilcox

said. "We've still got an hour before we play, right? I know our other kids are here and ready to go." He turned to Danny and Terrell. "Guys, this is Billy Tommasino. He's the camp director."

Tommasino looked to be about sixty. He had gray hair, a good-size paunch, and a ready smile. He shook hands with Danny and Terrell and then turned to the guy in the suit.

"Coach, fellas . . . this is Paul Judson. He's a vice president of Pro Styles, the management company that helps us market the camp and what we try to do to help youngsters. He just wanted to say hello to you guys."

Judson looked like a young politician to Danny. The suit was clearly expensive, and so was his haircut. He shook hands warmly with all three of them. "A real pleasure. Coach, I've really admired the way you've handled all the attention this past year. A lot of people in your position in the past haven't always put their kids first. That's clearly been your intent right from the beginning."

Danny wanted to ask Judson when "the beginning" had been, but his dad just smiled and said, "That's kind of you to say."

Judson was on a roll. "Anything we can do to help out now or in the future, please let me know." He whipped a card from his pocket. Instead of accepting it, though, Coach Wilcox jumped backward, as if the card was electrified.

"Whoa there! Thanks but no thanks," he said. "Honestly, I'm not sure I haven't already violated some NCAA rule by letting you shake hands with these two kids, and I *know* opening up a dialogue with an agent is not a road I want to go down."

Judson was still smiling, the card hanging off his fingertips, but the dripping phony charm quickly went down a notch. "Coach, I know the rules," he said. "I play by the rules. Check around. I'm not one of those agents who gets kids declared ineligible. The players I represent are the highest-quality young men. *You* are not a recruit. *You* have the right to deal with anyone you choose. Please don't think I'd do anything to jeopardize Terrell. I'd just like to be helpful to you two in any way I can."

"But not me, huh?" Danny said. "Not quite a high-enough-quality young man for you?"

Now Judson's smile was gone. "I didn't mean it that way," he said. "What I meant was—"

"We know how you meant it," Coach Wilcox said, his voice icy, the way it got when he was really angry but didn't want to shout. "We need to go register." He shot a disgusted look at Tommasino, and the three of them continued their torturous trip to the registration table.

"Danny, try not to antagonize everyone, okay?" Coach Wilcox grumbled under his breath.

"But, Dad, what a sleaze—"

"I know, but still. Let's make our biggest impression on the court, shall we?"

Danny and Terrell veered to the right, to the line marked "Player Check-in," while Danny's father headed for the coaches' check-in line. A smiling young woman in a Brickley outfit greeted them cheerily. "Welcome, gentlemen," she said. "Find your name on the list and sign in. We've got gifts for you."

A few moments later, now carrying massive red-and-blue Brickley bags that were stuffed with shirts and caps and sweatshirts and jackets and a brand-new pair of Brickley shoes—each player had sent in his shoe size with his application form for the camp—Danny and Terrell headed in the direction of the locker room.

Danny's dad had to go to a coaches' meeting. He told Danny and Terrell to find the rest of their teammates and tell them that they were playing on court two at 2:00 and that they should meet there at 1:30 to warm up and have their pregame talk.

Because there were twenty teams invited to the camp, with more than two hundred players, locker-room space was at a premium. Half the players were assigned to one locker room and half to the other. A lot of players would have to throw their clothes on benches or take them out to the court.

As they walked across the gym to the locker room, Danny could see that the Rothman Center had been set up with three courts running east to west, between the bleachers. He assumed that when Fairleigh Dickinson played, a single court was laid out north to south, with bleachers at each end as well.

There would be three sessions each day, and each session consisted of a total of six games, with three games being played simultaneously. In the morning session, there'd be three games at 9:00 and then another three at 10:30; in the afternoon session, the games would be played at 2:00 and 3:30; and the night session had games at 7:00 and 8:30. Each team would play seven games in four days—a lot of basketball. The top two teams in each of the four divisions in the camp would advance to the championship bracket on the weekend. Quarterfinals and semifinals would be played on Saturday, with the championship game and also the third-place game on Sunday. UBS's sports cable network was planning to televise the championship game. The thought of it made Danny tingle with excitement and nerves.

"Man, look at all these people," Terrell said as they crossed the court. "Games don't start for another hour, and this place is packed."

He was right. The bleachers were almost full. On one side of the court—opposite where the players who weren't involved in a game would be seated—were all the college coaches. They were easy to recognize because of their school colors.

Danny caught himself gaping at the sight of Roy Williams and Mike Krzyzewski, two of the sport's archrivals, laughing as they talked.

Terrell elbowed Danny and said, "Who's the black coach with Pitino?"

Danny smiled. There were advantages to having grown up with a basketball-obsessed father—he could pretty much identify any coach in the building. "That's Anthony Grant," he said to Terrell. "Coach at Alabama. Used to be at Virginia Commonwealth. He's really good. And heading right for us is Frank Sullivan. He's retired, but he used to coach Harvard."

Terrell shot him such a surprised look that Danny laughed. "I only know that one because he's friends with my dad."

Sullivan had a huge smile on his face as he walked up to Danny.

"Danny, I am so proud of you guys," he said, wrapping Danny in a hug. "I know this guy"—he looked at Terrell—"has been great, but your game has come *so* far this past year. . . ."

"It's a lot easier when you're open all the time," Danny said.

Sullivan nodded. "I get it, I get it," he said. He put his hand out to Terrell. "I'm Frank Sullivan," he said. "I work for the America East Conference. More important, I've known Danny since he was about three years old."

"Nice to meet you, sir," Terrell said.

"Coach, what brings you here?" Danny asked.

"Part of my job is to supervise the refs in our conference," Sullivan said. "A lot of the guys who will be working your games are young guys trying to move up the ranks. I'm here to watch them more than you guys—although I'll certainly be paying attention when you're out there playing."

Typical Coach Sullivan, Danny thought. His dad had told him once that if he had a weakness as a coach, it was that he was *too* nice. He just wasn't willing to do some of the cut-throat things a coach had to do to be a star on the college level—even in the Ivy League.

Danny and Terrell shook hands with Coach Sullivan again and then made their way across the court, following a group of players. They walked into a locker room that could comfortably fit about twenty-five people and found about a hundred players milling about.

"Don't even bother looking for a locker," said the guy at the door who was checking to make sure everyone who came in had a badge identifying him as a player. "Find an empty spot, change, and take your bag to the court with you. If you leave it here, I can't promise it'll be waiting when you come back."

"Aren't you supposed to make sure nothing gets stolen?" Terrell said.

"What do I look like, the FBI?" the guy said.

Danny shrugged at Terrell. "We're ten miles from the George Washington Bridge," he said. "Lot of New York attitude around here."

"It's called the real world, kid!" the attendant yelled at Danny's back.

They found an empty spot back near the shower room and began changing. Danny got a little chill when he put on the dark gray jersey he'd been given when he checked in. On the front, in huge red letters, it said "Brickley Shoes." Underneath, in smaller letters, it said "School Is Important— Camp 2012." On the back was another Brickley logo and a number—132—so the college coaches could identify him easily, and, surprise, surprise, the words "Brickley Shoes" (again) at the bottom of the jersey. If you turned it inside out, you had the identical jersey—only in white. The Rebels were designated as the visitors for their opening game, which would be against a team from California called the Orange Crushes. When they were the home team, they would simply reverse the jerseys and play in white.

"Pretty cool," Terrell said, standing up and smoothing out his jersey. He had number 133, but Danny knew most coaches wouldn't have to check their programs to identify him.

"Yeah, it is," Danny said, realizing again that he was about to play at a level he'd only dreamed about. He recognized a number of the players changing around them. There was little talk or banter. This was *not* your father's summer camp. This was serious business.

"Let's go find the other Rebels," Terrell said with a grin. "I am ready to *play*."

THREE

The gym was even more crowded when they walked back in, and Danny could see that many of the teams that would play in the two o'clock games were already warming up.

"Straight ahead to get to your court," said a security guard in a yellow jacket.

They walked to court two and found the rest of the Rebels warming up at the far end.

"Danny, Terrell . . . about time," called out a massive kid wearing the same kind of gray jersey. He waved at them as they approached. Alan Owens was by far the biggest of the Rebels. He was six foot ten and claimed to weigh 260 pounds, but Danny was convinced he weighed at least 280. He was grinning as they walked up, and the other players on the team, whom Danny and Terrell didn't really know very well, came over to say hello. He remembered Jason Marks as being really fast in their few pre-camp practices. Mike Roth was another point guard, who, he thought (hoped), was not as good as he was. And Ken Medley had a sweet shot.

"Coach Wilcox wants us to meet with him for a couple

minutes," Danny said as handshakes were exchanged. His dad was standing behind the basket talking to Frank Sullivan.

"You mean your *dad* wants to meet with us," said Jay Swanson, a six-foot four-inch shooting guard who happened to be the only other white kid on the team. He had made it clear to Danny during the tryouts for the team that he resented the fact that Danny pretty much had the team made regardless of how he played—at least that was Swanson's view.

"Same guy," Danny said, figuring there'd be plenty of time later to let Swanson know he thought he was an idiot. He gestured at his dad, who was waving them all over.

"Fellas, I want you all to meet Frank Sullivan," Coach Wilcox said as they formed a semicircle around him. "He's been a coach at Harvard, and he's scouted at this camp and many others. Frank knows all those coaches you're trying to impress and what they look for. So listen up, because he can help you."

They all turned to Sullivan, who smiled and said, "I know Harvard won't impress most of you guys, but I do have a pretty good idea what every coach in this camp is looking for. First, more than anything: team players. Everyone knows all you guys can dunk with one hand."

Danny almost laughed out loud at that one. He could dunk with one hand—standing on a ladder.

Sullivan seemed to read his mind, because he shot him a quick smile before continuing. "Most guys come to this camp thinking, 'I'm going to show these coaches what I can do.' If they're looking at you, they already know what you can do as an athlete. They want to see what you can do as a *basketball player*. There's a difference. A basketball player helps on defense, finds the open man, and sets good hard screens to get other guys open. An athlete goes one on three and makes a spectacular play but then turns it over the next three times he tries the same move. He hears the applause for the spectacular play, but believe me, the coaches see the turnovers."

He paused, started to say something else, and then looked around the semicircle. He was losing his audience. Some of the players were staring at the floor, and others were glancing around the gym. The one person who had his eyes locked on him was Terrell Jamerson.

"Okay, guys, enough from the old coach's textbook. Have fun out there," Coach Sullivan said, wrapping up.

When he was finished, Danny's dad told them to go get warmed up. As soon as they got into layup lines, Jay Swanson grabbed one of the balls being fed to them by the little kids who were acting as ball boys, took two dribbles, and dunked with one hand. "Tell your father's pal that coaches *do* notice a six-four white kid who can dunk with one hand," he said as he ran past Danny.

Already Danny knew one thing: Being Jay Swanson's teammate for the next week wasn't going to be much fun.

* * *

The team they were playing was supposedly from South-ern California, but they had apparently recruited a couple of ringers from Las Vegas. And their best player was Omar Whytlaw, from Chicago.

When Terrell had noticed Whytlaw's name on the Crushes' roster, he had asked Coach Wilcox about it.

"Highest bidder, I'd guess," he said. "I'm new to this, Ter-rell, but a lot of the best guys you'll face are playing for pay already."

"Don't they worry about the NCAA catching them?" Terrell had asked.

Coach Wilcox shook his head. "*I'd* be worried. But there are plenty of people who'll tell you different."

Whytlaw was similar to Terrell—perhaps an inch shorter but with a reputation as a better shooter. While Terrell had yet to talk publicly about any college he might be interested in playing for, Whytlaw had already announced five final-ists in what one of the ESPN recruiting gurus had dubbed "The War for Whytlaw." They were, as you might expect, powerhouses: Kentucky, North Carolina, UCLA, Florida, and—the one surprise—East Texas, a school best known until recently for having a great fencing team.

As the teams walked out for the tip-off, Danny noticed that the court was completely surrounded. It appeared that 80 percent of the people in the gym were watching court two. No doubt about it, the Jamerson-Whytlaw showdown on the very first day of the camp was the reason.

The game didn't start very well for the Rebels. Danny

tried to throw a pass on the wing to Terrell on the opening possession, but Whytlaw stepped right into the passing lane and caught the ball. He roared down the court, with Danny angling to cut him off for a second before realizing it was futile. Whytlaw leaped in the air at about the foul line, hung there à la Michael Jordan, and dunked with his right hand, his arm seeming to come out of the ceiling as the ball went through the net.

Danny heard the gym explode with noise. Maybe the coaches didn't notice one-handed dunks, but everyone else certainly did. This one had been hard to miss.

On the next possession, Terrell caught a pass in the post, spun on Whytlaw, and tried a five-foot bank shot. The problem was, the shot went about eight feet. One of the other Crushes grabbed the ball, and the Orange County kids hurtled down the court. Their point guard put his head down to go into the lane, and Danny tried to take a charge. He was lying on the floor when he heard another roar. The point guard had dropped the ball off to Whytlaw, who had gone in for another thunderous dunk.

Danny sat up and saw one of the officials indicate a time-out—he was pointing at Danny's dad, who had called it from the bench. The Crush point guard offered his hand to help him up. Over the din Danny heard him say, "You're not playin' in the suburbs anymore. This is real ball. Try to take another charge on me, and I'll put you through the freakin' floor."

Danny turned and jogged to his team's huddle.

"All of you, *calm down!*" his dad said, his palms down. "Stop worrying about what the coaches are thinking about you—just worry about playing a basketball game. You have to make these guys play defense. Terrell, that means you don't take the first shot available because you're trying to show everyone you're better than Whytlaw. And Danny, take care of the damn basketball!"

Danny knew his dad was angry—he hardly ever swore. He looked at Terrell, who nodded at him as if to say, *I'm okay now.*

Danny took a deep breath. Even though this was just a camp game, one in which the result meant little, he now understood that it was going to be as intense as anything he'd ever experienced. *Well,* he said to himself, *that's why you're here—to find out if you can play with guys like this.*

The Crushes had switched to full-court pressure. Clearly, their intent was to blow out and humiliate the Rebels in the first five minutes of the game. As soon as Danny caught the inbounds pass, he was double-teamed. This time, though, he didn't panic. He remembered what he'd been coached to do for years and years by his dad.

He could almost hear his dad's voice in his head talking him through it: "Don't try to dribble through a double-team. Ball-fake. Use their emotion against them." Danny pivoted as if to throw a crosscourt pass and put the ball behind his head as if to throw it. Both defenders leaped in that direction. That gave Danny a clear lane to look upcourt, where he saw Terrell streaking behind Whytlaw. Danny looped a pass in Terrell's direction as if he was an NFL wide receiver coming open on a post pattern. Terrell caught the ball in stride at the head of the key, took one dribble, and flew—Danny thought he actually *did* fly—in the direction of the hoop before slamming the ball through with his right hand.

The gym exploded with every bit as much glee as it had on Whytlaw's two dunks. They wanted to see a show.

Okay, Danny thought as he set himself in a defensive stance, *we'll give them one.*

What happened over the next seventy-five minutes was the kind of basketball game Danny had often fantasized about taking part in. There were no easy possessions at either end of the court. Every pass was contested, every shot, every rebound. The pace of the game was so fast, there was no need for a shot clock.

At halftime, the Crushes led, 47–44—a lot of scoring for just sixteen minutes of basketball. The break was only five minutes, so the players from both teams simply rested on their benches. Danny remembered reading in the camp brochure that the only game all week that would have a regulation fifteen-minute halftime was the championship game, and that game was being televised.

Coach Wilcox talked to the players briefly before the second half began. "Look, guys, they're going to try to play even faster this half," he said. "They're not happy that we're only down three. They don't just want to win this game;

they want to win by twenty and show people right away they're the best team in the camp."

He knelt down on one knee and looked at the players staring back at him. "The way we win is we use that against them. If you're patient—just a little bit patient—they'll overcommit trying to steal passes and making things happen fast. Just wait, ball-fake every once in a while, and good things will happen."

Danny looked around at the other players and realized that only he and Terrell were paying any attention at all. The buzzer went off, and it was time to play again.

"Hey, Wilcox." It was Swanson.

"What?"

"What's your old man doing, trying to get a job or something? Doesn't he know this camp isn't about winning? It's about showing the scouts what you can do."

"Showing the scouts that you can help your team win isn't a bad thing, Swanson," Danny said, turning to the official who was handing him the ball so he could inbound to start the second half. It was a good thing Jay Swanson was such a good player, Danny thought. Otherwise, there would be no reason for him to exist.

The second half was much like the first, except the Rebels didn't come out playing scared. A three by Swanson—who, Danny had to admit, could *really* shoot—put them up for the first time at 52–51. Looking around, Danny could tell that just about everyone in the gym was watching their game.

Early in the fourth quarter, with the game tied at 76, Terrell was double-teamed near the basket and quickly passed the ball to the perimeter to Swanson. But one of the Crushes got a hand on the ball, and Swanson had to run it down near the sideline. Trapped, he found Danny, who had alertly come to the ball-side in order to help. Danny caught the pass wide open and went up to shoot. But the ball caromed off the rim, and the Crushes grabbed the rebound.

As Danny sprinted back on defense, he saw Swanson jogging back. His man flashed past him. The Crushes' point guard quickly found him on the left side, and he went in uncontested for a layup that would not have happened if Swanson had run back.

"Swanson, you have to get back!" Danny screamed as he took the inbound pass and started back up court.

"If you could make a shot, I wouldn't have to run back."

For just an instant, Danny forgot where he was or how many people were watching. He snapped a pass in Swanson's direction that would have been perfect had it been thrown from twenty feet away. But he was no more than eight feet from Swanson, and the ball caught him square in the face, knocking him over.

Danny didn't even notice the Crush player picking the ball up and heading the other way for another easy layup. Neither did Swanson, who jumped to his feet, face red, and ran straight at Danny. The two of them went down in a heap, and Danny felt Swanson's fist catch him on the side of the face.

People were reaching in to pull them apart. Danny didn't try too hard to keep the fight going, because Swanson was bigger and stronger than he was. The officials and coaches stepped in between the two of them. One of the officials turned to Danny's dad. "Coach, I can't eject players from the same team for fighting each other," he said. "But I'd suggest you get them out and cool them down for a while."

"You've got it," Coach Wilcox said. "Give me a time-out."

"Time-out," the ref called, blowing his whistle. "Coach, you've only got one left."

"Everybody back to the bench," Coach Wilcox ordered.

They walked back, the others between Danny and Swanson, just in case either of them had an idea about starting up again.

"Sit!" Coach Wilcox said. "Wilcox, Swanson, you're done for these last five minutes."

"Whaaa!" Swanson said. "I didn't throw the ball in his face—he threw it in mine!"

"Don't be an idiot, Swanson," Terrell said before anyone else could say anything. "You don't loaf back on defense because someone misses a shot and then act like it's not your fault."

"Yeah, go ahead and stand up for your pal," Swanson said.

"Shut up, Swanson!" Danny's dad said. "One more word from you and you won't play in the next game, either!"

That seemed to get Swanson's attention. Mike Roth and Ken Medley were sent into the game. Danny sat at one end of the bench, Swanson at the other. Danny was really angry—at himself, for letting Swanson get to him. He was barely watching the game as it went on, dimly aware that both Terrell and Whytlaw were putting on a show. His dad's voice, screaming "Time-out!" brought him back.

He looked at the scoreboard and blinked. There were twenty-one seconds left, and the Crushes were leading, 94–92. The Rebels had the ball, and his dad had called time to set up a final play. Danny got up for the first time since he had been yanked and stood outside the huddle as his father talked.

"We're going to run a one-four for Terrell," his dad said, drawing on the miniature board he carried with him. It was set up like a basketball court, and he drew a circle out near midcourt that was Terrell and four circles down on the baseline, which was where he wanted the other four players to be to create space for Terrell.

"Terrell, you take what the defense gives you," he continued. "If it's just you and Whytlaw one-on-one, create something for yourself. If they run a double-team at you, find the open guy. Take the best shot—doesn't matter if it's a two off penetration or a three."

Everyone nodded, and the team walked back out. The place was going crazy—the game and the Whytlaw-Jamerson matchup had lived up to what they had all wanted to see.

Mike Roth was inbounding at midcourt. Terrell took a quick jab step toward the basket, then came into the backcourt to take the pass. The other four Rebels headed to the baseline, shadowed by their defenders. Terrell and Whytlaw were left alone, one-on-one, head-to-head. All eyes were on them.

"No help!" Coach Wilcox screamed at Terrell as the clock ticked under ten seconds. He was letting him know that Whytlaw was going to be left to guard him alone. The Crushes' coach knew great theater when he saw it.

Terrell almost smiled at the sound of his coach's voice. He was dribbling patiently, moving in the direction of the key, the clock melting away. Whytlaw came up tight on him.

The clock reached three, and Terrell made a move toward the right of the key. For a moment, Danny wondered if he had lost track of the time. But no. He took two hard dribbles to his right, then crossed over to his left as if he was going to go past Whytlaw that way. Whytlaw scrambled back to block Terrell's path to the basket.

But as Whytlaw went in the direction of the basket, Terrell took one lightning-quick step-back dribble so that he was beyond the three-point line and launched his shot just before the sound of the buzzer echoed through the building.

Danny knew as soon as he let it go that it was going in. He'd seen Terrell's shot-release so many times, he knew it was good the instant it left his hand. The ball swished. The referee's arms were in the air, indicating a three. Danny and seven teammates rushed the court to mob Terrell. It was only while he was pounding Terrell on the shoulders that Danny noticed Swanson, towel around his neck, in front of the bench, watching.

Whytlaw was standing on the edge of the celebration.

Danny and Terrell both noticed him. Whytlaw put out a hand. "Nice move, man," he said. "You're the real deal."

"So are you," Terrell said, and they shook hands.

"Next time, it's me," Whytlaw said, smiling.

"We'll see," Terrell said.

"Yeah, bro, we will," Whytlaw said. "We absolutely will." He turned and walked away.

FOUR

Omar Whytlaw was the only one of the Crushes who stuck around long enough to shake anyone's hand when the game was over. The rest of them just turned and headed to the locker room. Danny thought, *So that's how it's going to be.*

The moment Whytlaw walked away, camp director Billy Tommasino appeared, as if by magic. The agent that Danny's dad had wanted nothing to do with earlier was right by his side.

"Hey, Terrell, great job!" Tommasino said, making Danny feel a little bit like the invisible man. "Look, I've got some security guys right here to get you to the locker room. I don't want anyone bothering you."

"Uh, thanks," Terrell said, a little confused but not unhappy, Danny sensed, with the attention.

Tommasino put his arm around Terrell and walked him in the direction of three beefy security guys in yellow jackets. Judson fell in on the other side. Danny looked around for his dad but couldn't find him. The teams that were playing in the next game on court two had already come out to start their warm-ups. So Danny fell in behind Terrell and his little entourage.

Tommasino hadn't been joking about Terrell needing security. Danny saw lots of familiar faces as they made their way through the gauntlet. There were plenty of coaches, none trying to do anything more than be seen. That, Danny knew, was part of the recruiting game: Let the players see you, even if the rules won't allow you to talk to them at that moment. There were plenty of media types too: Jay Bilas from ESPN gave Terrell a pat on the back and a "Nice playing" as he went past him. Seth Davis, who worked for CBS and *Sports Illustrated*, was standing next to Bilas. Bobby Kelleher was a few feet away, although he didn't even look up when Terrell went by because he was scribbling something in his notebook.

Danny saw the dudes too; they were waiting just outside the door that led to the locker-room hallway, which was off-limits to everyone but the players and coaches. When Terrell saw them, he veered away from the yellow jackets to say hello.

"Dude, that was beyond awesome!" Maurice said, hugging Terrell as if he had just returned from serving overseas. "You showed all those TV dudes who *the man* is in this camp."

"Aw, I made one good shot," Terrell said, exchanging the usual high fives and hugs with the other dudes. "Whytlaw can play. . . ."

"Yo—dude can't *touch* you," said Chao. "I was talking to Bilas and he said it's not even close."

Danny wondered exactly how Chao had ended up in conversation with Jay Bilas. There was no time to ask, though, because Tommasino was practically shoving Terrell forward to keep him away from his buddies. "Terrell's got to go talk to the media," he said. "You'll see him later." He took Terrell's elbow, and the procession started up again.

Danny was about to follow when he felt a hand on his shoulder. It was Maurice. "What are you, his shadow?" Maurice said, nodding in Terrell's direction. "Why don't you go hang out with that other white boy on your team?"

"Other white boy can at least play," said Anthony, who was the number two dude as far as Danny could tell.

"I don't see *you* wearing a uniform," Danny said to Anthony. "And you don't even have the excuse of being white, like Maurice does."

For a split second, Danny thought he was about to get into his second fight in the past hour. But Maurice of all people saved the day. "Good line, white boy," he said, holding up his hand for a high five.

Danny didn't really want to high-five Maurice, but he figured it was better than fighting Anthony. Then he ducked into the hallway before anyone could say anything else.

His dad was waiting. "Danny—there you are. They want you and me and Terrell to go to some kind of interview area before you guys shower and change," he said. "I asked them to make it quick, because it's already been a long day for you both."

"No kidding," Danny said.

Someone in a Brickley uniform hurried up to them and said, "Coach, can you two follow me?"

They walked past the locker room into some kind of meeting room. There was a table at the front of the room, with chairs on one side. In front of each chair was a microphone. Billy Tommasino had somehow reappeared at the podium in the middle of the table. Danny could see at least a half dozen cameras in the back of the room and at least fifty reporters—maybe more—seated in front of the table.

Bobby Kelleher was standing by the door when they walked in. "Hey, Danny," he said, waving him over.

Curious, Danny made a detour.

"First of all, you played a nice game, even if you lost your cool for a minute there," Kelleher said.

"Thanks. I think."

Kelleher smiled. "Second, get comfortable up there, because no one in this room is going to ask you a question."

Danny rolled his eyes and again said, "Thanks. I think"— though he was pretty sure Kelleher was right.

As it turned out, Danny *did* get asked a question—about his fight with Jay Swanson.

The reporters had all been asked to identify themselves before asking their questions. "Danny, I'm Mike Presca from the *Norwalk Evening News*," one of them said, taking the handheld mike that was being passed around the room for questions. Danny sensed trouble. He remembered that Swanson was from Norwalk.

"Can you tell us why you threw the ball in your own teammate's face?" Presca asked.

"I got frustrated," Danny said. "It was a tense game. I didn't feel Jay had gotten back on defense and that he was somehow blaming me for it. I shouldn't have done it."

"Did you apologize to him?" Presca persisted.

"No, he didn't," Danny's dad said before Danny could answer. "Both kids were out of line. That's why I sat them the rest of the game."

"Coach Wilcox, don't you think you're a little biased toward your son?" said Presca, who was now officially getting on Danny's nerves.

"No, I don't," Coach Wilcox said, his voice measured, staring right at Presca, who finally sat down, shaking his head as if something was terribly wrong.

The rest of the questions were for Terrell: about the matchup with Whytlaw, the last shot, all the people watching, and where he stood in his decision on a college. They'd discussed how to answer that question in the car on the way down. "Just say, 'I'm flattered by all the attention from so many great schools,'" Danny's dad had counseled. "And say you'll decide where to make your visits before school starts in the fall."

That was Terrell's answer, almost word-for-word. Naturally, there was a follow-up. "Who will be involved in the decision?"

"My mom," Terrell answered. "And Coach Wilcox."

"That's it?"

"That's enough."

At which point Billy Tommasino jumped in and said, "In fact, that's enough for this session. We need to get these guys a shower."

Danny couldn't have agreed more. Even though he had thrown on one of the Brickley sweatshirts they'd been given, he was starting to shiver a little in the air-conditioning.

They walked back into the hallway and Danny noticed a clock on the wall as they headed for the locker room. It was four o'clock. They had been in New Jersey for all of three hours. It felt more like three days.

The good news about doing the press conference was that the locker room was now close to empty. Almost everyone who had played in the two o'clock games had cleared out, and all the guys playing in the second round of afternoon games were out on the courts.

"Man," Terrell said when they were alone inside. "I knew camp would be intense, but this is crazy."

"And it's only the first day," Danny said.

"I know. I'm beat," Terrell said. He smiled. "And I didn't even get into a fight."

Danny grimaced. "Funny. That guy is a total idiot."

"Yeah," Terrell said. "Tell you what, though, he's got some skills."

Danny sighed. "I know he does. But you're way better than him, and you're not in everyone's face about it. . . ."

"True, I am exceptionally modest," Terrell said, placing his hand over his heart.

"Mm-hmm." Danny couldn't help grinning. "Why is that?"

"Probably because I have friends who keep me in line," Terrell said with a laugh.

"Speaking of, I almost got into it with your pal Anthony outside."

"What are you, a hockey player?" Terrell said. "You just wanna fight with everyone you see? What happened?"

Danny told him, and Terrell laughed again. "They're not bad guys," he said. "They just don't like you."

"Well, that explains it," Danny said.

They showered, dressed, and walked out to the gym. The 3:30 games were wrapping up and the gym was beginning to empty, with people heading out for the dinner break before the evening session began. Danny and Terrell spotted Coach Wilcox standing at the far end of one of the bleachers with Frank Sullivan and a tall man with dark hair who had a thick looseleaf notebook in his hands. Another reporter, Danny figured.

"Danny, Terrell, I want you to meet someone," Frank Sullivan said as they walked up. "This is Tom Konchalski. He knows more about high school basketball than anyone alive."

"Stop it, Frank," Konchalski said. "You're always too kind to me." He reached out to shake hands with Danny and Terrell. "It's a pleasure to meet you both. That was a great win today, especially with Danny sitting out those last few minutes. Danny, you need to remember how much your dad and Terrell need you out there in tight games."

Danny instantly liked Tom Konchalski. For one thing, he hadn't looked right through him to get to Terrell. Plus, he had just said that Danny had an important role to play on the court.

"What do you do, Mr. Konchalski?" Terrell asked.

"I watch a lot of games," Konchalski said. "And, for some reason, people are willing to pay to find out what I think about what I see. It's a real scam, actually."

Frank Sullivan laughed. "This coming from the one guy in this business who *isn't* trying to scam anyone," he said. "Guys, Mr. Konchalski writes the *HSBI Report*, which is, without question, the most respected high school scouting service there is."

"What was it Seth Davis called you a few years ago?" Danny's dad asked.

"Oh, stop," Konchalski said, actually appearing to blush.

"'The only honest man in the gym,'" Sullivan said. "That's what he called you."

"Exaggeration," Konchalski said. "But I do try to tell people what I honestly think."

"So, Mr. Konchalski, what did you think today?" Terrell asked—surprising Danny, because if there was one thing Terrell was not insecure about it was his ability to play basketball.

"I thought you both did some things very well,"

Konchalski said, again impressing Danny by addressing both of them. "Terrell, you're a little bit of a black hole when you get the ball, especially inside. Ball goes in to you, it's never seen again most of the time. If you pass it back out of those double-teams more often, your teammates will get great shots *and* they'll love you for it."

Terrell was listening intently. "Anything else?"

"Yes. I know there isn't much defense played in these camps, but I saw a couple of games you played this winter. You're not guarding anyone at all. You're just playing for steals and blocks. I know Coach doesn't want you in foul trouble, but at the next level, you're going to have to play defense. You need to start working on that now."

Danny had never heard anyone—not even his father—talk to Terrell this way about his game. Most of the time people just gushed. Terrell had scored 41 points and had had 14 rebounds. And yet Konchalski was talking to him about what he was doing wrong. He looked at Terrell for a reaction. If Terrell was upset, he didn't show it.

Konchalski turned to Danny. "I really like your feel for the game, Danny," he said. "But your defense could use some work too. You play the passing lanes well, but you guard with your hands—that's why you had four fouls in a game where the refs called almost nothing. You need to guard with your feet. Get in position, and you won't need to use your hands so much."

"Yes, sir," Danny said, nodding. Foul trouble had been a problem for him in the past.

"And don't be a hothead," Konchalski said. "You can't help your team win sitting on the bench."

"Amen to that," Danny's dad said.

"Hey, we did win the game," Danny said.

"Yes, you certainly did," Konchalski said. "Terrell, you're now officially the sensation of the camp. If you think you had people trying to get close to you before today, just wait until tomorrow."

"You mean it gets worse?" Danny asked.

Konchalski laughed. "Today was like a play opening in New Haven. Tomorrow you're going to be on Broadway." He turned to Danny's dad. "Andy, how many agents did you have to deal with today?"

"Just one—that guy Judson, who's pals with Tommasino," Coach Wilcox said.

"Paul Judson is the Pope compared to what you're going to see after word gets around about today," Konchalski said. "All the bird dogs for all the agents. The bad, the bad, and the ugly—there are no good—will be reporting back. You'll notice it right away when you get here in the morning."

Danny, Terrell, and Coach Wilcox looked at one another.

"On that note," Frank Sullivan said, "how about we go eat? I'm sure you're all starved."

"Starved is right," Terrell said. "And a little bit scared."

"You should be," the only honest man in the gym said. "You should be."

FIVE

Tom Konchalski's prediction that things were going to get more intense proved to be correct. Only they didn't have to wait until the next day.

After dinner at a Houston's in a nearby shopping mall, they drove to the Teaneck Marriott, which was two miles and about a hundred traffic lights from the gym. Brickley apparently had some kind of deal with Marriott, because half the teams were staying in the Teaneck Marriott and the other half were in a Marriott a couple miles—and, no doubt a hundred more lights—down the road.

As soon as they set foot inside the lobby, Danny began to understand what Konchalski had been talking about. The place was teeming with people—all of them, it seemed, in sweat suits of some kind. If there had been a giant sign outside the hotel that said "Terrell Jamerson arriving here tonight at 8 p.m.," there could not possibly have been more people waiting for him, all of them calling his name at once.

Danny saw a look of genuine terror cross Terrell's face. So did his dad, who stepped directly in front of Terrell, turning himself into a human shield. But there was only so much he could do, because people were coming from all directions.

One guy stood out, if only because he was bigger than the others, probably about six foot eight, Danny guessed, and clearly still in playing shape. "T-man!" he said loudly, his voice somehow standing out from the cacophony around him. "You were great today, man. Ate that Whytlaw kid up at the end. Did Chuck reach you? He wanted your cell to give you a call."

While Coach Wilcox was explaining to several of the other worshippers that Terrell needed to get to his room and get to bed because the Rebels were playing at 9:00 the next morning, Terrell looked at the big guy—who was wearing a jet-black sweat suit with an Athena logo stitched neatly on the chest—and said, "Chuck?"

"Barkley," the big guy answered. "Some of the coaches called him today after your game. I think it might have been K or Graber—not sure. He wanted to check in with you in case you need someone to lean on who's been there."

Terrell was staring wide-eyed at the guy. "Charles Barkley?"

"Yeah, man. Give me your cell, and I'll pass it to him. He'll give you a call tomorrow."

Before Terrell could answer, Danny stepped in. Terrell always bailed him out on the court, so he made it his job to help off the court. His dad was now telling someone that Terrell most definitely did *not* want Spike Lee to make a point of coming out to see him this weekend.

"I have a better idea," Danny said. "Why don't you give Chuck's number to Terrell? That way he can call him tomorrow when he's got some downtime between games."

The big guy was looking straight down at Danny as if he had tried to reach into his pocket for his wallet. Which, in a certain sense, he had.

"T, who's this—your valet? Your walk-around guy?"

"I thought you saw the game today, A-man," Danny said. He always felt bolder when he knew someone just out-and-out hated his guts. "I play point guard."

"Who the hell is 'A-man'?"

Danny pointed at the logo on his jacket. "Athena. Isn't that your name?"

A-man was now looking at him as if he was nuts. Danny knew exactly what Athena was: It was one of the fastest rising shoe and apparel companies going, challenging Under Armour in the top-of-the-line category. Everything Athena made was expensive. Danny guessed the outfit A-man was wearing cost at least $500 retail. Although he was fairly certain A-man hadn't paid retail.

"You're funny, little point guard," A-man said. "Why don't you go to your room and let the grown-ups talk?"

"He *is* going to his room. And so is Terrell."

It was Danny's dad, who had always had good peripheral hearing.

A-man looked at Coach Wilcox for a second, then smiled. "That's all good, Coach." He threw his arms around Terrell and gave him a hug as if he were a father sending his son off to college. "I'll see you in the morning, my man. We'll hook you up with Chuck." He nodded at Coach Wilcox, ignored Danny, and walked away.

There were others milling around, waiting to give Terrell a handshake or a slap on the back, but the message had been delivered that Terrell was heading to the elevators and his room. The good news was that Brickley had done precheck-in for everyone and room keys had been part of their camp packet, so there was no need to stop at the front desk.

When they finally made it to the elevator, Danny's dad turned to Danny, pointing a finger. "We're going to have to deal with this all week," he said. "Don't pick fights with everyone. Terrell can take care of himself."

Terrell laughed. "Coach, I'm not so sure you're right. I need all the help I can get."

Coach Wilcox nodded as the elevator stopped at the fifth floor and they got off. "I know. And you're going to get it. But your point guard needs to cool his jets—on the court and off it."

"It's that hockey thing with him," Terrell said. "He always wants to drop the gloves."

"Yeah, well, he needs to stay out of the penalty box," Coach Wilcox said, causing both boys to laugh.

They had reached their rooms: Coach Wilcox was in 507, and Danny and Terrell were across the hall in 508.

"Get a wake-up call," Danny's dad said as he slid his key card into the door. "We need to be out the door at eight."

They both nodded.

When they opened the door to their room, sitting on one of the beds was the biggest fruit basket Danny had ever seen. The envelope on it said "Terrell Jamerson."

"Open the card," Terrell said.

Danny popped the envelope open. The note was typed neatly. "From all your friends with the Charlotte Bobcats. Great going today. Keep it up all week."

"So . . . the Charlotte Bobcats," Terrell said. "Who sent it?"

Danny held the note up in the air. "It's signed 'Mike,'" he said.

Terrell's eyebrows knitted into a question mark. "Mike?"

"Yeah," Danny said. "As in: the owner of the Bobcats. Most people call him Michael. Or Mr. Jordan."

Terrell's eyes went wide, and he sat down heavily on the empty bed. "Shut up."

"I know."

"Michael Jordan sent me fruit?"

"How do you like them apples?" Danny smiled.

"I don't know. Open it up—let's have some."

Danny ripped open the cellophane and tossed Terrell an apple, then took another for himself.

Terrell could barely chew, he was smiling so hard. "Sweet," he said, juice dripping down his chin.

Day two started early. The lobby was quiet except for a few players from other teams with 9:00 a.m. games. Andy Wilcox was sitting with a cup of coffee, reading the newspaper at a table with a spectacular view of the parking lot. "You guys need to hustle through the buffet so we can get going," he said as they started to sit down.

"None of Terrell's fan club around?" Danny said.

"Quit it, Danny," Terrell said.

"Yeah, Danny, quit it," his dad said. "I'm guessing the people you are referring to don't get up this early."

Apparently not. The only ones waiting for them when they pulled into the parking lot at the gym were the dudes. Even they seemed a little bit sleepy. Maurice was sipping from a giant Starbucks cup. "Hey, Terrell—you're going to tear it up today, dude. You should have lunch with us between games," he said as they headed for the back-door entrance.

"Yeah, maybe," Terrell said. "I'll have to check with Coach."

The place was alive with players warming up and coaches huddling with one another to talk. Most of them, Danny noticed, were clutching cups of coffee. He felt as if he needed a jolt of adrenaline himself, but he knew he'd get one when the game began.

As Danny and Terrell crossed the court to the hallway that led to the locker room, Paul Judson, the slick agent they'd met the day before, was blocking their path.

"Morning, guys," he said, trying to sound casual.

They both returned the greeting, and Danny kept moving, hoping that would be the end of the exchange. No such luck. Judson had positioned himself in such a way to make it pretty much impossible for Terrell to get around him and through the doors that led to the hallway.

"Terrell, I hope you have a few free minutes later today," Judson said. "There are some folks who saw the game yesterday who'd really like to meet you."

Before Terrell could answer, Danny jumped in, playing the role of his father. "We've got a tight schedule today," he said.

Judson gave him a smile that looked more like a smirk. "I know the schedule," he said. "I've already talked to Billy T., and he's fine with Terrell taking a few minutes."

Before Danny could answer, Terrell did. "Coach Wilcox decides my schedule, not Mr. Tommasino," he said. "I'll talk to him after we play this game. It'll be up to him."

Judson didn't seem thrilled with that answer, but it was enough to get Terrell and Danny past him and into the hallway.

"Man, this could get old fast," Terrell said as they walked to the locker room.

"You okay?" Danny asked.

"Fine," Terrell said. "I just want to play some ball."

Once again, the area around the court where they were playing was packed. The Rebels were playing a team from Ohio that must have been invited as some kind of favor to the coach. Danny's estimate was that the best player for Team Tire (they were from Akron) might have been about the eighth best player on the Rebels. The fact that he was able to go past the point guard at will whenever he wanted to told him early on that it was going to be an easy morning.

Terrell scored 32 points in twenty-four minutes. Danny actually had 16 and 12 assists, plus, most important to his dad, only one turnover. With the score 70–35 after the third quarter, Coach Wilcox ordered his players to make at least five passes before shooting on every possession to slow the game down. When Jay Swanson grabbed a rebound and went the length of the court with ease to dunk on the hapless Tires—who were looking *very* tired at that point— Coach Wilcox called time-out.

When the players reached the huddle, their coach was red-faced. "Swanson, you need to understand something," he said, his tone low but full of anger. "I don't care if we win this tournament or if we don't win another game. So don't think being one of the best players means you're going to play. Because if you ever disobey an instruction like that again, I promise that you won't play the rest of that game or in the next one, either. I told you guys *five passes!*"

"But, Coach, no one stopped me—"

"No one on that team has stopped anyone all day. You don't humiliate helpless kids like that. It isn't their fault that they don't belong here."

"It's not my fault, either, Coach."

The horn blew, ending the time-out. Swanson stayed in the game. Danny knew what his father was doing. Rather than bench Swanson, he wanted to test him. The next time the Rebels got the ball, Danny quickly snapped a pass to Swanson, who had come open on the wing. Swanson instantly passed the ball back to him without so much as a glance at the basket. Message received—at least for the moment.

As soon as the game ended, Terrell was whisked away by Billy Tommasino and the now-familiar coterie of security people. When Danny's dad asked Tommasino if he or any of the other players had been requested by the media, Tommasino gave him a disdainful look. "Coach, the media really isn't that interested in you."

He turned to follow Terrell and the security guys across the court. Danny looked at his dad. "What do you think that was about?" he asked.

"My guess is your conversation with Judson before the game was quickly relayed back to him." Danny had let his father know what had happened before the game began.

"But it was *Terrell* who told Judson you were in charge of his schedule, not you."

His dad smiled. "Danny, what do you think the chances are that any of these people are going to get mad at Terrell about anything?"

"Mmm," Danny said. "If it makes you feel better, I find you very interesting."

"That does make me feel better," his dad said. "Come on, you get into the shower while I go make sure Terrell isn't getting devoured by the wolves in there."

As they walked back down the hallway, Danny was convinced he heard howling all around him. The wolves weren't baying at the door; they were in control of the door.

SIX

Danny was hoping to get in and out of the shower and back to the gym. The Orange Crushes were playing in one of the 10:30 games. The buzz in the locker room that morning was that there were three teams that people had already decided were head-and-shoulders above the others in the camp: the Rebels, the Crushes, and a team from Mississippi called the Riverboats, which had two players who were being recruited by everyone in the country.

The Riverboats had also played a nine o'clock game, and as Danny was pulling off his jersey, someone dressing in the same row was pulling on a Riverboats T-shirt. Seeing Danny looking at him, he smiled and put out his hand. "Alex Mayer," he said.

"Danny Wilcox," Danny said, taking Mayer's hand.

"I know who you are," Mayer said. "Watched the second half of your game yesterday. I'd have done the same thing to that kid—what's his name, Swanson?—that you did."

"I lost my cool."

"Can't blame you. That was some finish, though. Your guy Terrell is the deal."

"Yeah, he is. I almost feel sorry for him right now, though. He can't turn around without five people in his face wanting to be his new best friend."

Mayer laughed. "I can only imagine. Even at my level it can get pretty obnoxious."

"Who's recruiting you?" Danny asked.

"Ah, you know—the usual suspects."

"'Usual suspects'?"

Mayer shrugged, clearly a little embarrassed. "Yeah. I guess I'm down to Duke, North Carolina, Kansas, and UCLA. I decided against Kentucky because they recruit so many one-and-dones. I'd like to have a chance to get to know my teammates."

"One-and-done" had become as much a basketball term in recent years as "jump shot" or "slam dunk." The NBA had established a rule saying that players had to go to college for at least one year before declaring for the draft. So now a lot of the elite players did just that—one year of college. Kentucky coach John Calipari had made one-and-dones his specialty.

Danny realized that Mayer must be one of the two stars from the Riverboats he had been hearing about. Mayer was probably six foot three, but he had long arms.

"Quite a list," Danny said.

Mayer shrugged again. "Actually, the kid who's playing up front with me this week is the one everybody wants. He might not be as good as Terrell or Omar, but he's not far behind. He's good enough to be a one-and-done, but he says he wants to stay at least three years wherever he goes."

Danny knew who Mayer was talking about because the player's name was impossible to forget: Michael Jordan. He was originally from Greenville, North Carolina—a town not far from where the real Michael Jordan had grown up—and he had moved to Covington, Kentucky, for high school. Danny had seen a *SportsCenter* feature on the fact that the entire state of Kentucky was obsessed with Coach Cal's recruitment of the "new" Michael Jordan.

Naturally, Jordan was being recruited by all the usual suspects also, including North Carolina, the real Michael Jordan's alma mater.

"Is Jordan going to go to Kentucky?" Danny asked.

"Don't think so," Mayer said. "Same reason as me—even though he'd be a lottery pick if he left after one year. He has a pretty good sense of humor about it all. Told me he might go to Duke just to make North Carolina fans root *against* Michael Jordan."

That was *funny*, Danny thought.

"So you guys could end up together," Danny said.

"Maybe," Mayer said. "We've had more than a few coaches approach us about being a package deal."

"I'm guessing you're talking about a real *deal*," Danny said.

Mayer rolled his eyes. "Seems like it. To be honest, it's hard to know, exactly. No coach will ever offer you anything directly—they're too smart to be that obvious. It's always one of those guys hanging from the rafters of this building every day. I had a guy I thought was a friend try to get me to visit a school I wasn't interested in. When I told him no, he started begging me and finally told me he'd been offered ten grand if he got me to visit."

"Ten grand just to visit?"

"Yup."

"So I'm guessing this guy became a close friend *after* people started recruiting you."

"Yup. Lesson learned. Then there's this guy Judson. I'm sure he's hit on you guys, right? He's all over us. Told Michael yesterday he would love to help the two of us choose a school. He said he likes to think of himself as an 'educational consultant.'"

Danny laughed out loud and then noticed he was getting looks from some other players in the locker room. "That's sort of like Kentucky calling their one-and-done guys 'student-athletes,' right?"

Mayer was nodding in agreement when someone called his name. "Alex, we gotta go do this thing with Tommasino."

"Danny Wilcox, Michael Jordan," Mayer said.

Jordan, who looked to be about six foot six, extended a huge hand and said, "Terrell Jamerson's point guard, right?"

Danny laughed. "Actually, that's my full name, Danny Wilcox, Terrell Jamerson's point guard."

"You could be called a lot worse," Jordan said, smiling.

"You got that right."

Jordan looked at Mayer. "Ready? They're outside waiting on us."

"Yeah, yeah," Mayer said. He looked at Danny. "We have

to go do some video promo thing about how great the camp is. Not sure how Tommasino talked our coach into it . . ."

"I am," Jordan said, shaking his head.

Mayer took his phone out. "Give me your cell," he said to Danny. "I'll send you a text, and then we'll have each other's numbers."

As they left, Danny looked at the clock. He needed to take a *really* fast shower. The time had been worth it, though. The more people he talked to, the more he learned about the world he, his dad, and Terrell were now living in. And what a strange world it was. . . .

Danny's dad was waiting for him outside the locker room.

"Did you take a shower or write a book while you were in there?" he asked.

"I could write a book about this place," Danny said.

"So where's Terrell?" his dad asked.

"Isn't he with you?"

"He was. I talked to him after his press conference. He said he was going to shower. That was fifteen minutes ago. You didn't see him in the locker room?"

"No, but maybe I missed him—although I don't see how. It isn't that big in there."

They walked back inside together and called Terrell's name. One of the players from the Akron team was walking out as they were walking in. "You looking for Jamerson?" he asked.

"Yes," Danny said.

"I saw him come in about ten minutes ago. He changed his shirt and went back out."

Danny and his dad looked at one another quizzically. Why would Terrell not shower? And where had he gone? "Let's go back onto the court and see if he's there," Danny suggested. "If not, I can call his cell."

"Or text," his dad said, which made Danny laugh, since his dad couldn't send a text if his life depended on it.

They walked back outside. The 10:30 games were under way, and the place was packed. Still, picking Terrell out would not be that difficult. Chances were good he'd be surrounded by all sorts of people.

Except he wasn't anywhere to be found. They bumped into Frank Sullivan and asked him if he'd seen Terrell.

"Yeah, a few minutes ago," Frank said. "He was going out the side door with those kids who were hanging around yesterday. Maybe someone else too—I'm not positive."

Danny's dad pointed at the phone in Danny's hand. "Call him right now. Tell him wherever he is to get his butt back here."

Danny was dialing before his dad finished the sentence. The phone went straight to voice mail. Not good. He waited for the tape and left Terrell a message: "Terrell, call me right away," he said. "We can't find you."

As soon as he hung up, he typed a text with the same message. Seeing what he was doing, his dad said, "Tell him if we don't hear back from him in fifteen minutes, he's not playing tonight."

Danny paused when he heard that. "Dad, that's kind of extreme, isn't it? It's just the dudes. We don't have a practice or a meeting or anything to go to, right?"

His dad looked grim. "I hope it's just the dudes. Terrell knows he has to be careful who he runs off with—especially around here." He pointed at the phone. "Tell him."

Danny shook his head. "Sorry, Dad," he said. "If you want to discipline one of your players, that's for you to do. I shouldn't be your middle man."

Coach Wilcox had always been very careful to try not to put Danny in a position where he was isolated from the other players on his team because he was the coach's son. This was the first time he had asked Danny to do anything like this.

For a moment, his dad said nothing. Then he took his cell phone out of his pocket and dialed. "Terrell, it's Coach Wilcox," he said in a tone that let Danny know he was talking to voice mail. "I don't know why your phone's turned off, but I need to hear from you very soon. Danny and I are going to Houston's for lunch with Tom Konchalski and another scout you should meet. I expect you to meet us there by noon. Call me for a ride if you need one."

"So you changed your mind about the game tonight?" Danny asked.

"His phone's turned off, so I can't be sure when he'll get the message."

He turned and began walking in the direction of the

door. Danny followed. He had known that the games here would be intense, but he hadn't thought that lunch would be also.

The only honest man in the gym was waiting for them at Houston's. He was with an older man who had jet-black hair that was clearly dyed and thick black glasses.

"Danny, this is Howard Garfinkel, the man who invented summer basketball," his dad said when they arrived at the table. "I can tell you for certain he is *not* one of the only honest men in the gym."

"Come on, Andy, let me up already," Garfinkel said. "I gave your player a five-minus twenty years ago and you're still holding a grudge?"

Danny was completely lost. He shook hands with Garfinkel, whose name he recognized, though he wasn't sure why, and said, "Mr. Garfinkel, nice to meet you."

"It's Garf," Garfinkel said. "No one calls me Mr. Garfinkel. Konchalski's the only one who calls me Howard, and *no one* calls me Howie."

"Except if they give you a good horse," Tom Konchalski said.

"That's different," Garf said.

"Garf started the first national basketball camp forty-five years ago," Konchalski explained as the Wilcoxes sat down. "Five-Star Camp in Honesdale, Pennsylvania. All the summer ball you see played now is because of Garf."

"You can't blame all of it on me," Garf said. "Our camp was a real *camp*. Kids learned fundamentals. We had all the best coaches come in to do clinics. Knight, Smith, Valvano, Pitino, Krzyzewski—all the greats. We had station thirteen *every afternoon*."

He was wound up now, waving his arms.

"And in forty years I never once put a number on a kid's back."

Danny noticed that both Konchalski and his dad helped Garf finish the sentence about never putting a number on a kid's back. Clearly, they had heard the speech before.

"What's station thirteen?" Danny asked.

His father and Konchalski both groaned.

"You have a game at seven tonight," Konchalski said. "There isn't enough time—"

"When I started Five-Star, I wanted it to be a teaching camp," Garfinkel interrupted. "I didn't want kids to come up, show off their skills for the college coaches, and go home. I wanted them to learn. So every single morning they had to go through twelve stations before they played a game. We did fundamentals: dribbling, passing, shot-fakes, moving your feet on defense—everything.

"Then in the afternoon, after they played a game, they had to go to station thirteen. That's where that day's clinician—like I said, *all* the best coaches—would be. You think a kid isn't going to listen to Bobby Knight tell him he doesn't know how to set a screen? All the greats—I mean, *all* the greats: Moses Malone, Ralph Sampson,

Michael Jordan, Charles Barkley—will tell you about station thirteen."

"Michael Jordan knows about station thirteen?" Danny said, truly amazed.

By now his dad and Konchalski had their faces in their hands.

"Are you kidding?" Garfinkel roared. "Andy, you didn't teach your kid anything about basketball, did you? Let me tell you about Jordan before he got to Five-Star. He was *nothing* . . ."

Mercifully, a waitress showed up at that moment.

"Can I get anyone a drink?" she asked.

"Black coffee and tell me where I have to go to smoke," Garf said.

"That would be out the front door," she said.

"Our society is crumbling," Garf said as he slid out of the booth. "I'll be right back."

"Should I keep your coffee hot, sir?" the waitress asked.

"No," Garf said. "Just keep it coming. Tom, you know what I want to eat."

He practically ran in the direction of the door.

"He's eighty-two and feeling every minute of it," Konchalski said. "Except when he needs a cigarette or has a horse to bet on. Then he moves like he's twenty-five."

By the time Garf returned, Konchalski had ordered him a cheeseburger and French fries and was explaining to Danny how Garfinkel really had been the first person to discover Jordan when he went to Five-Star at the end of his junior year of high school.

"Now kids get discovered in seventh grade—or sooner," Konchalski said as Garfinkel slid back into the booth. "Terrell is an exception because he's a late bloomer. That's why so many people are scrambling now—he's fresh meat."

Danny noticed his cell phone was vibrating. He saw that it was Terrell and said, "I'm going to take this outside."

As soon as he was out of earshot he answered, "Where the hell are you?"

Terrell laughed. "I'm in the same mall as you, man. Take it easy. We're at Morton's."

"Morton's? The steak place?"

"Oh yeah. I just had the biggest porterhouse you've ever seen. . . ."

"Who bought you the porterhouse? You know my dad is flipping out?"

"Why? I'm just with Maurice and the guys. We're going to hang out for a while, and I'll be back at the hotel in another hour or so."

Danny was shaking his head even though Terrell couldn't see him. "Maurice and the dudes did *not* just buy you a Morton's steak, Terrell," he said. "Who else is there?"

"Just this guy, Eddie J. He works with Mr. Tommasino, who set us all up. It's cool. He's not an agent or anything. Tell Coach not to worry."

Danny took a deep breath. "You need to come over here to Houston's, Terrell. We haven't eaten yet."

"No, man, I'm stuffed. Tell your dad I'll be back at the hotel by three. We don't play till seven."

It had now gone from he'd be back in an hour or so to

he'd be back in three hours. Danny knew this wasn't good. And he didn't trust anyone named Eddie J. "You should at least talk to him, Terrell," he said.

"You talk to him for me," Terrell said. "I have to go. I'll catch you later." He hung up.

Danny stared at the phone. He noticed that he was sweating profusely. It wasn't from the heat.

SEVEN

Terrell had walked into the mall to call Danny without saying anything to the others at the table other than "I'll be back in a minute."

When he returned, he could see that dessert—he had ordered a sundae—was being served. He slipped back into his seat and quickly grabbed a spoon.

"What's up?" Maurice asked, pointing at Terrell's phone, which he had put down on the table.

"Had to check in with my coach," Terrell said, figuring it wasn't a great idea to bring Danny's name up if he didn't need to.

"'Check in'?" Maurice said. "Is he your coach or your parole officer?"

That drew a laugh from the rest of the table. Terrell knew how Maurice and the other guys felt about the Wilcoxes, and he understood. Coach Wilcox was polite but not exactly friendly, and Danny was always in their faces about something.

"We have another game tonight," Terrell said. "He just likes to make sure everyone knows the schedule."

"Hey, Terrell, you can tell him if you're with me, there's no way you're going to miss game time," said Eddie J. "If that happened on my watch, my boss would fire me in about half a second."

More laughs. Terrell spooned some of the sundae—which was huge. "Coach is just looking out for me," he said, smiling so everyone would see he didn't think any of it was a big deal.

"I'd look out for you too if I was him," said Anthony. "Take you off the team, the rest of those guys couldn't beat *us*."

Of all the dudes, as Danny called them, Anthony was the one who made his disdain for the Wilcoxes most obvious. Maurice danced around it a little because he knew that Terrell and Danny were close. Anthony didn't care. But he also didn't care much if Terrell gave it right back.

"Anthony, man, I've seen your game," Terrell said. "Danny Wilcox could eat your lunch. And Swanson's kind of an idiot, but he's a big-time player."

"Yeah, the Swanson kid's got game," Anthony said, conceding half the point.

Terrell figured it was enough and focused on his sundae. He liked the dudes. He had met them soon after arriving in Lexington when he decided to check out the summertime hoops at the local rec center a few blocks from his house.

There were four outdoor courts—only one of them with nets hanging from the rims. This was clearly the place where the best players hung out and Terrell had stood off to the side to get an idea of how high the quality of play was in that court.

The first person to speak to him that day was Maurice. "Dude, what are you, like six eight?" he had said, looking up at him as if he had never seen anyone so tall.

"More like six seven," Terrell had answered.

"Well, I've got next," Maurice said, meaning that his team would play the winner of the game currently going on. "Can you play?"

"I'm not bad," Terrell said, knowing at a glance that he would easily be the best player on the court.

"Then come on. We need a fifth. One of my guys didn't show today."

"You sure? I just got here. I can wait a while."

"I'm sure. If you can't play, we'll know soon enough. I'm Maurice." He put out his hand.

A couple of minutes later, the game was over and Maurice was introducing him to the rest of his crew. "This is Anthony, Chao, and Sky," Maurice said.

Terrell nodded at all of them.

"He's Terrell," Maurice added. "He's with us for now."

They had taken the court against a team that had four African Americans and a gangly white guy who was a little taller than Terrell. There were no handshakes or nods and no referees. The other team simply inbounded the ball, and the game began.

One thing Terrell knew for sure about schoolyard ball was that the new guy always got tested right away. Sure enough, as soon as the ball was in play, the tall white guy whom he had been told to guard took up a spot to the right of the key with his back to the basket. He put up his hand to call for the ball. He caught it, and before Terrell realized what was happening, he took a hard step backward, right into him. In a real basketball game it would have been an obvious offensive foul. But this was a schoolyard, and there was no such thing as a foul. Terrell wobbled for a second and saw the guy turning to shoot. He caught himself, jumped straight in the air, and blocked the shot. He still remembered the stunned look on the guy's face.

The ball went the other way, and Maurice got it back to Terrell on the right wing. He took one dribble and dunked. As he turned to run down court, it looked as if the other nine players were frozen where they stood. They were all staring at him.

After that, Terrell played with the group—or, as Danny would later call them, the dudes—every afternoon. They pretty much dominated the court, giving it up only when they were tired or, often as not, bored. The dudes were Terrell's first friends in Lexington, and he wasn't about to forget that.

And if he could be their ticket to a steak lunch with someone else picking up the tab, well, that was cool too.

"So, who's up for a swim?" Eddie J. said, handing his credit card to the waitress.

"Swim?" Terrell asked. "Where are we gonna swim—the Hudson River?"

Eddie J. laughed. "Not exactly. Mr. Tommasino rents a house for the week near here. It has a sweet pool in the backyard."

"I told my coach I'd be back at the hotel by three o'clock at the latest," Terrell said.

"Your game's not till seven, right?" Anthony said. "What is he, your keeper?"

"No, but neither are you," Terrell answered, starting to get just a little bit annoyed with Anthony's constant carping.

"We'll have you back by three o'clock, no sweat," Eddie J. said. "Come on, Terrell, kick back a little. This camp is supposed to be fun."

"I don't have a bathing suit."

"There are plenty at the house. What are you going to do at the hotel—sit in the room and stare at the walls until it's time to go play?"

He had a point. A swim sounded very cool—literally. "How far from here to the house?"

"Five minutes. Ten, tops."

"Terrell," Maurice said. "It's a basketball camp, not boot camp."

Terrell nodded. *What the heck*, he thought, *what could possibly go wrong?*

Turned out, everything went wrong.

Terrell first sensed trouble when it took closer to twenty minutes, not "ten, tops," to get to the house. The place *was* spectacular, set way back from the road on a leafy street lined with big homes. They drove up the circular driveway and piled out of the car. Before they got to the door, it was opened by a girl Terrell guessed was about twenty or so, wearing a white bikini.

"Been waiting on you guys," she said. "I thought you'd be here sooner."

"Traffic," Eddie J. said. "Monica, meet Terrell . . . and, um, the guys."

Clearly, Eddie J. couldn't remember anybody else's name. But no one much noticed—they were too busy noticing Monica.

"Terrell!" she said, walking over to where he was standing, rooted to the spot. "I have heard *so* much about you. Come on inside. There are some other people here who really want to meet you. What do you want to drink?"

She linked her arm in his and began leading him to the door.

Terrell's head was spinning. Someone clearly wanted to show him a very good time. But who? Brickley, through Tommasino? Maybe. A college coach who was working with Tommasino? Also possible. He suddenly wished Danny was there with him.

Still, the next hour wasn't exactly unpleasant. Monica had four friends, all of whom looked very nice . . . in their bikinis. The guys were given bathing suits, and soon they were all splashing and laughing in the large L-shaped pool. There were speakers pumping music out to the pool and patio. Terrell drank water, but the dudes opted for beer. Even without any alcohol, Terrell felt intoxicated by the whole thing. This didn't feel like his life, but it sure didn't feel bad.

They were all sitting on chaises around the pool when Eddie J. came out of the house with a tray of drinks and cigarettes. He lit one, took a deep drag, and passed it to Monica, who was sitting next to Terrell. As soon as Eddie J. finished his drag, he began to cough. Then Terrell picked up the aroma coming from the cigarette and realized it was *not* a cigarette.

Because he was an athlete and hung around other athletes most of the time, and because his mother had put the fear of God in him, Terrell didn't know much about drugs. But now Monica was holding the joint out to him.

"No, no thanks," Terrell said. "Game tonight."

"It's okay, honey, a couple of hours from now you won't even know you've had it," she said. "It's weak weed."

Terrell had no idea what that meant, but he could feel a dozen pairs of eyes on him. He figured one quick drag couldn't hurt. He took the cigarette from Monica and puffed it quickly, turning to hand it to Dante, who was sitting on the other side of him.

"No, no," Monica said. "That's not how you do it. Let me help you."

She sat down on Terrell's lap, took the cigarette, and put it in her mouth. She breathed in, smiled, and handed it back to him. "Like that," she said, blowing smoke slowly out.

Terrell took it, put it in his mouth, and breathed in. In

an instant, he felt light-headed. It was a nice feeling, he had to admit.

Eddie J. had lit another one and was passing it around the circle. When it came to Terrell, he was feeling much more mellow about the situation and breathed in deeply again.

Monica was still sitting on his lap. "You like it, don't you?" she said.

Terrell nodded. She took it back from him. "This one will be just for you and me, okay?" she said.

Terrell didn't argue. That sounded just fine to him.

When Danny asked him later what happened after he first tried marijuana, Terrell's honest answer was, "I don't remember."

Most of what happened was a blur until the moment that Terrell realized he was in the backseat of Eddie J.'s car and had a pounding headache. "What time is it?" he asked.

"Almost four," Eddie J. said. "We'll be back at your hotel in ten minutes."

Terrell groaned. He had told Danny he'd be back at three. Maybe, if he was lucky, he could sneak back to the room and take a shower and Coach Wilcox wouldn't know he had been so late or, more important, why he was so late. Monica, he noticed, was nowhere in sight. Maurice was in the front seat with Eddie J., and Chao, Anthony, and Dante were squeezed in the backseat with him.

"Where's Sky?" he asked.

"Behind you," Maurice said.

They were riding in an SUV that had one of those way-backs that doubled as a trunk. Terrell turned his head and saw Sky curled up—sound asleep. He started laughing, which made his head hurt more.

They arrived at the hotel, and Eddie J. pulled the car up to the main entrance. As soon as Terrell climbed out into the heat, he felt woozy and light-headed. Apparently, it was noticeable, because he heard Maurice saying, "Whoa, big fella, let's get you inside and up to your room real quick."

That, Terrell thought, was an excellent idea. With Maurice holding his arm to keep him steady, they made their way through the revolving door and into the lobby. Terrell was seriously dizzy, and he was afraid he might get sick. He could see the elevators—nirvana!—across the lobby. If he could just get there and back inside the room . . .

"Terrell, where the hell have you been?"

Terrell didn't have to turn his head to know it was Danny. The last thing he needed right now was for Danny to be barking his name so people could hear. He was about to say something to that effect when he saw that Danny was walking toward him, with that reporter—what was his name? Oh, yeah . . . Bobby Kelleher—a couple of steps behind.

Crap.

Terrell stood up very straight, ready to act like everything was normal. They were just a little late. "Hey, Danny, whassup?" he said, trying to sound casual.

Danny had stopped in his tracks and was staring at him.

He was also looking at the rest of the group as if they had all grown two heads. "Jesus, Terrell, are you nuts?" Danny hissed. "We have a game in three hours."

"What about it?" Maurice said. "He's fine, white boy. Just butt out."

Danny took a step forward so he was right in Maurice's face. "No, Maurice, *you* butt out," he said. "You've done enough for one afternoon."

Normally, Terrell would have jumped between his two friends. But he was having enough trouble simply standing up. Fortunately, Eddie J. got between them. "Calm down, Wilcox. There's nothing going on here," he said. "Why don't you just get Terrell up to his room, okay?"

"You better get him something for those eyes first," Terrell heard someone behind him say. It was Kelleher. "Anyone sees him looking like this, even in a couple of hours, is going to know what he was doing this afternoon."

Terrell wondered what he meant. His eyes felt fine. But Danny was nodding as if Kelleher was making sense. "Come on. Let's find some eyedrops," he said, turning to Terrell. "My father sees you like this, it's big trouble."

"Chill out, man. We can take care of him," Maurice said.

"*Obviously you can't!*" Danny yelled.

Heads were turning. "Easy, Danny," Kelleher said. He took Terrell's arm. "We'll take it from here, fellas."

Terrell could see Maurice and Eddie J. glaring at Kelleher. At least he *thought* they were glaring at him. He really wasn't sure. Danny had taken his other arm. Kelleher and

Eddie J. were exchanging unpleasantries, but Terrell wasn't certain what they were saying.

They made it across the lobby to the gift shop, and Danny began searching the shelves. "Here," he said, pulling a bottle of Visine off the shelf and showing it to Kelleher, who nodded.

It suddenly occurred to Terrell that a *reporter* was buying him Visine. "Hey, man," he said to Kelleher. "Are you gonna write about this?"

Kelleher shook his head. "No, Terrell, I'm not," he said. "But I'd seriously advise you to choose your friends more wisely in the future. I don't know those other guys, but Ed Jackson? He's trouble. I'm the least of your worries. Your secret's safe with me."

"What secret is that?" Terrell heard a familiar voice say.

He turned and there, standing in the doorway holding the newspaper he had apparently come downstairs to buy, was Coach Wilcox.

Danny had once told Terrell about two guys who had showed up for practice one day clearly stoned. "Took my dad thirty seconds to figure it out," he said. "He's been around a lot of teenagers."

As it turned out, Danny had underestimated his father. It took him about ten seconds to figure out what was going on.

"Mr. Kelleher, I hope you meant what you said about keeping quiet," he said. "This gets out, it could really damage

Terrell, and he's a good kid." He looked up at Terrell. "Not always a smart kid, but a good one."

"No worries, Coach," Kelleher said, waving a hand. "I can tell the good guys from the bad guys in these stories. But I may need your help with the bad guys at some point."

Coach Wilcox nodded. "We'll talk." He shook hands with Kelleher, who gave Terrell and Danny a wave and walked back into the lobby. "My room, right now," he said to the two boys.

Terrell's head was pounding. "Coach, can I get some aspirin first?" he said. "I have a pretty bad headache."

The look on Coach Wilcox's face told him he wasn't going to get a lot of sympathy at that moment. "It's only going to get worse, Terrell," he said. "Let's go."

When they got up to the room, he proved his point. "Neither of you is playing tonight," he said. When Danny started to object, he held up his hand. "Terrell, you aren't playing because you just broke the law—for starters. To be honest, I'd normally suspend you for two games, but that's not fair to the eight guys on this team who had nothing to do with this. We can lose tonight and still advance, and I don't want to ruin their week because you did something stupid.

"Danny, you sit tonight because you were trying to help Terrell cover up what he did. You earn a few points for trying to be a friend, but you lose more for being an enabler. There are enough of those trying to weasel their way into his life now without you jumping on that bandwagon."

"But, Dad . . . ," Danny tried—futilely.

"No buts. And, Terrell, I think you know my policy on this: Two strikes and you're out. Do this again, and you'll need to find yourself another high school if you want to play basketball this winter. My advice would be for you to tell your mom what happened, because if she finds out you didn't play and wants an explanation, I'm not going to lie to her."

Terrell felt sick to his stomach. "Coach, a lot of people are comin' to see me tonight," he said. "Coaches and—"

"Terrell, *if* you stay out of trouble, they'll have plenty of chances to see you before the end of the weekend. That's your short-term goal. Once we're done here, you and I and your mom need to sit down and talk about longer-term goals."

"Like what?"

"Like learning to stay away from people who are going to ruin your life. Because that's what they're going to do, Terrell. I'll bet you all those guys were telling you that you don't need to put up with all my rules because you're a star. You can do anything you want. It's all just waiting to be taken—steaks, girls, money, drugs—anything you want. You think that was a free lunch today? Get real.

"You missed your free lunch today with two guys who could have really helped you. They've met hundreds of kids like you over the years, and they can tell you who succeeded and who didn't—and *why*. But you skipped that to hang with the dudes and, I'm betting, a bunch of girls, all of whom just kept telling you, 'Anything you want, big guy.'"

Terrell had heard those exact words not long before. "How'd you know that, Coach?" he said.

Coach Wilcox smiled grimly. "Older and wiser, Terrell. Now, go take a shower and get some rest. You've got a game to watch tonight."

EIGHT

The game that night went about as Terrell and Danny both thought it would after hearing Coach Wilcox's assessment of the Toreros, from Austin, Texas. "They don't have a lot of size inside," he said, "but they have a bunch of guys who can really shoot it, and they have a point guard who makes plays."

Without Terrell to power the offense or Danny to lead the defense, the Rebels looked lost from the start. Almost everyone on the team took a turn trying to slow down the Toreros' point guard, William Nagy, but he was too quick and too smart for all of them. Every time he got inside, one of two things happened: Alan Owens or Jay Swanson would try to cut him off, and he would coolly pitch the ball to an open shooter on the perimeter. Or, if Owens and Swanson stayed with their men, Nagy went all the way to the basket for an easy layup.

Terrell felt as if everyone in the gym was staring at him as the game wore on. Danny was apparently thinking the same thing. "Look in the stands," he said at one point. "All the coaches are pointing at us."

Danny had a knack for finding a black cloud in every silver lining. This time, though, Terrell couldn't argue. The Toreros won going away, 85–66.

Billy Tommasino was waiting at the end of the court as the Rebels headed for the locker room. The fake smile Terrell had seen since their arrival was nowhere in sight. "Coach, what the hell was all that about?" he said as soon as Danny's dad was within earshot. "Why didn't you play the kid? You've got half the basketball world here to watch him."

"Billy, I sat two players out because they violated team rules. Normally, it would be a two-game suspension, but out of respect for the fact that this is a short-form event, I reduced it to one."

"Damn it, Andy, this isn't real basketball," Tommasino said, turning red. "It's a summer camp. It's entertainment. It's a showcase for these players. You don't suspend kids. Your team didn't even exist a month ago."

"Were they keeping score?" Coach Wilcox asked. "Were there referees out there? Am I supposed to be teaching these kids something? What's the name of the camp again, Billy?"

That seemed to throw Tommasino a little bit. The "School Comes First" name he had slapped on his camp didn't exactly match up with what he had just described. "He plays tomorrow?" he said at last.

"You mean, do *they* play tomorrow—right, Billy?" Coach Wilcox said. "You're concerned about *all* your campers—I know that. Yes, *they'll* play tomorrow morning *if* they stay out of trouble tonight. So you might want to keep your guy Jackson away from them."

Tommasino turned a little bit pale at the mention of Eddie J.'s name. "I'll talk to him," he said in a much softer tone.

"Brilliant idea," Coach Wilcox said, throwing a profanity in between "brilliant" and "idea."

Terrell did a double take. He hadn't heard Coach Wilcox swear more than two or three times since he had arrived in Lexington.

Tommasino headed off. As soon as he was gone, Coach Wilcox turned to his two nonplaying players. "I would advise both of you to go straight back to the hotel, call room service if you're hungry, and go to bed," he said. "That way there's a fifty-fifty chance you can stay out of trouble between now and nine o'clock tomorrow morning.

"Terrell, you're luckier than Danny. If you don't want discipline, there's nothing I can do to stop you. There are about five hundred high schools that will take you tomorrow if you want to leave Lexington. Danny's stuck with me. You're not."

"I don't want to go anywhere, Coach," Terrell said.

"Good," Coach Wilcox said. "I'm glad to hear that. Now prove it."

Terrell sighed. He knew he had made a mistake—a dumb one. And yet he couldn't help wondering just how long he was going to have to hear about it.

Their nine o'clock game the next morning was against a team from the Bronx called the Pinstripes.

When Danny and Terrell walked onto the court for pregame warm-ups at 8:30, Jay Swanson, who had been surprisingly quiet the night before when Coach Wilcox had told the other players that Danny and Terrell wouldn't be playing, was waiting. "So the word around camp is that you guys didn't play last night because Coach caught you getting high," he said in greeting.

Terrell was about to tell Swanson that only one of them had gotten high, and if he wanted to get angry at someone, it should be him, when Danny pointed his finger in Swanson's chest and said in that subtle Danny way, "Shut up, Swanson!"

Swanson returned Danny's menacing look. "No, Wilcox, you shut up!" he said. "You're only on this team because your old man is coaching, and your old man is only coaching because he's got Jamerson."

"What happened yesterday is none of your business," Danny said. "We screwed up and got punished like anyone else would get punished."

"It *is* my business," Swanson said angrily. "It's the whole team's business. We lost because you guys are stupid. Now we have to win all four games the next two days or we might not play the weekend. So don't tell me it isn't my business!"

Terrell knew he was right. Which hurt almost as much as not playing had the night before.

Danny apparently realized it too. "You're right," he said. "We screwed up. I apologize." He put his hand out as a peace offering.

Swanson looked at it for a second as if deciding what to do in response. Then he shook his head, turned, and walked away.

Terrell felt slightly sick to his stomach. He took a step in Swanson's direction, but Danny cut him off. "What are you doing?" he said.

"I'm going to tell him it was only me. It's not fair. . . ."

Danny was shaking his head. "It doesn't matter. Let's just beat these guys and put it behind us."

But that was easier said than done.

The game was almost as good as the opener two days earlier against the Crushes. The Pinstripes didn't have anyone as good as Terrell, but they had five very good players, and their bench was solid too. The two teams must have traded the lead a dozen times, but neither could really pull away. With forty-four seconds left, the Rebels had the ball and were leading, 85–84.

Terrell saw Danny look at his dad as he brought the ball up court to see if he wanted a time-out. Coach Wilcox simply put his left fist in the air, which indicated he wanted Danny to let the shot clock get to ten seconds and then get the ball to Terrell in the low post. Fortunately, the Pinstripes decided not to double-team Danny, so he was able to dribble the clock down without anyone coming to help. Terrell, who had been standing on the left wing, spun down to the low block and called for the ball, which Danny delivered to him with six seconds on the shot clock and fifteen on the game clock.

Not surprisingly, the instant the ball reached Terrell, two Pinstripes left their men on the perimeter and dropped down to help their center, who was directly behind him and was trying desperately to push him away from the basket. Seeing the extra defenders coming at him, Terrell took one quick dribble, then picked the ball up before anyone could swipe at it.

Swanson had come out from the corner to the right wing, just outside the three-point line. Terrell spotted him and flicked a quick pass to him. Swanson was stepping into his shooting motion as he caught the ball, and no one came close to him. The shot-clock buzzer went off just as the ball hit the bottom of the net.

The Pinstripes called time-out right away, and Swanson ran straight to Terrell and gave him a high five. "Great pass," he said.

"Great shot," Terrell replied.

The Pinstripes missed a three at the buzzer that wouldn't have mattered anyway, and the Rebels walked off with an 88–84 win. After they had gone through the handshake line, Terrell saw Swanson turn and point a finger at Danny. He started to make a move to get between them, but there was no need.

"Good game," Swanson said. "You ran the offense perfectly on the last possession." Without waiting for Danny to answer, he turned and jogged to the locker room.

Danny and Terrell looked at each other, baffled. "Maybe he's just happy that he hit a big-time shot with all the college coaches watching," Danny said.

"He's also right," Terrell said. "You played great."

They were about to head for the locker room when an attractive woman in a Brickley outfit stopped them. She appeared to be in her late twenties and was almost as tall as Danny. "Terrell, Danny. Hi, I'm Kristin Martz. I'm the TV coordinator for the camp," she said, offering her hand and a big smile.

Terrell was baffled. "What's a TV coordinator?" he asked.

She laughed as if the question was somehow remarkably clever. "It just means I'm the liaison between all our players and coaches and our TV partner. Most of the time I work in marketing for Brickley."

Terrell still wasn't sure what any of that meant, but he nodded as if he did.

"The folks from UBS were hoping to tape something with the two of you after you get through showering and changing," she said. "It'll be for airing on Sunday, when they televise the championship game."

"UBS?" Danny said. "Oh, wait—you mean UBS College or whatever they call it. Why would they want to talk to me? I would think they'd just want Terrell."

Kristin's smile faded just a bit. "It's called UBS Sports Network, and it's very much a part of the UBS family. And they'd like to talk to you about Terrell and your dad and the great relationship the three of you have."

Terrell almost choked when she said that. "Did you see our game last night?" he said.

"Well, no, I didn't. Why?"

"Never mind," Danny said, jumping in. "It's fine. Where should we go?"

"Just go out the back door and turn left. They have a set out there."

"Did you clear this with our coach?" Terrell asked. He wasn't about to agree to do *anything* without Coach Wilcox's approval. He didn't want to miss any more games.

She shrugged. "Mr. Tommasino is talking to him right now about his interview time. So I'd guess the answer is yes."

Terrell wasn't so sure about that guess. He'd have to ask himself.

"So did you play in college?" Danny asked.

"I played at Maryland," she said. "I was a senior on the national championship team in 2006."

"Congratulations," Danny said.

"That must have been awesome," Terrell said, figuring if Danny was going to be polite, he would be too.

"Anytime you beat Duke, it's thrilling," she said. "See you in about twenty minutes?"

They both nodded. Terrell had no idea that Maryland had beaten Duke in 2006 in the women's championship game. All he remembered about the 2006 NCAA Tournament was George Mason beating Connecticut to get to the men's Final Four. As a UConn fan living in Hartford, that had been less-than-thrilling.

After they had showered and changed, they went to look for Coach Wilcox. They found him talking to Tom Konchalski and Howard Garfinkel. If the two of them knew anything about what had happened the day before, they didn't let on.

"Hey, Dad, this woman wants us to talk to these TV people . . . ," Danny said as they walked up.

"Yeah, yeah, I know. UBS whatever-it-is," his dad said. "Tommasino and the guy from the network got very put off when I asked if anyone ever actually watched. I told them it was fine for the two of you, but I wasn't going to do it."

"Why not?"

"Because they should focus on you guys. Any coach who goes on is just doing it to promote himself."

Konchalski snorted. "I got a call last week from some guy who wanted to know if I would do some analysis of the players during the game. I told him no, thank you, I don't do that kind of thing. He got very huffy and said, 'Do you know how many homes we're in?' I told him I had no idea, but I was betting it wasn't many, unless they paid extra, and from what little I'd seen of his network, I'd only pay extra if they took the network *off* my cable package."

Terrell laughed. Konchalski was honest *and* funny.

"Go do the interview," Coach Wilcox said. "And then let's get lunch. Tonight's game will probably decide if we make the semis. You guys need to rest."

"Who are we playing tonight?" they both asked.

"The Gauchos. Don't you look at the schedule?"

Terrell shook his head and smiled semi-sheepishly. "My coach always tells me one game at a time."

The three adults laughed. "He's coachable," Garfinkel said.

"The Gauchos may be the most famous AAU team of all time," Coach Wilcox said. "We beat them and we probably make the quarters, because we should win both our games tomorrow. But if we lose, we're out."

Terrell saw Danny smiling. "In other words, if we don't win tonight, this interview we're about to do will probably never air, since we'll be long gone by Sunday."

"You got that right, son."

They had no trouble finding the set. The trouble was fighting their way through all the people standing underneath the tented area where the set was located.

There were hangers-on everywhere. Agent types in suits, Brickley people in tracksuits, security people in yellow, and others who Terrell figured were with the network. Even the dudes were all standing in the back.

They finally got close enough to the front to see a player Terrell didn't recognize being interviewed. Tommasino was off to the side with Kristin Martz. When he spotted Terrell, he waved him over. "You're up next, Terrell," Tommasino whispered when they walked up.

"Do I go on with Danny?" Terrell asked.

Kristin gave him a tight smile and said, "We're going to talk to you next, and then we'll see about Danny. If Omar Whytlaw shows up, Danny'll have to wait while we interview Whytlaw."

The interview with the player Terrell didn't recognize was wrapping up.

"So you really don't need me very much, then, do you?" Danny said, which was exactly what Terrell was thinking.

"We need you because your father wouldn't talk to us," said a man who had just taken off a headset. "The only coach we've asked who said no."

"My dad likes to be different," Danny said. Terrell could see that he was a little ticked off.

The headset guy said, "Okay, Terrell, we're ready for you."

Terrell looked at Danny. "I'm nervous. I've never done anything except local TV before."

"This is a lot like local TV. Almost no one watches this network. Don't be nervous."

Headset guy pointed a finger at Danny. "You know, you don't have to appear on our network. We don't have to interview you at all."

Terrell knew that was the wrong thing to say to Danny.

Danny shrugged. "Fine with me."

Terrell paused for a moment, deciding what to do. He remembered how Danny had taken the heat for him before the game. That made his decision easy. He looked at the headset guy. "I'm going too."

The headset guy's expression quickly changed from a sneer to a phony smile. "Oh no, Terrell, don't misunderstand. We're thrilled that you're taking the time to do this."

Terrell shook his head. "You dragged Danny over here, you tell him you only want him if he doesn't mess you up with Omar, and only then because his dad wouldn't talk to you, and then you get all pissed off because he's not acting

like this is the greatest moment of his life. Hell with you."
He turned to Danny. "Come on—let's go."

The two of them walked off. The last thing Terrell heard
was Billy Tommasino's voice. "Hey, Wilcox, tell your father
he'd better enjoy the rest of the week," he said. "Because
this is the last time a team of his will ever be invited to *my*
camp."

Terrell could tell by the look on Danny's face that he was
thinking about turning around and going back. He put his
hand on Danny's shoulder to keep him going in the right
direction.

"Don't worry," Danny said. "I'm fine. Thanks for that."

"Least I could do," Terrell said, meaning it. With all eyes
on them, they walked away from the tent and back into
the gym.

NINE

Terrell could sense a buzz in the crowd. There seemed to be more people in the gym each day, and with the Rebels facing a team that had three bona fide Division I prospects and a well-known summer hoops heritage, the open areas between the courts were packed.

The Gauchos were a very good team, but they didn't have anybody who could guard Terrell. He just blew by everyone and had 22 points at halftime.

With the game well in hand, Coach Wilcox rested both Danny and Terrell on a couple of occasions, and they spent the time coach spotting. Terrell picked out Roy Williams, Rick Pitino, Mike Krzyzewski, Jim Boeheim, and John Calipari. But Danny knew even more. Terrell nudged him and pointed to a young African American coach standing next to Krzyzewski.

"Tommy Amaker," Danny said, and smiled. "Harvard. My dad said he might be here tonight."

"Who's the guy next to him?" Terrell asked. "Not K—the guy on the other side."

"Fran O'Hanlon," Danny said. "Lafayette. I wouldn't mind playing there, either."

In the second half, when the Gauchos doubled him whenever he touched the ball, Terrell remembered Tom Konchalski's advice and found shooters—notably, Danny and Jay Swanson—wide open on the wings.

Danny spent most of the night guarding D'Andre Dunigan, who was considered one of the better point guards in the camp—and in the country—and totally held his own. Terrell noticed that Dunigan had been sent to double on him in the post, but after Danny drilled a couple of threes, they sent someone else to double him, which opened things up for Terrell inside. The Rebels won with surprising ease, 91–78.

In the handshake line, Terrell found Dunigan. "Nice game," he said.

Dunigan gave him a warm handshake and then turned to Danny, who was right behind Terrell. When Danny offered his hand, Dunigan grabbed it and pulled him close, so he could whisper in his ear. Terrell was close enough to hear him anyway. "Don't let anyone say your boy is the only one on this team who can play," he said. "*You* got game."

"Thanks," Danny said, clearly surprised.

Terrell had rarely seen Danny either flustered or surprised.

Dunigan smiled. "And tell your boy he needs to stay away from Eddie J. and those guys. Nothing but trouble there."

Terrell turned around to look at the two guards. "I know," he said. "I know."

He and Danny headed for the locker room. "Seems like a good guy," Terrell said.

"Yeah," Danny said.

Terrell nodded. "He's got a bunch of guys hanging out with him too, you know. I've seen them."

"And?"

"Nothing. Except that sometimes players have guys hanging out with them whether they want them around or not."

"You think that's true of Dunigan?"

Terrell shrugged. "Don't know. But it *is* true of me. You should remember that."

Danny was still thinking of an answer when one of the Brickley functionaries grabbed Terrell to tell him he was needed in the media room. As Terrell was hustled off, Danny looked around for his dad, who was nowhere in sight. He was about to head for the locker room when he heard someone call his name. He looked around and found Alex Mayer.

"Funny, I was just thinking about you," Danny said.

Mayer gave him a questioning look, then smiled. "You were thinking that Dunigan could kick my butt, right?" he said.

Danny laughed. "No, but it did have to do with Dunigan."

"We've got the eight-thirty game right now," Mayer said. "But I'd like to hear more, and I'd *really* like to know what happened yesterday that got you and Terrell benched. In case you didn't know, it's the talk of the camp."

Danny didn't know, but he could imagine. "I don't think I've got anything going on for lunch tomorrow," he said.

"How about Houston's at twelve thirty?" Mayer said.

"Michael's got a car. He's meeting some other people at the mall. We can hitch a ride with him or I can meet you."

"Michael's got a car?"

Mayer grinned. "Oh yeah. I'll tell you about it. Listen, meet us in the back lot at twelve twenty-five tomorrow—or text me if something changes."

He jogged off in the direction of the court. Danny headed for the locker room. He was nearly there when someone tapped him on the shoulder. He turned and saw Bobby Kelleher.

"We need to talk," Kelleher said.

"We do?" Danny said.

Kelleher nodded. "Not tonight. You play early again tomorrow. After your morning game. We'll go someplace quiet."

Danny didn't argue. Friday was apparently going to be a very social day for him.

The Rebels, as Danny's dad had predicted, had no trouble with a team from Montana Friday morning. He and Terrell hardly played in the second half because the game was such a blowout.

That didn't mean the media didn't have a million post-game questions for Terrell. Danny had showered and was heading out of the locker room just as Terrell was heading in.

Danny raised an eyebrow to ask how it had gone. Terrell rolled his eyes. Enough said.

Danny found his father outside the interview room and filled him in on his plans. "Bobby Kelleher wants to talk to me, and then I'm going to meet Alex Mayer for lunch. Okay?"

"The kid from Mississippi?" his dad said. "Good player." His eyes narrowed a little bit. "What's Kelleher want?"

"I don't know. But given what he saw the other day, I probably should talk to him."

"Yeah, I guess so. I noticed I had a message from him, but I haven't called him back. Konchalski says he's a straight shooter, and if Tom trusts him, I guess I trust him. Remember, though, you have to be back here at three thirty for that media seminar."

Danny had forgotten. "Do I have to do that?" he asked.

"Yup. It won't be so bad. You might learn something."

Danny nodded. "Okay. What are you doing for lunch?"

"Going out with Tom and Garf and Gary Williams."

"The old Maryland coach?"

"Yeah, he's just up for the day seeing old friends." He patted Danny on the back. "You've played really well the last couple of games. People are noticing."

Danny allowed himself a smile—his dad didn't hand out all that many compliments.

"Call and let me know what happens with Kelleher, okay?"

Danny nodded and headed out to the courts.

He found Kelleher talking to two big-time coaches—Tom Izzo of Michigan State and Jamie Dixon of Pittsburgh.

"Danny, I won't introduce you to these guys because I think that would be a violation of some kind of NCAA rule," Kelleher said.

"More like about ten NCAA rules," Izzo said, smiling. "If I *could* talk to him, I'd tell Danny I really admire the way he runs a team."

"And I'd tell him I'm willing to bet he's a lot better player than he knows he is," Dixon said. "But, of course, I can't talk to him."

"Too bad," Kelleher said. "I bet he'd really like to hear all that."

So, Danny thought, his dad was right, people *were* noticing him. "Yeah," he said, "I would definitely like to hear all that." He turned to Kelleher. "You think they mean what they're not saying or is that just polite coach-speak?"

"Hey, Bobby, have you ever known me to be polite?" Izzo said.

"Absolutely not," Kelleher said. "But Jamie *is* polite."

"I never tell kids what they want to hear," Dixon said. "I tell them the truth. But, of course, right now I'm not talking to a recruit. In fact, I'm not even talking to you because the rules say I can't talk to the media about specific players."

"What *don't* the rules say?" Danny said, still looking at Kelleher.

"I think breathing is allowed," Kelleher said.

"Not on Sundays," Izzo said. "But you didn't hear me say that."

"Okay," Kelleher said. "I probably should get Danny out

of here before you guys are on probation for five years and Danny is ineligible until 2020."

They all laughed, and both coaches gave Danny a friendly nod as he and Kelleher turned to go. *No doubt*, he thought, *that's a violation too.*

"Good guys?" he asked Kelleher as they walked down the hall in the direction of the back door.

"Very good guys," Kelleher said.

"Even if they're blatant rule breakers?" Danny said, laughing.

"Yeah. Exactly," Kelleher said.

They walked through the searing heat to Kelleher's car. He put the air-conditioning on full-blast as soon as the engine was on. "You okay on time?" he asked.

"I'm supposed to meet Alex Mayer at Houston's over at the mall at twelve thirty."

"You guys friends?" Kelleher asked.

"Just met the other day," Danny said. "But I like him."

"There's a pretty good pizza place at the far end of the mall," Kelleher said. "We probably won't run into many of the camp people there. I can get some pizza, and if you don't want to eat yet, you can get soda or coffee or something."

Pizza sounded good to Danny. He had only eaten a bagel for breakfast since they were playing so early. "I can probably eat twice," he said. "We don't play again until seven."

"You have that media training thing this afternoon, right?"

"Yeah, at three thirty."

"One piece of advice: Whatever the guys they bring in tell you to do, always do the opposite."

Danny laughed. "You aren't a big fan of the people running this camp, are you?" he said.

"I'm not a big fan of anyone who tries to buy kids off," Kelleher said. "And that's what these guys do."

He ran a yellow light and turned into the mall.

While they found a parking spot, Danny sent Mayer a text saying he would meet him at Houston's rather than at the gym.

Kelleher was right about the pizza. It reminded Danny of Regina's, his favorite place in Boston. They ordered slices at the counter and then walked out into the mall and found a quiet place to sit.

Once they had both taken a couple bites of pizza, Kelleher got straight to the point. "What's the deal with Terrell?" he asked. "Does he get high a lot?"

Danny wasn't exactly shocked by the question, but he wasn't really prepared for it. "Terrell doesn't get high," he said finally. "That's not who he is."

"Well, then, who was that I saw in the hotel the other day?"

Danny paused. His instinct was to like Kelleher and to trust him. But he was still a reporter.

"Is this on the record?" he asked. "Are you writing this?"

Kelleher smiled and shook his head. "No. What you need to understand about me is that I'm not looking to write a story that makes Terrell look bad. That's not what I do.

What I'm trying to do, maybe months from now, is write a story that explains what the culture of stardom does to young athletes. My sense is that Terrell's in a very delicate place right now. He's a late bloomer, so people are lining up to get a piece of him. He's got a lot of options being thrown at him, and not all of them are good. Not all of them are legal. *That's* the story. A rising high school senior smoking pot is not a story. It's an issue for him, but it's not a story for me."

"So if I talk to you now, what I say won't show up in your paper six months from now?"

"No, it won't. I need information so I can go and get more information. I need to know who the good guys are and who the bad guys are. I'm pretty sure I've got most of them pegged, but I need to be certain."

Danny nodded, trying to take in everything Kelleher was saying. "Still, why ask me?"

"Because people will be talking to you and your dad and Terrell in ways they won't talk to me. And because you seem like you're trying to keep Terrell out of trouble. So I'm wondering who looks like trouble to you."

"Well, that guy Eddie J. is bad news," Danny said.

Kelleher smiled. "Danny, have you heard? Man landed on the moon."

It took Danny a second to get the joke. When he did, he nodded. "Look, Mr. Kelleher . . ."

"Bobby. My dad is Mr. Kelleher."

"Okay, Bobby. You seem to know more than I do, really,

but . . . Tommasino is clearly annoyed that my dad isn't falling in line. And that agent he hangs around with—"

"Paul Judson."

"Yeah—him. Some of the players said he offered to be their 'educational consultant' and help them pick the right schools. Which feels suspicious."

"Very."

"And my dad says some of the coaches have their hands out."

Kelleher grunted. "Not some—most."

"Huh. And I'll tell you what, those TV guys aren't real impressive, either."

"They don't worry me so much. They're full of themselves but mostly harmless. Now, there are some big names at the networks who I think get involved some of the time. But no one much cares what these guys think." Kelleher shrugged, then continued. "Okay, none of those bad guys surprise me. I need to know if there are any *good* guys."

"My dad's a good guy. And I like that scout Konchalski. Terrell's a good guy. There are some guys on other teams who I think are good guys."

"You sure about Terrell? What about his pals, those guys he hangs out with?"

"'The dudes.' They hang out with *him*," Danny corrected, remembering Terrell's comment from the night before. "Until the other day, I'd have said they're just annoying groupies who want Terrell around to help them get girls. Now, I'm not so sure."

"My guess is their interest in Terrell goes beyond getting girls," Kelleher said. "'The dudes'? Where does that come from?"

"It's just what I call them because they think everybody's name is dude."

Kelleher laughed. "I like it."

"But they never offered Terrell drugs before that I know of—I think that came from Eddie J."

Kelleher nodded thoughtfully. "You mentioned kids on other teams. Who?"

"Alex Mayer, the kid from Mississippi. D'Andre Dunigan, the guard we just played against last night."

"Hmm. Those are two highly recruited kids. What about Michael Jordan?"

"Don't know him. But he *is* driving a car here that someone loaned him or gave him."

Kelleher's eyebrows went up. "That's certainly interesting. I'm a little surprised you mentioned Dunigan. He's supposed to be an entourage guy."

"You look at Terrell from the outside, you'd think he's an entourage guy too," Danny said. "But he's not. And Dunigan made a point of warning us about Eddie J. But I talked to him for all of two minutes."

"Sounds like you've got pretty good instincts," Kelleher conceded. "You want another slice?" He was pointing at Danny's empty plate. Danny was meeting Mayer and Jordan for lunch in fifteen minutes. Still, it was really good pizza.

"Absolutely," he said.

TEN

After a quick shower, Terrell headed back out into the gym and saw Michael Jordan and Alex Mayer waving at him from across the court. They were warming up for their game but clearly not all that focused on it yet.

"What's up?" he said, walking over to the two of them. "Don't you guys play in about five minutes?"

"Yeah, we do," Jordan said. "Coach says we could play with one hand tied behind our backs and win by twenty."

Terrell knew for a fact that Coach Wilcox would never describe *any* opponent that way. Everyone was different—apparently.

"Hey, we're meeting your boy Wilcox for lunch at twelve thirty," Jordan said. "Why don't you come?"

Terrell wavered. The dudes had been bugging him to hang out this afternoon, but he didn't know if he could stand listening to Maurice tell him—again—that he was sorry about the other day, that they were just trying to show him a good time.

"Got a little out of hand, I guess," Maurice had said.

"Ya think?" Terrell had answered.

"Come on, T-man, you know we've got your back. Don't start listening to your white-boy friends just because of one little incident."

"Maurice," Terrell had said. "*You're* white, remember?"

"You know what I mean, dude."

Terrell did, kind of. And the dudes *had* been his first friends in Lexington. But lunch with someone else sounded pretty good right now.

"Well, I was going to go back to the hotel and order some room service before that three-thirty media thing. . . ."

"Come on," Jordan said. "No way you can get into trouble hanging with us."

Terrell wondered what they knew about the other day. But he didn't want to ask. "Okay," he finally said to Jordan. "How do I get there?"

"Meet us in the locker room at twelve twenty," Jordan said. "I've got a car."

"You do?"

"Yeah, man. Don't sweat it. See you in a couple hours."

Terrell nodded. But suddenly this lunch didn't feel all that safe, either. Maybe Danny was right. Maybe everyone in the camp *was* on the take.

He found a seat in the bleachers and settled in to see if Michael Jordan was as good as his name.

Danny thanked Kelleher for the pizza and walked to the other end of the mall for his second lunch. Alex Mayer and Michael Jordan were already seated at a round table in the back of the restaurant, and they weren't alone. Terrell was there, along with a man he hadn't seen before. The man stood up when Danny approached and introduced himself as Ray Leach.

"Enjoyed watching you play this week," he said, shaking hands. "I'm hoping you guys will end up playing Alex and Michael's team on Sunday."

It hadn't occurred to Danny that the Rebels could end up playing against the Riverboats in the knockout rounds. He'd been so focused on just trying to get from one day to the next that the weekend had felt light-years away.

"We've got a lot of work to do before Sunday," he replied, sliding into the empty seat at the table. "Terrell, I thought you had other plans," he said.

"The guys invited me," Terrell said. "I figured you-all would keep me out of trouble."

"That remains to be seen," Danny said, drawing a too hearty laugh from Ray Leach.

Jordan hadn't looked up from his cell phone when he arrived, but now he put it down and explained—sort of— who Ray Leach was. "Ray's a friend of our coach," he said. "He helps out a lot. Since we don't play until the afternoon Sunday, he's got us tickets to the Yankees game Saturday night."

Danny smiled. "You're pretty sure you're going to play on Sunday, huh, Michael?"

"Oh, they'll play," Ray said. "So will you. Remember, if you make the semis, you play Sunday, win or lose. You're welcome to come see the Yankees Saturday night if you want. I can get more tickets, no problem."

Danny loved baseball. He did not, however, love the idea of Ray Leach. He gave off the same sort of vibe as Paul Judson. "So, Ray," he said, "who do you work for?"

Leach gave him a smarmy smile. "Everyone," he said. "And no one. Really, I just work for guys like you and Michael and Alex. I try to make sure you get involved with the right agent when the time comes, with the right shoe company, with the right college, with the right money manager—which sounds ridiculous now but won't in a few years. I went through it all myself a long time ago, so I try to keep guys from going in the wrong direction."

"Ray's a good dude," Jordan said. "You can trust him."

Danny resisted the urge to say, "Yeah, right." Instead, he asked Leach where he had played.

"I went to Rutgers," Leach answered. He shook his head sadly. "Got hurt as a freshman. Knee. That's when I found out I didn't have nearly as many friends as I thought. That's why when I graduated I decided I wanted to try to make sure younger guys didn't have an experience like mine."

"So you graduated from Rutgers, even though you got hurt?"

Leach shook his head. "No, I finished at Six Flags."

"Isn't that a theme park?"

"It's also a college in Arizona."

Danny made a mental note to look that one up.

The waitress came and took their order. When Danny

ordered only soup, Ray Leach waved a hand at him. "Order whatever you want, Danny," he said. "It's on me."

"I'm okay," Danny said. "I had kind of a snack right after we played."

Alex and Terrell ordered hamburgers. Michael Jordan ordered soup, shrimp, and the roast beef platter.

When the waitress was gone, Leach leaned forward and took Danny's arm. "I've heard you're thinking D-3," he said. "You're a lot better than that, my man. I've talked to a bunch of coaches here, big-time coaches, who think you can play for them."

Terrell clapped Danny on the shoulder. "That's what I've been telling him too. But he won't listen to me."

"I always listen to you," Danny said. "Just not to some of the guys you hang out with."

Leach leaned back, smiling, clearly thinking he had gotten their attention. "I can put them in touch with you if you want."

"If they want to contact me, they can just go through my father. . . ."

"Of course they can," Leach said. "And they will. But if you go through me, it works better."

"How so?" Terrell asked, a split second before Danny could.

"Just does," Leach said. "Like Mike said, you can trust me."

Jordan, who was back to looking at his cell phone, looked up and nodded. "It's true," he said. "You can."

Mayer hadn't said a word.

Leach turned his attention to Terrell. "I can help you too—but in different ways. You don't need any help with coaches, but I can steer you clear of some of the bottom feeders who will try to make you offers. You need some guidance there."

That was touching, Danny thought. Leach wanted to help Terrell.

"Guidance, huh?" Terrell said, smiling. "Is that what I need?"

Danny smirked, pleased to see that Terrell wasn't buying this. His first instinct was to tell Leach exactly what he thought of his offers of help and guidance. But then he wondered if Bobby Kelleher knew about Ray Leach. If he didn't, he should. So he decided to play along for the moment. "Why don't you give us your card," he said. "In case we need anything."

He saw Terrell and Mayer both flash him looks of semi-horror.

Then his soup arrived. It wasn't very appealing, either.

Danny and Terrell got a ride back to the gym with Jordan and Mayer. Danny was relieved to find that Leach had his own car. During the short ride, Jordan kept going on about everything Leach was doing for him.

Mayer, who had been almost silent throughout lunch, finally couldn't contain himself any longer. "Michael, the guy's a sleaze bag," he said. "Everything he's doing is against the rules. Hell, we probably violated half a dozen rules just by letting him buy us lunch. He could get you into big trouble."

Jordan waved him off. "Come on, Alex, don't be like that," he said. "Everybody does this stuff, and you know it. Terrell, tell him about all the guys hanging out with you."

"They aren't *all* bad," Terrell said. "Just some of them."

"What'd you think of Leach?" Danny asked.

"Not very much," Terrell said.

"Yeah. I don't think I need his kind of help, either," Danny said.

Jordan glanced in the rearview mirror and gave Danny a patronizing smile. "No offense, but who's recruiting you? Vermont? BU? Or maybe you're a really good student so you've got the Ivy League looking at you. But you think you're ever gonna play in the NBA? Ever gonna have a shoe deal? A billboard? No. But I will. Terrell will too. It's different for us."

Danny looked at Alex, who clearly didn't want to argue with his teammate. Terrell rolled his eyes and looked out the window. And really, what did he care what Michael Jordan did or said? But Danny could never quite resist a fight. "You're right. You and Terrell are different from me. But every year there are a dozen high school players just like you. And they don't all end up with billboards. Most of them end up like Lenny Cooke."

"Who the hell is Lenny Cooke?" Jordan asked.

"Exactly," Danny said. "He and LeBron James were both at this camp. They were the 'next ones.' Cooke was rated ahead of Amar'e Stoudemire *and* Carmelo Anthony. He tried to turn pro without playing in college. Never got drafted, never played a minute in the NBA. He and LeBron were Terrell and you or Omar Whytlaw a dozen years ago. One of them's an icon. The other one's forgotten. Maybe you'll be the icon and Terrell will be Lenny Cooke. Or maybe it will be the other way around."

"Or maybe we'll both be LeBron," Jordan shot back.

"Possible," Danny said. "But the odds are better you'll both be Lenny Cooke. Most of the guys making the big NBA money weren't big stars in high school. A few, but not many."

They were wheeling into the parking lot now. Jordan headed right for the front row of parking spaces nearest the building. A yellow-jacketed security guard was blocking the road, but as soon as he saw the Lincoln approach, he moved out of the way and waved at Jordan, who waved back. They pulled into a spot no more than fifteen yards from the back door.

"Ray took care of these guys at the start of the week," Jordan said as he put the car into park.

"What a surprise," Danny said.

Jordan turned and looked right at him. "Listen, Wilcox, I really don't need any life lessons from a slow-assed white point guard who will be lucky if he gets to be on court with me next year so I can dunk on him all night. I know how good I am, and I'm not the only one who knows it." He looked at Terrell. "And I'll tell you something, choir boy, you're a fool if you listen to him and his father. There's just too much candy on the table to walk away. And if you're afraid of being some lame Lenny Cooke, then you'd better take what's on offer *now*."

He turned around, jumped out of the car, and slammed the door, leaving Danny and Terrell sitting there with Mayer. It took only seconds for the car to start to feel hot with the air-conditioning turned off.

"He's headed down a bad road," Danny said as they watched Jordan stop to high-five several people as he headed for the door.

Mayer shrugged. "You might be right," he said. "But a lot of guys go down that road and end up just fine. If you can play, people will always take care of you. Michael can play."

"How're his grades?" Terrell asked.

Mayer laughed. "Come on, Terrell, now you *do* sound naive. You know that doesn't matter. If he needed someone to take the SAT for him, it would get done. If he needs to change schools to 'get his grades up,' that'll be done. Seriously, when was the last time you heard of a star player who wasn't eligible to play? All these guys like Ray and the shoe guys and the big-time college coaches—they've figured the system out. The NCAA doesn't *want* to catch them."

Danny sighed. Mayer was right. The rules, he realized, might exist for someone like him or possibly even for Alex. But for Terrell Jamerson, Omar Whytlaw, and Michael Jordan, they didn't.

Terrell also suspected Mayer was right. But even though the game was rigged in his favor, he felt a little sick.

The three of them got out of the car before it turned into an oven and walked inside the gym, their path unimpeded by any dudes or hangers-on or even coaches.

Most people were watching the two o'clock games. Since their meeting wasn't until three thirty, they had some time to kill, so they went and sat high up in the players' section of the bleachers to watch.

"So why didn't you guys play yesterday?" Alex asked once they sat down.

Danny started to say something, but Terrell put up a hand. "Honestly?" he said. "I screwed up. I went out with my pals and got high, and Danny tried to cover up for me, which our coach didn't appreciate."

If the revelation surprised Alex, he didn't show it. "Yeah, I think Michael's friends hook him up too," he said.

"Really?" Danny asked.

"I'm just guessing. We're friends, but not like you and Terrell. We go to different schools back home."

"That was my first time," Terrell said.

"Seriously?"

"Very seriously."

They watched in silence for a while, although Terrell wasn't really paying attention. Which might have been why he didn't notice the man in the suit walking up through the bleachers in their direction. He stopped one row short of where Danny, Terrell, and Alex were sitting. Even then

Terrell avoided eye contact. He really had no interest in dealing with another agent, and the suit—even though the man was wearing an open-collared golf shirt, as opposed to a button-down and a tie—made it clear that this was yet another agent.

"Terrell Jamerson? Danny Wilcox? Alex Mayer?" the man said.

"Uh-huh," Danny said in a bored tone, hoping rudeness would convince the man to leave them alone.

"I'm Frank Parsons, from NCAA enforcement," he said, flashing his wallet as if he were a cop—which, in a sense, he was. "I need to speak to the three of you right now."

Terrell looked up at Parsons, who appeared to be in his midthirties. He was African American, with short-cropped hair and a look that would best be described as no-nonsense. Terrell's heart skipped half a beat. Why would he want to talk to him and Danny and Alex? Before he could say anything, Alex, who was still leaning against the back of the bleachers, said, "What do you want to talk to us about?"

"Come with me and I'll tell you," he said.

"I'm not going anywhere until you tell me what this is about," Alex said.

"I'd advise you to change your attitude in a hurry, Mr. Mayer," Parsons said. "You're already in trouble."

"For what?" Danny blurted.

"You'll find out in about five minutes," Parsons said. He turned and began walking down toward the floor.

Terrell looked at Danny and then at Alex. "What do you think?" he said.

"I think we'd better go," Alex said. "If only to find out what this is about."

The three of them followed Parsons in the direction of the locker room. Terrell noticed that Parsons never turned to check to see if they were behind him.

Parsons walked into the locker-room hallway and paused at the room where the press conferences had been held all week. Terrell saw Danny smile. "What's so funny?" he whispered.

"Who would've thought I'd be hoping there were reporters inside," Danny whispered back.

There were no reporters. Instead, they found Michael Jordan; the coach of the Riverboats, whose name Terrell didn't know; and another man dressed a lot like Frank Parsons.

"This is Michael Olander. He works with me," Parsons said. "I believe you both know Mr. Jordan. And this is Coach Woolard, who's coaching the team Mr. Jordan and Mr. Mayer are playing on here."

"Dave Woolard," the coach said, standing to shake Danny's and Terrell's hands. "I'd say it's nice to meet you both, except for the circumstances."

"What *are* the circumstances, Coach?" Alex asked.

"Have a seat," said Olander, who was leaning against the podium at the front of the room. He had barely nodded at Terrell, Danny, and Alex. Now he pulled a notebook from his breast pocket, flipped it open, and began to read. " 'Four players, identified as Jordan and Mayer from the Mississippi team and Wilcox and Jamerson from Massachusetts, were observed having lunch at Houston's restaurant in Teaneck with a Ray Leach. Mr. Leach has been employed in the past as a bird dog for several agents, as a representative for at least two apparel companies, and as a representative for a number of Division One basketball programs.'"

"Has he ever actually been sanctioned by you guys for any violations?" Coach Woolard asked.

"We can't sanction him, because he doesn't fall under our jurisdiction," Olander said. "But he has been named in a number of our investigations that have led to sanctions." He whirled on Danny, pointing a finger. "How did you come to have lunch with Mr. Leach?"

Danny opened his mouth to answer, but Terrell gave him a shove. "Before we answer any questions, I'd like to have my coach here," Terrell said. "I'm sure Danny feels the same way."

Danny nodded, grateful.

"You don't need your coach," Parsons said. "This isn't a police station. No one has read you your rights. We're just asking a few questions."

"But Mike and Alex have *their* coach here," Danny said. "We should have ours here too."

Before Parsons or Olander could say anything, Coach Woolard jumped in. "He's right, and you two know he's right. Either let them call their coach or we're all leaving."

The NCAA duo did not look happy.

"Go ahead and call your daddy," Olander said in a sneering voice. "You've got five minutes."

Danny didn't argue with the ridiculous deadline. He pulled out his phone and hit his father's number on the speed dial.

ELEVEN

Danny breathed a sigh of relief when his dad picked up the phone right away. He was even happier to learn he had just walked back into the gym after lunch. When Danny told him he needed him to come to the interview room to meet with some people from the NCAA, his dad didn't ask any questions. Maybe he could tell by Danny's tone that he would get answers once he got there.

If the scene that greeted Coach Wilcox when he walked in shocked him, he didn't show it. He patted Danny and Terrell on the back as if to say "Stay calm," and he shook hands with Coach Woolard. The NCAA men introduced themselves and said they were looking into possible viola-tions committed by the four players in the room.

Danny's dad folded his arms and said, "Okay, what have you got?"

Olander, still reading from his notes, repeated what he had witnessed inside the restaurant.

Coach Wilcox nodded and looked at Coach Woolard. "Unless there's something I'm missing, it sounds like these four kids have been accused of eating lunch with a bad guy. I know the NCAA rule book is something like five hundred pages long, but I didn't know there were rules about who you could and couldn't eat lunch with."

"Actually, you're wrong," Parsons said. "There are very explicit rules about student-athletes socializing with representatives of universities that might recruit them, registered agents, or anyone who might represent the athletic interests of a college."

"And which of those categories does this Leach guy fall into?"

"There's a long list based on his past. In this case, we're trying to find out which one. The student-athletes can answer our questions now—or later, when we open a formal investigation. Your choice. Or theirs."

Danny's dad shook his head and laughed. "Can you just call them players? Save the 'student-athlete' crap for your press releases. Dave, I'm okay with my guys answering a couple questions before that three-thirty meeting. Are you?"

Woolard nodded. "Let's get it over with."

Olander again looked at Danny. "As I was saying, Mr. Wilcox. Can you tell me what you were doing with Mr. Leach in the Houston's restaurant today?"

Danny shrugged. "Sure. I was not eating the bowl of soup I ordered. It was cold."

"Who paid for the soup?"

"I assume Mr. Leach. I had no idea who he was. Never met him before today."

"Did he offer you anything else?"

"Yeah," Danny said, trying to hide a smirk. "Dessert."

Both Terrell and Mayer laughed out loud at that one, earning glares from both the NCAA men.

"You want to try that one again without being a smart-ass?" Olander said.

"I'm telling you the truth," Danny said. "I got there late. I had actually already eaten with someone else."

"Who would that be?" Olander said.

"Bobby Kelleher," Danny said.

"The reporter?" Parsons asked.

"Yes."

"And he'll back up your story?"

"Of course."

Olander decided it was time to change his focus. "Mr. Mayer, how did you come to have lunch with Mr. Leach?"

It occurred to Terrell that this might be a dicey question for Mayer. Saying that Jordan had made all the arrangements would put the spotlight squarely on him—which was, he suspected, what the NCAA guys wanted. Alex didn't blink. "Mr. Leach seems to know a lot of players here," he said. "And I know he's friends with Mr. Tommasino. He offered to buy us lunch. Neither one of us is exactly dripping with money, so we figured why not? We were told not to talk to coaches or agents. He didn't appear to be either."

Olander turned to Jordan. "All this true, Mr. Jordan?"

"Yeah," Jordan said, his tone a lot different than the cocky "I'll do what I want" tone he'd been using on the car ride back. "Yeah. We just had lunch with the dude. That was it."

"Did he offer any of you anything other than lunch?" Olander asked.

"He said he could get us tickets for the ballgame Saturday night," Mayer said. He glanced at Jordan for a split second. "We told him no."

Jordan, clearly picking up the hint, was nodding. "That's right. We told him no."

Terrell was waiting for the NCAA men to ask Jordan about the car he was driving. He didn't think Jordan would have an answer for that one.

As expected, Olander asked next about the car. But he didn't ask Jordan. "Mr. Mayer, how did you get from here to lunch and back today?" he asked.

"Divide and conquer," Danny whispered, leaning close to Terrell.

"Do you have a comment, Mr. Wilcox?" Parsons said.

"No," Danny said. "Absolutely not."

"I got a ride," Alex said.

"From whom?" Olander said.

"Mike. He said that Mr. Leach was already at the shopping mall and had asked him to drive the car over there for him."

Wow, Terrell thought. *That was pretty good.*

"How did Mr. Leach get to the mall?" Olander asked.

Alex shrugged. "I have no idea."

Olander made a face indicating that Mayer had upset

him by not falling into his trap. He turned to Jordan, who looked a little more relaxed than he had a couple of minutes before. Alex had handed him a possible escape route.

"Mr. Jordan, do you know how Mr. Leach got to the mall? You know we'll question him later."

"Well, then, I'm sure he'll explain," Jordan said. "Before we played this morning, he asked me if I'd do him a favor and drive his car to the mall when we met for lunch because he had to be over there earlier for another meeting."

"How did you meet Mr. Leach?" Olander asked.

"Mr. Tommasino introduced us," Jordan said with so much confidence that Danny suspected he was telling the truth. "He said he was a 'friend of the camp' and that it was okay to talk to him while we were here."

Parsons and Olander appeared upset. They looked at each other, as if searching for another direction to go in.

"Besides loaning you a car and taking you to lunch, what else has Mr. Leach given you this week?" Parsons finally said, looking at Jordan.

"He didn't loan me the car—he asked me to bring it to him," Jordan said. "And that's it—lunch." He smiled. "Like Danny said, we didn't even have dessert."

Danny's dad had apparently heard enough. "Unless you two have some kind of real evidence that any of the boys did something wrong, they have a meeting they're supposed to be at in about two minutes," he said. "So are we done here?"

Parsons glared at him. "We're done," he said. "For now."

* * *

Danny was about to say something to Alex Mayer, like "quick thinking," once the three players and the two coaches were out in the hallway, but before he could open his mouth, his father said, "We'll talk to you guys a little later. Danny, I need you for a minute before your meeting. Terrell, wait here a second."

He put his hand on Danny's back and began steering him down the hall before any of the Mississippi-three could say anything beyond "Catch you later."

They walked straight out the back door and into the broiling heat.

"I want you to listen to me, Daniel, because I'm pretty much through with pulling you back from the cliff every damn day," his father began.

Danny knew that his father saying "damn" was a bad sign, and calling him Daniel was even worse. That name only came up when he was in serious trouble.

"Dad, I swear I didn't . . ."

His father put a hand up. "You did. And I know you like this Mayer kid, but he looked those NCAA guys right in the eye and lied cool as could be just now. That's the sign of an experienced liar. And if you think for one second they bought that story, you're crazy. What were you thinking, taking Terrell to lunch with a guy like Ray Leach?"

"I didn't, Dad," Danny said, almost pleading. "He was with Jordan and Mayer when I got there after talking to Kelleher."

His dad's face softened a little. "Okay, okay. Look, those guys won't let up. They'll try to find a way to take it out on *you* because they couldn't nail Jordan and they have nothing on Terrell. And you'd better drop that smart-ass tone I heard in there."

"Dad, the guy was a complete jerk—"

"They're *paid* to be jerks. This Jordan kid is being bought and paid for right under their noses, and you and Mayer give them attitude and a bunch of lies. What do you expect them to do, clap you on the back and say, 'Good luck tonight'? Grow up, Danny. Now go to your meeting. Try not to get into trouble there. You're wearing me out."

He turned around and walked back inside. Danny stood there alone for a moment, wishing he had the keys to Jordan's Lincoln, which was sitting a few yards from where he was standing. If he'd had the keys, he would have been seriously tempted to get in the car, drive away, and not look back.

Instead, he squared his shoulders and walked back inside to find Terrell.

And then he *did* get into trouble in the meeting.

It wasn't his mouth this time, it was his eyes—which at some point closed during the presentation by someone who apparently worked in public relations for the NCAA. Maybe Danny had just had his fill of NCAA people for the day, but soon after he heard the guy say, "And remember, print reporters are always looking to create controversy. Always remember that, as a student-athlete . . ." he felt someone shaking him by the shoulder.

"Whaa, huh?" he said.

"Wake up, Wilcox."

He looked up and saw Paul Judson, the agent he'd met the first day, standing over him. Judson had been introduced as someone who would explain to them how to know an agent you could trust from an agent you couldn't trust. Hearing that, Danny had thought about what Bobby Kelleher would have said in response: "If the agent is breathing, don't trust him." He hoped he might have somehow slept through Judson's presentation, but no such luck; the NCAA drone was still standing at the front of the room.

"You need to party less and pay attention more," Judson said as the room tittered.

Terrell, sitting next to him, sat up very straight in his seat after that comment but said nothing.

Danny remembered his dad telling him he'd better stay out of trouble, so rather than come back with another smart-ass answer, he sat up straight and said he was sorry. The drone continued.

The meeting lasted almost two hours and Danny was pretty sure he saw others nodding off before it was over. No one shook them awake. As they walked out the door, Terrell fell into step with him. "Kinda funny, wasn't it?" he said.

"There was something funny in that meeting? I missed it."

"It's kinda funny that a two-hour meeting on how to

deal with the media is all about why everyone in the media except TV is evil."

Actually, Danny thought, that *was* funny. The entire message had been: Don't tell the media anything. It had been two hours' worth of the famous Crash Davis speech in *Bull Durham*, in which he tells Nuke LaLoosh to always say noncommittal, noncontroversial things when talking to the media: *I just want to give 110 percent every day. . . . I love my teammates. . . . I want to thank the fans for everything. . . . I thank God for giving me the chance to play this great game.* He wondered how many athletes had learned their lines from that movie.

Because the meeting let out so late, the camp had arranged for a buffet-style meal for the players, so they would be able to eat and digest before playing at seven o'clock.

"They should have had this set-up all week," Danny's dad said as they sat down. He had joined them and had brought Tom Konchalski and Frank Sullivan with him. "Then there would have been less riding back and forth to restaurants with unsavory types. . . ."

Tom Konchalski had been briefed on Danny and Terrell's latest misadventure, and he wasn't laughing even a little bit. "Let me tell you something about these NCAA guys," he said. "In their own way, they're every bit as corrupt as Ray Leach or Paul Judson or any of these other hangers-on. They have an agenda too. They're after scalps, so they can show their bosses that they're doing their jobs. They don't care what's fair or whether they're nailing big offenders or little ones. They just want to nail *someone*."

"What's the old Tark line about NCAA justice?" Frank Sullivan asked, referring to Jerry Tarkanian, the former coach at Nevada–Las Vegas who had spent most of his career battling with the NCAA.

Coach Wilcox smiled and filled in the story for Danny and Terrell. "Years ago, an overnight-mail envelope en route from the Kentucky basketball office to the father of a Kentucky recruit accidentally opened, and a thousand dollars fell out of it. The mail guy turned the money in, and Kentucky got investigated by the NCAA. Tark said, The NCAA is *so* mad at Kentucky, they're going to put Cleveland State on probation for another three years."

Everyone laughed ruefully. It was hardly news that the NCAA would rather put the hammer to a relatively small program like Cleveland State than to a big-time program like Kentucky.

"The point of the story should be important to you," Konchalski said, looking at Danny. "They'd rather nail you than Terrell or Michael Jordan, because those guys are more likely to drive TV ratings when they get to college. Terrell, you're lucky—they'll only go after you if you *really* screw up. Danny, you they're more than happy to go after."

Danny remembered the feeling in the interview room. The NCAA guys had made sure Jordan's coach was there. They hadn't even asked Terrell a single question. They had gone after him first as if he was somehow the main culprit. "So what should I do?" he asked Konchalski.

"Everything your father tells you to," Konchalski answered. "Play by the rules. You too, Terrell. Because the more they think you're on the take, the more likely they'll be to go after Danny."

They both looked at him closely to see if he was smiling. He wasn't.

Given all that had gone on that afternoon, Danny was afraid the game that night might be a disaster. He'd forgotten, though, that the rest of the Rebels hadn't been involved in the ongoing soap opera. He also hadn't been paying much attention to the team they were playing, the Texas Rangers, who, as it turned out, were probably more qualified to play baseball than basketball.

Early on, it became apparent that no one on the Texas team wanted anything to do with Terrell. At the end of the first quarter, with the Rebels leading 18–9, Coach Wilcox looked at Danny and said, "Throw it in to Terrell every time until they stop him."

They never did. All the starters came out two minutes into the fourth quarter with the score 81–38. Terrell had scored 44, and, although he didn't know it, Danny had 21 assists. The only reason he found out was because someone rushed over to him when the game was over to tell him he had set a camp record—whatever that meant—with the 21 assists.

Jay Swanson was behind Danny in the handshake line when the camp PR person told Danny about his "record."

"My cat could get twenty-one assists feeding Terrell in a game like this," Swanson said. "All this team is about is trying to get you a D-1 scholarship."

Danny was tempted to start another fight, but there was no point. He only had to put up with Swanson for two more days. Still, he couldn't resist a small jab. "How many threes did you hit tonight, Jay?" he asked.

"Five," Swanson said, not surprising Danny by knowing his stats off the top of his head.

"How many of those came on passes from me?"

Swanson didn't answer that one.

Before Danny could say anything else, he heard a familiar voice.

"Jay, *my man*. You had twenty-three and it could have been double if you'd have gotten the ball more."

It was Ray Leach.

"No kidding," Swanson said.

There was an angel sitting on Danny's shoulder telling him to just keep walking. But there was a devil on the other shoulder whispering in his ear. He listened to the devil.

"Hey, Ray," he said. "Do you want to meet up with Terrell and me after we're showered?"

Leach looked like a kid who had found Santa eating his cookies by the fireplace.

"Yo, dude, absolutely. Tell me where and I'll meet you."

"Yeah, perfect," Danny said. "Meet me in hell."

He headed for the locker-room hallway with a huge grin. He didn't have to look back to know that both Leach and Swanson were glaring daggers at him. He really did need to try harder not to pick fights with everyone . . . starting tomorrow.

TWELVE

The easy victory over the team from Texas clinched a spot in the quarterfinals for the Rebels. Saturday morning they would play DC Assault, a team out of Washington. A win would most likely set up a rematch with the Orange Crushes, the team they had played on the first day of camp. To Danny, that game felt like a hundred years ago. The Riverboats were in the other bracket, meaning they couldn't meet the Rebels before the championship game. Just as well—Michael Jordan had scored 54 points in the Riverboats' last game of the round robin.

According to Tom Konchalski, there were now three players being touted by the scouts as potential one-and-done college players: Jordan; Omar Whytlaw, from the Crushes; and Terrell. Konchalski had also told Coach Wilcox that Danny had been one of the surprises of the camp. "My phone is filled with texts," his dad confirmed. "You are no longer considered a marginal D-1 prospect. You're well above that. Don't get a big head."

Danny was too tired to get a big head. The games had

been good—but all the off-court stuff had been exhausting. As he pulled on his uniform Saturday morning, he knew he needed to focus. There were plenty of lockers available now because twenty-four of the thirty-two teams were no longer playing. Some had gone home; others had stayed to watch the remaining eight teams.

As it turned out, the quarterfinal didn't require all that much focus from Danny. The game was almost as much of a blowout as the one the night before. DC Assault's best player, Carlos Ruiz, who was their point guard, had rolled an ankle the previous day and didn't play. Without Ruiz, the DC team had trouble running any offense at all. The game was close for a half, before a spate of turnovers led to a 17–2 run for the Rebels, who pulled away to win, 94–74. Terrell finished with 27 points, Swanson had 22, and Danny had 12 points and 12 assists.

The dudes were out in force after the game. Terrell gave them the usual high fives but didn't linger. "We have to play the semis in a couple hours," he said. "I'll catch you guys later."

The semifinals would be played back to back. The Riverboats were playing High Five from Detroit at 2:00. After that, the Rebels would have their rematch with the Orange Crushes at 3:30. There was another buffet set up for the players because the timing was so tight, but they did have the option of eating on their own.

"Trouble in paradise?" Danny asked as he and Terrell headed for the buffet.

"What?" Terrell asked.

"You and the dudes," Danny said. "You kind of blew them off back there."

Terrell shrugged. "Listen, I know I screwed up the other day, but I'm not stupid. So you can lay off a little, okay? I'm not sayin' I'm never going to hang with those guys again, but I *am* going to be more careful."

Danny nodded, surprised at Terrell's serious tone.

"All I want is to win two more games and get out of here. It's been one long week."

"So you think we can crush the Crushes and sink the Riverboats?" Danny asked, earning a small smile from Terrell.

"Everyone loves a rebel."

"You know it," Danny said, nodding. "Let's go overthrow the establishment."

Terrell shook his head. "Danny, Danny—always looking for a fight . . ."

"You got a problem with that?" Danny said, getting up in Terrell's face.

"Not at all, man," said Terrell, laughing. "Not at all."

Crushing the Crushes was—not surprisingly—easier said than done.

The gym was packed. Gone were the three courts and the three games being played at once. The regular baskets were in place, with the court now running north and south, and all eyes in the building were on one game, because only one was being played.

Terrell and Danny got a chance to briefly congratulate Alex Mayer as the Riverboats were leaving the court after winning their semifinal. They had been in the locker room for the final few minutes but had seen enough to know that Jordan had been brilliant again. While Danny and Terrell were chatting with Alex, Jordan walked by with a phalanx of security and camp PR people.

"Nice playing, Mike," Danny said.

Jordan glanced at him, shook his head, and kept going.

"What's his problem?" Terrell asked Mayer.

"He's decided what happened the other day was your fault, that you guys somehow tipped off the NCAA guys," Mayer said.

"That's crazy," Danny said, feeling a surge of anger. "He's the one driving around in the big car, hanging with Leach. I never even heard of the guy until you two brought him to lunch."

"Me neither," Terrell put in.

Mayer waved a hand. "I know, I know," he said. "I told him that. But he's scared now. It never occurred to him the NCAA would actually check up on him. He isn't going to blame Leach or any of his boys, so he's decided to blame you two."

"That's his problem, then," Terrell said.

"You're right," Mayer said. "But if we play you guys tomorrow, don't try to take a charge from him."

Danny snorted. "I may be dumb, but I ain't stupid."

Mayer laughed.

A camp PR person hustled up. "Alex, you're needed right now in the interview room," she said urgently.

"Good luck, guys," Alex said. "I hope we're playing against each other tomorrow."

No matter what Danny's dad had said about Mayer lying so coolly to the NCAA guys, Danny couldn't help but like him. He hoped they would play tomorrow. Of course, there was the not-so-small matter of the Orange Crushes and Omar Whytlaw to get past first.

It became clear very early in the game that Whytlaw wanted very much to get even with Terrell for nailing the three-pointer at the end of their first game. But Whytlaw's obsession with proving he was better than Terrell turned out to be a bigger problem for the Crushes than the Rebels because he didn't want to give up the ball. Coach Wilcox quickly recognized what he was doing and ordered Danny to double-team him whenever he caught the ball in the low post with his back to the basket.

The smart thing for Whytlaw to do when he saw Danny coming at him was to pitch the ball to Danny's man, who was wide open on the perimeter. Instead, with Danny in front of him and Terrell behind him, he tried to bull his way to the basket. By halftime, Danny had stolen the ball three times. Whytlaw had twice been called for charges when trying to get past Terrell and had made just three of eleven shots. At the other end, Terrell was handling the Crushes' decision to double-team him perfectly: He waited for the perimeter defender to leave his man and then passed to the open Rebel. Terrell had seven assists at halftime, and Danny and Swanson had each hit four three-pointers. The Rebels led, 43–29.

"You have to expect Coach Welch to adjust and tell Whytlaw he has to pass the ball out of the double-teams," Coach Wilcox said during the break. "He's probably already said it, but now he's got to insist."

"Should we stop doubling?" asked Jason Marks, who occasionally doubled instead of Danny, just to surprise Whytlaw.

"No, not until he actually starts to pass the ball," Coach Wilcox said. "If he starts finding shooters, we'll make the adjustment."

On the first play of the second half, Danny found Terrell inside, and no one doubled him. Not wanting to commit a third foul, Whytlaw played matador defense on Terrell, allowing him to spin right past him for an easy dunk. The Crushes came down, and Whytlaw posted up, calling for the ball. George Smalls, the point guard who had threatened to put Danny through the floor if he tried to take a charge the first time the teams had played, actually looked away from Whytlaw, clearly wanting to go somewhere else with the ball. But his teammates were just watching, not moving, figuring the ball was going to Whytlaw.

Terrell could see Smalls visibly sigh before angling left so he could get a pass into Whytlaw in the post. Instantly, Danny turned to double. Whytlaw saw him coming, took one quick dribble, and tried to power through Terrell, who had excellent position. Terrell went down, and the whistle blew. Sitting on the floor, Terrell saw the referee signaling Whytlaw for a charge—his third foul.

"You got to be kidding!" Whytlaw said to the ref, clearly frustrated. "Dude is acting, man. Can't you see that?"

Having signaled the foul, the ref turned to Whytlaw. Danny knew from his dad that the officials, most of whom were aspiring college referees, had been told to be patient with the players and try to explain to them what they'd done wrong. "Son, he had clear position on you. Even if he hadn't gone down, it would have been a charge. You went right through him."

"Ah, f— you, man," Whytlaw said.

The officials had been told to be patient, but they had their limits. Right away the ref called a technical foul on Whytlaw for cursing. Since a technical also counted as a personal foul, that meant Whytlaw now had four fouls—one away from fouling out. Coach Welch was way out on the court, taking Whytlaw by the arm to get him away from the referee before he got teed up again.

Terrell saw Danny start to the free throw line to shoot the technical. Danny was a 92 percent free throw shooter, so he always shot technicals in Lexington games. This was the first technical that had been called all week here, though, and Swanson was also walking to the foul line. Clearly, he was also used to taking the technicals.

"What are you doing, Wilcox?" Swanson said. "Does Daddy let you shoot technicals to make you happy?"

"I do usually shoot them, yes," Danny answered.

"Yeah, well, when you make eighty-five percent, then you can shoot them," Swanson said. "In the meantime, get out of my way."

Terrell looked at the bench to see what Coach Wilcox would do. He was waving Danny away from the foul line, indicating he should let Swanson shoot. Swanson made one of the two shots. Terrell saw Danny walk stiffly past Swanson to go and inbound the ball, clearly aching to say something but holding himself back. He felt no such compunction. "My boy shoots ninety-two percent from the line," he said to Swanson. "Next time, he takes the shots."

Swanson said nothing.

They were up, 46–29. They just needed to get this game over with and get ready for the final. That turned out to be difficult. With Whytlaw on the bench, the Crushes spread out their offense and, with nothing to lose, began bombing threes. By the end of the third quarter, they'd cut the lead to 65–55. A few minutes later, it was 79–75, and Coach Wilcox called time-out.

As the players huddled around him, Terrell noticed Whytlaw reporting to the scorer's table to check back into the game.

"Coach," Terrell heard Danny say, catching his father's eye and nodding toward the table. Danny was always careful to call his dad Coach in front of other players.

Andy Wilcox nodded. "Fellas, it looks like Whytlaw is back in," he said. "You *still* need to get back on defense better, but Danny, Jay, Jason—be prepared to double him in the post if they're running their regular half-court offense."

As they walked back on court, Terrell nudged Danny. "Would you put him back in?" he said quietly.

"Nope," Danny said. "But their coach is probably worried

about the coaches who are watching, the people running the camp, and Whytlaw's posse."

The whistle blew, and as Danny started the ball up-court, Coach Wilcox held up three fingers, pointed downward. That meant he wanted Terrell to show himself in the low post and then come around a screen for a quick pass and shot. It was one of a handful of plays they had worked on during their three pre-camp practices. They hadn't run the play very much during the week because the screener on the play was Swanson and his weak attempts at screening had done nothing to free Terrell.

Danny looked surprised, but the call was clear. Danny held up his three fingers pointing at the floor and dribbled to his right. Terrell, having set up briefly in the low post, popped up from his stance, sprinted to the baseline, and turned back in the direction of the key, angling to the left of the lane. As Whytlaw tried to follow, he slammed full-force into Swanson, who had set a perfect screen. Danny fed the ball to Terrell, and Terrell caught it with his feet squared up just outside the three-point line, wide open thanks to Swanson's jarring screen.

The ball swished through with 3:37 on the clock for an 82–75 lead.

The Crushes didn't quit. Whytlaw had finally figured out that he couldn't go through Terrell or put the ball on the floor when he was doubled. On two occasions, he pitched the ball to the perimeter and found open teammates for threes. On two other occasions, they threw the ball right back to him and, before Danny or Swanson could recover, he turned for short jumpers over Terrell in the lane.

The Rebels led by two, 91–89, after another Whytlaw jumper with 5.7 seconds to go. The Crushes were out of time-outs, so Terrell grabbed the ball and inbounded it quickly to Danny, knowing the Crushes would foul right away—which they did. The clock was at 3.9 seconds as everyone walked to the far end for Danny to shoot. The Rebels were in the double bonus, so Danny had two shots.

"No fouls!" his dad was screaming. "If Danny makes both, just let 'em go! If he misses one, run ninety-four."

Ninety-four was their full-court defense. If he missed a shot, the Crushes would need to get a three to tie the game, so the Rebels would do their best to kill off the clock before they could do that.

Danny took a deep breath as the referee handed him the ball, and went through his routine. He calmly swished the first shot, and the lead was 92–89. If he made the second, they'd be in the final. Danny stepped back and nodded at the Crushes' point guard George Smalls. "I've got ten," he said, making sure everyone else knew who they were supposed to cover in case he missed.

But Terrell knew he wouldn't. He had never seen Danny miss when it mattered. Still, he took note of Whytlaw, who was standing at midcourt, hands on hips.

Danny took another deep breath. Two dribbles and the ball was in the air. Swish again. He allowed himself a smile as he raced over to pick up Smalls, who was inbounding.

Smalls tossed a quick pass to Whytlaw, who was a few steps beyond midcourt. Terrell wasn't going to go anywhere near him and risk fouling him while he was attempting a three. That was the Crushes' only chance—to make a three and get fouled in the act of shooting.

Realizing that no one was near him, Whytlaw took the ball, dribbled straight to the basket, and went up for a ferocious two-handed dunk, no doubt figuring he might as well show off for the crowd since the game was lost and his run at this camp was over. Terrell heard the buzzer go off while Whytlaw was still swinging from the rim—a move that would have earned him a technical foul for showboating if the game hadn't been over.

Terrell was about to head for the handshake line when he noticed that Whytlaw was losing his grip on the rim. He saw him try to grab it, but to no avail. He plummeted downward and landed squarely on his back with an ominous thud that seemed to shake the whole gym. Terrell heard him let out a scream of pain. Instinctively, he began running in Omar's direction.

Coach Welch was the first one to get to Whytlaw. His teammates quickly surrounded him, and Terrell heard Coach Wilcox turn to the scorer's table and say, "Call the EMTs—quick!"

Terrell had seen an ambulance parked out back, which he knew was routine at an event like this, but he had never given it any real thought. Whytlaw was still lying flat on his back, his arms at his sides, eyes wide open. He was moving his head from side to side, moaning loudly. Terrell didn't know if it was from pain or fright or both.

"Omar, don't try to move," Coach Welch said. "Stay calm. Help is on the way."

Terrell saw a man with short-cropped blond hair pushing through the crowd just as he noticed the back door open and saw a stretcher being pushed through it.

"I'm a doctor," the blond-haired man said. "Let me get a look at him."

He knelt next to Whytlaw. He was speaking very softly, but the gym had gone so quiet that Terrell could hear him.

Terrell saw him squeeze Whytlaw's leg. "Omar, did you feel anything just now?" he asked.

Terrell could see Whytlaw crying. "Nothing, nothing. Doc, am I paralyzed?"

"Easy, Omar," the doctor said. "We're just checking a couple things here."

He reached up and grabbed his arm. Whytlaw winced. The doctor nodded.

"Good, Omar, your upper body seems fine."

Without saying anything, he reached down again, and Terrell saw him squeeze Whytlaw's leg hard. There was no reaction from Whytlaw. The EMTs had now arrived with the stretcher. The doctor pulled one of them aside and spoke to him quietly. When he was finished, the EMT said, "Folks, we need some room here."

He knelt next to Whytlaw. "Omar, just to be extra careful, we're going to put some apparatus on you to keep you from moving while we put you on the stretcher. This means nothing except we want to be sure we don't hurt you when we move you."

Whytlaw was still crying, but he nodded.

Terrell watched the doctor head slowly over to talk to Coach Wilcox and Coach Welch.

"It's definitely spinal," Terrell heard him say. "No way to tell here if it's permanent."

Terrell shuddered. He looked at Danny, who just shook his head, eyes wide.

"You mean it might be?" Coach Welch asked.

The doctor took a long, deep breath. "He's got no feeling in his legs at all. That could change in an hour. Or it might never change at all."

THIRTEEN

It took a solid twenty minutes for the EMTs to strap Whytlaw to the stretcher so they could roll him out to the ambulance. None of the players left the court, and many of the fans stayed where they were. Everyone had witnessed such a scene before, more often in football than in basketball. Most of the time the procedure was just a precaution. In this case, the words of the doctor echoed in Terrell's head.

As the EMTs worked, Terrell told Danny what he'd heard the doctor say. A few minutes later, Alex Mayer, who had been watching the end of the game from the stands, joined them.

"This is worse than Lenny Cooke," Mayer said quietly.

"Way worse," Terrell said. "I mean, what if—"

"Don't 'what if,'" Danny said. "The doctor said he might be up walking around in an hour."

Or, Terrell thought, *he might not*. He shuddered and vowed to never again swing on the rim while dunking—something he often did in practice just for fun.

When Whytlaw was finally on the stretcher and the

EMTs began to roll him in the direction of the door, all the players formed what could have been a reception line as he went past. Some just said, "Good luck, Omar" or "You'll be okay, Omar." Others shook his hand. When the stretcher came by Terrell, Danny, and Alex, Terrell grabbed Whytlaw by the hand. The EMTs actually stopped for a moment. "You listen to me," he said, leaning down. "You're gonna be okay. *Believe it*, okay?"

"You have a great life," Whytlaw said softly.

Before Terrell could answer, one of the EMTs said, "I'm sorry, but we've got to get going here. Time's important."

Terrell nodded. He had tears in his eyes. So did Danny, who gave Whytlaw a quick handshake as he went by, as did Mayer. The people in the stands were applauding respectfully as the stretcher rolled out, and Whytlaw managed to give everyone a thumbs-up just before he disappeared through the door.

"Okay, guys, I know this is tough, but we've got to get you all showered and dressed."

Terrell turned and saw Billy Tommasino standing behind the circle of players—some in uniform, some in street clothes, like Alex. Other camp functionaries had magically appeared, and now they were all practically herding the players in the direction of the locker room. No doubt Tommasino was noticing all the TV cameras that had gone from taping game highlights to taping the grisly scene that had just unfolded and was having nightmares about the news reports around the country that evening that would begin,

"Tragedy struck this afternoon at the Brickley Shoes 'School Comes First' Camp in Teaneck, New Jersey . . ."

Danny's dad was waving everyone in the direction of the locker room, and so was Coach Welsh. They all followed instructions. No one was talking very much. Once they were inside the locker room, Tommasino raised his voice to get everyone's attention.

"Fellas, if you can all listen up for just a second," he said, and everyone turned to him. "Look, I know we're all upset about Omar, but the fact that he has use of his upper body is a very good sign, so let's stay optimistic. There will be a lot of media outside wanting to talk about this. You were all at media training yesterday. Remember what you were told: In a crisis—and I'm not sure this is a crisis—don't say more than you have to. So let's all just say 'We're praying for Omar. We're sure he's going to be okay' and leave it at that."

"How can we say we're sure he'll be okay?" Terrell asked, no doubt voicing what most people in the room were thinking.

Tommasino looked annoyed, then forced a smile. "Terrell, I understand what you're saying. But remember, we want to look at the bright side as best we can."

Uh-huh, Terrell thought. That and Billy Tommasino didn't want any negative vibes coming out of his camp—especially with the championship game on national TV the next day.

"Let's get everyone out of here as soon as possible," Coach Wilcox said. "Both teams have games to play tomorrow."

They all showered and dressed quickly. Terrell couldn't remember ever being in a quieter locker room. When he and Danny walked back into the gym, the lights had been turned out and it was empty—except for a cadre of waiting media. TV lights immediately came on, blinding them for a moment, and then came a lot of shouted questions.

Terrell was the focus of most of their attention, so Danny was able to slip away when he spotted Bobby Kelleher standing a few yards from the scrum. Terrell wished he could hear that conversation. Instead, he just heard reporters shouting questions he couldn't begin to answer.

"Don't you want to hear what Terrell has to say?" Danny asked Kelleher.

Kelleher shook his head. "Every kid who's walked out that door has said the same thing: 'We're praying for Omar. We're sure he'll be okay.' They might as well be reading off cue cards."

Danny nodded. "Do you have a secret camera set up inside the locker room?"

"Don't need one," Kelleher said. "This isn't my first rodeo. You were standing over there with the doctor and the EMTs. What'd you hear?"

Danny shrugged. He had no problem telling Kelleher the truth. "The doctor said he could be up walking in an hour. Or he might never walk again."

Kelleher sighed. "That's probably all they can know until they get an MRI and see how bad the damage to the spine was. It's weird with falls like that. I've seen guys get back up and run downcourt after what looks at least as horrible as that one. And then, other times, they don't move."

There was none of the usual Kelleher smart-guy tone as he spoke. Clearly, he was as shaken as everyone else. "Your games tomorrow should be called off if the word comes back that the kid is seriously hurt," he said after a pause. "But they won't be. TV won't allow it, and Tommasino won't pass on the national publicity."

Danny thought that might be an overreaction. "Call off the games?" he said. "Everyone's worked pretty hard to get this far."

"Really?" Kelleher said. "You've been here since Tuesday. It's a *camp* tournament. Everyone is just here to show off for the college coaches. You know that. And you've all already done that. But what the hell. The Olympics went on in 1972 after the Israeli athletes were murdered. That set the standard for tastelessness. Relatively speaking, this is nothing."

Danny didn't really know what to say to that. But he was curious. "Why do you do this," he asked, "when you're so disgusted by everyone here?"

Kelleher smiled. "Not *everyone*." Then, after a pause, he continued. "I guess I like tilting at windmills. And this sport is about the biggest one out there right now."

They did play the games on Sunday.

The news on Omar from the camp officials wasn't

encouraging: "He's in the hospital, being observed and undergoing further tests." But as far as Danny could tell, there was never even any discussion about calling the games off.

Coach Wilcox had met with camp officials and the TV network people on Sunday morning to go over what would be expected of them during the telecast.

"I suggested that the players wear some kind of patch, to acknowledge that Omar had been hurt," he told Danny and Terrell. "One of the TV guys practically jumped down my throat. He said, 'The kid wouldn't have been in the championship game anyway. The game his team is playing today isn't on our air. You wear patches and the announcers will have to explain what they're for. Forget it.'"

Omar Whytlaw, as far as the TV and camp people were concerned, had already ceased to exist.

But most of the players couldn't forget. The championship game between two powerhouse teams was oddly slow. Even the fans, many of whom had been in the gym when Whytlaw went down, seemed muted. Terrell knew he felt sluggish, and he could see that Danny, who loved to play so much, was having trouble putting his heart into the game. Even Jay Swanson wasn't himself. Once, when Danny fired a wayward pass to him on the wing that he had no chance to get more than a hand on, Swanson just shook his head and said, "Don't worry, Wilcox. Next time."

There was one player on the court who seemed completely unaffected by what had happened to Whytlaw:

Michael Jordan. Alex Mayer had mentioned to Terrell and Danny during warm-ups that Jordan hadn't stayed for the second game, so he hadn't seen what had happened to Whytlaw.

"All he cares about is showing everyone he's better than you," Mayer said to Terrell. "He's like all these camp and TV guys—Omar Whytlaw doesn't exist anymore."

Jordan certainly played that way. He looked a step quicker than everyone on the court. Terrell was trying as hard as he could, but he felt as if he was running in mud. Danny and the rest of the Rebels looked the same way. The Riverboats kept going back to the same play: a clear-out for Jordan, leaving him one-on-one with Terrell. Jordan couldn't miss. If Terrell came up on him, he drove past him and simply soared over anyone who came to help as he went to the basket. If Terrell took a step back, Jordan was happy to shoot a three. By the end of the first quarter he had made four threes and four twos on ten shots, and he was four-of-four from the foul line. That gave him 24 of his team's 28 points. The Riverboats led, 28–14.

During the break at the end of the quarter, the sideline reporter from the UBS cable outfit asked to speak to Terrell on-camera. This wasn't so much a request as a demand: The teams had been told before the game that there would be in-game interviews and the coaches had to deliver whoever was asked for.

Coach Wilcox sighed when the production assistant tapped him on the shoulder and said, "We need Terrell."

"I need him more than you do," he replied, but he nodded at Terrell, who slumped his shoulders and walked over to where the sideline guy was standing, microphone in hand.

"What do you guys need to do better to stop Jordan?" was the first, entirely predictable question.

"Play better," Terrell said, shrugging. "He's more ready to play, I guess, than the rest of us. No excuses, but it's hard to come out and play after what happened to Omar last night. It was scary, and I think we're all kind of shaken up."

That clearly wasn't the answer the sideline guy was looking for, and Terrell was standing close enough to hear shouting coming through the guy's earpiece.

"Terrell, there's been a lot of emphasis put on nonbasketball things, like your education, at this camp. What have you learned this week?"

Terrell wasn't up for playing the Gee-this-camp-has-been-great game, especially since what the guy was saying was dead wrong. "What have I learned?" he repeated. "I've learned to watch what I say to the media and to be careful who I trust." He heard more shouting from the earpiece.

"Thanks, Terrell," the guy said, sounding glum.

At last, Terrell was allowed to go back to basketball. It didn't do a lot of good. Jordan cooled a bit in the second quarter, but he had 33 points at halftime, and the margin was the same: Riverboats 51, Rebels 37. Terrell saw the sideline guy interviewing Coach Welsh as everyone else trudged to the locker room. Unlike the round-robin games, there was a real fifteen-minute halftime for the championship game.

They were all just sitting down and opening bottles of water and Gatorade when the door burst open and Billy Tommasino came in. He was followed by one of the people Terrell remembered as being from UBS.

"You listen to me, Wilcox," Tommasino said, his face red. "You tell your players that when they're asked about what they've learned at this damn camp, they say nice things—not this crap about not trusting people! And *no more* talk about Omar Whytlaw! You got me?"

Andy Wilcox smiled. "I don't tell my players what to say or not say, Billy," he said. "And if they weren't bothered by what happened to Omar, I'd be worried about them. You're more than welcome to not talk to them the rest of the game."

"That's just what we'll do," the UBS guy said. "We'll give all the national exposure to the Mississippi kids and their coach. In fact, we don't need any of your players when you come back out, Coach. We'll talk to the people from the team that's kicking your ass instead."

The two men turned and walked out. Coach Wilcox tossed the piece of chalk he'd been holding into the corner. "You guys need a pep talk now?" he said. "You want to prove them right, or you want to stick it to them?"

Their answer came in the form of their play. They were all angry enough to focus by the time the third quarter began. Terrell wasn't thinking about Omar Whytlaw, something he would later admit with some chagrin. He was thinking only about humiliating Jordan. Clearly surprised by Terrell's sudden burst of energy, Jordan suddenly couldn't get off a shot, much less hit one, because he was being smothered. On offense, Terrell, Danny, and Swanson began working inside out: If Terrell was double-teamed, he pitched it to one of them for an open three. Everyone was playing defense. The bench, silent in the first half, was alive.

At the end of three quarters, the lead was down to 74–68. The Rebels finally got the score tied with ninety seconds left, when Danny hit a three from the corner to make it 91–91. Neither team scored on the next two possessions. With less than thirty seconds to go, Jordan posted up and Terrell heard Coach Wilcox yell, "Don't double!" He wanted Terrell taking Jordan on alone.

Jordan caught the ball and tried to shot-fake. Terrell didn't move. Jordan looked up to see if anyone was open, but no one had left his man. Finally, he took a dribble and tried to go *through* Terrell to the basket. The whistle blew. It was an easy call: charging. The Rebels got the ball back with sixteen seconds to go. They inbounded, got the ball to midcourt, and called time with twelve seconds left.

"Terrell, Coach Welsh isn't as dumb as I am, so he's going to double you as soon as you get the ball," Coach Wilcox said in the huddle.

"Do you want me outside?" Terrell said.

"No. Jordan's quicker than you. Your advantage is inside. They'll have to double you there. Danny's been hot, so they won't leave him." He turned to Swanson. "You ready to win this game, Jay?"

Swanson looked surprised. But after stiffening for a split second, he nodded. "Damn right I am."

"Okay. Remember the play we've run a couple times today—'Weak right'? I promise it'll be wide open."

The play was fairly basic: Danny would dribble to the left of the key and get the ball to Terrell in the post. They were counting on Danny's man—probably Alex Mayer—staying with him, because he had made three threes in the fourth quarter. Swanson had missed twice. So, in all likelihood, Swanson's man would leave him on the right side of the key to double Terrell. As soon as that happened, Terrell would reverse the ball to Swanson for what should be an open shot. If, by some chance, there was no double-team, Terrell would be on his own to get a shot over Jordan.

They inbounded. Danny swerved left as Terrell posted up, arms extended, calling for the ball. Danny got the pass to him with five seconds left. Terrell saw that Mayer had stayed with Danny as he drifted toward the corner. Just as Coach Wilcox had predicted, Swanson's man bolted through the key to try to strip Terrell if he put the ball on the floor.

Terrell saw him coming and never dribbled. He made one quick fake and then coolly pitched the ball to Swanson on the far side of the court. He could see that Swanson was almost into his shooting motion as soon as he caught the ball.

The buzzer went off with the ball in the air.

Swish.

Everyone was rushing to mob Swanson, Terrell, and

Danny included. The final score was 93–91. When they unpiled, the UBS sideline guy was standing there with a big grin on his face, saying, "Jay, let me get you here for a minute."

"Sure," Swanson said, grinning.

Terrell saw Danny start to say something, but Swanson shook his head. "I got this."

He stood next to the very short sideline guy as they waited for a cue. "Thanks, guys," the TV man said. "Jay, tell us what happened on that last play."

"No," Swanson said, looking down at him. "One of your people told us at halftime that you didn't need to talk to us. So go talk to the Riverboats. We dedicate this win to Omar Whytlaw."

Before the sideline guy could say another word, Swanson turned and walked away into the waiting arms of his teammates, who pummeled him as if he'd just hit the winning shot all over again.

PART II

FOURTEEN

After his performances in Teaneck and at the other all-star tournaments he played in during July, Terrell Jamerson was rated the number one high school player in the country going into his senior season. Michael Jordan was number two.

Terrell's mom was proud and amazed. She knew her son was a standout player, and she'd certainly noticed the flood of phone calls and letters from college coaches and a staggering number of other "interested parties"—they'd already changed their phone number three times to try to escape the constant ringing. Still, somehow, the number one ranking crystallized things for Melinda Jamerson. Her son had a huge opportunity here.

But every time Terrell looked at those rankings, he thought about Omar Whytlaw, who was now in a rehabilitation center in Chicago trying to learn how to live his life without the use of his legs. Things change.

In September, they decided which coaches to invite for official home visits. Mike Krzyzewski from Duke was high on

Terrell's list. He was college basketball's all-time winningest coach—a no-brainer. In addition, Terrell had asked Roy Williams from North Carolina; Mike Todd, the coach at Massachusetts State; Grant Hathaway from the University of Atlanta; and Ben Howland, the coach at UCLA.

Terrell suspected his mom wasn't going to let him go to college in California, but when he'd visited UCLA, mostly to see what Los Angeles was like, he'd been really impressed. Hathaway and Atlanta had made the cut because Barrett Stephenson, the coach at Concord High School—who happened to be dating Terrell's mom—felt that the U of A was an up-and-coming program.

It was slightly surreal, having coaches he'd watched on TV now sitting in his living room, telling him how he could be a star at their schools and, later, in the NBA. On the court, Terrell felt at home—in control. But oddly, here—at home, surrounded by coaches singing his praises—he felt out of place. It was hard to think. Hard to know how to choose.

After each set of college coaches had gone, Coach Wilcox, Coach Stephenson, and his mom would turn to him, and Terrell would shrug and say, "They were nice. I'd like to visit the campus and get to know some of their players."

But then came Coach K . . .

Krzyzewski bowled Terrell over with his humor and his honesty. Terrell felt like Coach K was talking *to* him rather than *at* him. He'd brought Jeff Capel and Steve Wojciechowski, his two top assistants, with him and Terrell liked them too. Coach K's pitch wasn't that different from what the other coaches were saying, except for two things: He didn't act as if Terrell was the greatest player he'd ever recruited in his life.

And, maybe more important, he'd told him very specifically he was *not* going to recruit Danny Wilcox. The other coaches made it clear they'd love to have Danny if that would make Terrell happy.

"I believe Danny's good enough to play a role for us," Krzyzewski had said. "But I'm not going to recruit him for two reasons. First, it's not fair to him to have people say we only recruited him so we could get you to come to Duke. Second, I know Tommy Amaker would love to have him at Harvard, and Danny can be a star there. He can also get a pretty decent education."

Terrell wondered what Krzyzewski would have said if he'd told him that he was going to go to college with Danny—period. He and Danny had talked about it but had decided it was a bad idea—for almost exactly the reasons Krzyzewski had brought up.

After Krzyzewski and his assistants left, Coach Wilcox had looked at Terrell and said—as usual—"What'd you think?"

This time Terrell smiled. "Where do I sign?"

"I agree," his mom said.

Coach Wilcox and Coach Stephenson nodded.

Since it was September, he couldn't actually sign a letter of intent to go to Duke. The first chance to do that would come in November. Still, they all agreed that he would call Coach K the next day to tell him he'd decided. Then there'd be press conferences and the inevitable media, but for once Terrell didn't mind the idea.

That night before he went to bed, Terrell had sent Danny a two-word text saying, "It's Duke."

Danny had apparently been staring at his cell phone, because about five seconds after Terrell hit send, a reply came flying back: "Fantastic!"

Terrell slept better that night than he had in weeks.

But the clear picture he had in his mind when Krzyzewski left his house quickly became murky the following day. When Terrell came down to breakfast, Coach Stephenson was sitting at the kitchen table with a coffee mug in his hands.

Even though his mom and Coach Stephenson had been seeing each other for over a year, he almost never spent the night, and, at least in Terrell's memory, he had never done it on a school night. But his mom was standing at the kitchen counter making eggs and bacon, like it was a regular morning.

"Morning, Mom . . . Coach," Terrell said, trying to not seem surprised by Coach Stephenson's presence. He sat down and took a sip of the orange juice that was on the table. His mom raised an eyebrow at Coach Stephenson, who clapped Terrell on the shoulder—something he had never done before. "Quite a night, wasn't it?" he said.

"Yeah—the best," Terrell answered.

"You comfortable with your decision?" Coach Stephenson asked.

"Oh yeah," Terrell said. "I can't wait to tell everybody. Can't wait for the signing date, so people will stop bothering me."

Coach Stephenson laughed—not a real laugh but a fake, forced laugh. Terrell caught his mom giving him a look. What was going on?

"Listen, Terrell, I understand why you want this over with. I get that . . . ," Coach Stephenson said. His voice trailed off.

"But . . . ?" Terrell said.

"But I'm not sure you should rush into this just to get it over with. It's too important to rush. You want to be sure so you don't make a mistake."

Terrell was confused. "How could it possibly be a mistake to pick Duke and Coach K?"

Another fake laugh. Terrell had never seen Coach Stephenson look so uncomfortable.

"You're right. Obviously. Duke. Coach K. But . . ."

"But *what?*" Terrell snapped, finally out of patience.

"Terrell, watch your tone," his mother said, finally proving she hadn't lost her voice overnight.

"Sorry," Terrell said. "But I don't get what's going on here. Last night you said—"

Coach Stephenson cut in. "Last night I didn't want to say anything in front of Andy . . . Coach Wilcox. He's not family."

Now Terrell was mad. He liked Coach Stephenson, but there wasn't anyone he trusted more than Andy Wilcox—

especially when it came to basketball. With the possible exception of Danny. "'He's not family,'" he repeated. "And you are?"

"Terrell!" His mom again.

"I'm sorry, Mom, but what the hell is going on here? Ten hours ago we all said Duke. Now all of a sudden it's, 'Let's think about this.' What happened?"

His mom set a plate of eggs and bacon in front of him, but Terrell couldn't eat.

"Terrell, I know how important this decision is and how emotional it can be," she said as she sat down at the table. She leveled him with a look. "But you know how I feel about using profanity in this house."

Terrell's mom was about five foot seven, meaning she was a foot shorter than he was, and she weighed about a hundred pounds less than he did. That didn't mean he wasn't scared of her.

"Yes, ma'am," he said.

"We just think you need to visit all the schools before you make a decision," Coach Stephenson said. "I mean, you haven't even made your official visit to Duke. How can you be *so* sure?"

"I was there in August, remember? Danny and I took that trip and stopped at six different schools, including Duke and Carolina. You even said back then it was better to just walk around on our own rather than get the grand tour on an official visit. I've seen the place. I know exactly what I'm getting."

"But you don't know what you might get at another school—" Coach Stephenson stopped suddenly.

"What does that mean?" Terrell said.

"It means," his mom said, "that Duke may very well be the right place for you. But you owe it to the other coaches who came here to talk to us to at least see their schools."

"Mom, I made my official visit to UCLA, and I've seen Duke and Carolina—"

"That leaves Mass State and Atlanta," Coach Stephenson said. "You haven't seen either of them yet."

"I'm not all that interested in Mass State—we've talked about that," Terrell said. "I want to go someplace warmer."

"Atlanta's warmer," his mom said.

He nodded. "I know. But I thought Coach Wilcox was right when he said we should watch out for newer programs trying to use me to get to the big time. Plus, none of us liked Coach Hathaway all that much." He was giving his mom the pleading look he used when he wanted her to trust that he knew what he was doing.

But she wasn't looking at him. She was looking at Coach Stephenson, who said, "Terrell, you need to carry the process through to the finish line, *then* decide. We're *all* agreed on that, right? So make the rest of your visits, and then we'll reconvene. If your choice is still Duke, I'll be one hundred percent behind you."

He spoke with an air of finality. As if he was Terrell's father. As if Terrell needed his permission. And that pissed Terrell off as much as anything. Terrell's father had died when he was a baby, so he'd never really known him. It had always been just him and his mom, and that was enough—more than enough.

But his mom was clearly with Coach Stephenson on this. And Terrell was so thrown by that fact that he gave in. Fine. He'd go through the motions and make the visits in October. Whatever.

Terrell was sound asleep when he became vaguely aware that the phone was ringing downstairs. This wasn't unusual, although his mom had just changed their phone number again.

It was Saturday, and practice wasn't until 11:00. Specifically, this morning was the first practice of his senior season, and he knew it was going to be kind of a media circus. Danny had told him that his dad said close to a hundred media members were planning to come.

He groaned and was about to roll over when he heard his mother's voice from downstairs. "Terrell, you've got a call down here," she said.

"Who is it?" he yelled back, thinking whoever it was could call back later.

"Mike Krzyzewski," his mom said.

Terrell sat straight up in bed. "Be right down!" he called back.

He scrambled out of bed and took the stairs down three at a time.

"Did I wake you?" Coach K asked.

"No, Coach. I mean, I was just, you know, waking up."

Terrell heard Krzyzewski laugh. He felt embarrassed that he was stumbling over his words.

"What time is practice today?" Krzyzewski asked. His tone was that of a friend calling a friend. He could have been Danny. Except that Terrell wouldn't have sprinted down the steps to talk to Danny.

"Eleven o'clock," Terrell said.

"Listen, Terrell, I called just to tell you one thing, and it has nothing to do with whether you're going to come to Duke or not. You already know how I feel about that. I talked to Coach Wilcox last night, and he told me about all the media coming today and how tough it's been for you since the summer, dealing with everyone who wants to be your new best friend."

Terrell laughed. *That*, he thought, *is an understatement.*

Krzyzewski went on. "Don't worry about any of it. It will all take care of itself. Play basketball—enjoy basketball—and keep trying to get better. Take care of your classes and your grades. And remember who your *real* friends are. Just worry about those three things and you'll be fine. More than fine."

Terrell wanted to blurt out, *Coach, I'm coming to Duke!* but his mom was standing nearby. So he settled for "Thanks, Coach. It's great of you to call."

"Have fun today, Terrell," Coach K said. "Okay?"

"Got it."

"We'll talk soon. And if you ever want to talk to me, you know where to find me."

"Thanks, Coach."

He hung up. His mom was still standing there. "What was that about?"

"He just wanted to wish me luck starting practice and to remind me to have fun."

His mom nodded. "Uh-huh. And to remind you he wants you to come to Duke."

Terrell looked at her for a moment and started to say something. He stopped himself, hearing Coach K's words in his head: "Remember who your real friends are."

"He never brought that up," he finally replied.

"Hmm," his mother said. She turned and walked toward the kitchen. "I'll make breakfast."

"I'll go shower."

He walked slowly back up the stairs, wondering who his real friends were. He trusted Danny implicitly. And Coach Wilcox, even though the dudes had told him over and over again that he shouldn't. Was it possible that his mom wasn't one of his real friends? The thought actually made his head hurt. But she and Coach Stephenson had been acting strange since Coach K's visit.

Terrell shook his head. No. He *did* trust his mom. They might not always agree, but he knew she wanted what was best for him. Coach Stephenson, though . . . there was maybe just a tiny seed of doubt in his mind.

FIFTEEN

Danny picked Terrell up a few minutes after ten. Terrell had been offered cars by more people than he could remember. Most had offered to "loan" him a car. A couple of them had said they would like to give him a car because they knew he was the kind of guy who wouldn't forget the favor and would pay it back when he was in a position to do so.

He had politely turned them all down. His mom, who was a history teacher at Concord High School, had told him she would try to buy him a used car for his birthday in January, but he didn't really want her to do that. And Danny was more than willing to drive him anywhere.

Danny had bought his car with money he had made working summers and weekends at the golf club. He hadn't worked that much this past summer because of all the basketball tournaments, but by September he'd amassed enough to buy a used Honda. It had 157,000 miles on it when he'd bought it, and Terrell was sure he'd added another thousand in the past month.

As Danny pulled into the back parking lot at school,

they noticed a host of TV satellite trucks parked near the door they normally used to get to the locker room. Seeing them, Danny kept going and swung around to the front lot, which was virtually empty on a Saturday.

"What're you doing?" Terrell asked.

"They're all camped out waiting for you at the back door," Danny said. "So we'll go in the front."

"It's locked on Saturday."

"I know. But I have a key."

Sometimes it paid to hang out with the coach's son.

"So we're sneaking in the *front* door," Terrell said, laughing.

Before they went on the court, Coach Wilcox gathered everyone together in the locker room. It wasn't as if they hadn't seen one another all fall—they informally played pickup every afternoon and worked out individually with Coach Wilcox and his assistant, Joe Kress, who was an English teacher but helped out with the team because he loved basketball.

But today was the first day under the high school rules in Massachusetts that teams were allowed to hold a formal practice. It was also the first day since the end of July that Terrell would be talking to the media. Coach Wilcox had told everyone—even ESPN, who had asked to come to do a feature on Terrell and his recruitment—that he was off-limits until practice began. The temporary reprieve from the spotlight was over.

"Okay, fellas," Coach Wilcox said. "You know there are

going to be a lot of cameras and a bunch of media types out there this morning. We also know they aren't here because they think we've got a shot at the state championship."

Everyone laughed.

"So we have to stay focused, because that's what *we* care about. This team, all of us together, is going to do great things this year. And we're going to do it by working hard every day. I've told the media folks that if they don't stay out of the way, I'll clear the gym. So don't concern yourselves with them. For the next two hours I want your full effort and full attention on the court. We'll worry about the media after that.

"So, let's start with our layup drills the way we always do and then get to work."

They came together around Coach Wilcox and put their hands in.

"On three," Coach Wilcox said.

They counted to three and yelled, "Work hard!"

Terrell had known there would be a lot of people waiting for them when they made their way up the stairs from the locker room to the gym. Even so, he wasn't prepared for what he saw—or what he didn't see because of the glare of the TV lights—when he reached the court.

It wasn't just the media, although they were hard to miss. Terrell counted at least thirty camera crews plus all those carrying tape recorders and notebooks. But there were also fans. The Lexington High gym seated about 1,800 people, and it must have been three-quarters full. Terrell saw some familiar faces, fans who came to the games, but they were outnumbered by newcomers.

There were no college coaches—thank goodness—because October was a period when they weren't allowed to travel for recruiting. But he saw enough suits and expensive sweat suits to know that a lot of the agent types and shoe-company reps and hangers-on he had encountered during the summer were also present. "It's like we're back in Jersey again," Terrell murmured to Danny as they each went to take a basketball from the ball rack at midcourt.

"Worse," Danny said. "They've invaded our territory now."

Terrell sighed. He looked around the court where his teammates were forming layup lines. For the next two hours, at least, he would be safe inside the white lines of the court.

They went through the basics you would expect in any first practice. There were three new players, all sophomores, who had to learn the offense and whom Coach Wilcox had to remind about defensive responsibilities. But only one starter from last season had graduated, so the other players on the court were already a cohesive team. Monte Torre ran great screens. And Tommy Bonk was a much better shooter than his name implied.

Two national polls had placed Lexington in the top five teams in the country, behind traditional powers like DeMatha of Maryland, Saint Anthony's of New Jersey, and Simeon of Chicago. Seeing Lexington's name mixed in with those names was amazing. The USA *Today* poll, which had ranked Lexington number four, gave a thumbnail sketch of each team. The one for Lexington: "Two words say it all: Terrell Jamerson."

Terrell thought that was unfair, especially to Danny, whose stock had soared at the end of the summer. Before the summer tournaments, he hadn't been in anyone's rankings. Most of the high school scouting services ranked the top five hundred players in the country and then the top one hundred at each position. Danny had gone from nowhere to as high as number ninety-four nationally in one poll and number twenty-seven among point guards.

Tom Konchalski didn't rank players in *HSBI*. He just gave them grades, with a 5-plus being the highest possible grade. Only three players in the country had been given a 5-plus by Konchalski at the end of the summer: Terrell Jamerson, Michael Jordan, and Anthony Johnstone, a South African who had moved to the United States as a high school junior and was playing at Oak Hill Academy in Virginia—another perennial national power. Danny, who had been rated a 4 by Konchalski at the end of his junior year, was now rated a 5-minus, which meant he was one step shy of being considered a lock for high-school All American.

The practice seemed to fly by, at least for Terrell. When he was playing, everything made sense. *He* made sense. At six feet seven inches, Terrell was often uncomfortable. Classroom desks were too small. Doorways were too low. His elbows were always knocking into things. But in the gym, his long arms were an asset. His big hands were perfect for palming a basketball. And his long, powerful legs propelled him high above his defenders. Here, on this court, in purposeful motion, he was perfect.

Much too soon, he was standing with his teammates at the center jump circle listening to Coach Wilcox tell them that he was pleased with the way they had practiced, but they had "miles"—his word—to go on defense. Terrell suppressed a grin. Danny had told him that to his father the perfect game would be one where his team never had the ball to start a possession. It just played defense and tried to win by getting enough turnovers to outscore the other team. Now *that* was basketball.

Coach Wilcox finished by reminding them that they would be taking the team picture at 3:30 on Monday before practice. "So if you want to look good in a photo you'll probably show your grandkids, you might get a haircut later today and shave on Monday morning," he said.

Finally, he called over Mr. Robertson, who taught senior history but also was in charge of the weekly student newspaper, the *Patriot*.

Coach Wilcox explained that Mr. Robertson was acting as "our public relations guy" and then asked him to explain what was going to happen once they were finished with their meeting.

"Terrell, at the far end of the court there's a podium with a microphone," Mr. Robertson said. "That's where you'll go. You can see that the camera crews are setting up over there right now. The rest of you guys just fan out and see who wants to talk to you. If after about five minutes no one has sought you out, you can head for the showers.

"One thing: Some people may ask for your phone number or email or Facebook address. Don't give it to them. Tell them if they need to contact any of you about anything, they can contact me or Coach Kress. I've given them a sheet with our contact info on it.

"Questions?"

There was one, from Carson Simpson, who backed Danny up at point guard, although his most important role on the team was to keep everybody laughing. "Mr. Robertson, since we're spending all this extra time talking to reporters, can I turn in my paper on Napoleon on Tuesday instead of Monday?"

This drew a laugh from the entire team—especially the other four seniors.

"*No,*" Mr. Robertson said, but he had a big smile on his face. "My guess, Simpson, is you'll be heading for the showers in about five minutes. You should have plenty of time."

Terrell couldn't resist. "What about me?" he said. "I'll probably be here longer than that."

"Which is why I'm really glad you have the rest of the day today and *all* day tomorrow to finish," Mr. Robertson said.

"But it's Patriots and Jets tomorrow," Danny blurted out. "We *have* to watch that."

Mr. Robertson turned to Coach Wilcox. "Your team is ganging up on me, Coach," he said.

"They have a point about the Patriots and Jets," Coach Wilcox said, unable to resist a grin.

"Tell you what," Mr. Robertson said. "I'm going to send out an email to everyone in the class. If the Patriots win, papers aren't due until Tuesday. If they lose, you better get 'em in, because I'll be in a very bad mood on Monday."

The seniors clapped and everyone else laughed. Terrell wondered what the media, who were all standing around the court waiting for them to finish, imagined was going on.

They huddled and put their hands in. "On three . . . Pats win!" Coach Wilcox said.

They yelled, "One, two, three, Pats win!" in unison and headed for their assigned places. The fun part of the day was over.

Mr. Robertson escorted Terrell to the podium, leading him through the gauntlet of cameras and notebooks. Chris Pullman, who worked on the tech crew for school plays and assemblies, was standing next to the microphone. "I already checked it for you, Terrell," he said. "The mike's working. Andrea is out there with a wireless for people to use to ask questions."

"Thanks, Chris," Terrell said. "I appreciate it."

Mr. Robertson was standing at the mike asking for quiet. "Folks, just for the sake of keeping this civilized, I'm going to ask you to request the wireless mike from Andrea"—he pointed to where Andrea was standing next to a reporter—

"and then, when you have the mike, to ask your question and pass it on. So now, as Ed McMahon would say, 'Here's Terrell.'"

Terrell stepped gingerly up to the microphone.

The guy standing with Andrea had the mike now, and Mr. Robertson pointed at him.

"Terrell, I'm Pete Thamel from *Sports Illustrated*," he said. Terrell had to admit that was a pretty impressive starting point—someone from *Sports Illustrated*. "There's been a report floating around that you've pretty much decided you want to go to Duke. Can you give us some idea of how true or not true that may be?"

Whoa, Terrell thought. *Nothing like a nice easy first question.*

He paused, trying to make sure he chose his words carefully. "I think people know I had five schools come to my house," he said finally. "Duke, North Carolina, UCLA, Mass State, and the University of Atlanta. I like them all. I still have two visits to make—Mass State and Atlanta—and after that I'll make a final decision." He decided that was a good place to stop. Someone else had the mike.

"Terrell, any truth to the story that you and Danny Wilcox are going to go to school together as a package deal?"

Terrell thought he saw Mr. Robertson take a step in his direction as if to cut off the question—or the answer. But he was happy to answer on his own. "If you've seen Danny play, you know he doesn't need to go anywhere with me as a package deal. The only school on his list that's the same as mine is UCLA. We both really wanted to see LA." That got a laugh. "But neither of us has decided anything yet."

The next few questions were pretty basic: What was he looking for in a school and in a coach? What was the best part of this sort of attention? The worst part of it?

"Doing this," Terrell said in response to that question, drawing more laughter.

"Two more questions," Mr. Robertson said after almost thirty minutes. Terrell noticed all the other players had finished talking. He noticed Danny standing out near midcourt. Bobby Kelleher was with him. Good.

The second-to-last questioner had the mike. "Terrell, do you have a girlfriend?"

Again, Terrell saw Robertson starting to wave his hand as if to ward off the question.

"No, I don't," Terrell said quickly. "But if you hear that Beyoncé is available, tell her she can give me a call."

That got a big laugh. He was almost starting to enjoy this.

"Last question," Mr. Robertson said, pointing at a guy who had to be what Danny called a TV talking-head. He was too well groomed and coiffed to be anything else.

"Terrell," the guy said, clearing his throat for effect. "As you probably know, I'm Ronald Archer, anchor of *The Top One Hundred*, on ESPNU. What I'd like to ask is if you can explain to me and to our cameras why your coach has refused to allow you to appear on our program? All the other top high school stars not only appear but often they practically beg us to come on the show."

"I guess you should ask my coach that question," Terrell said. "But it sounds like you have so many stars already, you don't really need me."

That got a big laugh too, although Terrell figured that had as much to do with the stunned look on Ronald Archer's face as the cleverness of his answer. Still, he couldn't help thinking that he was starting to get good at this.

"Okay, thanks, everyone," Mr. Robertson said, taking the mike. "Thank you for coming to Lexington High School. I'm sure we'll see you back here again."

Mr. Robertson had him by the arm. "Walk with me across the floor to the locker-room stairs," he said. "If you stop, people are going to try to grab you for one more question."

Before Terrell could take a step, an attractive young woman with a camera crew in tow was blocking his path. "Terrell, can I get you for one more question?" she said.

"If he stops for you, he'll be here another half hour," Mr. Robertson said.

"But you never called on me during the press conference," she said in a pouty tone. "I should have a chance to ask one question, just like everyone else did."

Terrell definitely would have called on her. "It's okay, Mr. Robertson, I'll do this and you can tell the others I'm doing just this one question with Miss . . ."

"Van Engstrom," she said. "Amber Van Engstrom. I'm from WJYE in Atlanta. Call me Amber."

She was, Terrell had to admit, pretty dazzling. Very tall,

with jet-black hair, dark brown eyes, and, for now at least, a big smile.

"Okay, Amber," Terrell said, trying to sound cool. "Fire away."

She turned to her cameraman and sound guy, took a mike from the sound guy, and said, "Ready?"

They both nodded.

"Terrell," she said as the camera light came on, "can you tell us the exact nature of your relationship with a man named Raymond Leach?"

For a split second, the name didn't register at all with Terrell. Then he remembered: Leach was the guy who'd brought the NCAA officials running after he'd bought lunch for Terrell, Danny, Michael Jordan, and Alex Mayer back in New Jersey. He had also tried to join them one night at dinner during a tournament they had played in down in Orlando. There he'd been told in no uncertain terms by Danny and Alex Mayer that he wasn't welcome.

"If you're talking about who I think you're talking about, he showed up at lunch one day in New Jersey during the camp there, and I think I met him again for about ten seconds at a restaurant in Orlando," Terrell said.

"That's it?" she said. "You didn't actually *have* dinner with him in Orlando? Or let him *buy* you dinner?"

Now Terrell was getting worried. Leach *had* bought lunch in New Jersey. But that wasn't what she had asked him. He took a deep breath. "No, Amber. Like I said, I was having dinner with some other players, and he walked over to our table and acted like he was pals with one of the guys. That guy wasn't very happy to see him, though, and so he left."

Amber started to ask another question—maybe about the lunch in New Jersey?—but Mr. Robertson cut her off. "You said one question," he said. "You're way past one."

Amber wasn't going to let anyone see her sweat, that was for sure. The camera swung from Terrell to Mr. Robertson.

"Who exactly are you, sir?" Amber asked. "Does Terrell have something to hide?"

"I'm the person telling you this interview is over," Mr. Robertson said. He smiled as he said it, making it clear he wasn't going to be baited.

She signaled to her cameraman to turn the camera off.

Without saying another word to Amber, Terrell headed in the direction of the locker room. He would be safe—he hoped—in there.

SIXTEEN

Danny and Bobby Kelleher had been standing close enough to hear Terrell's exchange with Amber, but as Terrell approached, Kelleher nodded at Danny and headed for the door.

"Where—" Terrell started to ask, but Danny shook his head.

"Later."

Two burly members of the wrestling team were standing in front of the steps that led down to the locker room. Once Terrell and Danny were safely in the locker room, Danny explained that he'd asked Kelleher to meet them downtown at Carol's for lunch.

"He's talked to a lot of people over the last couple months. Sounds like we need to hear what he has to say."

"Is your dad coming too?"

Danny shook his head. "No. He's busy. But he knows, and he's okay with it."

They showered and dressed quickly, then ducked out the way they had come in—through the front door. It was a bright, windy October afternoon, and the fall foliage had turned Lexington into a picture postcard of a New England town. For all that Terrell had said about wanting to go to college somewhere warmer, he did love it here.

Carol's was a favorite local restaurant, with a counter up front and tables in the back, though most of them were empty since it was after two o'clock. There was a TV in the corner of the room that had a college football game on. Boston College was leading Maryland, 17–7, in the third quarter.

"There's a guy waiting for you," Polly Shannon, one of the waitresses, told them as they paused by the television set.

"Thanks," Danny said, and they walked to the back of the room, where there was a door that led to a small private room with two tables. Coach Wilcox often used it after games to gather a few friends in a quiet place. It had now become a place where Danny and Terrell often went so they wouldn't be interrupted constantly. It wasn't as if the room was a secret; everyone in town knew about it. There was just an unspoken rule that during basketball season, you didn't go back there unless invited.

Kelleher was sitting at one of the tables, reading the *Boston Globe* and sipping coffee. There was a TV in the corner, and Kelleher had it on with no sound. He had found a different game: West Virginia at Texas Tech.

"This is what it's come to," he said, looking up from the paper and gesturing at the TV. "West Virginia in Lubbock, Texas, to play in the Big Twelve."

Danny wasn't that much of a football fan, but he knew that conference realignment had completely turned college athletics upside down. Boise State and TCU had joined the Big *East* then quit. The Big Ten would soon have fourteen teams, and the Big Twelve had ten teams. Danny had joked to Terrell that he should forget all the big-time schools and go with him to Harvard so they could play in the Ivy League, which would always have the same eight teams no matter what other changes occurred in college athletics.

They sat down, and Polly showed up a split second later to take their orders. On Danny and Terrell's recommendation, they all got cheeseburgers, French fries, and milkshakes.

Once Polly had left, Danny looked at Kelleher and said quietly, "So, Bobby, why don't you tell Terrell what you told me back at the gym."

Kelleher looked at his watch. "Have you guys got a while?"

He explained that he had spent about four months, "so far," working on a story about how corrupt college recruiting had become. His paper, the *Washington Herald*, had initially given him the summer to work exclusively on the project, but by the time Labor Day rolled around he had unearthed more questions than answers.

"Are you getting close to anything?" Terrell asked.

"Yeah, a nervous breakdown," Kelleher said. He smiled grimly. "I'm close to a lot of things. I know a lot of things. But getting it on the record is the hard part."

"So what do you know?" Terrell asked.

Kelleher picked up a file folder that had been sitting on

the chair next to him and slid it across the table. "In there are profiles I've put together on the top twelve high school seniors in the country, according to a consensus of the major scouting services. Look at the names; see if you think I've left anyone out. You met all of them during the summer except for Anthony Johnstone and Jonathan Blixt."

"Blixt, the kid from Utah?" asked Danny, who seemed to know every player alive. "He's seven-four. His parents wouldn't let him go to any of the camps or play summer tournaments. He's pretty much a lock to go to Brigham Young."

"You don't need to read any of the details," Kelleher said. "Just tell me if I've left anyone out who you think is a sure-fire NBA player. These are the kids the scouts have pegged as one-and-done, or at the very most, two-and-out."

Terrell and Danny glanced through the folder. The names were familiar. Omar Whytlaw was included for some reason. The only one that surprised Danny a little was Alex Mayer. "Alex Mayer told me he wanted to stay in college for four years," he said. "And why is Omar Whytlaw in there? He'll never play again from what I've heard."

Kelleher nodded. "I know about Mayer. But he's good enough that he could go sooner. As for Omar, you're right. But that's one reason why he's willing to talk to me. He's got nothing to lose."

"You've talked to Omar?"

"Several times. He's in a rehab center. He's hoping to walk on crutches by the end of the year."

Terrell shut the folder. "Okay, so what's the point of this list?"

"My point is that I am about ninety-nine percent certain you're the only guy on the list who hasn't yet taken a handout of some kind."

"Alex hasn't taken anything," Danny said.

"Yes, he has. Not as much as some others, but he definitely has taken things."

"Like what?" Danny said defensively.

"Like a car," Kelleher said. "Technically, his father bought it for him. But I've got the bank wire records that show Paul Judson sent his dad forty thousand dollars about a month before he bought the car."

"How'd you get that?" Danny asked, eyes wide.

"I have friends," Kelleher said. "I can't use the info right now, but I know it happened. Still, Alex has been given considerably less than these other guys."

"Except me," Terrell said.

"Right." Kelleher paused. "But . . ."

"But what?"

"*You* haven't taken anything," Kelleher said. "But there are people in your life who have been negotiating on your behalf. Normally, these guys try to get to your summer AAU coach, because they always have a hand out. But you were coached by Danny's dad during the summer, and Coach Wilcox made it clear he'd blow the whistle in a second. So they've had to go around him."

"To who?" Terrell asked.

Kelleher sighed. "To Coach Stephenson. And, through him, they hope, to your mom."

Terrell felt a hot flash of anger. His first instinct was to reach across the table, grab Kelleher by the shirt, and call him a liar. But he knew that Kelleher wasn't lying. He might be wrong—he *hoped* he was wrong—but he wasn't lying.

It was Danny who responded first. "I just don't believe that," he said. "I think someone is giving you bad information. Terrell's mom wouldn't sell him out that way."

"I don't think she's sold him out at all so far," Kelleher said. "But I think people are making repeated and persuasive arguments that she owes it to Terrell to help him take advantage of his situation. Unfortunately, Terrell, these days if you're a star the way *you're* a star and you just take the scholarship, most of your peers are going to think you're a chump. It's a one-way deal: The school makes millions off of you and you aren't guaranteed a dollar.

"Let's say you go to Duke. Krzyzewski is about as straight a shooter as there is in this crooked business. Midway through your freshman season, you tear up your knee and you lose a step and you go from being a lottery pick to a D-league player—"

"D-league?" Terrell said.

"NBA Developmental League. The minors. Minimum salary in the NBA is about $500,000 a year. Minimum salary in the D-league is about $500 a week. You know what Krzyzewski does? He sighs, says he's really sorry—which he is—but then goes out and recruits another player. Duke keeps making millions from TV and from athletic fundraising and from selling Terrell Jamerson jerseys as artifacts.

What do you get? Because Krzyzewski's an honorable man, he'd probably keep you on scholarship. A lot of coaches wouldn't."

"Well, that's worth something, isn't it?" Danny said.

"Yes, it is," Kelleher said. "But it's not the big payoff you *could* be getting. Right now."

"It sounds like you're saying I *should* be taking stuff from all these guys," Terrell said.

Kelleher shook his head emphatically. "Absolutely not. Because then they own you. If Danny's buddy Alex Mayer doesn't do what Paul Judson wants him to do, Judson will out him. If that happens while he's in college, he could lose eligibility and not be able to play. If it happens after college, well, not as bad. The NBA doesn't much care about the NCAA's rules. But it will taint him in the eyes of corporate America. That billboard you guys all dream about? Not gonna happen."

Terrell had to admit he *had* fantasized about seeing himself up on a billboard promoting Nike or Under Armour or Brickley someday.

"So the system is corrupt on both sides," Danny was saying. "You play by the rules: The colleges get rich and you don't. You don't play by the rules: Some sleazy agent or sneaker company guy ends up owning you."

"Danny, you advance to the lightning round," Kelleher said. "You've got it exactly right. Pretty picture, isn't it?"

Terrell didn't want to discuss Kelleher's dark vision of basketball at that moment. "Can we get back to my mom and Coach Stephenson?" he asked.

Kelleher opened up one of the files. "Okay," he said. "Here's what I know so far."

When Kelleher closed the file, Terrell didn't know whether to laugh, cry, or just get up and walk out of the room.

The way Kelleher told it, Barrett Stephenson had been approached by Athena, the up-and-coming apparel-and-sneaker company that was trying to take on Under Armour. According to what Kelleher had found out, it started with Athena expressing interest in supplying Stephenson's team at Concord with gear. This wasn't uncommon. In fact, many high school coaches were paid by the big-name companies to put their players in their gear and to promote the company. Concord wasn't exactly a name program and Stephenson wasn't coaching anybody who was going to be a big-time recruit. The Athena rep, someone named Aubre Andrews, had told Stephenson that Athena was just looking for exposure anywhere it could find it to build the brand.

Soon after Stephenson accepted that offer, Andrews came back with his boss, Stan Montana, offering to pay for Stephenson's summer camp. The camp was hardly a big deal: two weeks of day camp at Concord. Stephenson ran it with three other high school coaches in the area, but it was a modest business. The four coaches usually ended up splitting between $10,000 and $15,000 in profits each year.

Athena wanted to pay for the camp and expand it to three weeks because it could use its contacts to bring in some semi-high-profile players. It would also supply the gear for all the campers. The offer meant that Stephenson and his partners would double their profit—or more.

There was just one small catch: Stephenson needed to convince Terrell Jamerson to attend the camp for one week. This would be good for everybody: Athena, the camp, and, of course, Stephenson and his partners.

Stephenson had been unsure at first but had ended up saying yes.

Terrell knew that was true because he *had* spent a week at the camp.

"He was honest with me about it," Terrell said to Kelleher. "He said Athena was interested in the camp, and me being there would help a lot."

"Uh-huh," Kelleher said. "That's how they get, if you'll forgive the expression, their foot in the door." He turned to another page of notes. "Terrell, you remember being introduced that week to a guy named Donald Tucker? Big guy, about six-six, former player? Very outgoing."

Terrell nodded. "Yeah, he said he had played at Kansas."

"He did. Sort of. He averaged 1.4 points a game for four years and never graduated. But he's real smart and he helped start Athena. He came to town partly to meet you but also to tell Coach Stephenson that he was so pleased with the camp, he was going to put him on the payroll in the fall."

"Is that legal?" Danny said.

"Absolutely. In fact, I don't think anyone involved here has broken a rule yet."

"Yet," Terrell said.

Kelleher nodded and went on. "Everyone was happy with

the new arrangement—especially when you announced the five schools you were going to visit. Tell me, Terrell, how'd you put that list together?"

It had actually been pretty simple. Terrell and his mom and the two coaches he trusted—Wilcox and Stephenson—had sat down one night after dinner with a list of about thirty schools that had already been in touch and had whittled them to nine very quickly. Three were automatics as far as Terrell was concerned: Duke, North Carolina, and UCLA. The first two had Hall of Fame coaches and he had seen the campuses—both were beautiful. UCLA had a very good coach in Steve Alford, and he'd really *wanted* to see the campus.

That left six others for two spots: Kentucky, Connecticut, Kansas, Indiana, Mass State, and the University of Atlanta.

Kentucky was a one-and-done school. That was what Coach John Calipari sold: Come here and you'll be NBA-ready in a year. No thanks. Connecticut had a great tradition, but they also had a brand-new coach and had just been on NCAA probation. No thanks. He didn't know that much about Kansas and Indiana, but both had storied basketball traditions and coaches who came across as good guys: Bill Self at Kansas, Tom Crean at Indiana. Mass State and Atlanta were up-and-coming programs whose coaches, Mike Todd at Mass State and Grant Hathaway at Atlanta, were selling the notion that Terrell would be the breakout player who would take their school to places they had never been before.

In one letter, Hathaway had written, "You'll be an icon

the day you set foot on campus. From there it will only get better."

Terrell's mother had snorted. "No one should be an icon at the age of eighteen."

She hadn't said much during that meeting. Now that Kelleher was asking, Terrell remembered that Coach Stephenson had pushed very hard for Atlanta. "It's a great city, the weather won't be too cold, and I think Grant Hathaway has a chance to be one of the next great coaches." He added that he thought Terrell should consider at least one school with an African American coach. Mike Todd fit that bill.

Coach Wilcox liked the idea of Mass State too. "You should visit one school close to home," he said. "You may decide you don't want to go too far away. I was thinking UConn, but I understand your reservations there. I don't know Mike Todd that well, but clearly he can coach."

Coach Stephenson nodded. "Actually, he did a clinic at my camp this summer," he said. "The kids loved him."

So it had been decided: Duke, North Carolina, UCLA, Atlanta, and Mass State.

"Stephenson likes Atlanta and Mass State," Kelleher said. "That mostly makes sense. I have sources—granted, biased ones—who say Stephenson will make a lot of money if he delivers you to Atlanta. I don't know of a Mass State connection yet—but I'm still digging."

Danny couldn't stop shaking his head. "It all seems so . . . complicated. All this maneuvering and scheming. Do they really want Terrell that bad?"

"Think, Danny. Terrell could be their ticket to the Final Four, a national championship, enormous revenues for their school. All the money they're laying out to entice players like Terrell or Michael Jordan or Jay Swanson? It's *nothing* compared to what they stand to gain when their team wins. So, yes, they want Terrell that bad."

Danny studied Terrell, wondering how he felt about that. But Terrell wasn't really paying attention. He was still focused on what he'd been told about Coach Stephenson. And the question he was almost too afraid to ask. Finally, he said, "Does my mom know all this?"

"That I don't know," Kelleher said. "That I do not know."

SEVENTEEN

There was another question that Bobby Kelleher hadn't addressed. What was Terrell supposed to do with this information?

And: "Why are you telling me all this?"

"Danny tells me you're going to make your visits to Mass State and Atlanta over the next couple weekends," Kelleher said. "I'd like to know what goes on during those trips. I'd like to know who you meet and what they say to you and what they tell you."

"And what they offer me?"

"Yeah—that too," Kelleher said.

"Why would I do that?" Terrell asked.

Kelleher shrugged. "Because you don't seem like you want to play their game. Because exposing these guys is the right thing to do."

"And because you'll get a big story out of it?"

"Yup," Kelleher said. "I will. Is there something wrong with doing a story that tells the truth on a subject this secret and this corrupt?"

Danny had told Terrell that he liked Kelleher for three reasons: He was smart, he was honest, and he was direct.

"Tell you what," Terrell finally said. "Let's talk after I get back from the visits."

"Deal," Kelleher said. "Now, what do I have to do to get more coffee in this place?"

Six days later, Terrell was headed for Atlanta. He and Danny drove to Logan Airport together as soon as school was over on Friday. Danny was flying to Nashville to visit Vanderbilt for his official recruiting visit.

Vanderbilt was in the Southeastern Conference, and the fact that they were recruiting Danny, even though they had no chance to get Terrell, was proof of how high Danny had risen in the eyes of college coaches since the summer. Danny's other visits had been to George Washington, Richmond, and UCLA. And then there was Harvard.

Terrell knew Danny was torn: He had loved his visit to Washington, D.C., and thought that living on GW's campus, a few blocks from the White House, would be cool. Richmond's campus, he had told Terrell, was just as pretty as Duke's or North Carolina's. Playing at Vanderbilt, a great school in a top conference, might be a good fit for him. But they both knew that Danny's dad wanted him to go to Harvard. Yes, he was impressed with Tommy Amaker, Harvard's coach. But mostly he wanted him to go because it was, well, Harvard.

"I know he doesn't do it on purpose," Danny said as they

searched for a place to park at Logan. "But every time we talk about Harvard, he brings up how much it would have meant to my mom to have her son go to Harvard."

"You *sure* he's not doing it on purpose?" Terrell said.

Danny gave him a look. "Good point," he said.

They were on the same flight to Atlanta because Danny had to change planes there to get to Nashville. They managed to get aisle seats across from each other, which was especially important to Terrell. Squeezing his six-foot seven-inch frame into a coach seat was tough.

The flight was packed, which was not surprising on a Friday afternoon. Just before the doors closed, a tall man dressed in an expensive suit hustled down the aisle and sat in what appeared to be the last empty seat—right in front of Terrell.

He gave Terrell and Danny a friendly smile and nod as he sat down. A minute later, the plane backed off the gate. They taxied to the runway where—surprise, surprise—the pilot told them they were twenty-first in line and should be ready for takeoff in "twenty minutes or so."

Terrell looked at Danny, who already had that week's *Sports Illustrated* open in front of him. "The 'or so' means it could be forty-five minutes, you know," he said.

Danny nodded. "Nothing we can do about it," he said. "Might as well read or sleep."

Terrell was about to put his head back when the late arrival seated in front of him leaned around his seat and put out his hand. "Glenn Hitchcock," he said. "I'm surprised to see you in coach, Terrell. Figured you'd be in first class."

Terrell glanced at Danny, who shrugged and buried his

head in the magazine. "If being in first class would get us going, I'd be all for it," he said.

The guy laughed much too hard at Terrell's little joke. "Where you headed?"

Terrell was tempted to simply say "Atlanta," but figured the truth would be easier. Technically, schools weren't allowed to announce official recruiting visits, but somehow the news always leaked out. He knew there had been a number of stories in the past week about the fact that he would be visiting Atlanta and Mass State the next two weekends. So he said, "Going to visit the University of Atlanta."

"Really? Very cool. Great school. I think you'll like it."

"Did you go there?"

Hitchcock laughed too hard again. "No, no. But I live down there. I'm a season ticket holder. I know Coach Hathaway pretty well. Good guy . . . very good guy."

"So you're heading home, then," Terrell said, trying to figure a way to wind down the conversation.

"Yeah, I was up here seeing some clients. I'm an investment banker."

Terrell wasn't a hundred percent certain what an investment banker did, but he figured Glenn Hitchcock was in the business of trying to make rich people richer.

"I actually represent quite a few athletes and coaches. Couple guys with the Celtics. That's who I was up here to see."

"Really?" Terrell asked. "Who?"

Hitchcock smiled. "They don't like me to talk about it. Part of our deal. I don't use their names to help me attract other clients. But let me put it this way: The players don't spend a lot of time on the bench."

Terrell nodded. Six months ago he would have been awed by the notion of talking to someone who knew two members of the Celtics well. Now, he not only wasn't awed, he wasn't even sure he believed the guy. If he was such a hotshot, why was *he* traveling in coach?

"Look, here's my card," Hitchcock said, a card magically appearing in his hand. "If there's ever anything I can do for you, let me know."

Terrell took the card and looked at it: GLENN HITCHCOCK, MAGIC INVESTMENT CO. "What could you do for me?" he asked. "I haven't got any money to invest."

Hitchcock laughed. "I know that, Terrell, but that'll change someday. In the meantime, if you need NBA tickets—any city—or tickets to just about anything, I can help. Concerts too. If you end up at U of A, I know all the good restaurants and clubs. You won't lack for a social life, I can promise you that."

Terrell was wondering when the guy was going to tell him that Charles Barkley wanted to give him a call. He leaned back in his seat and closed his eyes. Hitchcock was still talking just as the pilot came on to say the delay would be a "few more minutes."

"Anything I can do to help," Hitchcock was saying as Terrell tried to drift off to sleep.

Just once, Terrell thought, *I'd like to meet someone who doesn't want to do anything he can to help.*

The flight landed almost an hour late. Terrell had expected to be greeted at the gate by one of the assistant coaches, but it was Grant Hathaway who was standing right there, along with one of his assistants—having magically gotten through security without a ticket.

"I thought you guys were never going to get out of Boston," Hathaway said, greeting Terrell and Danny like long-lost friends. "Danny, I know your connection's very tight, so we've got a guy with a cart waiting over there to get you to your gate. Tell Kevin Stallings I'm jealous we couldn't convince you to visit."

Kevin Stallings was the coach at Vanderbilt. Danny looked a little bit stunned that Hathaway knew his schedule. "Thanks, Coach," he said. "That's really nice of you." Then he and Terrell exchanged a quick handshake, and he was off by cart to catch his connecting flight.

Terrell was about to say something to Coach Hathaway when he noticed that Glenn Hitchcock was hovering.

"Hey, Glenn!" Hathaway said, appearing surprised. "Were you on this flight too? Hey, come and meet one of the next great players, Terrell Jamerson."

"Actually, I sat one row in front of him," Hitchcock said. "First class was sold out. Come on, Grant, you know I keep up. I know just who Terrell is."

Hathaway had his arm around Hitchcock. "One of the good guys," he said to Terrell. "Someone you can actually trust. I don't let very many people hang around our guys, but Glenn's an exception." He turned to Hitchcock and asked, "What were you doing up in Boston?"

"Went to see some of my guys."

"Doc and Rondo?" Hathaway said, referring, Terrell knew, to the Celtics' coach, Doc Rivers, and point guard Rajon Rondo.

"You know I don't talk about that," Hitchcock said.

"Yeah, yeah, sure," Hathaway said. He turned back to Terrell. "You got bags we need to pick up? Or are you set?"

"All set," Terrell replied.

They were walking through the crowded concourse now, picking their way between people.

"You guys need a ride?" Hitchcock said.

"No, no, we're fine," Hathaway said. "My car's right outside."

"You guys going out to eat?"

"My guess is Terrell's a little bit hungry. Or were the peanuts on the plane enough for you, Terrell?"

Terrell grinned. "There were some cookies too," he said. "But I'm starving."

"Good!" Hathaway said. "Ever heard of the Palm?"

Terrell had heard of it. In fact, that was where he'd been taken out to eat during his visit to UCLA. He hadn't realized there was more than one. "You mean, like the one in LA?" he said.

"Yeah, exactly," Hathaway said. "Glenn, you want to join us?"

"Can't," Hitchcock said. "Meeting someone down the road."

"Well, bring her by for a drink later if you want," Hathaway said.

"How'd you know it was a her?" Hitchcock said, with a big smile on his face.

"Because I know you," Hathaway answered.

The coach and his friend had a good laugh at that one. Terrell decided to focus on the steak he was going to eat at the Palm.

An hour later, he was doing just that. Coach Hathaway hadn't been kidding about his car being right outside. After they had ridden the underground train from concourse C to the terminal, they walked outside the door, where a man in a red cap stood waiting, seemingly just for them.

He flipped a set of car keys to Hathaway, who pointed to a silver Tahoe sitting right at the curb. "Hop in."

Terrell did while Hathaway waved at the red cap and said, "Thanks, Jake. See you soon."

"Get us a good one, Coach," Jake yelled back.

"Do you always get to park like this?" Terrell said as they buckled in and Coach Hathaway peeled out into traffic.

"Pretty much," Coach Hathaway said. "You'd be amazed the support we have in this town right now. We've left Georgia Tech in the dust as Atlanta's college basketball team."

Georgia Tech had been to the Final Four, and Atlanta

had only been playing Division I ball for six years. But Tech had struggled in recent years, and Atlanta's run to the Sweet Sixteen the previous year had brought it a lot of national attention. As if reading his mind, Coach Hathaway said, "You know we're playing twelve games on ESPN this season?"

"All on ESPN?" Terrell asked.

"No, but these days there's not much difference between ESPN, ESPN2, and the U." Then he added, "Next season, if we have another good year, we'll be on *Game Day*."

Terrell caught himself smiling at the mention of *Game Day*. That was the show ESPN aired during both football and basketball season where its announcers went to a campus and broadcast before and after the so-called big game. The ESPN publicity machine had hyped it to the point where, well, coaches mentioned it to recruits. Terrell remembered watching it once with Danny and his dad. When the cameras showed a shot of a group of students with painted faces screaming and mugging for the cameras, Coach Wilcox had turned to them and said, "If I ever hear that either one of you even *knows* a kid who acts like that, I'll disown both of you."

Terrell had laughed. "Coach, you aren't my father."

"Whatever. I'll disown you anyway," Coach Wilcox had answered.

When they arrived at the Palm, which was located in the lobby of what was clearly a very upscale hotel, everyone—from the valet parker to the maître d' to the waiters to the chef, who came out of the kitchen to ask Terrell exactly what he wanted to eat—treated them like kings.

"Is this really Terrell?" the manager of the restaurant said when he rushed over to the table after they'd been seated. He pumped Terrell's hand. "I'm not sure what's more exciting, having you in my restaurant or the thought of you in a U of A uniform next season."

"I'll take the latter, Jerry," Hathaway said. "Even though I love you and your food."

It was like that all night. Terrell was devouring the massive porterhouse he had ordered when he heard Coach Hathaway say, "Hey, Derek, Carlos—come and meet someone!"

Terrell looked up to see Derek Rose and Carlos Boozer walking over to the table. He remembered that the Bulls were in town for a game the following night.

"Terrell Jamerson," Boozer said, shaking hands. "Coach K has told me all about you."

"Hey, alumni aren't allowed to talk to recruits!" Hathaway said, half joking. Boozer had gone to Duke.

"Yeah, yeah," Boozer said. "Well, I'll be honest and tell you that if you want to have a good time in college, this is the coach for you."

That became more apparent as the night went on. Terrell lost track of the number of attractive women who came by the table to say hello to them. Just as they were finishing dessert and Terrell was beginning to feel extremely tired, another couple wandered over to the table to say hello.

The guy was, Terrell guessed, about forty. He was extremely well dressed. His date—Terrell guessed she was his date because he had his arm wrapped around her waist—was considerably younger, barely out of college.

"Grant, I see you've brought the Messiah," the guy said. "Terrell, good to see you here. I'm Stewart Jenkins from Athena. This is my friend, Brandi."

"Do you spell it with an 'I' or a 'Y'?" Terrell asked.

"With an 'I,'" she answered. "Why do you ask?"

"Just curious," Terrell said, hoping he didn't have a foolish grin on his face. He remembered reading somewhere that 90 percent of the women who entered beauty pageants were named Tiffany, Amber, or Brandi—as opposed to Brandy.

"Sit down, join us," Coach Hathaway was saying.

Brandi sat down next to Terrell, and Stewart Jenkins sat down next to Coach Hathaway.

"So, Terrell, you have any Athena gear?" Jenkins asked as he signaled a waiter to refill his and Brandi's drinks.

"No, I don't," Terrell said. "It's kind of expensive."

Jenkins laughed as if Terrell had just told him the funniest joke he'd ever heard. "We can fix that, can't we, Grant?"

Coach Hathaway shook his head. "I can't fix anything, Stewart—you know that. NCAA rules. I can buy Terrell dinner and take him to our football game tomorrow and make sure he's well fed until he flies home Sunday morning. That's about it."

Terrell wasn't really listening because Brandi had moved so close to him that she was brushing up against him. It was, to say the least, distracting. If either of the men sitting across from him noticed, they didn't say anything.

"Well," Stewart Jenkins said. "There's nothing in the rules that says I can't help him out, is there? I'm not a representative of the school. Terrell's already met my boss, Stan Montana. Right, Terrell? Heck, if what I've read about Terrell here is true, I work for the competition just as much as I work for you, right?"

"Terrell *is* visiting Mass State next weekend," Coach Hathaway said. "Unless, of course, we can convince him this weekend that the trip will be a waste of time." He smiled at Terrell just as Brandi pushed up against him a little bit more. "Any chance we can do that, Terrell?"

"Don't think so, Coach," Terrell said. "I promised my mom I'd visit all the schools who came to see me. But it's nice of you to make me feel wanted."

"Oh honey, you're wanted," Brandi said. "Trust me, you're wanted."

EIGHTEEN

Terrell was about to tell Coach Hathaway he was exhausted when, as if reading his mind again, the coach announced that it was time for Terrell to get some sleep, since he had to wake up early to have breakfast with his "future teammates."

Terrell hoped no one noticed his sigh of relief. They all got up, and both Stewart Jenkins and Brandi hugged him to say good night. When Brandi looked up at him and said, "Oh my, you certainly *are* tall," Terrell was convinced he was in a bad movie.

"Hope you had fun," Coach Hathaway said when they were back in the car.

"Oh yeah, it was great, Coach," he said. "The food was fantastic."

Coach Hathaway gave him a sideways glance as if trying to read his face in the darkened car. "I'm sorry if Brandi came on a little strong," he said. "There are a lot of good-looking women in Atlanta who love our team."

Terrell wasn't sure how to answer that—so he didn't. A couple of minutes later they pulled into the Ritz-Carlton,

Buckhead, which was where Terrell would be spending the night. UCLA had put him up at the Four Seasons in LA, so the trappings of the five-star hotel weren't new to him. Still, having everyone in the place say, "Hello, Coach Hathaway," as they walked to the front desk was impressive.

"I'll leave you with Tony," Coach Hathaway said once Terrell had been given a room key and a bellman had come to take his one and only bag from him. "Just follow him. He'll take care of you." As Tony started in the direction of the elevator, Coach Hathaway leaned closer to him and said, "Don't worry about the tip. It's taken care of." Terrell was glad to hear that.

Tony jabbered on about all the stars he'd "gotten to know" while working at the Ritz as the elevator took them upstairs. "They got you a suite," he said, putting the key in the door. "You must be a big-timer. Most of our recruits just get regular rooms."

Our recruits? Terrell thought. He wondered if Tony used that line on everyone who the U of A—as everyone in town called the school—put up at the hotel. Actually, he didn't really care. He just wanted to be alone so he could get some sleep.

The phone rang at 7:00 a.m. Terrell had been dreaming that a dozen women who all looked like Brandi were chasing him down a hallway. He rolled over and answered it, and a cheerful voice reminded him he was being picked up in the lobby at 7:30.

Right, he remembered. Breakfast with his future teammates.

Two of them were waiting for him when he got downstairs, still blinking sleep from his eyes even after a lengthy shower. Both wore black-and-red Athena sweat suits, and he knew who they were right away: DeMarcus Suliman, the sophomore shooting guard, and James Tennyson, the junior center. Every story he'd read about the U of A indicated that one or both wanted to turn pro at the end of the season, so their status as "future teammates" was questionable.

Even so, he liked them right away. The three of them piled into Tennyson's jeep and headed toward campus, which, they explained, was about five miles to the north.

"So . . . you get the treatment last night?" Suliman asked as they pulled onto Route 400.

"The treatment?"

"Let me guess," Tennyson said. "The Palm for dinner. Stewart Jenkins showing up with some hot woman and everyone coming over to tell you why U of A is the place for you."

Terrell laughed. "I thought she was more obvious than hot," he said.

"Most of them are," Suliman said, and they all laughed.

Breakfast was in the student center, which was quiet on a Saturday. Even so, the team had its own table in a private room. He was introduced to everyone. No coaches were in sight. He was surprised. He had figured Coach Hathaway would be monitoring everything said to him.

"Look, let's be honest," Tennyson said as he dug into a huge stack of pancakes he had served himself from the middle of the table. "We all know the score: We're here to get ready for the NBA and to have a good time while we're at it. Coach H makes sure of that. Does he pile it on a little heavy in recruiting? Sure. But who doesn't?"

Suliman took over. "I'll tell you what, though. The guy makes sure you get your props from the media, and he knows all the people you want to know. Stewart Jenkins is full of it, but the dude *will* take care of you. Wait till you get home. You'll have enough Athena gear to last until about your fifth year in the league. And it will just keep on coming."

"The gift that keeps on giving," said Twan Mobley, the point guard, who was sitting across from them. "Jenkins can get you more than gear too."

"You mean like Brandi?" Terrell said.

"Was that her name last night?" Suliman said. "Yeah. He knows about a hundred just like her."

Terrell decided to change the subject. "Can Coach Hathaway coach?" he asked.

They all laughed. "Back when Bob Knight was still coaching at Texas Tech and Coach H first got here, they were both recruiting a kid from Texas named Bobo Alexander," Tennyson said.

Terrell vaguely remembered the name.

"Anyway, when Bobo told Coach Knight he was going

to Atlanta, Coach Knight said, 'That's fine, Bobo. Go play for a guy who couldn't coach lions to eat red meat. See how that works out for you.'"

"Where's Bobo now?" Terrell asked.

They all looked at each other. "D-league," Mobley finally said. "I think he's playing in North Dakota or something."

"So why would I come here if Coach H isn't a good coach?" Terrell asked.

"Because *you* don't need to be coached," Tennyson said. "You don't come here because of what you get on the court, you come here because of what you get off the court. And, trust me, that isn't a bad deal."

When breakfast was over, Anton Bennett, one of the assistant coaches, showed up to walk him over to the football game. Any doubts Terrell had had about Atlanta were long gone. This was exactly the kind of program he knew he wanted no part of.

He genuinely liked the players, but he suspected their honesty was as much strategy as anything else: Tell him what it's really like here—lots of parties and freebies, lots of exposure and celebrities. Sure, Coach can't coach, but that's not what the place is about. For some people, Terrell knew, the U of A would be the perfect place. Just not for him. He'd learned a ton from Coach Wilcox. And from Danny, too. About strategy, and anticipating what the other team would do. And about how to play defense—Coach Wilcox was all about defense. Yeah, the talent and the effort was all him, but Terrell was a smarter player because of the Wilcoxes. And he knew he had more he could learn still.

The football stadium was brand-new, built to house a rising program. It had 30,000 seats and was about two-thirds full. Coach Bennett explained on the walk over that Atlanta had started playing football only four years before and was still in the Football Championship Subdivision, meaning it played one level down from the powerhouse schools that made up what was called the Football Bowl Subdivision.

"In the old days, they called it 1-A and 1-AA, but you know the NCAA. They don't like to imply that anyone is bigger or more important than anyone else, so they came up with the new names," Coach Bennett explained. "We're scheduled to move up in two years. Right now we draw about twenty thousand a game, which puts us in the top five nationally in our division, and we're ranked eighth in the country. Today's a big game for us because Delaware is always good."

The stadium sparkled with newness. There was enough parking for tailgating, and it was a perfect fall day, so the lot was full of cars sporting red-and-black flags. Terrell almost laughed out loud when he saw the name on the stadium: "Athena Field of Atlanta."

"So . . . Athena paid to have its name on the stadium," Terrell said to Coach Bennett as they walked inside.

"Athena basically owns this campus," Coach Bennett admitted. "We're practicing right after the game. There will be about five thousand people watching us in Athena Arena."

"Athena Arena—seriously?"

"Only if you consider twenty million serious. That's what they're paying for the next ten years to have their name on both places."

Terrell swallowed his next question. Stewart Jenkins had said the night before that it was okay for him to give Terrell gear since he didn't represent the university. Really? His company was paying twenty million—not to mention whatever they were paying Coach Hathaway—and he didn't represent the university?

Now, *that* was funny.

They rode an elevator up to what was labeled "The President's Level." It was packed with well-dressed people holding drinks that didn't look like sodas to Terrell. He glanced at his watch: it was 11:40 in the morning.

"Come on. We're supposed to meet Coach Hathaway at the president's private reception," Coach Bennett said. "Dr. Haskell really wants to meet you."

Dr. Wayne Haskell was the president of the U of A. Terrell had read a bio that described him as "one of America's most forward-thinking academicians." He had no idea what that meant.

Coach Bennett led Terrell down a hallway filled with people dressed in black and red. At the end was a door with a guy standing guard who looked like he was in the Secret Service. He was wearing a dark suit, had a wire coming out of his ear, and looked very serious. Remarkably, he smiled when he saw the two of them coming. "Coach. Good morning," he said. "This must be Mr. Jamerson."

"It is," Coach Bennett said. "Terrell, this is Owen Taylor. He's our head of security."

Terrell shook hands with Owen Taylor, who pushed the door open for them. Inside were still more people in red and black. Coach Hathaway, who stood out because he was in red and black sweats, spotted them immediately and waved them over. Terrell noticed that there was a huge picture window that had a panoramic view of the stadium and the field. There was a door that led outside to two rows of seats where, he assumed, President Haskell and his friends went to watch once the game began.

"Terrell, how was your morning?" Coach Hathaway said, greeting him as he and Coach Bennett walked up. "If you didn't get enough food, there is *plenty* here to eat." He pointed to a buffet table on the far side of the room right in front of another picture window. There were no fewer than six people lined up to serve food.

One thing about attending the U of A, Terrell thought, *I'll never starve.* "I enjoyed meeting the guys," he said as he and Coach Hathaway shook hands. "They were great."

"Well, come on over and meet Dr. Haskell," Coach Hathaway said. "He told me he was going to fire me if he didn't get to meet you before kickoff."

Terrell laughed, and they walked over to where a small man in a gray suit, wearing (naturally) a red shirt and a red-and-black tie, was standing with several people. As soon as Dr. Haskell saw Terrell coming, he broke off his conversation. "Grant, it's about time!" he said in a drawl so Southern that Terrell thought he might be acting. "Terrell, I'm Wayne Haskell, and it is an *honor* to have y'all here at the U of A. Come on over and meet some folks."

He had grasped Terrell's hand and wouldn't let go, dragging him in the direction of the folks who wanted to meet him. Or was it "him-all"? Terrell wasn't sure. The next few minutes were a whirlwind of names. Terrell didn't even try to keep up. He just kept repeating "Very nice to meet you" until he thought his tongue and his arm were going to fall off.

After Dr. Haskell had finally introduced him to the last couple in the informal receiving line, he took Terrell by the arm and steered him to the front of the box, where they had some breathing room. He waved an arm in the direction of the field and the view. "Like it?" he asked.

"It's spectacular," Terrell said.

"Once we move up to play with the big boys, we'll expand and sell the place out every Saturday," Haskell said. "We're playing South Carolina next year, you know. Wanted to play Georgia Tech, but they're afraid of us."

Terrell figured if he kept smiling and nodding, that would be enough. If it bothered Haskell that he wasn't oohing and aahing, he didn't show it.

"You know, Terrell, I leave athletics to my athletics

people," he continued, changing subjects without missing a beat. "I pay Grant a lot of money, and he's worth every penny. You should have seen the way our fund-raising sky-rocketed last spring after we made the Sweet Sixteen."

He had now pushed up very close so he could whisper in his ear as best he could since he was about a foot shorter than Terrell. "Grant tells me you're the guy who will put us over the top. He's never said that about a player before. He's gushed about guys who he said would make us better and get us to the places we've already been. But when he told me you were coming to visit us, he said, 'Dr. Haskell, this is *the* guy. We get Terrell, we're going to the Final Four.'"

Haskell paused as if he was letting the weight of those words sink in. "Ever been to the Final Four, Terrell?" he asked at last.

"No sir."

"I have. They put seventy-five thousand people in a dome to watch basketball. Can you imagine that? If you take the U of A to a Final Four, I can tell you without hesitation that your future is assured."

That got Terrell's attention. What exactly was the distinguished president of a major university saying to him? "My future will be assured?" he repeated.

Haskell nodded. "You know how much money there is right here in this box? A lot of these people could buy and sell most NBA owners. Ask our players how appreciative they were last year. This is a dream world for a basketball player, son. You have my word on that."

Terrell was a little bit stunned. President Haskell had just offered him a massive bribe. On the other hand, he hadn't technically offered him anything—which proved that he was no dummy. If Terrell went public and said, "Dr. Haskell offered me a bribe," the first question would be, "What, exactly, did he offer you?"

The answer to that would be, "Well, he said people would be very appreciative if we got to the Final Four and that the U of A was a dream world for a basketball player."

Part of Terrell wanted to ask Haskell to be specific so he could take the information back to Bobby Kelleher. But he knew it was pointless. Haskell wasn't going to make that mistake and, even if he did, unless Terrell had him on tape, he'd just deny it. Before he could respond at all, Coach Hathaway returned, carrying a heaping plate of food.

"Terrell, figured you should eat something before kick-off," he said. "Dr. Haskell, what'd I tell you?"

"Great young man!" Dr. Haskell said. "You were a hundred percent right, Grant. I say, let's sign him up right now."

Haskell turned to Terrell. "What do you say, Terrell, you want to make your commitment to U of A right now?"

Terrell did his best to smile. "I think if I committed to anyone without checking with my mom, she'd kill me," he said.

"Where's your mama?" Dr. Haskell asked, looking around. "Didn't you bring her?"

"No sir. She's back home."

Dr. Haskell said, "Well, next time you come down, I want your mama here as my personal guest. We Southern men understand about treating your mama right."

Another non-bribe?

"Come on, Terrell, let's find you a place to sit down and eat," Coach Hathaway said, which sounded very good to Terrell.

Dr. Haskell shook his hand and gave him a hug.

These people, Terrell noticed, were big huggers.

"I want you in the U of A family, Terrell," Dr. Haskell said. "You are just the kind of student-athlete we want here. I know this will be the right place for you. I can tell just talking to you."

"Yes sir," Terrell said, wondering exactly how much Dr. Haskell knew about his record as a student. "Thank you, sir."

"Anything—I mean, *anything*—I can do to help, you let me know."

Terrell knew he meant that. Just like everyone else did.

NINETEEN

Terrell breathed a deep sigh of relief the next morning when Coach Hathaway gave him a hug (naturally) as he dropped him off at the curb in front of the airport terminal.

Coach Hathaway wanted to walk him to his gate, but Terrell told him it was really okay, he didn't have to go to the trouble. He was surprised and relieved when the coach didn't argue with him. Danny had texted that his connecting flight from Nashville had left on time and that he would meet Terrell at the gate for the flight back to Boston.

Terrell couldn't wait to tell Danny about all the "helpful" folks he had met in Atlanta. There had been more of them at the party the players had taken him to Saturday night after the football game. During the game, various professors and deans had taken turns sitting with him, along with several other boosters. All of them wanted to tell him why the U of A was the place for him.

After Atlanta had beaten Delaware, 17–13, he had been taken out to dinner—this time at Morton's—by several of the players. If anyone paid for the meal, he didn't see it happen.

"Don't we need to pay?" he had asked James Tennyson as they were getting up to leave.

Tennyson laughed. "Already taken care of, buddy. One thing about coming to the U of A, you needn't worry about bringing any cash with you."

They had gone from there to an off-campus party at some kind of club where there were two guys who weighed at least three hundred pounds apiece standing at the door.

They hugged and high-fived Tennyson, who was Terrell's official escort, and then did the same with Terrell.

"Bouncers?" Terrell asked as they walked inside a room that was so loud, he knew there was going to be no way to talk the rest of the night.

"Football players," Tennyson screamed back. "The linemen rotate on the door to make sure no one comes in we don't want."

Terrell looked around and saw that just about every male in the room appeared to be an athlete and every female a future runway model. As if reading his mind, Tennyson shouted, "Dudes don't let in any girl that's less than a nine."

If he was joking, Terrell didn't see any evidence of it.

Tennyson led him to a table in back that had been commandeered by several basketball players and several of the women who had passed the "nine" test. There was a good deal more hugging, much of it from the women.

One, who was introduced to him as China, told him he would be the most popular guy on campus the day he arrived.

"What about these other guys?" Terrell asked.

"Everyone says you'll be the best player we've ever had here," China told him. "Best player gets the best girls. Of course."

The rest of the night was more of the same. Terrell had to admit that the attention from China and her friends was a lot more fun than the attention he'd received from Dr. Haskell and *his* friends. He couldn't help but wonder if these were all U of A students.

At one point, when the throbbing music had been turned down for a little while, he asked a girl who'd been introduced to him as Destiny if that was her real name.

"Destiny Marie Watson," she said. "I'll show you my driver's license if you want."

"What's your major?" he asked.

"Marketing," she answered. "I'm on the volleyball team."

He could easily look at the school website to see if Destiny Watson was on the team. When he thought about it, it wasn't that much of a stretch on a campus of fifteen thousand that twenty or twenty-five great-looking women would show up at a party thrown by the campus jocks.

At midnight, Terrell mentioned that he had to be up early to make his 9:45 flight. Grudgingly, Tennyson agreed to take him back to the hotel. It took another fifteen minutes at the door, what with all the hugging and promising to stay in touch.

"So this is a typical Saturday night around here?" Terrell asked as they walked to Tennyson's car.

"Nah, when *we're* playing and we win, then it really gets wild," Tennyson said.

He stopped and looked Terrell in the eye. "Listen, man, everything I hear, you're probably only going to college for one year," he said. "You pick a place like Duke or North Carolina, you're going to have to go to class, keep up your grades—stuff like that. Here, you'll just have a great time, go to parties like this one every weekend, never have to worry about anything except winning games and fighting off the ladies."

"What if I want to actually graduate?"

Tennyson laughed. "Then you shouldn't go here."

He unlocked the car and started to climb in. Terrell had one more question. "If going to school here is about fighting off the ladies, how come you're leaving with me?"

Tennyson smiled at him as he pulled the door shut. "Soon as I drop you off," he said, "I'm going back."

Right, thought Terrell. *I knew that. . . .*

As promised, Danny was waiting at the gate, reading the *Atlanta Journal-Constitution.* When he saw Terrell coming, he stood up to greet him.

Terrell put out his hand quickly and said, "You know I love you, man, but please don't hug me. I can't take any more hugging."

Danny laughed. "That bad?" he said.

"Worse," Terrell said. "Tell me about Vanderbilt."

"Loved it," Danny said. "The players are good, smart guys. I think I'd fit in. Coach Stallings seems like a straight shooter. He told me he thought I could play for them but that he'll have two senior guards next year and I'd probably be fighting for minutes behind them. I already knew that, but he didn't try to BS me about it. . . . I did find out something pretty interesting after what Kelleher told us last week."

"What's that?" asked Terrell.

"They were recruiting Alex Mayer early on. He was very interested until the summer. Then when they tried to contact him about making a home visit, he told them he'd narrowed his list and they weren't on it."

Terrell shrugged. "So? I had places like Texas and Notre Dame on my list, and when I had to cut down, they didn't make the cut."

"Yeah, but I remember Alex telling me specifically that he didn't want a school where almost every guy was one-and-done. You know who's on his list now? Kentucky, Atlanta, Memphis, Mass State, and Mississippi State. The only one on that list that isn't a one-and-done type school is Mass State."

"Atlanta?" Terrell said. "No one mentioned to me at U of A that he'd visited."

"He hasn't, not officially," Danny said. "Next week. The kid's got like a three-point-six GPA and he's not interested in Vanderbilt? Doesn't sound like he's looking for a great *education*."

There was an announcement calling their flight.

"Harvard is still where you should go," Terrell said to Danny. "It would make your dad *so* happy."

"It also might make him broke," Danny said. "It's hard to pick a place that's not offering you a scholarship. Though I've heard they have great financial aid. . . . Oh, we'll see. Maybe you can go with me when I visit?"

"No need—I'm sure it's *exactly* like the U of A." Terrell laughed. "Though I'm willing to bet there's not a single girl there named China or Destiny."

Terrell reported on his Atlanta visit to his mother that night. He was glad to be able to talk to her without Coach Stephenson around.

"It sounds like a place you'd have fun," his mom said when he had finished. "It also sounds like we have to decide if you're choosing a college or a basketball team."

Terrell was a little shocked. "I didn't think that was a question for you."

His mom nodded. "I know. But I'm trying to keep an open mind. I mean, I've been thinking of basketball as your ticket to a great college, a great education. But all this attention you've been getting . . ."

"What are you saying?" Terrell was almost afraid to know.

"I guess I never saw the NBA as a real option before. So few people can really play at that level. . . . But I'm beginning to believe *you* could. If you want to. *Is* that what you want, Terrell? To play professional basketball?"

"Well, yeah, of course . . . ," Terrell answered. He'd certainly fantasized about it anyway.

His mom took a deep breath. "Okay. Well. Then maybe we should be asking ourselves which school—which team— will help you achieve *that* goal."

Terrell's head was spinning. Had he been leaning toward the more academically oriented schools and going for four years because he thought it's what his mom wanted? Or was it what he wanted?

Did he have to decide right now?

No, he thought. *Not really.*

"Mom, that's the thing about Duke. There I can get both a great coach and a great education. I can keep my options open."

His mom smiled. And did she look a bit relieved? "That makes sense," she said. "But let's keep our word to Barrett and go through the entire process before making a decision. There's no way that can hurt. Maybe you'll go to Mass State next weekend and love it and decide to stay close to home."

Then she grinned and said, "Or maybe that girl Destiny will call you and convince you to go to Atlanta."

Terrell rolled his eyes. "For a date maybe."

The next week was the most fun Terrell could remember having since Lexington's march to the state championship game the previous spring. There was no doubt that the Minutemen were good, and the addition of a sophomore forward named James Nix was clearly going to make them even better. As a player, Nix reminded Terrell a lot of Jay Swanson: a very good shooter who was able to run the floor very well. The difference was that he clearly wanted to be part of a good team and was willing to work on defense and try to fit in with his new teammates.

Not surprisingly, Coach Wilcox wasn't oohing and aahing about his team's play at practice. Even if he thought he was coaching the greatest team in the history of high school basketball, the last thing he would do was tell his players that. He didn't need anyone thinking they were unbeatable a month before the first game.

And there *was* a lot to work on. Terrell had played most of last season in the low post, with his back to the basket, largely because he was too quick for most big men to guard there. But his perimeter game had improved so much during the summer that it would be silly not to use him that way too. Coach Wilcox had put in a series of plays built around screens on the baseline that freed Terrell up in the corners and out on the wing. From there he had two options: shoot if he was open or, if he found himself double-teamed, get the ball back to Danny or Nix on the perimeter.

As sound as that offensive strategy was, it was an adjustment for everyone, especially Danny, who was used to looking for Terrell in the low post and having space to himself outside.

On the night before Terrell was scheduled to make the drive to Mass State, he and Danny took James Nix out for a getting-to-know-you dinner at Nettie's, which was a local staple known for their pizza. Danny and Terrell both liked the pizza, but they also really liked the waitresses who delivered them.

After they had ordered, Nix held up his iced tea to deliver a toast: "To you two guys, for letting me be part of this team." He turned to Danny. "And especially to you, Danny, for not getting upset with your father for changing the offense."

Terrell could see that Danny was caught off-guard. "How'd you know we changed our offense?" he said.

"When I knew I was moving here, I asked your dad if he had some tape from last season. I figured it would be good to know how you guys played. From what I saw, you had a lot more space to do your thing last year because Terrell was always near the basket. Now you've got to share that space and make more decisions. It isn't just, 'Get the ball in to Terrell' anymore."

Terrell grinned. They rarely encountered another player who thought the game through the way Danny—who had learned from his dad since he was little—did.

Danny took a sip of his drink and nodded. "Yeah, it is a little bit tougher," he conceded. "But we're a better team this way."

"True. But it makes it harder for you to show the college coaches what you can do."

Danny shook his head. "Now, that you're wrong about," he said. "Running an offense that relies on just dumping the ball to the best player in the country isn't that challenging.

I may get fewer shots this way, but it will show coaches I can adapt and make decisions on the fly."

Terrell nodded. "One thing you'll find out, James, if you've got skills, Coach'll find a way to use 'em. He knows Danny can run a more complicated offense. And that I need more variety in my game."

"Is that why he's your number one adviser about where to go to college?" James asked.

"Who said that?" Terrell said.

"I've read it," James said. "In fact, a lot of the scouting services say that some college coaches have been frustrated because they don't think they've been given a fair shot at you—it seemed like they were implying Coach Wilcox was keeping them away."

"What would you expect the coaches who aren't on his final list to say?" Danny said. "They have to be able to explain to their alumni and boosters that it isn't *their* fault they don't have a shot at Terrell."

James nodded. "Good point," he said. "I gotta admit, I knew it would be a little bit crazy when I came here because of you, Terrell, but I never dreamed it would be like this."

Terrell was about to tell him about Destiny and China and friends when he heard someone calling his name. He looked up and saw Maurice and the dudes approaching the table. He was a little surprised—he hadn't seen them much since school started.

"Terrell. Long time no see, dude," Maurice said, walking to the table, followed by the four other dudes and someone

Terrell didn't recognize. He gave Terrell a fist-bump and turned to James. "So is this the new guy I've heard so much about?"

"It is," Terrell said. "James Nix, Maurice Evans."

"Pleasure," Maurice said, surprising Terrell by giving James an actual handshake. "Meet Chao, Anthony, Sky, Dante, and Felipe. Hey, Terrell, you haven't met Felipe yet."

Terrell shook Felipe's hand and introduced him to James and then to Danny—who was leaning back in his chair, glaring daggers at Maurice. When it came to the dudes and Danny, Terrell had a simple goal: keep Danny and Maurice from getting into a fight.

Without even looking at Maurice, Danny shook Felipe's hand and said, "So, Felipe, where are you from?"

"New York," Felipe said. "I'm goin' to the community college over in Waltham."

"Really?" Danny said. "You have to be the first college student to ever hang out with this crowd."

Maurice gave a disgusted half laugh, half grunt. "Your boy here still thinks he's the funniest guy in the room, huh, Terrell?"

"I'm impressed, Terrell," Danny said, still not looking at Maurice. "One of the dudes actually picked up on my humor. That's pretty good."

"Come on, you guys," Terrell said. "Let's all try to get along this season, okay? No reason not to, right?"

"Yeah, right," Maurice said.

At that moment, Laurie Walters, their waitress, arrived

with their pizzas. "Hot stuff coming through!" she said, forcing the dudes to give her a path to the table.

Laurie was a senior at Lexington, and Terrell had been trying to convince Danny to ask her out for almost a year. The two of them were always making eyes at each other. For now, though, that was as far as it had gone.

"Hot stuff is right," Maurice said as Laurie put the pizzas down.

"Down, boy," Terrell said lightly, seeing the look that crossed Danny's face.

"What, somebody got a problem with me noticing a little hottie when I see one?" Maurice said. He stepped into Laurie's path as she was leaving the table. "You don't mind it, do you, little hottie?"

Before Laurie could do or say anything, Danny jumped from his seat and was in Maurice's face. "Leave her alone, Maurice," he said. "She's not for you."

"Whoa, white boy. Did I hit a nerve?"

"You want to see something hit, just keep doing what you're doing."

They were chest to chest. Terrell was pretty certain Maurice would back down. On the other hand, he knew Danny *wouldn't*. Terrell quickly got between his best friend and Maurice. He didn't want Danny to get in trouble for beating the crap out of him. "Cool it, would you? Maurice, do me a favor and just let us have our pizzas. I've got a big day tomorrow."

It was Anthony who responded. "Yeah, all your days are

big ones these days, aren't they, Terrell? Too important to hang with your friends."

"He *is* hanging with his friends," said Danny, who was still glaring at Maurice even though he had taken a step back.

"Yeah, right," Anthony said. "All of his friends these days are rich white people. Why is that, bro?"

"Nah, man, it's cool," Maurice said, shaking his head. "We'll catch you later, Terrell. Good luck with your 'big day.'"

The dudes all left, which was good, but Terrell felt bad. He could have sworn that tough-guy Maurice had looked kind of . . . hurt.

TWENTY

Mass State was about as different from the University of Atlanta as basketball was from hockey. It was almost rural, just a few miles from the Massachusetts-Vermont border, with trees everywhere—or so it seemed.

"If you're looking for big-city parties, this ain't the place for you," Jordan Augsburg, a junior from New York, said as they walked across the campus. Terrell had gone to the basketball office upon arrival and had been greeted by Augsburg and sophomore point guard Jerrell White. White was from LA and had been recruited by all the top schools, but he had chosen Mass State over UCLA at the last possible moment, stunning much of the basketball world.

"That's why I came here," White said as they headed for the union building, where they were supposed to meet the rest of the team for dinner. Clearly, there would be no meals at Morton's on this trip. "I just loved the quiet," he continued. "It gets cold in the winter, but the snow is beautiful."

Augsburg laughed. "Says the guy from LA."

"Yeah, okay," said White. "So I was pretty stoked about my first snowball fight. . . . And the skiing is awesome. We can go down to Springfield or Hartford if we want city stuff. But really, everything I want is right here."

"Yeah, you get used to it," Augsburg put in. "Coach will make you work—I won't lie to you. But if you work hard, there's a lot of good that comes from that. Look what it did for us last season."

Mass State had made the NCAA Tournament the previous spring for the first time since it had joined Division I in 2001. It was one of the last four at-large teams into the field and had made it all the way to the Elite Eight before losing in overtime to Kentucky. Along the way, the Freedoms had become media darlings. Four seniors had graduated—Coach Todd always pointed out that they had, in fact, *graduated*—so this was a rebuilding year.

"We'll be better than people think this season," Augsburg went on. "Next year, though . . . we get you, there's nothing we can't do."

Terrell couldn't help but notice that everywhere he went, his arrival on campus was apparently going to change school history. That said, it might be more true at Mass State than at any of the other places he had visited. Duke and North Carolina had won multiple national championships and would always be top-ten teams. UCLA hadn't won for a while but had more championship banners than any program in history. Atlanta and Mass State were the new guys on the block, but Terrell's sense was that Mike Todd and his program would be around longer than Grant Hathaway and his program.

After dinner, Augsburg and White drove Terrell to Coach Todd's house, where he was introduced to everyone on the coaching staff and to their wives. There were a number of other people there too, some of them clearly boosters, but they all blended together in Terrell's mind. There was no one who reminded him of China or Destiny.

"We'll talk more at breakfast tomorrow," Coach Todd told him. "For now, I just wanted you to meet everyone and get a feel for what we're about here."

At breakfast the next morning, it was just Terrell and Coach Todd. No assistants, no hangers-on—just the two of them. Coach Todd was waiting for him in the hotel lobby at eight o'clock, as he had promised, and they sat in a corner of the dining room and talked for almost two hours.

"I'll be honest with you, Terrell," Coach Todd said. "If I was a high school senior and Duke or North Carolina recruited me, I'd have a tough time saying no to either one. They're both great schools and they've got great coaches." He leaned in and lowered his voice. "But think about this. You can *never* mean as much to those places as you would mean to us. You go there and win four straight national championships, which even for a player as talented as you, isn't going to happen—you're still just building on what's already been done.

"You come here and you can *be* Mass State basketball. That's no knock on the guys who have gotten the program to where we are right now. But none of them has your talent—they all know that. You can be to Mass State what Bill Russell was to the Celtics, what Michael Jordan was to the Bulls, what LeBron James should have been to the Cavaliers."

"Should have been?" Terrell was curious to hear what Coach Todd thought of LeBron.

Coach Todd shrugged. "He left too soon—the job wasn't finished. Coach Wilcox told me he believes you when you say you don't want to be a one-and-done. If that's true, I think you'll stay here to finish the job. And with you here, I can recruit players who will make sure you do that."

It was heady stuff. Coach Todd had seemed nice enough in Terrell's living room in Lexington, but there had been five other people there—two assistant coaches, Coach Wilcox, Coach Stephenson, and his mom. Now it was just the two of them. Man to man.

And somehow this felt more real than all the wining and dining of the previous weekend. The players here seemed more grounded than those at Atlanta or even at Duke or North Carolina, where, even though they went to class and graduated, they were given plenty of special treatment. Terrell could suddenly see the appeal of a quiet campus in the middle of nowhere.

* * *

The rest of the weekend was great. Mass State didn't have a football team, so the players took him to a soccer game, where they stood around on the sidelines for a half before deciding to take off. They went to a place called the Redcoat Inn, where they were greeted the same way Terrell and Danny were greeted at home in Lexington. They piled into a corner booth right next to a fireplace.

The next few hours were full of story swapping. Everyone had recruiting stories to tell. Two of the players—Johnson Highsmith and Tony Alexander—had visited Atlanta. They weren't surprised to hear about Destiny and China.

"Mine were named Amber and Britney," Highsmith said.

"I think I had Lola and Tonya," Alexander said.

"You gotta admit," Augsburg said, laughing, "you *do* remember them."

Terrell felt completely at home with the players. They went to a movie after dinner that night, and he had a farewell breakfast with all the coaches the next morning.

"We aren't going to call you or text you every day," Coach Todd said. "You know what's here for you. You know what you could mean to us and, I hope, what we could mean to you. I'll only ask one thing of you."

"What's that?"

"Don't sign early. I know most guys like to sign early because it gets the biggest decision of their lives behind them before the season starts. Sometimes it makes sense. But not for you. You became a star late, so you started your recruiting late. I know you've seen a lot, but I think you should wait and see who everyone signs with and how everyone's season plays out."

He smiled. "Of course, if you want to sign early with us, I withdraw everything I just said."

Terrell laughed. He really did like Coach Todd. And, he had to admit, the decision that had felt so clear-cut the night Coach K had been in his house felt less so now. "I'll think about everything you said," he promised.

"That's all I can ask," Coach Todd said. "That and your signature on a letter of intent."

On Friday, Terrell would have found that request laughable. Now, he nodded his head and said, "We'll see."

Coach Wilcox had scheduled practice for four o'clock Sunday afternoon in order to give Terrell and Danny plenty of time to get back from their final campus visits. Danny had been at Harvard, meaning he had spent the night at the Marriott Long Wharf, a really nice downtown hotel, and not in his own home, even though they were about equidistant from Harvard.

"If I could spend four years staying in that hotel, I'd commit to Harvard right now," Danny said as they were getting into their practice gear. "Place is right on the water, across the street from Faneuil Hall."

"Yeah, but what'd you think of Harvard?"

"Where?" Danny said. Then he laughed. "Honestly—it's a great place. I loved Coach Amaker, just like on his visit, and the players are cool. The campus is amazing. But do I want to go to a place where I can't get a scholarship? Do I want to be so close to home? Do I want to study that hard?"

"And?"

"I don't know! Why don't you go there with me and we can make history. Take 'em to the Final Four."

Terrell laughed. "Now you sound like Coach Todd," he said.

Practice was spirited, since they'd had two days off. Terrell would have liked to have gone out for post-practice pizza with the other guys, but he had homework, so he begged off, showered quickly, and was the first one out the back door to the parking lot. He was tossing his gym bag into the back-seat of his mom's car when he heard a familiar voice behind him.

"You've lost your white shadow, Terrell. Amazing."

He turned and saw Maurice leaning against a car a few spaces away from his.

The rest of the dudes were there too: Anthony, Chao, Sky, Dante, and the new guy, Felipe.

"What's up, Mo?" Terrell said, trying to sound friendly and not impatient.

"We're heading over to Norm's," Maurice said. "We thought we'd pick you up on the way."

Norm's was a divey bar/restaurant named after the *Cheers* character.

"Can't do it tonight, Mo," he said, smiling. "Just got back from a college visit. I've got homework, and my mom's waiting on me. That's why I'm out of here so much faster than anyone else. Next time, okay?"

He started to pull open the front door.

"No, not okay," Maurice said, pushing himself away from the car to walk over to Terrell. He was about a foot shorter than Terrell and yet, for some reason, Terrell always found him intimidating. "You're coming with us. In fact, I'm going to ride over there with you. We need to talk."

TWENTY-ONE

Terrell didn't say a word during the drive to Norm's, and neither did Maurice. When they walked in, the place was almost empty—not too many people out on a rainy Sunday night. The rest of the dudes were already seated at a booth way in the back.

Terrell sat down on one side while Maurice sat down on the other. Somehow this felt like a showdown.

"You want something?" Chao asked. "Drink? You hungry?"

"Starving," Terrell said. "Which is why I'd like to go home for dinner, and do the pile of homework I've got waiting. But apparently Mo has something he wants to talk about."

Anthony grunted. "Dude, if you're breathing, you'll get into any college you want. They don't care 'bout your history grade."

"But my mother does," Terrell said. "And she's more important than the colleges. And more important than you, for that matter." He started to stand up.

Maurice leaned across the table, put a hand firmly on Terrell's shoulder, and pushed him down. He was surprisingly strong for his size. "Terrell, don't be like that. Give your old friends a minute. We're worried about you."

"Worried?" That was unexpected. "Why would you be worried about me?"

"We think you're missing your main chance," Maurice said. "Your straight-arrow coach—he wants you to take a scholarship and that's it, right?"

"What else would I take?" Terrell said, though of course he knew.

Maurice sat back and looked at the other dudes. "Told you," he said. "They've got him snowed." He leaned forward again. "Terrell, you know how much all these people are gonna make off you? You're worth millions to any college you go to, to the TV networks, to the shoe company that has their deal, to the coach, to the coach's agent, to the president of the college—hell, to the entire athletic department, which will be selling your jersey. While you get *nothing*. Everyone gets rich except you."

"I get rich if I make it to the NBA. And if I don't make it to the NBA, if I do what I'm supposed to, I get a college degree."

"Excuse me for sayin' so, 'cause I don't really know you that well, but are you kidding?" Felipe said. "You sound like one of those commercials they play during games, where everyone's a student-athlete and is goin' to end up as president or something."

Terrell actually laughed. Felipe was right—he *did* sound like one of those stupid commercials. He and Danny loved to hate them—they were like parodies of themselves. Their favorite was the one where someone was a swimmer but also a concert violinist. "I hear you," he said. "And I know there's a lot more on offer. Trust me, I know. But I don't want to owe anything to anyone."

"You don't need to," Maurice said. "People should owe *you*."

Terrell shook his head. He was pretty sure he knew where this was going. "What've you got in mind?"

"A win-win for everyone." Terrell said nothing, so Maurice pushed on. "There are people who someday are going to want to do business with you—who want to start doing business now. If you want to play by the NCAA's rules, no reason you can't. You never even have to meet any of them. We'll be their bridge to you until the day you turn pro."

"Bridge?"

"We'll be, like, your agents—even though we're not officially agents, so no one can say you have an agent. People can pay us, but really the money's for you, see? Less a small percent, of course. The point is, you can start making money—and earning interest—right now, instead of having to wait."

"And how are you going to convince these 'people' that I've given you permission to represent me—officially or unofficially?"

"Easy," Maurice said, clearly prepared for the question.

He pointed at Sky, who reached into his jacket pocket and produced a piece of paper, which he handed to Maurice.

"Sky's got a friend who's a lawyer. All it says is we're your unofficial reps until you turn pro. Nothing binding, except it shows people you know that we're helping you out. No one will ever even know about it except the people we show it to as proof you're with us."

Terrell knew that what Maurice was proposing was ridiculous. But he didn't want to just laugh it off and make him mad. "Let me think about it," he said.

Maurice looked at him suspiciously. "You're just trying to stall, aren't you?"

"Yes," Terrell admitted with a sigh. "Maurice, you know I can't sign anything like that. For about a hundred reasons."

"You got a better idea?" Maurice said, sounding irritated again.

"No. *I* haven't been thinking about this," Terrell replied.

"Which is why you need us to think for you," Maurice shot back. "Your old friends. Who knew you when. Who know all your secrets. Those things you'd rather keep between us . . . you know, like what a partier you are."

Terrell just stared at him. "I'm not—you know it was just that one time. . . ."

"I'm *kidding*, come on." Maurice grinned, but his tone was anything but light. "Loyal friends like us, we'd never let anything bad happen to you. Friends take care of each other. Right?"

What could he say to that? "Tell you what," Terrell said finally. "When these 'people' come to town, I'll come meet you and them. I won't commit to anything, but I'll let them know that we're friends. I'm pretty sure they'll *take care* of you."

Maurice looked at the other dudes. "What do you think?" he said.

"I think, screw that," Anthony said. "Dude isn't talking anything but a free meal every now and then."

"No, it could be more," Felipe said. "He comes out with us, it tells people we're tight. I think we can work with that."

"I do too," Maurice said. "Being friends makes everything work, right?" He reached his hand across the table to Terrell.

Terrell had never found the word *friends* quite so frightening. But he took Maurice's hand.

Terrell filled Danny in on what had happened the next day at lunch. Danny kept shaking his head in disgust. "Why would you agree to hang out with them at all?" he said. "Maurice clearly showed his hand when he brought up what happened in July."

Terrell popped a couple of French fries into his mouth and nodded. "Of course he did," he said. "But I'm not really worried about that. You think any of the schools that are recruiting me will care that I smoked pot once?"

"So why . . . ?"

Terrell smiled. "Bobby Kelleher."

"What?"

"I think the story he's trying to do is a good idea. And if

the dudes can convince some of those sneaker reps or agents or the guys who do the dirty work for coaches that they're the way to get to me, they'll come running."

Danny shrugged. "They'll come running if *you* call them. What do you need the dudes for?"

"Because with me they'll be more subtle about it. I'm sure the word is already out that I don't want to be bought and paid for. So they'll be careful. But if the dudes can convince guys that I'm in but that I want to keep a low profile, *then* we'll find out what they're offering."

Danny picked up the bottle of Coke he'd been drinking and drained it. "You know, for a dumb jock you're pretty smart," he said.

"I need your help, though," Terrell said.

"What?"

"I need you to be totally pissed off at me when I start hanging out with the dudes again. If you're not, they may wonder if something's up."

"Act pissed off at the dudes?" Danny said with a big smile. "I think I can do that."

After talking it over with Coach Wilcox, Terrell asked his mother if Coach Stephenson could come over to the house for a talk. When his mom asked what it was about, Terrell said, "I want to tell you both together."

Shortly after eight o'clock, the three of them sat down in the living room. Coach Stephenson looked about as tense as

Terrell could ever remember seeing him. There was none of his usual joking or questions about practice. The early signing period would begin in exactly seven days.

"I've given this a lot of thought," Terrell said. "You guys were right about me taking those last two visits to Atlanta and Mass State. I learned a lot on both trips. If I had to sign today, I would sign with either Duke or Mass State. . . ."

"Terrell, you need to really think this through before you make a final decision," Coach Stephenson said, breaking in—though not really, because Terrell had paused briefly to see if he would.

"Yeah, Coach," he said. "That's what I was about to say. I think I need more time, and, really, I don't *have* to sign early. I know that means I'll have to deal with all the recruiting stuff during the season, but I've handled it for six months. I can handle it a little while longer. And I know all the coaches will understand that I don't want to be pressured too much."

"Do you think Coach Todd and Coach K will be willing to wait?" his mom asked.

"For Terrell, they'll all wait," Coach Stephenson said.

"I think so," Terrell agreed. "I mean, Coach Todd *asked* me not to sign early. And that made sense to me. That way I'll be able to see what happens at all five schools with their seasons, and maybe see who signs where."

Coach Stephenson was nodding. "You're doing the right thing, Terrell," he said. "You need to take your time and gather as much information as you can."

"Barrett, don't you think we have more than enough information already?" his mom said.

"Sure we do," Coach Stephenson said. "But if Terrell isn't sure, there's no reason to rush him."

His mother sighed. "It's your decision, honey," she said finally. "I'll back you, no matter what."

Terrell was relieved to hear that. He knew his mom was still standing behind him. It was also pretty clear where Coach Stephenson was standing.

TWENTY-TWO

The next few weeks flew by for Terrell.

There wasn't a lot of free time. His weekdays were all pretty much the same: school, practice, dinner, homework, bed.

The weekends weren't a lot different. There was still homework, and there was practice on Saturday morning. On Friday nights, he satisfied his unofficial commitment to the dudes and spent time with them. He insisted on going to Nettie's—in part, because he liked the pizza; in part, because Valerie Dove worked there. He and Danny had made a pact: Danny would ask Laurie Walters to the Thanksgiving dance and he would ask Valerie Dove.

"If we both get shot down, we can stand in the corner by ourselves all night," Danny had joked.

"We won't be alone," Terrell had answered. "The dudes will hang out with us."

Fortunately, they didn't have to test the theory. Laurie all but jumped up and down when Danny finally asked her after about five minutes of um-ing and uh-ing and trying to seem casual. "I thought I was going to have to ask you," she said with a mischievous grin.

Valerie Dove was another story. Terrell liked her not only because she was pretty and smart but also because she made it clear that his status as a basketball star didn't mean anything to her. She was considered a shoo-in to be the class valedictorian and had applied early decision to Harvard. If anyone was awed, it was Terrell—not the other way around.

He didn't want to ask her in front of the dudes, so on the Saturday before Thanksgiving he and Danny and James Nix went to Nettie's for a post-practice lunch. Laurie had told Danny that Valerie would be working. The opening game of the season was six days away; the dance, seven days away.

As soon as they sat down, Danny noticed Valerie delivering a pizza to a table that was halfway to the men's room. "Go ask," he said. "Now."

"Now? I was thinking I'd ask on our way out," Terrell said weakly.

Danny just smirked. So did James, clearly enjoying seeing the guy who was so in control on the basketball court dealing with something he had almost no control over.

Terrell got up and started walking slowly in the direction of the men's room, hoping Valerie would finish refilling the iced tea before he got there.

For once, he got lucky. She turned from the table almost at the moment he arrived. For just a split second, she smiled as if she was happy to see him. Terrell hadn't seen her smile all that often, but when she did, her eyes sparkled. "So, it's the BMOC," she said. That was what she called him—Big

Man on Campus. Often when she took their order she'd say, "What'll it be, BMOC?"

Terrell wasn't going to be intimidated today. He'd seen the smile, even if only for an instant. "Yup, it's me," he said. "You know we start the season on Friday night."

"Oh, really?" she said.

"Why don't you come?" he said.

"Working," she answered. "You guys are supposed to kill Burlington anyway."

Aha! She *was* paying attention to basketball.

Someone was waving from a booth to get Valerie's attention.

"You working Saturday too?" he asked quickly.

"Lunch," she said.

"Well, then, why don't you go to the dance with me Saturday night?"

He said it so fast that it came out more like, whydontyou gotothedancewithmeSaturdaynight?

She stared up at him for a second as if she wasn't sure what he had said. He wasn't 100 percent sure, either.

Then she raised one eyebrow. "You know how to dance?" she said.

"A little," he answered.

She smiled, showing the dimples again. "Guess I'll have to teach you, then. Can't have the BMOC tripping over his big feet and getting hurt."

Terrell wanted to let out a whoop. Instead, he just smiled—dopily, no doubt. The guy in the booth was calling now, getting impatient.

"We'll talk later," she said.

He nodded, but she was gone, heading for the booth. No matter. He'd scored. He could return to the table with his head up.

"Well?" James said as he sat down.

"She said yes," Danny said before he could answer. "Just look at his face."

"She's gonna teach me how to dance," Terrell said, knowing he still had the dopey smile on his face.

"I'd buy a ticket to see that," Danny said.

Valerie's prediction for the Minutemen's season-opening game proved accurate. Terrell had scored 37 points and dunked five times before Coach Wilcox took him out with four minutes left. Danny had 16 points and 16 assists, and James Nix, in his varsity debut, had 18 points and 10 rebounds. The final score was 92–47.

Before heading for the locker room, Terrell scanned the crowd in the stands for his mom. She never yelled or cheered during games, but she was always there. He spotted her halfway up on the home side. As she did after every game, she put her hand on her heart and then pointed to him and smiled. He nodded and waved and headed for the showers.

The lobby was a mob scene after games and Terrell's mom hated crowds, so she wouldn't wait. Mrs. Jamerson also knew Terrell really wanted to go out with his friends after games, so she got a ride home with a neighbor and left the car for Terrell.

Terrell was intensely grateful they'd worked out this routine last season, because the dudes were waiting in the lobby
and they'd brought "friends."

Maurice introduced him to at least a half-dozen people,
including a tall man wearing a fashionable—and no doubt
very expensive—sweater with an Athena logo on it.

The guy looked familiar. "Stan Montana," he said, shaking hands with Terrell. "We met briefly in Jersey over the
summer. I'm director of East Coast marketing for Athena.
Great playing tonight, my man."

Terrell remembered him. He had been the guy who had
tried to get his cell phone number in the hotel lobby to pass
on to "Chuck" Barkley. Terrell was about to say something
about that when he heard Danny coming up behind him.

"Well, if it isn't A-man," he said, looking at Montana—
who was a good eight inches taller than he was. "Where's
Chuck? You didn't bring him? How about Mike? Or Kobe?"

Montana was looking at Danny with so much loathing
that Terrell almost laughed out loud. He loved his point
guard: fearless on the court, completely nuts off it.

"Oh, yeah," Montana said, either remembering Danny
or pretending he had just remembered. "You're the point
guard who has never had an assist passing the ball to anyone
but Terrell."

"Interesting," Danny answered. "Terrell, how many baskets did you have tonight?"

Terrell had looked at a stat sheet so he knew the answer.
"Eleven," he said.

"Two off steals, right?"

"Right."

"So, at most, I could have had nine assists throwing the ball to you, right?"

"Yup."

"And yet I had sixteen assists," Danny said. He turned to Montana. "What's the deal, A-Man, they don't value math skills at Athena?"

For a split second Terrell thought he was going to have to jump in between them.

Instead, Montana turned pointedly away from Danny back to Terrell. "Maurice tells me you have a great pizza joint in this town," he said. "Why don't we head there and let your little D-3 point guard go home and do his math homework."

"He's not a D-3 point guard, Mr. Montana," Terrell said. "And if you watched the game tonight, you know it."

Montana didn't argue—not with Terrell.

Danny and Terrell had agreed that Danny should give him a hard time about going out with the dudes after the game, but this was even better. "I'm going, Terrell," Danny said, looping his gym bag back over his shoulder. "Laurie and Valerie are working tonight."

"I'll probably see you there, then."

Danny paused, looking genuinely pissed off at Terrell and the dudes and Montana. Then he shook his head and stalked off with James Nix.

Maurice, who had been strangely silent through the entire Danny-Montana exchange, finally spoke up. "Stan, don't worry about the white boy—he's always picking fights. Terrell, got a couple more people who want to meet you." He turned to two men who had been talking to Chao and Anthony. "Dennis Murphy, Brad Burford, I want you to meet Terrell Jamerson."

Terrell had grown accustomed to the gushing way basketball people greeted him. Murphy and Burford were no different.

Murphy, who was dressed in an expensive Athena sweat suit, looked to be about forty. He wasn't very tall but had an air of confidence about him. "Always nice to meet the next great player," he said, shaking hands. "I would have loved to have coached you this summer."

"Coach Murphy runs the Total Hoops program in Hartford," Maurice explained. "His summer team is New England Jam. You guys were in a couple tournaments with them but didn't play them."

"Lucky for me," Murphy said with a fake laugh. "Hey, I talked to Coach H today. He's up in East Lansing to play Izzo's guys tomorrow night. He sent regards."

Coach Hathaway and his assistant coaches had sent several texts making sure Terrell knew that Atlanta was playing at Michigan State and that the game was on ESPN Saturday night. Texting was the one way the NCAA allowed coaches to be in regular contact with recruits. Which suited Terrell, because if he didn't want to respond—which was most of the time—he didn't feel he had to.

"Brad's also a coach," Maurice was saying.

"Well, I'm a money manager in real life," Burford said. "But because I'm still kind of addicted to the game, I take a couple of teams to play in Europe every summer. I've got a team for high school juniors and another for guys transitioning from high school to college."

Guys who no doubt would be turning pro and making money pretty soon, Terrell thought. But he just nodded and said, "I'm starving. How about we go eat?"

Everyone seemed to like that idea, especially since Terrell's attention kept getting pulled away by people offering congratulations and kids asking for autographs.

As they headed for the door, Burford, who was just about as tall as Terrell, fell into step with him. "Mind if I ride over with you? Give me a chance to talk to you quietly for a little bit."

Terrell would have preferred to ride alone, but he couldn't be rude. "Sure, no problem," he said. "It's only about five minutes away."

"That's plenty of time," Burford said. "I can talk fast."

Terrell didn't doubt it.

By the time they arrived at Nettie's, Burford had dropped the names of about half the players in the NBA and explained to Terrell why *he* was the one guy Terrell should trust, because being involved with him couldn't possibly get Terrell into trouble with the NCAA.

"I don't represent any school," he said. "I played at Kentucky State twenty-five years ago, but I have nothing to do with them now. My business is helping kids who may need financial guidance. The coaching thing is just for fun. You want my advice on something, I'm there to give it. You don't want my advice, I just shut up."

If only, Terrell thought.

Nettie's was packed, but Maurice had apparently made arrangements to get them the huge booth in the back. Danny was across the room with Nix and some other guys from the team. He was talking to Laurie and gave Terrell a thumbs-up—whatever that meant—as he walked by.

A moment later, Valerie appeared at their table. "Laurie made me switch so she could take Danny's table," she said, clearly addressing Terrell. "What can I get for you-all?"

"We're more than happy to have you take care of us," Dennis Murphy said. He was looking at Valerie in a way that made Terrell very uncomfortable. But if it bothered Valerie, she didn't show it, and she took the drink orders—beer for the out-of-towners, iced tea for everyone else—and disappeared.

That seemed to be the signal for Montana, Murphy, and Burford to start their pitches. Montana wanted Terrell to understand that any Athena gear he wanted, all he had to do was ask. "No rules against it, in case you're worried," he said.

Murphy was so sad that Terrell wouldn't be eligible for AAU ball the following summer. But then he had a brilliant idea. "You can come work for me at camp," he said.

"You won't play forever. You might want to see if you enjoy coaching and get some experience."

Burford thought Terrell might enjoy playing on one of his teams in Europe over the summer—it was a great way to keep up his skills and meet the guys who he'd be seeing soon in the NBA.

When the drinks arrived, they ordered pizzas. Maurice and the dudes kept telling Montana how much *they* admired Athena gear and how happy Terrell would be if his buddies were wearing Athena too. Terrell played along.

Valerie came back to check on them. The pizzas were half eaten and disappearing fast. "Anything else I can get you?" she asked. Terrell was hoping the answer would be no. He was ready to go home. But the dudes wanted more iced tea, and then Montana gestured for Valerie to come closer so he could talk quietly. "Why don't you bring us another round of beers too. And bring me the check—with your cell number on it. I'm going to be back in town again soon."

Terrell knew Valerie must deal with this sort of leering all the time, but he still wanted to leap across the table and throttle Montana.

There was no need. Valerie gave Montana a look that could have frozen the sun. Then she pasted on a smile. "Iced teas, beers, and the check," she said. "But I don't give my number to idiots." She looked at Terrell. "That includes you, BMOC." She turned and walked away.

Terrell jumped up and followed her. "Hey, listen, I'm

sorry about that guy," he said, catching up to her just as she was about to go back into the kitchen. "I don't know him at all. I'm sorry he's such a lowlife."

"If you don't know him, why are you sitting with him? What are you doing with Maurice and that crowd? Why aren't you sitting with Danny and the other guys?"

Terrell sighed. "It's a long story."

"Mmm-hmm, and I'm sure plenty of girls would like to hear it. But I'm not one of them."

"Come on, Valerie, cut me a break," he said. "It *is* a long story and I promise you I'm not the bad guy. Danny will back me up on this. Come to the dance tomorrow and I'll explain."

She looked at him, clearly trying to decide what to do.

He jumped on her hesitation. "I'll pick you up at six thirty," he said.

"I'll meet you there at seven," she answered.

He decided not to push his luck. "That's great. I'll meet you at seven in the lobby."

Valerie headed into the kitchen, and Terrell walked back to the table. "I gotta get going," he said.

"Come on, Terrell, don't overreact," Montana said, standing up. "I was just joking with her. I'll apologize when she comes back."

"You do that," Terrell said stiffly.

"Man, I should have known the hottest girl in town belonged to you," he said, laughing. "I didn't mean to cross you up there. My bad, okay?"

He put out his hand. Terrell would have loved to walk away. But he had set this scene in motion for a reason.

"Yeah . . . okay," he said finally, shaking Montana's hand.

Montana leaned in for a hug. "I'll leave a great tip. That should keep her sweet."

Terrell bolted for the door. Of course Montana thought he could fix things with cash. . . . Money was what everyone wanted, right?

TWENTY-THREE

Valerie Dove proved to be a very good dance teacher. And a very good listener.

She had managed to keep Terrell from making a complete fool of himself on the dance floor for almost two hours, and then she and Laurie suggested that they all duck out to get something to eat. That sounded like a great idea to Danny and Terrell, who were eager to get the dance floor behind them and some food in front of them.

There was no chance they were going to Nettie's. Valerie and Laurie made it clear that being anywhere close to that place when they didn't have to work was out of the question. Carol's was also out of the question because Danny's dad might be there. So they went to a place called Burgers and Fries for, well, burgers and fries. Since it was already nine o'clock when they arrived, the place was relatively empty, which suited everyone fine.

They were a little overdressed, especially the girls, who were both wearing a dress and heels, but that somehow made them all feel festive. Once they were seated and had ordered something to drink, Valerie cut to the chase. "Okay,

BMOC, why don't you explain about that table full of low-lifes you were sitting with last night?"

This is not a girl who lets things slide, Terrell thought.

"You mean the dudes and their traveling circus?" Danny said, helpful as always.

"The dudes?" Laurie put in.

"That's what Danny calls Maurice and his buddies—because they call everybody dude," Terrell said:

"I'm more interested in the traveling circus," Valerie said. "Everyone knows about Maurice and Anthony and those other guys. They're just parasites, sycophants. You like sycophants, BMOC?"

Terrell wasn't positive he knew what a sycophant was. He looked at Danny for help, but it was clear he was just as clueless.

"Yes-men, toadies, people who live off others' talents," Valerie said, slightly exasperated. "You guys *are* seniors, right?"

"But I'm not going to Harvard," Terrell said.

"I'm not, either—not yet anyway," Valerie said.

"Danny, I thought you said you might go to Harvard," Laurie said.

"Not if I have to know what 'sycophant' means to get in," Danny said.

"We're off track," Valerie said. "Tell us about the traveling circus."

So they did. In detail. By the time they were finished, both girls looked shocked, even Valerie. "Okay. I understand how all these guys want a piece of you—I think. What I don't understand is why you don't just tell them to get lost."

Terrell looked at Danny. They had left out one key element of the story: the time when Terrell had gotten high with the dudes and Eddie J.

Danny nodded encouragingly, so Terrell told the rest of the tale, and included the dudes' implied threat to go public.

"Do you really think smoking pot once is going to change the way all those coaches feel about you?" Laurie asked when he had finished.

"No. But they might claim it was more than once. Or they might claim it was more than pot. Who knows? Plus, I want to help Bobby Kelleher with the story he's trying to do. If I'm going to help expose these guys, I need to string them along and see what they offer me."

"But say you manage to discredit these particular guys, aren't there a million others?"

"Yeah," Terrell said. "But maybe they'll finally make some rules that affect the traveling-circus guys. And maybe players will be a little more skeptical when they start to suddenly have all these new best friends. It took me a while to figure it out. If I'd known more, maybe it wouldn't have."

"Skeptical. That's a good word," Valerie said.

"A Harvard word?" Terrell said.

"Maybe Yale," she answered with a smile, and stole his last French fry.

He really liked this girl.

* * *

The first few weeks of the season were pretty close to perfect as far as Terrell was concerned. The team was winning easily, racing to a 9-0 record before they took their pre-Christmas break for finals. He was seeing Valerie on a regular basis when they both had free time—which wasn't often enough for Terrell. Best of all, because the college coaches weren't allowed to travel prior to semester break at their schools, the attention he had been getting had finally quieted down. The text messages still came daily, but he could handle that.

Even the dudes had backed off a little—though Terrell noticed they were now all decked out in Athena gear. Terrell suspected that the Athena guys, notably Stan Montana, were working as middlemen for the U of A and that if he committed to Atlanta, Maurice would make a killing. He had no intention of being delivered to anyone, but Maurice didn't need to know that.

The Minutemen had been invited to play in a prestigious post-Christmas tournament that was being held just outside Washington, D.C. The trip down there would be interesting both for the company—Danny and Terrell were supposed to see Bobby Kelleher while they were in town—and the competition. Norwalk High School would be playing, led by their "old friend" Jay Swanson. Also in the field was Oak Hill Academy, one of the real power programs in the country. Oak Hill's star was a last-second transfer from Mississippi named Michael Jordan. And then there was Starkville Academy, which was led by Alex Mayer.

"Be like old home week," Danny said to Terrell when they looked down the list of teams that would be playing.

"Yeah, I'll bet you can't wait to talk to your pal Swanson about the good old days," Terrell said, grinning.

"He got better as the week went on," Danny said. "I was training him in the art of being a human being."

"I'm sure he appreciated the help."

With so many powerhouse players, it was interesting that none of them had taken advantage of the early signing date in November to commit to a college. This was becoming something of a trend. A lot of players had been burned in recent years by committing in November and then finding out in March that the coach they thought they were going to play for—the coach who had said over and over that his life's dream would be fulfilled if the player committed to play for him—was leaving for more money or more glamour (or both) someplace else.

Once you'd signed, that was it. You had to go—or sit out for a year. The NCAA insisted that a player was "committing to a university" when he signed a letter of intent. It was a nice thought, but there wasn't an elite athlete alive for whom the coach he was planning to play for wasn't the key reason he made his college choice.

The second reason a lot of star players waited to announce their college choices until the spring was publicity. Many made deals with ESPN to announce their decision during one of the high school all-star games that would be televised in the spring. Rumor had it that Michael Jordan had already told ESPN he would make his decision at the "Jordan Brand All-Star Game," as long as he could do it with the man for whom the game was named standing alongside him. That fueled a lot of speculation that, in spite of what he had said during the summer, he was going to attend North Carolina, Jordan's alma mater.

When he read that, Terrell laughed. Just as well he'd pretty much ruled out North Carolina himself. No way did he want to spend more time with Jordan than he had to.

The Minutemen flew to Washington on the day after Christmas. Almost all the big-time holiday tournaments were owned and operated by one of the shoe companies, and the teams had their expenses paid for them, allowing them to fly rather than drive and also to stay in a nice hotel. Not long after they arrived, they were on a bus heading for Georgetown Prep, where they'd be practicing and playing. Georgetown Prep had the look of a small college campus. They pulled in through the gates and saw tennis courts—indoor and outdoor—and both a football stadium and a baseball field nearby. The bus circled to the back of the gym, which was in a building that also housed a swimming pool.

"Not a school for the poor," Danny said to Terrell as they made their way inside.

"All boys," Terrell said. "Not for me."

"Yeah, well, that's just because you're in love."

Danny had him there. If he wasn't in love with Valerie Dove, he was pretty close to it. The only bad thing about being in this tournament was that he would be away for four days when neither of them had school to worry about. Valerie had been accepted to Harvard on December fifteenth, and Terrell could see that a great weight he hadn't really known she'd been carrying had been lifted from her shoulders. She was still full of one-liners and had little patience for fools, but she laughed more easily and smiled more often. And sometimes she looked at him in a way that made Terrell feel at least partly responsible for her newfound happiness.

Oak Hill Academy had just finished practicing when they walked in, and there were TV cameras and reporters all over the place. The practice schedule was set up with a thirty-minute break after each one-hour session, so that the media would have a chance to talk to the coaches and players.

Terrell saw Jordan being led from one TV crew to another. Jordan looked up when he heard the sound of the Lexington players coming and smiled when he spotted Terrell and Danny.

"The boys from Boston are here," he said to no one in particular. But then Terrell noticed familiar faces standing not far from Jordan: Billy Tommasino, the director of the Brickley "School Comes First" camp; his pal Paul Judson, the agent; and Stan Montana—aka A-man. There were a couple of other men standing with them whom Terrell didn't know but was afraid he would before the tournament was over.

"Oh, goody," Danny said. "The gang's all here."

Jordan was waving them over to where he was about to conduct a TV interview. A tall blond woman was waiting, microphone in hand, to get started. She looked less than thrilled with the interruption.

Jordan gave Terrell the full soul shake and hug. Danny had to settle for a handshake. Terrell noticed the TV woman looking at her watch while Jordan rattled on about how fired up he was to play against Terrell again. "I got some *players* with me now," he said. "We've got four D-1 players on our team. You've just got you."

"And Danny," Terrell replied. "He's being recruited by Vanderbilt, GW, Richmond, and Harvard."

Jordan laughed. "Harvard?" He looked at Danny. "You gonna go to Harvard? Who do you play at Harvard? Yale? Princeton?"

"Yup, they play Yale and Princeton," Danny said. "They also played Connecticut, Florida State, and Boston College last year. They beat Florida State and BC. In fact, they've beaten BC five years in a row and, in case you missed it, they beat New Mexico in the tournament."

Jordan looked unimpressed. So did the TV woman.

A short, older man who had been standing a few feet away jumped in. "Terrell, I'm sorry to interrupt," he said. "I'm Charlie Brotman, I'm doing PR for the tournament. I know you have to get ready for practice, and we need to get Michael going with this interview."

The TV woman immediately reacted to hearing the name *Terrell*. It was as if someone had plugged her in and flipped a switch. "Terrell Jamerson?" she said, her bright eyes blinking. "Lorraine Yarney, from Channel Seven here in Washington. I'm *so* looking forward to talking to you after practice."

"Oh, thank you," Terrell said. "This is my point guard, Danny Wilcox."

Ms. Yarney did not appear quite as excited to meet Danny. "Oh yes," she said. "I know your name."

The person least happy with the exchange, clearly, was Michael Jordan. "We going to do this?" he asked. "I've got people waiting on me, you know."

"Absolutely," Lorraine Yarney said. "See you later, Terrell. Let's do this, guys."

She stepped back into position and turned on a bright smile.

"Come on, Terrell," Danny said. "Let's see if we can get to the locker room without a full-on reunion."

Needless to say, that proved to be impossible. They hadn't taken three steps before Billy Tommasino began calling their names. "Terrell, Danny—over here!" He was waving them over as if something very important was about to happen. Terrell wished Coach Wilcox was there, but he was at a pre-tournament coaches' meeting. The other Minutemen had already disappeared into the locker room.

"Let me handle this," Danny said.

"Bad idea," Terrell said. "You're gonna say something to piss them off."

"Which is why it's a *good* idea," Danny said.

He had a point.

They walked over and Billy Tommasino enveloped Terrell in a hug worthy of a long-lost brother. Paul Judson mercifully settled for a handshake, as did Montana.

"Terrell, got a couple more people here you need to meet," Tommasino said. "This is David Forcier—he's a money manager. Genius, I'm telling you, he's a genius. You got five bucks on you? Give it to him. He'll turn it into a hundred by the end of the day."

"He's exaggerating," Forcier said, offering Terrell a handshake. "Anyway, I only work with guys who have a lot more than five dollars in their wallet."

"Then you don't want to work with us," said Danny, who no one had acknowledged yet. "We need to go get ready for practice."

"You coaching the team now, Danny?" Tommasino said.

"No, but my dad's at a coaches' meeting, and Terrell and I are in charge of making sure everyone is ready to go when our practice time starts. We've only got an hour." He gave Tommasino a smile that meant he was seriously considering starting a fight.

Judson, ignoring Danny, turned to an older man dressed in an expensive suit. The man had silvery white hair and the look of someone who had once been an athlete.

"Terrell, I'd like you to meet my boss," he said. "This is Donald M. Johnston the Third—the founder of our company."

"Terrell, it's a pleasure," Donald M. Johnston III said. "Paul tells me you are *exactly* the kind of young man we like to represent. When the day comes that you need representation, I would very much like to talk to you about it personally. I'm semi-retired, so I only work with a handful of special clients. I suspect you are that kind of special."

Terrell was about to say something, but Danny jumped in first. "A semi-retired agent," he said. "So does that mean you steal from people part-time instead of full-time?"

There was a moment of stunned silence, and then Paul Judson said, "Watch your mouth, punk. You don't know who you're talking to."

"It's all right, Paul," Mr. Johnston said. "This, I take it, is the angry young point guard? Every team has one of you, Mr. Wilcox. The player who isn't good enough to merit attention, so he yaps at people in order to call attention to himself."

"Yup, that's me," Danny answered with a smile. "You know what, though? I may not make a living playing basketball someday, but I promise you I *won't* make it calling myself 'The Third' and hanging out in high school gyms, sucking up to teenagers."

Terrell could tell by the look on Mr. Johnston's face that Danny had scored. Judson took a step in Danny's direction. Terrell grabbed Danny's arm and turned to go.

"Right. Like Danny said, we've got to get ready for practice," he said. "Maybe we'll see you all later."

Danny was half resisting as Terrell pushed him away, still shooting looks at the five men behind them.

"You know what you said about pissing them off?" Terrell said.

"Yeah?"

"Mission accomplished."

TWENTY-FOUR

Terrell and Danny managed to escape from the gym after practice without any further incidents. Apparently, Tommasino and company had decided that hanging around and trying to get "Terrell Time," as Danny had taken to calling it, wasn't worth the effort, especially since there was a fairly sizeable media contingent waiting to talk to Terrell, Coach Wilcox, and, surprisingly, Danny.

"Hey, you got some pub," Terrell said when Charlie Brotman finally excused them after Terrell had told the fifteenth different interviewer he still had no idea where he was going to college. "About time. What'd they ask you about?"

"You," Danny said, without cracking a smile. "Every question was about you."

"Ah, man, I'm sorry . . ."

Danny waved him off. "Don't sweat it. I'm used to it."

As instructed, they walked out of the gym and headed in the opposite direction from where their bus was parked. Terrell spotted a hand waving inside a car that was idling about halfway across the lot.

"There he is," Terrell said, nodding in the direction of the car.

The car pulled up, and Danny and Terrell jumped in quickly to get out of the cold.

"So, how'd the media blitz go?" Bobby Kelleher said.

"It was fine," Terrell answered. "Usual stuff."

Kelleher laughed. "This is the world today, eighteen-year-olds being bored by talking to the media."

"You won't be bored by who we saw," Danny said as Kelleher drove through the snow-covered campus.

"Let me guess. Billy Tommasino . . . Paul Judson and his boss, that guy who always calls himself The Third . . . and Stan Montana."

"You missed one," Danny said. "Some money manager. How'd you know?"

"Saw them leaving as I arrived," Kelleher said. "The other guy must have parked someplace else. I'll bet it was David Forcier."

"Bingo," Terrell said. "That's impressive."

Kelleher had pulled into traffic after leaving Georgetown Prep. "Not really. I know the players," he said. "I even know how they work. What would be impressive is if I could prove it."

Terrell smiled. "I might be able to help you there."

They drove a couple of miles down a busy road that Kelleher said was packed no matter what time of day. "The lights are perfectly coordinated; you can never make two in a row."

They finally pulled into the parking lot of a large shopping mall. "Pizza or Chinese?" Kelleher asked as they got out of the car.

"You have good taste in pizza," Danny said.

They walked into a place called Bertucci's, which was virtually empty because it was 3:30 in the afternoon. Once they were seated, Terrell updated Kelleher on what had been going on since the season started, including the time he had been spending with the dudes. He and Danny filled Kelleher in on their encounter at the gym with the money guys.

Kelleher shook his head and, much to Terrell's surprise, pointed a finger at Danny. "How many times do you have to be told that pissing these guys off is *not* the way to get the information we need?" he said. "Do you always have to prove you're the smartest, toughest guy in the room? You've got two new players in this thing, and instead of giving Terrell a chance to find out what they're up to, you drive them away."

"They'll be back," Danny said.

Kelleher rolled his eyes. "You're right, they will be. But next time will you please keep that big mouth of yours shut?"

"I wouldn't hold my breath on that," Terrell said with a laugh.

"Hey!" Danny punched him. "No piling on."

Kelleher sighed. He took a long sip of the coffee he had ordered when they sat down. "Listen to me a second. Believe it or not, your friend Maurice may be the key to this whole thing," Kelleher said. "Someone is paying him to try to steer you someplace—and I don't mean just to college. It could be Judson or some other agent. It could be Montana, although I don't think that's likely because he's been around a lot and doesn't need a runner."

"Or it could be someone we've never seen," Terrell said.

"Right," Kelleher said. "The really smart guys are the ones who stay invisible so they can deny any involvement if things go bad."

"So what do we do from here?" Terrell asked.

"Keep doing what you're doing. Next time one of them talks to you, apologize for Danny. Tell them he's got a temper and that you understand they're just doing their job. Let them give you the 'We just want to help you out' speech again and act as if, at the very least, you're intrigued. They'll buy in. Fortunately, *they* all think they're the smartest guys in the room too."

The pizza arrived.

As he was digging into his first slice, Terrell had a thought. "Have you been trying to talk to any of the other guys? You know, the other highly recruited players? Jordan? Alex Mayer? Jay Swanson?"

Kelleher paused a second to swallow and nodded. "I talked to Jordan and his people some. And I hate to tell you, Danny, but I think Alex Mayer has gone over to the dark side. He talked to me most of the summer, but lately he's been spending a lot of time with that Forcier guy, who mostly steers kids to the SEC or, lately, to Atlanta."

"A lot of guys are being guided there, I think," Terrell said.

"Oh yeah," Kelleher said. "It's Athena's signature school right now. I'm not surprised to hear Forcier is hanging out with Montana. I've seen them together before."

"What about Jay Swanson?" Danny asked.

"Very interesting question," Kelleher said. "I had him pegged this summer as a guy with his hand out. In fact, I'm pretty sure he *did* have his hand out. Everyone thought he was going to sign early with Kentucky. Then there was a lot of talk that Tom Bogley was going with him in a package deal someplace."

"Who's Tom Bogley?"

"High school coach."

"But Swanson didn't sign early," Terrell said.

"No—which was a surprise. Now I'm hearing that Duke and North Carolina and—get this—Penn are involved."

"Penn? Ivy League?"

"He's a Northeast kid. Very good student. Apparently, his dad is from Philly, and he's gone to games at the Palestra all his life."

"Yeah, but Penn's not paying," Danny said. "Neither is Duke or Carolina."

"I know. That's what I can't figure out. I need to talk to him here this week."

"Are you going to come to the games?" Terrell asked.

"I'll be there," Kelleher said. "But I'm going to keep a low profile. No sense making myself any more visible than necessary."

"Boy," Terrell said. "Wouldn't it be fun to just play basketball for three days?"

Danny laughed. "That ship sailed long ago, my friend."

In truth, the three days that followed weren't all that bad, if only because Coach Wilcox kept the team on a pretty tight schedule.

They played their first game at 11:00 a.m., so Coach Wilcox made plans for them to go sightseeing in Washington in the afternoon. Less than an hour after finishing off an easy 87–65 win over Georgetown Prep, Terrell and Danny found themselves on the steps of the Lincoln Memorial. They had not been terribly happy when they learned they would be eating a box lunch on the bus as soon as the game was over instead of going back to the hotel, but they had to admit that standing on the top step of the memorial, with Lincoln sitting in his chair behind them and the Mall and the Washington Monument in front of them, was pretty cool.

"Looks even better in person than on television," Terrell commented.

"Yeah, impressive," Danny said. "But I don't know why we couldn't have come here on Sunday, after the tournament's over."

"Because it's packed around here on Sunday," Coach Wilcox said, coming up behind them. "Come on, we're going on a tour. The tournament people set this up for us.

You both better shut up and listen, because if I ask you what was said later and you don't know, you'll be running all next week." He was smiling when he said it, but there was no doubt that he was completely serious.

Terrell and Danny both groaned but followed their coach to where the tour guide was waiting for them. It turned out to be a lot more interesting than Terrell thought. He had always liked history—it was his one consistent A in school—and the guide told them stories about Lincoln, Jefferson, Washington, and a lot of the Founding Fathers who didn't have monuments in their names.

As they headed back to the bus, Coach Wilcox said, "I hope you guys enjoyed that. Tomorrow, we're going to the Vietnam Memorial."

He wasn't kidding. They didn't have a game until five o'clock, so they were back on the bus the next morning for the trip downtown.

What struck Terrell about the Vietnam Memorial was how quiet it was. At the other monuments, there was a constant cacophony—people laughing, talking, shouting. Along the wall of the Vietnam Memorial, people spoke quietly to one another. There were people standing silently in front of the wall, staring at the names, or Terrell assumed, one name, in particular. Many had tears in their eyes.

Terrell could see that Danny had noticed too. He was standing with his hands in his pockets, taking it all in.

The bus ride back to the hotel was noticeably quieter than normal. When they walked back into the hotel lobby,

Terrell was shaken from his thoughts about the Vietnam War and the wars going on right now by a sight he hadn't expected to see on this trip: the dudes.

Coach Wilcox spotted them too. "Maurice, guys, good of you to make the trip," he said. "We're eating our pre-game meal in ten minutes, and I need Terrell there."

"Not a problem, Coach," Maurice said in a friendly tone, giving him a big smile. "We just want to say hello."

Coach Wilcox nodded. "See you in ten, Terrell." He turned in the direction of the elevators.

Maurice's eyes followed him until he rounded the corner. The fake smile was gone when he turned back to Terrell. "Surprised to see us?" he said.

"Well, yeah. It's a long way to come for a tournament," Terrell said.

"We weren't planning to come, actually," Maurice said. "But we got a phone call saying we should probably make the trip."

"A phone call? Who from?"

"Here's the thing. You need to get your pit-bull point guard to stop being rude to people."

"What?" Terrell said, jaw dangling.

Maurice moved closer to him. "There are important people here who want to help make you rich, Terrell. Don't let the Wilcoxes get in the way of that. They're not the ones with millions at stake here. You are."

Terrell started to ask, *How much have you got at stake, Maurice?* but thought better of it. Instead, he said, "I hear you. I'll talk to Danny. But those guys need to give me some space, especially when we have important games to play. Which we do—starting tonight."

Maurice nodded. "You go ahead. We'll be there to cheer you on."

The other dudes hadn't said a word the whole time. Now they all pushed forward for hugs and handshakes. Terrell escaped a few minutes later and breathed a sigh of relief when the elevator doors closed.

So . . . Danny was rude one day and the dudes got called in to run interference the next. Very interesting. He figured Athena would be picking up the tab for the dudes' stay.

As the elevator pinged and opened on his floor, Terrell had a sudden thought: Had someone paid for the dudes to come to the camp, back in July? To get him away from the Wilcoxes? To set him up with Eddie J.? He had zero proof, but in his gut he knew it was true. And somehow he found it as depressing as anything he'd discovered so far.

Not surprisingly, that night's game was a lot more difficult than the opener had been. The reason was Jay Swanson.

Norwalk High School was a lot like Lexington. It had one true star and a number of solid players who understood that their best chance to win was to get the ball to the star. Terrell had leafed through the tournament's media guide, which included the statistics for every player on all eight teams. Swanson's numbers were actually better than his. He was averaging 29.6 points per game to Terrell's 26.4. Terrell was out-rebounding him, 13.8 to 8.4, but Swanson was a guard. Swanson was also averaging 7.7 assists a game, better than Terrell's 4.5. Both teams were now 10–0 after their first-round wins. Terrell was impressed.

Coach Wilcox decided to start the game with James Nix guarding Swanson. James was a little taller and just about as quick, and he had picked up Coach Wilcox's defense quickly. Even so, both Danny and Terrell were on alert to double-team Swanson anytime he made a move in the direction of the lane. "If we're lucky, his ego will get involved, and he'll force shots instead of finding the open man," he had said. "Either way, he's too good to ask anyone to guard him one-on-one."

The plan made sense, except for two things: Swanson began the game acting as if the lane was radioactive. He kept coming around teammates screening for him near the three-point line, catching, and shooting. By the end of the first quarter he had made four out of five three-point shot attempts and had two other jumpers from inside the three-point line. He hadn't been to the foul line, because Nix hadn't gotten close enough to foul him. Norwalk led, 22–20.

"No need to change anything," Coach Wilcox said. "We're getting good penetration on offense, and Swanson can't keep making those shots all night. Just keep doing what we're doing."

So they did—and Swanson kept making shots. He had

28 points at halftime, and the score was tied, 39–39. By the end of the third quarter, with the crowd oohing and aahing every time he touched the ball, he had 40, and Norwalk had the lead again, 60–59. Terrell hadn't been bad himself with 26, and Danny and Nix had chipped in 12 apiece.

Swanson was still hot in the fourth quarter. When he scored his fiftieth point on a three from the corner with Nix practically tackling him, Norwalk had the lead one more time, 83–81.

Coach Wilcox called time-out with thirty-four seconds left. "I swear to God, I'm tempted to play for one, if only so Swanson doesn't get to shoot again," he said in the huddle. "But we can't do that."

He called a play called Circle, which meant that Terrell would start the play in the low post and pitch the ball back to Danny or James when the ball came in to him. Danny or James would have the option to shoot if they were left alone, but, if not, Terrell would circle back to the outside, get the ball back, and then use a screen to start a drive to the basket. If the defense collapsed on him, he could pass. If not, he would try to tie the game with a layup or by getting fouled.

The play ran as scripted. Terrell passed out of a quick double-team to Danny, but Swanson was all over him. Terrell circled outside, got the ball from Danny, and drove the left side of the lane with what looked like the entire Norwalk team racing to meet him. He saw Nix in the far corner with his hand up and he found him. Without any hesitation,

Nix stepped into a three and drained it with 6.8 seconds left for an 84–83 lead.

Now Norwalk called time-out.

There wasn't a soul in the packed gym who expected anyone to take the last shot other than Swanson.

"He's going to take the inbounds and go end to end," Coach Wilcox said. "I want everyone inside the lane except Terrell. If he passes to someone, fine, we'll take our chances. Terrell, *you've* got him."

"Me?" Terrell said.

"Yeah, you. I don't care how close he gets to the basket, you have *got* to stay in front of him. Just get those long arms up and make him shoot the ball over you. And do *not* foul. He doesn't miss free throws."

They walked back on court with the place buzzing with anticipation. Swanson was standing almost on top of his teammate who was going to inbound the ball. As they waited for the horn to tell the officials to resume play, Swanson looked up and saw Terrell was on him. "Now, *this*," he said, "is an honor."

"For me too," Terrell replied.

Swanson grinned. "How much fun is this?" he asked as the horn ending the time-out sounded.

As soon as the official handed the ball to the inbounder, Swanson darted to his left to take the pass. Terrell scrambled to get back as Swanson sprinted across midcourt. The ball looked like it was connected to his hand on a string as he dribbled.

As Swanson crossed midcourt, Terrell heard Danny's voice above the din. "Screen!" Danny screamed, and Terrell darted to his right just an instant before he would have collided with Norwalk's burly center, Thomas Jones. That move gave Swanson a half step on him, and he wheeled in the direction of the key, Terrell trying to accelerate to catch him.

Danny, in spite of his father's orders, came out to slow him down. That move forced Swanson to dribble to his right, allowing Terrell to get back in front of him.

Basketball instinct and the sounds of the crowd told Terrell the clock was close to zero. Swanson knew it too. As he approached the foul line, with Terrell slightly on his heels, he rose up to shoot. Terrell reacted quickly, jumping toward Swanson but not straight at him, not wanting to foul. The ball cleared Terrell's fingers by no more than an inch and everyone turned to see where it was headed.

Terrell was convinced it was going in. The ball did a 360° spin around the rim, hung there for an instant, and just slid off the left side of the rim. Terrell saw Swanson go down into a crouch, burying his head in his hands—as much in shock as in disappointment.

Terrell's teammates had their arms in the air and were rushing in his direction, but he went over to Swanson, leaned down, and helped him to his feet. He noticed that Danny was right behind him. "Turns out Coach Wilcox was right," Terrell said.

"What do you mean?" Swanson said.

"He said you couldn't keep making those shots all night and he was right—you missed *one*."

Swanson smiled wanly and gave Terrell a hug.

Danny hugged him too. "You're a hell of a player," Danny said.

"You know what?" Swanson said. "So are you."

TWENTY-FIVE

Terrell and Danny were having breakfast in the hotel dining room the next morning when they saw Jay Swanson approaching their table. "Mind if I join you guys?" he asked.

"Have a seat," Terrell said. "How's your arm?"

"My arm?" Swanson said.

"I thought it might be sore from all those shots you made last night."

Swanson laughed as he sat down. "My arm's fine. The rest of me is pretty sore. I'm afraid Alex Mayer may school me tonight."

Mayer's team, Starkville Academy, had lost to Oak Hill in the second semifinal. Terrell, Danny, and their teammates had watched the first half and had left with Oak Hill leading, 41–27. They had been surprised to hear that the final score was 80–76, until they learned that Michael Jordan hadn't played in the fourth quarter because he had rolled an ankle on the last play of the third.

Starkville would play Norwalk in the third-place game at five o'clock before the Minutemen took on Oak Hill for the championship at seven.

"You know I haven't seen Alex for five minutes since we got here," Danny said. "How'd he play last night?"

"Had thirty-seven," Swanson said. "You'll see him in about another minute. I ran into him in the lobby and told him I was coming in here to see you guys. He said he'd stop by."

"How'd you know we were here?" Terrell was starting to feel as if everyone knew his every move.

"I ran into your coach buying a paper. He said you'd just come in."

Almost on cue, Alex Mayer, dressed in what looked like the latest model Athena tracksuit, walked into the dining room. There were handshakes all around, and he sat down after asking a waiter to bring him some coffee.

"Nice playing last night," Terrell said.

Mayer laughed. "If Michael had faked his injury a little bit earlier, we might have won and gotten to play you guys. Instead, I have to spend the night chasing the mad bomber here." He nodded at Swanson.

"*Faked* his injury?" Terrell said. "What are you talking about?"

Mayer shrugged. "He doesn't want to play against you, Terrell. His stock went down a little when you outplayed him in New Jersey, and he doesn't want to take any risks. You kick his butt again, he might not have quite as many suitors."

"I'm guessing you aren't talking just about colleges," Swanson said.

Mayer laughed. "Hardly. Heck, he's claiming he's going to North Carolina and they don't pay anybody. It's the same guys chasing you, Terrell—the so-called money managers, the agents, the equipment guys. He's even got some production company that wants to do a reality series with him during his freshman year."

"Speaking of getting paid, that's a nice outfit," Danny said.

Terrell was surprised it had taken Danny this long to bring it up.

Mayer took a long sip of his coffee. "Yup, it is," he said. "No sense letting the parade pass you by, I figure."

"That's not what you were saying last summer," Danny said. His eyes were narrowed in a way familiar to Terrell. He was angry.

"That was last summer," Mayer said. "Things change. Man, everyone around me is cashing in—including whichever coach I'm going to play for in college, who's going to be making seven figures while I help him win games. So why shouldn't I cash in too?"

"Maybe because it's against the rules?" Swanson said, surprising Terrell. "There are a lot of things in life that aren't fair. Is it fair that we get our butts kissed all the time because we can play basketball, but the really talented kids in the band get nothing—in fact, are considered geeks?"

"What are you talking about with the band?" Mayer said. "People pay to see *us* play. The band's the sideshow."

"I know, it's different. You're right. But it's not really fair."

Terrell and Danny looked at each other. It was almost as if Mayer and Swanson had somehow swapped personalities since the summer.

"Jay, what happened to you?" Danny asked. "At camp, I honestly thought you were on the take."

Swanson nodded. "I was. But I realized after a while that those guys thought they owned me. And a while after that, I realized they kind of *did*. Which sucked. So I backed out. The money will be there down the road if I make the NBA."

"What if you get hurt?" Mayer asked. "What if you become Omar Whytlaw?"

"Then all the money in the world won't really matter, will it?" Swanson said. "Look, Alex, I'm not busting on you at all. I totally understand where you're coming from. I just got sick of that scene."

Not surprisingly, the championship game was a bust. With Michael Jordan sitting on the bench, Oak Hill was no match for Lexington. It still had a number of good players, but no one who could guard Terrell. And when they tried to double- or even triple-team him, Terrell was alert enough to find his shooters—notably, Danny and James Nix. The final score was 79–62. Terrell was named tournament MVP, and Danny and James were picked to the all-tournament team, along with Jay Swanson and Alex Mayer, who had both had big games in Norwalk's victory in the consolation game.

After the game, Terrell did all the media interviews,

including a fairly lengthy one with someone from ESPN. Coach Wilcox had told them that ESPN was planning to televise Lexington's season-ending game against Waltham in late February as part of a "high school showcase night."

The college coaches weren't allowed to talk to them because it was an evaluation period—no contact allowed—so they had to settle for positioning themselves so that their top recruits could see that they were there, watching every play.

The bad news was that all the hangers-on weren't restricted from talking to them. Terrell noticed Jordan chatting with Billy Tommasino and a couple of other guys in suits. No surprise there. Mindful of Kelleher's warning to not scare people off, Terrell spent a few minutes making nice, accepting congratulations, and listening to the "If there's anything you need . . ." refrain for about the millionth time. When he saw Danny standing under one of the baskets talking to Tom Konchalski, he used that as an excuse to break away.

"Mr. Konchalski, I didn't know you were here," he said as he walked up to the group that consisted of Danny, his father, and the only honest man in the gym.

"Terrell, you played wonderfully," Konchalski said. "The improvement in your passing since July is noticeable."

"Thanks," he said. "I've been working on that since you mentioned it. Of course, it's a different game if Jordan plays."

Konchalski shrugged. "Sure it is. But from what I'm hearing, he wanted no part of you. If I'm a college coach, that would tell me something about him."

"You think anyone recruiting him will back off if they think he ducked Terrell?" Coach Wilcox asked, clearly surprised.

"No, I don't," Konchalski said. "You can't overlook a talent like that. But it'll be on the mind of whoever ends up coaching him next year."

"Who do you think that will be?" Danny asked.

"I think he wants to go to Kentucky," Konchalski said. "I think he believes John Calipari is the best coach you can play for if you're going to be one-and-done because he's had so much experience with it. But I think the people around him are pushing him to Atlanta."

"What about North Carolina?" Terrell said.

Konchalski shook his head. "Don't see it. Roy's loaded anyway. He doesn't need that kind of headache."

Across the court Terrell could see Jordan surrounded by a coterie of suits—one of them being Paul Judson, another being David Forcier, the financial planner they had met the other day. He could also see the dudes, standing near the door—waiting expectantly, no doubt, to talk to him.

"I'm exhausted," he said. "Danny, you gonna walk with me to the bus?"

Danny raised an eyebrow but then nodded. "I'll make sure everyone's on the bus and call you. Okay, Dad?" he said.

"Good idea," Coach Wilcox said. He looked at Konchalski. "Early flight in the morning."

Konchalski nodded. "Never fun." He shook hands with Danny and Terrell just as Tom Bogley, the Norwalk coach, came over to say hello. Clearly, everyone in high school basketball knew Tom Konchalski.

Terrell and Danny started across the gym.

"What was that about?" Danny asked. "You need an escort or something?"

In reply, Terrell nodded in the direction of the dudes. "If you're in a mood to piss somebody off," he said, "now would be a good time. I just don't want to deal with these guys tonight."

Danny grinned. "Happy to oblige," he said.

Maurice led the parade to congratulate Terrell, followed closely by Chao, in the ever-present "Yao Rules" T-shirt. Terrell wondered if anyone had told him that Yao Ming had retired. "Dude, you're killing it," Maurice said as he gave Terrell the obligatory hug.

"It's too bad Jordan no-showed on you," said Felipe, the new dude, whom Terrell found to be less of a pain than the others.

"He was hurt, I guess," Terrell said, shrugging.

"He was scared, man," Chao insisted. "Dude's a wimp."

"But he's gonna be a rich wimp," Maurice said. "Terrell, there's a really good burger joint right down the road from here. . . ."

This was Danny's cue to jump in. "He can't," he said. "Bus is leaving in about five minutes, and we have an early flight in the morning."

"Daddy make you the assistant coach, angry boy?" Maurice said, flaring at the sound of Danny's voice.

"What if he did?" Danny said in a tone laced with sarcasm. "Either way, what the team is doing is none of your damn business."

"Terrell *is* my business," Maurice said.

"Yeah, that's how you see him, isn't it?" Danny shot back. "As a business opportunity . . ."

Without warning, Maurice launched himself at Danny. It was the culmination of months of bad blood.

Maurice had the advantage of forward momentum, surprise, and sheer, pent-up anger. He took Danny down while everyone stood frozen, too stunned to move. Danny recovered quickly and was able to use his size—he had about five inches on Maurice and at least twenty pounds—and strength to push Maurice off him, regain his balance, and put him in a headlock.

As soon as the dudes saw that Maurice was in trouble, all four of them rushed Danny. Seeing that, Terrell stepped in. He grabbed Chao from behind and tossed him out of the fray.

Now tournament people were coming over to try to help break up the fight, too.

Anthony finally managed to pull Danny off Maurice. He shoved him away and then started after him. Terrell tried to slow Anthony down, but it was like stepping in front of a charging bull. One of Anthony's elbows caught him right across the chest and sent him flying backward. The next thing he heard was a thud—which was the sound of his head hitting the floor.

He squinted up at the lights of the gym. Then darkness filled his vision until there was only a tiny pinpoint of light. And then everything went black.

Terrell blinked and saw Danny and Coach Wilcox kneeling next to him. Somehow he knew he'd been out, but he had no idea for how long. He could tell there were a number of other people around, but his vision was still a little bit blurred. He started to say something but instantly felt sick so he closed his mouth.

"Easy, Terrell," Coach Wilcox said. "Paramedics are coming right now."

That word panicked Terrell. "Paramedics?" he repeated. "How long—?" His voice was a croak, but at least he got the words out.

"Not long," Coach Wilcox said. "Maybe a minute. Paramedics were right outside. Here they come now. The hospital is nearby."

"Hospital?" Terrell said. "Why?"

"Stay calm, Terrell," Coach Wilcox said. "They just need to check on you because you were unconscious."

He could hear sounds behind him, and a moment later someone in a uniform was kneeling next to him and talking to Coach Wilcox.

"How long was he out?" he said.

"Probably about a minute," Coach Wilcox said.

The uniformed man turned to Terrell. "I want you to lie

very still, young man—okay? I just need you to answer a few questions for me so I can decide what we're going to do next. You with me?"

Terrell nodded. Things were still a bit blurry, but he felt as if he had a strong sense of what was going on. He knew he'd hit his head—if only because it hurt—and he knew this guy was a paramedic who wanted to figure out how seriously he'd been hurt.

"Okay," the paramedic said. "What's your name?"

"Terrell Jamerson."

"Good. Where are we right now?"

Terrell needed a second to think about that one. "We're in a gym. We just played a game."

"Good. Very good. Do you know what gym we're in? Exactly where we are?"

Uh-oh. That one was blank. "We're at a tournament," he tried, hoping that might fool the guy.

"Good, Terrell. Where? What's the name of the school where the tournament was played?"

Terrell didn't know. He felt his heart pounding. He just shook his head in response. That was a bad idea because pain rocketed through him.

"Okay, Terrell, don't worry. You're doing fine," the paramedic said. "Tell me what day today is."

He had that one. "Saturday," he answered.

"And who did you guys play? Did you win?"

"We won."

"Who'd you beat?"

He had no idea.

The paramedic quickly realized it and patted him gently on the chest. "Okay, Terrell, listen to me. I think you're going to be fine. You've probably suffered a fairly mild concussion. You remember a lot of things but not everything. My guess is by morning it'll all come back. But for now, just to be absolutely safe, we're going to put you on a stretcher and take you to a hospital not far from here for some tests. Nothing strenuous."

"Hospital?" Terrell said. His mind was clear enough to know that wasn't a good thing.

The paramedic was nodding and smiling. "Just to be safe, okay? My partner here is going to help me get you on the stretcher. I don't want you to try to stand up because you might get woozy. We're just going to make this as easy and comfortable as we can."

Terrell nodded, but he knew he had tears in his eyes. How could this have happened? One minute he and Danny were walking to the bus, dealing with the usual annoyance of the dudes, and now they were putting him on a stretcher?

As he was lifted onto the stretcher, he could see that a lot of people were standing around watching. All his teammates were there, and so were the players from the other team. Wait! Oak Hill, that was who they had played.

"Hey," he said as soon as he was on the stretcher. "I've got it. We played Oak Hill."

"Good, Terrell—that's a good sign. The more things come back to you, the better we feel."

"But I still have to go to the hospital?"

"Yes."

Danny and Coach Wilcox were both standing next to the stretcher. "We're going to meet you there," Coach Wilcox said. "I'm going to call your mom so she doesn't hear something second-hand and think this is worse than it is."

"Can I go home tomorrow?"

Coach Wilcox looked at the paramedic. Terrell couldn't see whatever response he got. "Let's hope so, Terrell," he said. "Let's just make sure you're okay and then we'll figure out what to do next."

Terrell closed his eyes as they wheeled him in the direction of the door. He could hear people applauding, the way they did when injured players were taken off the field in the NFL. This wasn't football, though—it wasn't even basketball. It was just a stupid fight. He felt the cold when they pushed the stretcher outside. When he opened his eyes, he could see the blinking lights of the ambulance.

He closed his eyes again. *Maybe,* he thought, *if I keep my eyes closed long enough, I'll wake up and this will all have been a bad dream.*

TWENTY-SIX

"Danny, wake up."

Danny snapped from the dream he'd been having about punching out all the dudes one by one and saw his father standing over him. The discomfort in his back reminded him that he had fallen asleep in a chair in the hospital waiting room.

"What time is it?" he asked.

"It's late," his dad said.

Coach Wilcox had put his team on the bus back to the hotel after Terrell had been taken to the hospital and had left Joe Kress, the volunteer assistant coach, in charge of getting everyone up and to the airport in the morning. Danny had insisted on going with his dad to the hospital, figuring they would run some tests on Terrell and then they'd all go back to the hotel and eat.

It hadn't turned out that way. After what seemed like an eternity, a doctor had come out to talk to them. Terrell had authorized him to speak to them as if they were family, so he explained what was going on. "He's got a concussion, and it's really impossible to tell how serious it is right now," he said. "He took a pretty hard blow—that's the bad news. The good news is I'd say his memory is close to intact. He's in there right now spewing facts to prove he's okay so we'll let him get out of here."

Danny smiled at the thought.

"So *can* he go?" Andy Wilcox asked.

The doctor shook his head. "No. I want to keep him here overnight, as a precaution. I don't want him moving around at all for the next few hours, and a good night's sleep will help him. He has no appetite right now, which is pretty common, but it's also a sign that he needs to get things unscrambled before he leaves."

"So do you think it's okay to book a flight for tomorrow?" Coach Wilcox asked.

"No, no," the doctor said. "Last thing you want to do right after a concussion is fly. I understand you guys are from Boston, right? You could take the train, but I'd recommend renting a car. That way if he starts to feel sick, you can pull over whenever you need to. But flying is out of the question for at least the next few weeks."

Whoa, Danny thought. *This is serious.* He felt responsible. Maurice and the dudes had disappeared quickly when Terrell hit his head, although he'd gotten a text from James Nix saying that Maurice had called him at the hotel to find out how Terrell was doing.

"What about basketball?" Danny asked the doctor. "When can he play?"

The doctor shook his head. "Impossible to say. I would recommend you find him a specialist when you get home, someone who deals with this sort of thing regularly. There are tests that can be done to determine when and if he can play."

"*If?*" Danny said.

"Danny . . . ," his dad said.

"Yeah, Dad, but '*if*'?"

He could tell by the look in his father's eyes that he was thinking exactly the same thing.

"With a concussion, it's always if," the doctor said. "It doesn't look that serious to me, but it's been less than twenty-four hours. He could be fine in a few days, or he could have lingering post-concussion symptoms."

"Like Sidney Crosby," his dad said.

The doctor's brow furrowed. "Who?" he said.

"Hockey player. Had what looked like a minor concussion and then didn't play for almost a year."

The doctor nodded. "That can happen. Everybody's different."

"Can we see him?" Danny asked.

"Follow me."

They walked down a long hallway and found Terrell sitting up in bed, sipping from a container of apple juice. He gave them a big smile when they walked in. "The doctor says I can get out of here soon," he said. "I feel fine. He says the concussion was a mild one, so I should be okay."

"How's your appetite?" Coach Wilcox asked.

Terrell's smile disappeared. "Not great right now," he said. "But the doc thinks that will change soon."

"Did he tell you about flying?" Danny asked.

"You mean, *not* flying? Yeah. I texted my mom, and she said she can drive down and get me."

"Don't be silly, Terrell," Coach Wilcox said. "I'll rent a car and drive you back."

"Yeah, it'll be fun," Danny said. "Like our driving trips last summer."

"Not exactly," his dad said. "You're flying back with the team."

"But, Dad . . ."

"No buts. What Terrell needs most is rest. And I know you've got schoolwork that needs doing."

Terrell agreed but for a different reason. "Could you check up on my mom? I told her it was just a bump on the head, but I'm sure she doesn't believe me. She said the online *Globe* had it on the front page of sports."

"I imagine they did," Coach Wilcox said. "I'm not going to even get into it while we're here, but you two have *got* to stop getting into trouble all the time."

"Dad, I didn't start it," Danny said. "Maurice came after me—remember?"

"And why did he come after you? Because you were complimenting him on his wardrobe or because you were baiting him?"

"I wasn't baiting him."

"Yes, you were," Terrell said. "But, Coach, it was my

fault. I wanted him to. I didn't want to talk to them and asked Danny to be the reason."

Coach Wilcox put up a hand. "Like I said, we won't discuss it here."

The doctor came back into the room. "Gentlemen, Terrell needs to get some sleep," he said. "The more he rests, the sooner he can get out of here."

They both said goodbye to Terrell and headed for the door.

"What do we do now?" Danny asked as they walked down the hall.

"We're going back to the hotel so you can pack and get a couple hours of sleep. I need to cancel my flight and Terrell's flight and rent a car."

"How long do you think the drive is?" Danny asked.

"Probably about eight hours. Give or take."

"Dad . . ." Danny paused, but he couldn't help asking, "Do you think he'll be okay?"

"We'll see," his dad said, and put an arm around him. "It's a concussion. There's really no way to know."

That wasn't the message Danny delivered when he got back home.

A bus met the team at Logan Airport and took them back to Lexington High. Danny's father's jeep was in the parking lot where they'd left it, and Danny drove straight to see Mrs. Jamerson, as requested. He did his best to reassure her, but he didn't think she was buying it. Probably the black eye he'd sprouted overnight didn't help . . .

He went home for a nap and a shower before trying it again with Laurie and Valerie. They were at Nettie's, working, but when Danny walked in around four, their shift was just ending. The three of them went and sat down in a back booth.

Apparently, Valerie had talked to Terrell on the phone earlier in the day.

"He told me he's coming home tomorrow," she said after they were all sitting down. "He says everything is fine. Now I want you to tell me the truth."

"That is the truth. He seems fine. They're just being really cautious."

Valerie looked at Laurie, then at Danny. "I've spent a lot of time today studying concussions on the Internet," she said. "You know what I now know for sure?"

"What?"

"That no one knows what happens next after one of these. He doesn't know if he's fine, and neither does the doctor. He can't fly for a month at least. What does that tell you?"

"That you have to be very careful with concussions," Danny said.

"Exactly," Valerie said. "Which means he's going to need to see a doctor when he gets back here—a doctor who might tell him not to play for a while. And if he isn't playing, what happens to all his new best friends?"

Laurie laughed.

"What's so funny?" Valerie asked.

"You," she said. "First of all, two months ago you didn't know the difference between a basketball and a hockey puck. Second, nothing in the world would make you happier than if the hangers-on went away forever."

Valerie managed a sad smile. "The hangers-on, yes. The coaches, no. He needs to go to college."

"The coaches aren't going to go away because of a concussion," Danny said. "Even if it took a *year*, he could just red-shirt as a freshman. Plus, his grades are good, and his SATs were very good. He'll go to college, no matter what."

"What do you mean, red-shirt?" Valerie asked.

"Oh, I forgot, there are a few things you still don't know," Danny said with a smile. "It means you don't play for a year but don't lose any eligibility. Some guys do it because they're hurt; others just do it so they can grow or work on their games or their academics."

"You mean there are coaches who care about academics?" Valerie said.

"They *all* care about academics," Danny said. "They need their players to be eligible."

That actually got a laugh out of Valerie. For a second, she seemed to relax, leaning back in the booth.

Then Danny spotted Felipe, the newest dude, walking in their direction. He groaned, causing the girls to sit up. Danny stood up, not wanting another fight but ready for it if it came.

"Sit down, man," Felipe said, perhaps seeing the look on Danny's face. "I'm not here to start anything. I just need to talk to you."

"What about?" Danny said. "How'd you know I'd be here?"

"I didn't," Felipe said. "I came to ask the girls where you were and how Terrell is doing."

"He's fine," Danny said. "Not that you care."

"Listen to me, man," Felipe said. "I'm trying to help you. Maurice is really, really upset. . . ."

"Well, he should be," Valerie said. "He started the fight."

"No, you're not hearing me," Felipe said, looking at her and then at Danny. "He really wants to hurt you, Danny. All those guys—the Athena dude, the money manager, the agents, I think some of the coaches too—they've been feeding him money on a regular basis to keep an eye on Terrell, tell them who he's spending time with—you know. And there's a big payoff if he delivers him to any of them.

"Last night, after Terrell went down, all those guys were texting him saying there's no more money until Terrell plays again and they know he's okay. We drove all night to get back here, and the whole way back Maurice kept saying that if Terrell was hurt bad, he would get you, hurt *you* bad."

A little chill went through Danny. He wasn't afraid of Maurice in a fair fight. But he didn't trust Maurice to fight fair. Even so. "Tell him to come and try," he said, not wanting to show any fear.

Felipe gave him a hard look. "Come on, man, don't try

to be so tough. Maurice can be scary. I know that now. You have to watch yourself. That's what I came to tell you."

"If he's scary, why are you hanging out with him?" Laurie asked.

"I'm not," Felipe said. "Not anymore. I'm new in town, I met these guys, they seemed okay. I think the others probably are—they're just kind of stupid, really. Not Maurice. He's not stupid and he's not okay. I'm done with them."

"Aren't you afraid Maurice might come after you, too, if you stop hanging with them?" Danny asked.

"Yeah, a little," Felipe said. "But me not hanging with him won't cost him any money. Terrell getting hurt *will* cost him money. And he blames you for it."

Valerie stood up. "Sit down, Felipe," she said. "I'm going to get us all something to drink."

An hour later nothing had been decided except for one thing: Danny was not to wander around anyplace by himself—at least not until Terrell was back on a basketball court. His father would be told what was going on, but Terrell would not.

"If Terrell thought Maurice was looking for me, I'm afraid he'd go and look for *him*," Danny said. "We don't need that."

He was surprised at how calm he felt about the whole thing. It wasn't that he didn't believe Felipe—in fact, he *did* believe him. It was just that it seemed kind of stupid compared with what was going on with Terrell.

He and Felipe stuck around long enough to eat some dinner. When Felipe asked Laurie for a check, she just gave him a "You must be kidding" look.

"Now I see why you like this place so much," Felipe said.

"The pizza's good," Danny said. "But that's not what I like about it the most."

Felipe laughed. "Understood. Come on, I'll walk you to your car."

"What are you, my bodyguard?"

"Yeah," Felipe said. "I guess I sort of am."

As it turned out, they were parked right next to each other behind the restaurant.

"I'm sure you think I'm overreacting about this," Felipe said as he unlocked his car door. "But you weren't there last night. Maurice is pissed. And he's crazy."

Danny nodded. He wasn't looking forward to going home to a dark empty house.

PART III

TWENTY-SEVEN

"Not yet, Terrell. Maybe next week."

Terrell groaned in disbelief. "Doc, it's been a *month*. I feel fine."

Dr. Mazzocca shook his head. "You said you felt fine the first day you came in here, and when you stood up after I examined you, I had to catch you before you fell down."

Terrell stood up fast now. "Look, I just stood up and I'm fine." In truth, he had felt the room spin just a little bit when he got up.

"No, you don't. I saw your eyes roll there for a second. I'm a doctor, remember?"

Terrell sighed. Since his first visit to Dr. Mazzocca after returning from Washington, two things had been abundantly clear: The doctor knew what he was doing, and he wasn't going to let Terrell play basketball until he was 100 percent sure that Terrell was 100 percent healthy.

For a month now, Terrell had not been allowed to do anything more than shoot free throws. He wasn't even allowed to dribble or pull up to shoot. Well, truth be told, he had tried it once when no one except Danny was around, and he had gotten light-headed.

"Am I gonna play again this season? Tell me the truth."

"Sit down, Terrell," Dr. Mazzocca said. "Yes, I think you'll play. In fact, I think you might be okay in the next week or so. You've been better every time I've seen you, and that's important. Sometimes people don't get better for a long time. You stood up too fast there. But let's try this: Play some easy one-on-one with your pal Danny after practice tomorrow and see how that feels. But *don't* keep playing if you feel dizzy at all. How's that for a deal?"

Terrell nodded. "You really think I'm ready for that?"

"I do. But you have to go slow. No dunks, nothing really physical. And remember: You aren't in playing shape right now, so don't play too long, even if you feel good."

"And if I feel okay?"

"Like I said, come back next week. I'll run you through the tests again and see how you do."

"The sectionals start in three weeks."

"I know, Terrell. Last week you told me they started in four weeks. Now, do me a favor, stand up slowly, walk out of here, and try to remember your basketball career is about more than the sectionals."

Terrell nodded. "You're right. The states are more important. But we have to win the sectionals first."

Dr. Mazzocca smiled at that one. "Patience, Terrell," he said. "Patience. That's the most important word in your life right now."

"Sectionals, Doc," Terrell said. "Sectionals. That's the most important word in *your* life right now."

Terrell would never say it to anyone, not even Danny, but he had sort of enjoyed his forced respite from basketball.

Well, once his mom had stopped fussing over him quite so much.

Coach Wilcox had told him not to come to practice, in part because he knew how much it would frustrate him to sit and watch but also because he thought his time was better spent doing other things.

School suddenly became easy. His friends were all at practice, so he would go home after classes were finished and get his homework done right away. He had to take breaks because if he read or sat at the computer for too long, he would start to feel a little bit dizzy. But with all the extra time, that was no problem.

He had also been able to spend more time with Valerie. She didn't work on Mondays or Tuesdays and had at least half a day free on weekends. On game nights, Terrell would go to watch Lexington play, and then he and Danny, and most of the other guys on the team, would head for Nettie's.

The tough part of game nights was that, not surprisingly, Lexington struggled without him. In their first game without Terrell, Concord kept things close. Danny had to force a shot at the buzzer and it rimmed out, leaving the Minutemen 55–54 losers.

Three nights later at Waltham, Danny and James both got into foul trouble. Terrell was convinced the officials were trying to give Waltham—the team with the best chance to challenge Lexington if Terrell was healthy—every break possible. With Danny, James, *and* Terrell all watching for most of the evening, Waltham blew the game open and won, 71–57.

Danny and Terrell had a long talk that night while sitting in a back booth at Nettie's. Both of them were amused by the fact that there was almost no one around. There had been virtually no sign of the dudes since the fight in Washington. The only coaches showing up were from the schools recruiting Danny. Terrell was still getting a steady stream of texts, though.

Hey, T, can't wait to see you back playing—Coach H

Terrell, know your teammates want to see you back soon—Wojo

(Coach K, he had learned, didn't know how to text.)

T-man: Hear you may be back soon. Don't lose faith in yourself—Coach Williams

Kelleher had come to see him to give him a pep talk as much as anything else. He said he was "close" to being ready to write his story. But Terrell wasn't in a position to help him anymore—the agents were nowhere to be found. Ditto for the apparel reps and the money managers.

"You know, I can honestly say I haven't missed any of them. If there was a way to somehow play and not have any of these people around, life would be perfect," Terrell said.

Danny laughed. "Well, you could just play badly," he said. "That would keep them away."

Terrell shook his head, suddenly serious. "This is killing me. I sit and watch the games and I want to sneak into my uniform and get out there because I figure that even if I'm fifty percent, I could help."

"You *could* help. But that's not the point, and you know it. We'll hang in there until you get back."

"We have to win the league to make the sectionals. Another loss and we're in trouble."

"We'll get Waltham and Concord at home at the end of the season and even things up. You'll be back by then. I promise."

"Don't make promises that aren't in your control."

Valerie's shift had ended a little early, and she slid into the booth next to Terrell. "You tell him?" she said.

"Tell me what?" Danny said, looking at her quizzically.

"Nothing," Terrell said. He had had an idea, but he'd decided to talk to Coach Wilcox before mentioning it to Danny.

"You tell me right now, Terrell, or I swear—"

"Okay, okay." Terrell held a hand up. He knew Danny wouldn't be put off. "I was just noticing some things during the game. And I had some ideas for how you should change the offense."

"Like how?" Danny asked.

"Coach is still running the same plays as if I'm out there. Tommy Bonk is a good guy, but let's face it . . ."

"He's not you or even close to you."

"Right. *You're* the best player we've got right now."

"There's James—"

Terrell shook his head. "No. James is good, but *you* are our best player. Your dad has to set more high screens to get you shots, and he's got to bring Tommy away from the basket more to open up space for you. Everything needs to run through you, from the start of the offense to whenever you decide whether to pull up or get in the lane and create from there."

"He doesn't want to do that."

"I know, and I know why—because he doesn't want it to look like he's trying to make his son the star. I get it. But he has to think like a coach and not a dad. He's always done that when you screw up. He's got to do it now because it's the best thing for the team." Terrell could see Danny turning things over in his mind. He could tell by the look on Danny's face that he'd struck a chord.

But Danny just said, "I don't know."

"Well, I do," said Terrell, suddenly becoming even more sure. "Look, I'm going to talk to him. So be ready to work on some new plays, because you've only got two days to practice before we play Sudbury on Tuesday."

Danny smiled. "You're pretty pushy for someone who hasn't scored a point since New Year's."

Terrell smiled back. "And who do you think I learned that from?"

* * *

Three nights later, Danny scored 31 points and had 10 assists, and Lexington, with its new Danny-in-charge offense, buried Sudbury, 81–60.

Terrell went down to the locker room after the game. He had been staying away, wanting to give the guys space, but Danny had texted him before the game and told him the guys missed him. Coach Wilcox was standing at the door with his assistant coach Joe Kress giving the players a minute to celebrate, as he always did after wins. When he saw Terrell, he broke away and came over and wrapped him in a hug. "Coach Jamerson," he said. "Come on inside for a second. We've got something for you."

Coach Wilcox picked up a ball and gathered everyone around. "Fellas, that was a great win. Every one of you played about as well as I could possibly ask you to play. Especially you, Danny."

Terrell didn't think he'd ever seen Danny blush quite so deeply.

"Now," Coach Wilcox continued, "you all know we changed our offense for this game, and you executed brilliantly. But we never would have gone this route without Terrell's bold new vision, and, frankly, relentless badgering."

Now it was Terrell's turn to blush.

"So, Terrell"—Coach Wilcox paused and flipped him the ball he had been holding—"this is for you from all of us. No one ever deserved a game ball more."

Terrell was so surprised, he almost dropped the ball.

Everyone was clapping, and he didn't know what to say. Then he did: "I couldn't have done it without my players."

Everyone cracked up.

After that night, the Minutemen went on a tear. Some of the games were down-to-the-buzzer nail-biters. Others they won easily. But one way or another, they were keeping their season alive—waiting, praying for Terrell to come back. . . .

Terrell's one-on-one workouts with Danny had gone well, though they'd hardly proved he was ready to play.

Which is why he was surprised when Dr. Mazzocca smiled after his weekly exam and said, "Almost."

"What's that mean?"

"Stand up quickly."

Terrell did as he was told. He felt nothing.

"Sit down and then stand up again."

He sat down, then stood up. Nothing. "I feel fine," he said.

"That's what I thought," Dr. Mazzocca said. "If you walked in here right now and I ran all the tests and I didn't know you'd had a concussion, I would never suspect you'd had one."

"So I can start practicing?" Terrell said, realizing his heart had skipped a beat.

Dr. Mazzocca shook his head. "No, not yet. But you can start running and you can play real one-on-one with Danny. If you don't have any setbacks in the next week, I think you'll be ready for a real practice."

Terrell nodded. If he was cleared in a week, he would have two days to practice before the game with Billerica—a game the Minutemen should win easily. That would mean he'd be really ready to go for the two season-ending games against Concord and Waltham that were must-wins to get into the sectionals.

"Which means that, yes, you should be able to play the last three games of the regular season," Dr. Mazzocca added, reading his mind.

"Why am I better today?" Terrell asked.

Dr. Mazzocca shrugged. "Your body has healed. Some people never completely heal from a concussion like the one you had. Others can recover in a week. You've done the right things, we've been cautious, and it looks like it's working out. The reason I want to wait, besides being careful, is I want you to go back out there feeling completely confident that you're healed. In a week, after you play some more one-on-one and feel the way you feel now, you'll be more comfortable going out to play. I don't want you timid when you start playing again. I want you to be Terrell."

"Doc, I never knew you were a fan."

"I'm a fan of keeping good kids healthy," Dr. Mazzocca said. "And I *did* graduate from Lexington once upon a time."

The following Friday was the best night Terrell could remember having since he had first started being noticed nationally. It was Valentine's Day, and Valerie and Laurie both had the night off and were in the stands when Billerica came to town.

Even though the team had been instructed not to say anything, the whole town seemed to know that Terrell was coming back. The gym was already packed when the team came out to warm up thirty minutes before tipoff, and the entire crowd was on its feet screaming as soon as they saw Terrell in uniform. He spotted at least a dozen signs that said "Welcome back, Terrell" or something like it as he went through the layup line.

"Maybe my dad should start Bonk and really mess with them," Danny said as they jogged through early warm-ups.

"Shut up, Danny," Terrell said.

"Yeah, you're right," Danny said. "Some of the older folks might have heart failure if you sit on the bench."

"*I* might have heart failure if I sit on the bench."

He did end up sitting—but only in the fourth quarter.

Coach Wilcox ran Terrell's favorite play to start the game—a pick-and-roll. He came up to the foul line to set a screen and then rolled to the basket, looking up into the air to see that Danny had put the ball right where he could bound into the air, grab it, and dunk it.

As Terrell came down, he heard the crowd explode and felt a surge of energy and power. *God,* he thought, *I can't believe how much I've missed that feeling.*

The whole night was like that. Billerica wasn't very good and had no chance to guard Terrell. When the Indians tried to double-team him, he found open teammates for easy shots. By halftime, both of Billerica's big men had fouled out and Terrell had 25 points. At the end of the third quarter, Coach Wilcox pulled all the starters with the score 75–35. Even with JV players in the game for most of the fourth quarter, the final score was 89–52.

There wasn't a single moment when Terrell thought about or worried about his concussion. He was completely comfortable running up and down the court, although he got tired a little quicker than normal. He'd need to build his stamina back up.

When he and Danny sat down on the bench at the start of the fourth quarter, Danny asked him how he felt.

"Great," Terrell said. "It's almost as if it never happened."

"Too bad," Danny said.

"Too bad?"

"Yeah. I guarantee you come Tuesday night, all your old friends are going to be back in force."

Even so, Terrell couldn't stop smiling. For now, he was just happy to be a basketball player again.

TWENTY-EIGHT

Terrell was surprised to find his mother sitting at the kitchen table when he got home that night. She had never been one to wait up for him. But here she was, after midnight, sitting in her bathrobe, with a glass of milk and a couple of the chocolate cookies she liked in front of her.

"Everything okay?" he asked as he shucked his coat.

"Fine," she said, smiling. "I guess I was a little wound up from the game. Couldn't sleep, so I came down to get something to drink."

"And eat," he said, pointing at the cookies.

"Guilty," she said.

He went to the refrigerator, pulled out a bottle of water, and sat down across from her.

"Did you have a good time?" she asked.

"Oh yeah. Went to Nettie's. It was nice because the super friends didn't know I was playing tonight." Terrell and his mom had taken to calling all the hangers-on the super friends somewhere along the way in honor of a cartoon he had watched as a kid. "So it was just the guys on the team and—"

"Valerie and Laurie."

"Yeah."

"I like Valerie," she said.

He had introduced them just before the Washington trip, and his mom had dealt with the idea of his first serious girlfriend far better than he'd imagined. The fact that Valerie was brilliant and not a basketball groupie probably didn't hurt.

"She likes you too," he said. "She says I need the two of you to balance things out, because the men in my life only ever think about basketball."

"I've heard there are other things in the world," his mom deadpanned.

"Who knew?" Terrell shook his head.

There was silence for a moment, and then Terrell said something he hadn't planned on saying—something he hadn't even fully admitted to himself. "Mom, I'm a little scared."

"Of what?" she said, clearly surprised.

"Getting hurt again."

She nodded and thought. "I know it scared *me* to get a call from a hospital. I think my heart rate has just about gone back to normal. . . . But your concussion was a fluke. Bad luck. . . . There's no reason to think it will happen again."

"All injuries are a fluke," he said. "Omar's fall was a fluke. He'd made that move a thousand times before and been fine."

"But that serious an injury, one where you can never

play again—that's rare. The kind you've just been through is more common—an injury where you just have to stop and give your body time to heal. It was scary, but you *did* get better. You're fine now."

Terrell knew she was trying to be reassuring, but she was missing his point. "Yeah, but it could have gone the other way. There's no guarantee I'll always come back strong."

She grunted. "Terrell, honey, there are no guarantees in life. But that doesn't mean you should live scared."

"I know," he said. "I just wonder sometimes . . ." He trailed off, not sure he could actually say this out loud.

"Wonder what?"

"I wonder if the guys who say I'm crazy to not even consider some of the offers I'm getting have a point. I mean, maybe it does make sense to get paid now—while I'm healthy and people want me. If someone's willing to set us up for life *right now* and can guarantee we'd get the money even if I got hurt, why take the risk of getting hurt again and ending up with nothing?"

She didn't answer for a while. "What would Danny say to that?" she asked at last.

"He'd say if I take the money now, these guys will own me, and he's probably right. But what's the difference if they own me now or later? I *will* sign with an agent someday. I *will* sign with an NBA team and a shoe company and maybe more. I know it's against the NCAA's rules—but it's not *illegal*. And from all I've heard, even the NCAA doesn't really want to catch guys like me. They only go after non-stars, so there's less of a scandal. If the people making the rules are corrupt, do I still have to follow the rules?"

His mom narrowed her eyes. "Terrell, I hear what you're saying. But I can also hear *you*—and you sound like someone who is trying very hard to convince himself that what he's saying is right."

Terrell groaned and put his head down on the kitchen table. "I don't know. I don't know what to think anymore."

She sighed and reached over and rubbed his shoulder. "I never thought that being good at something would be so difficult," she said. "When you were little, I always hoped you would find a niche, something that would make you happy. I never dreamed that finding that niche would come with so many terrible choices. . . . I just want you to do something that you love doing."

"Mom, I *do* love playing basketball. But getting paid to do something you love isn't necessarily a bad thing, is it?"

"No," she said quietly. "No, it's not."

Danny's prediction that all of Terrell's super friends would be back turned out to be accurate—in spades. He had forgotten that the NCAA had opened a new recruiting window for coaches during the last two weeks in February, allowing them to go on the road before March Madness cranked up.

It was impossible not to notice the star-studded lineup spread around the gym when they went out to warm up before the Concord game. Since it was a Tuesday, a night when only a handful of college teams had games, none of the schools recruiting Terrell had just sent assistants. The big-name head coaches were all there: Mike Krzyzewski, Roy Williams, Steve Alford, Grant Hathaway, and Mike Todd—the five finalists in the Terrell sweepstakes. They weren't alone, though, Danny noticed. Kevin Stallings from Vanderbilt was there, and so were Mike Lonergan from George Washington and Tommy Amaker from Harvard. They were there, he knew, to see him one more time. Several other big-name coaches wandered in—perhaps, Danny thought, to get an early look at James Nix.

And then there were the usual suspects: the dudes, who had been completely absent during Terrell's absence, were there, and so were the shoe company reps and the agents. There were others in suits that Danny didn't recognize. Clearly, Terrell-mania was back in full force. The national signing date was only a few weeks away. It occurred to Danny as he went through the layup line that he had been so focused on Terrell's health the last few weeks that he hadn't made any real progress toward his own decision.

In a sense, the game was a disappointment. Everyone had been waiting to play Concord again since the loss in January. This game was, if nothing else, concrete proof of how much Terrell meant to the team—if there had been any doubt at all beforehand.

For some reason, Coach Stephenson started the game trying to guard Terrell one-on-one, putting Terry Schaefer, his six-foot ten-inch center, behind Terrell in the low post.

But Terrell was much too quick for Schaefer. Danny made no pretense of even trying to run an offense. Instead, he simply threw the ball in to Terrell, who made poor Schaefer look silly. Terrell might have scored every point for Lexington in the first quarter if not for a couple of Concord turnovers and run-outs by the Minutemen that led to fast-break baskets. By the time the first quarter was over, Lexington led, 24–7, and Terrell had 16 points.

"Terrell, he's got to double you sooner or later," Coach Wilcox said at the end of the quarter. "As soon as you see it, find your shooters on the perimeter."

As the second quarter started, Concord did begin double-teaming Terrell, but perhaps Coach Stephenson hadn't been so crazy to try to guard him with one player at the start. At least that way, Lexington was only scoring two points a possession. When they double-teamed him, Terrell found Danny or Nix consistently open for three-point attempts, most of which they buried. By halftime it was 52–20.

The final score was 89–56. Basketball game over. Let the recruiting game begin.

Which it did as soon as Danny and Terrell had showered and changed and emerged from the locker room. The media had returned too. During the time that Terrell was injured, there hadn't been more than a handful of reporters at the games: the school paper, the local weekly paper, and a blogger or two. It was as if Lexington had ceased to exist outside the town limits.

No more. Coach Wilcox had to enlist some of the school

staff to handle the renewed media onslaught. Terrell and Danny were led to a riser where two microphones awaited them.

"Maybe we should sing a song or two," Danny said to Terrell as they walked onto the riser.

"How about 'Can't Get No Satisfaction'?" Terrell suggested with a grin.

Instead, they went through the usual battery of questions—most directed at Terrell. Once he had assured people that his 35-point, 15-rebound, 11-assist performance did, in fact, mean that he felt pretty good, the questions about his future began.

"Are you any closer to making a college choice?" asked a tall blond woman who was wearing impossibly high heels.

"I guess I'm closer in that it's late February and I hope to decide by early April," Terrell said. "I can promise everyone that as soon as I know where I'm going, I'll tell you, if only so people will stop asking me."

"Did you ever worry your career might be over, given the nature of your injury?" asked another reporter.

"Not really," Terrell said. "But mostly because I forced myself not to think about it."

He had been prepared for the question. What surprised him was how badly he felt lying about it. He had thought about it constantly.

The questions went on like that for a couple more minutes before someone asked Danny if *he* was close to making a college choice.

"Yes, I am," Danny said. "I have decided I definitely want to go to college."

That got a laugh and gave the teacher who was more or less running the press conference the chance to thank everyone for coming and wrap it up.

Danny and Terrell were heading for the door when they realized there was no way to escape without going through the gauntlet of Terrell's many, many admirers.

"Maybe we should go back downstairs and slip out the back," Danny suggested.

"No point," Terrell said. "They'll follow us to Nettie's."

They waded in.

Mostly it was handshakes and congratulations and "Glad-to-see-you-back" hugs. Terrell hated the hugs.

Danny saw Tommy Amaker and Kevin Stallings and started to go over to say hello.

Amaker held up a hand. "If I could talk to you right now, Danny, I'd tell you that Kevin and I aren't allowed to talk to you," he said. "I'd also tell you, nice playing. But obviously I can't talk to you because of the no-bump rule."

"You'd just want me to know you were here, right?" Danny said, smiling.

"Right," Amaker said. "I'd also want you to know I can't be here Friday, but I'll be pulling for you because I know how important that game is."

"And if I could talk to you," Stallings said, "I'd want you to know that I flew up from Nashville as opposed to driving over from Cambridge. But you'd probably know that anyway. Not that I would bring that up, even if I *could* talk to you."

They all laughed, and Danny waved a hand in a non-goodbye. Terrell was completely surrounded by agents and shoe company reps—some whom Danny recognized, others whom he didn't. New players in the game. Standing on the outside of the circle, Danny noticed the dudes watching pensively.

Maurice glanced over and saw him staring. He and Danny exchanged glares for a moment. Maurice looked away first.

Maybe now that his human ATM machine was back in service, Maurice wasn't as eager to confront Danny again. Still, Danny didn't think they were finished by a long shot.

The school was humming with anticipation the next three days.

The game on Friday with Waltham would decide the league championship and who would advance to the sectionals. There were four sectionals held around the state, and the winner of each sectional would advance to the state championship series at the TD Gardens in Boston, the home arena of the Celtics.

It snowed on Wednesday but not enough to create a snow day. It took a blizzard to call school off in Lexington. A little three-inch storm just meant everyone stayed inside at lunchtime.

By Friday, the bad weather had moved out and a warm

front came through, sending the temperatures soaring into the fifties. Since seniors didn't have to stay in school for lunch, Danny and Laurie decided to take a walk. There was an old-fashioned drugstore about four blocks from the school that had very good hamburgers and milkshakes. Danny was craving a chocolate milkshake.

"You sure it's okay for you to eat like this on the day of a game?" she said as they walked over.

"It's noon. We play at seven. I'll be fine. Since when did you start worrying about basketball?"

"Since I started dating you," she answered. "Heck, even Valerie is paying attention. I think she was more nervous Tuesday night than you guys were."

Danny laughed. "My dad always says it's harder to watch than to play or coach, because you can't do anything." He knew, though, that there was more to it than that. While he and Laurie had fun together, Terrell and Valerie had gotten serious—very serious. He could tell by the way they acted around each other and by the way Terrell talked about her. He even seemed jealous that Danny might be going to Harvard with her and he wasn't.

They were still joking about Valerie's nerves when they pulled open the door to Peggy's. Peggy herself was behind the cash register when Danny and Laurie walked in. "No booths open," she said when she saw them. "There's one table, I think, in the back. Or there's room at the counter."

"We'll sit in the back," Danny said. "Thanks." He spotted the empty table and was about to point Laurie in that direction when he saw who was sitting around the large table at the very back of the room.

There were at least ten people in the party. Danny didn't recognize all of them, but he didn't need to. Paul Judson was looking directly at him. He was flanked by Billy Tommasino and Stan Montana. Next to Montana was the U of A Coach Grant Hathaway, and directly opposite Hathaway was Maurice.

It was the person sitting next to Hathaway, the one clearly trying to duck his head when he saw Danny, who brought Danny up short. Barrett Stephenson.

Bobby Kelleher had told them that Coach Stephenson was likely in Athena's pocket. But Danny had been so distracted by the dudes that he'd lost track of him. Now here they all were together . . .

Without saying a word to Laurie, Danny headed straight for the table. "So what brings all of you to town?" he said, looking straight at Coach Stephenson.

"Danny, don't overreact the way you do," Coach Stephenson said. "This is just a bunch of basketball guys having lunch, nothing more."

"Sure it is," Danny said. "And all of you just want to help Terrell in any way you can."

"Is that so hard to believe?" Paul Judson said. "Yes, we're all in the basketball business. That doesn't mean we don't have the best interests of players at heart."

"Oh, please," Danny said. "Where were all of you when Terrell was hurt?"

"Recruiting rules didn't allow me to leave town," Grant

Hathaway said. "You know that, Danny. None of the coaches recruiting you were in town during that time, either. They couldn't be."

"I'm not talking about you, Coach. I'm talking about the rest of these sycophants."

"Big word, white boy," Maurice said. "But maybe you should stop running that mouth of yours before someone gets hurt."

"You want to fight *again*, Maurice?" Danny said. "How 'bout just you and me outside where no one else can get hurt."

Maurice smiled and shook his head. "Nah, I'm not gonna fight you again." He glanced over at Laurie and cocked an eyebrow. "But I know you and Terrell don't want to see anyone else get hurt."

Coach Stephenson stood up to get between Danny and Maurice. "Both of you, stop it," he said. "No one's getting hurt. Danny, you have my word that I'm only here to help Terrell. So is everyone else at this table."

Danny laughed angrily. "That's a good one, Coach," he said. "Where's Terrell, then? While you're all plotting about how to help him?" He turned to Laurie. "Let's go. There's a bad smell back here."

Danny was still shaken when he and Laurie walked back to school. They were arguing about whether he should let Terrell know what they had seen.

"Let it go, Danny," she said—for about the fifth time.

"Telling Terrell won't accomplish anything. You'll only upset him right before the biggest game of the year."

"He should know," Danny argued.

"And you'll let him know—tomorrow," she said.

Danny finally decided she was right, mostly. "I'll wait until after the game," he said as they walked back into school. "But he's gonna know before he leaves the locker room."

"Fine," she said. "Unless you lose. Then let it wait."

He gave her a sharp look. "We're not losing," he said. "We lose, and the season's over."

Laurie just nodded.

"What's wrong?"

"I just don't want to see you too down if by some remote chance you lose tonight," she said. "It's not the end of the world, you know." She slid her hand inside his. "You've still got a lot that's good in your life." She smiled, showing her dimples.

He tried to smile back and couldn't do it. "I know you're right," he said. "But losing isn't an option tonight."

TWENTY-NINE

Danny knew that losing wasn't an option. But clearly the Waltham team felt exactly the same way.

Waltham Coach Jack Kvancz had been at the school for about a hundred years and had twice won state championships. This wasn't one of his best teams, but the Hawks were still 20–5 and 17–2 in league play. The Minutemen had played three extra games because of the Christmas tournament so they were 26–2 overall but also 17–2 in the league. The winner would go on to sectionals the following week. The loser would start looking forward to spring break.

Kvancz knew what had happened to Concord in its rematch with Lexington on Tuesday. He knew with Terrell in the lineup his team would probably suffer a similar fate if it came out and tried to play straight-up basketball.

So it didn't.

Every time the Hawks had the ball, they made no attempt to get into their offense until the shot clock was under ten seconds. On a couple of occasions they didn't get a shot off, but on a number of others they managed to find a good shot with the clock under five seconds. Playing good defense, staying in a stance for thirty seconds on every possession, was tiring. Danny was just glad that Massachusetts was one of a handful of states that *had* a shot clock. Otherwise, Lexington might never have touched the ball.

At the other end of the court, Kvancz put his team into what Danny's dad called a junk defense, meaning there were two players around Terrell at all times. There was no dropping down from the outside to double-team him, just two guys with him. The other three defenders guarded Danny, James Nix, and Monte Torre man to man. That meant that Alan Inwood was essentially unguarded. There was a reason for that: Inwood averaged under four points a game, and it showed in the first quarter, when he missed four straight wide-open shots.

It was 11–11 at the quarter and 21–21 at halftime. Coach Wilcox kept trying different players in Inwood's place, but they weren't much better offensively. He moved Terrell away from the basket to clear some space, and that helped because it gave Danny and James some room to operate, but they were still having trouble denying Waltham good shots at the end of the clock.

The game crawled into the fourth quarter. The crowd, which had been crazed at the beginning, was now tense, almost imploring the Minutemen to figure out a way to pull away from Waltham.

It wasn't happening. When Corey Allenson hit a three with the shot clock at one second, Waltham opened the biggest lead of the game, 41–36, with fifty-three seconds to play. Coach Wilcox called time-out.

"Okay, here's the deal," he said. "Terrell or Danny has to be our shooter here. Danny, you're bringing the ball up. Everyone else is on the baseline. Terrell, you come out to screen"—he was drawing this on his grease board as he spoke—"and Danny, if the shot's there, take it. If someone switches, it will be one of Terrell's guys. Then you get him the ball, and Terrell you go in there and dunk it as hard as you possibly can. They'll foul you, I promise. But you've got to make the shot. We need three here, not two. Got it?"

They all nodded. Danny noticed his dad was sweating.

He brought the ball up as quickly as he could. He could almost hear the fear in the crowd's noise. Kvancz had dropped his defense back, content to kill clock without risking a foul. Danny veered left near the key as Terrell popped out and set a hard screen on Allenson, who was guarding Danny. As soon as he did, one of the two guys guarding him switched, coming to get a hand in Danny's face. Waltham didn't want to give up a three right now.

Without even looking to see if Terrell had rolled away, Danny threw a semi-lob toward the middle of the key. He saw Terrell's hand reach to grab it and a second later he was in the air, slamming the ball down with the authority Danny's dad had demanded a moment earlier. And, as promised, he was fouled. The noise level doubled—the pleading became screeching.

Danny glanced at the clock. There were 41.2 seconds

left. As Terrell went to the line, he heard his father's voice over the din. "If he makes it, call time-out," he said.

Danny nodded. Terrell swished the free throw, and Danny, standing next to one of the officials, called time. It was 41–39.

"*No* fouls," his dad said in the huddle. "There's a six-second difference between the shot clock and the game clock. That's plenty of time. You've got to play defense one more time *and* get the rebound. *We have no time-outs left.* Once we've got the ball, get into our scramble offense and take whatever shot is there—a two or a three. Got it?"

They nodded. Danny's heart was pounding so hard, he was afraid it was going to burst through his chest. He looked at Terrell coming out of the huddle.

"When I get the board," Terrell yelled in his ear, "be ready to get the ball from me and go!"

Danny just patted him on the shoulder to let him know he understood.

Allenson brought the ball up court and dribbled the clock down. Danny gave him room. The look on Allenson's face told him he was surprised. Clearly, Waltham had expected them to foul. With the shot clock at 10 seconds, Kvancz shouted at Allenson, "Run red, Corey. Run red!"

"Red" was almost a universal call. It meant the point guard was supposed to drive the ball at his defender and create space to get a shot before the clock went to zero. Danny dug in. Sure enough, Allenson came right at him as if he intended to drive the lane. Danny knew he wouldn't do that because Terrell was back there. Sure enough, Allenson pulled up right at the three-point line and started to go into his shooting motion. Danny was there, hand up, getting as far off the floor as he could. He saw Allenson lean back just a tad to get the shot off over him. The shot-clock buzzer went off as the ball came out of Allenson's hands.

Danny saw the shot glance off the rim and right into Terrell's hands as he outleaped everyone around the basket. Danny curled back and Terrell flipped him the ball.

Everyone was sprinting in the other direction. Danny could see the clock slip from five to four as he put the ball on the floor and raced across midcourt. Allenson had come to cut him off. Danny faked as if to veer right and went left. He could see Terrell trying to race into position in the key, but there was no time for a pass.

He couldn't afford to look at the clock again, so he let his basketball instincts take over. As he neared the key, he knew he didn't have time to dribble the ball more than one more time. He took as big a step as he could with that dribble, so he could step into his shot as he released it.

Allenson, not wanting to foul him, flew past, arms flailing. Danny knew his body was squared to the basket as he released the ball and he heard the buzzer sound with the ball in the air. For a split second, it felt as if time had stopped, but Danny knew he had made the shot. He could tell by the way it felt when he released it. A photo in the newspaper the next morning showed him with his arms up while the ball was still en route to the basket.

It finally splashed through the net, and Danny felt as if an earthquake was happening around him. He was swallowed by teammates and students stampeding the court. As they lifted him onto their shoulders, he had one thought: *Thank God that wasn't the last shot of my high school career.*

There was another game to play next week.

When Danny's shot swished through the hoop, Terrell felt an almost overwhelming sense of relief. He was so exhausted after being hounded by double-teams all night and chasing Waltham through each lengthy possession on defense that he could barely get his arms up in the air in celebration of the shot and Lexington's stunning 42–41 victory. He was glad to see Danny being carried around the court as the hero. He deserved it.

As the chaos around Danny continued, Terrell was thinking of the Waltham players, who had worked so hard and come within a second of pulling off an improbable upset. Three of them were still on the floor, shocked by the ending. He went and offered a hand to Corey Allenson. Terrell had been camped out under the basket to try for a desperation tip if the shot missed, so he had a perfect view of just how close Allenson had come to deflecting the shot. He helped Allenson up and saw tears in his eyes. He gave him a hug and said, "Great game, man," which was all he could think of to say. Allenson said nothing. He just returned the hug and sobbed quietly.

Out of the corner of his eye, just outside the circle of mayhem, Terrell could see the two coaches shaking hands. Coach Wilcox was giving Coach Kvancz the same kind of hug he was giving Allenson. There wasn't much to say. Somebody had to lose.

As Allenson walked away, a few of the revelers grabbed Terrell to try and bring him into the circle. Even though he was very glad not to be in Waltham's shoes, he just didn't feel like jumping up and down. What he felt wasn't joy; it was relief. All their dreams had almost blown up. One more tick and they would be in the locker room right now listening to Coach Wilcox tell them they'd had a great season, no matter what. Now, they still had a *chance* to have a great season, but they were at least five more wins—maybe six— away from that.

THIRTY

The sectionals for the Minutemen would be held in Worcester, at Holy Cross. Eight teams were vying for one spot in the state championships. The four section-winning teams would go to the TD Garden in two weeks and play on Thursday night and Saturday afternoon—there was a hockey game in between on Friday night. Then, on Sunday afternoon, the Massachusetts state champion would play the Connecticut state champion. This was a brand-new concept created by the high school associations. The theory was that the team who won that game would move up in the final *USA Today* national rankings—which had become so important in the world of high school basketball.

Following their two losses, the Minutemen had dropped out of the top twenty-five. They were back in this week at number twenty-one. Only one other Massachusetts school, Central High School in Springfield, at number twelve, was ranked higher than they were. The state high school association hoped that the state champion, if it beat the Connecticut champion, would at least crack the top ten.

After the nail-biter with Waltham, the sectionals felt like a cakewalk.

Terrell had looked forward to playing in the Hart Center, the gym at Holy Cross, because Danny had filled him in on some of Holy Cross's basketball history. Notable to Danny was that it was the school that had produced Bob Cousy. Terrell wasn't the hoops junkie that Danny was, but he knew who Bob Cousy was—arguably the first truly great point guard in NBA history.

There was a statue of Cousy in front of the Hart Center, and they all stopped to look on their way in to their first practice. "So I guess he was pretty good," Terrell said as they read the plaque. He was goading Danny—he knew that Danny thought the two greatest guards in NBA history were Cousy and Walt Frazier. Danny liked guards who were great passers, because that was what he did best. He loved Chris Paul too. When Terrell brought up Magic Johnson, who was as great a passer as he had ever seen when he watched old NBA games, Danny shook his head. "Doesn't count. He was six nine. Make me six nine, and I could do stuff too."

"Stuff like *that?*"

"Well, maybe not like that . . ."

The Hart Center seated 3,600, and it was situated right at the top of the hill on which Holy Cross was built. Looking down toward Worcester, Terrell thought the town appeared almost pretty—markedly different from the feel it had when they had driven through it the night before en route to their hotel. The day was bright and sunny but very windy—especially on the hilltop. "What did you call the weather around here?" he asked Danny.

"Worcestering," Danny said. "Actually, it isn't Worcestering today. Worcestering is a constant drizzle or snow flurries and a gray sky. This isn't bad."

The entire weekend was actually pretty good. The wind never seemed to go away, but the sun stayed out. More important, the Minutemen were never challenged. Framingham, their first opponent, tried the Waltham approach, spreading the floor and running the shot clock. But Coach Wilcox was ready this time. Instead of having his players chase for thirty seconds, he had them sit back in a zone and then jump into man-to-man when the shot clock hit ten and Framingham started to run its offense. Framingham was one-for-nine in the first quarter and Lexington led, 19–2. That was the end of the delay offense. The final was 69–36.

There wasn't much suspense the next two days, either. No one in the section had anyone who was even close to Terrell, so it was a pick-your-poison situation for the coaches: try to guard him one-on-one and watch him score every time he touched the ball or double him and get buried from the outside. When Worcester tried to double-team Terrell, Coach Wilcox sent him to one corner with two defenders and Alan Inwood to the other corner with no defenders. That left Danny, James Nix, and Monte Torre to play three-on-three in the open court.

They were considerably better than the three Worcester kids who were guarding them. Nix kept going past his man for easy layups. On one play, one of Terrell's two bodyguards left him to try to deny Nix another layup. Nix flipped the ball to Terrell, who made a quick move and dunked.

Terrell scored 29 in the last three quarters, and the final was 84–58.

Natick was the opponent in the final. The school's most famous graduate was Doug Flutie, the Heisman Trophy–winning quarterback. According to Coach Wilcox, they had two players who were being recruited by Division I schools. When Terrell saw that they were going to play straight-up man-to-man defense and not play stall-ball, he felt his heart start to pound. He knew he was ready for a big night. So did Danny, who kept getting him the ball in places where he could score—inside and out.

The two of them came out of the game with about three minutes to go and Lexington leading, 71–47. Terrell had 39 points, and Danny had 18 assists, which they would learn later was a sectionals record. Terrell was voted the MVP. He happily accepted the trophy that came with it but was much happier when he and Danny, the team co-captains, were given the sectional championship trophy for the second straight year. They were back in the state Final Four.

The "We just want to help Terrell" Club had been smaller than usual in Worcester. It was March now, so the coaches couldn't travel for recruiting; they were all busy with their current teams in the run-up to the Final Four. The dudes were all there, though, and so was Stan Montana and a couple of other guys Terrell had seen before but not met. There was no Paul Judson, but there were enough people in suits sitting near Montana and the shoe reps to make Terrell think they were agents or financial advisers.

Danny had told him about his encounter with Coach Stephenson and the super friends on the day of the Waltham game, but so far no one had made any sort of direct move. He suspected it was coming soon.

Coach Wilcox had kept the team on a pretty tight leash since it had to play three nights in a row, so the super friends had to be satisfied with quick handshakes as the team walked straight from the locker room to the bus.

"It'll start again in Boston," Coach Wilcox warned both Terrell and Danny on the trip home after the championship game. "I've asked Tom Konchalski to come, because he can ID anyone new who shows up. And Frank Sullivan will be there for the same reason. They're going to come at you in all directions, hoping to tempt you."

"To do what?" Terrell asked. For all the talking and jabbering and "We'll do anything to help," no one had actually offered him anything specific besides Stan Montana's invitation to all the Athena gear in the world.

"Who knows?" Coach Wilcox said. "Maybe they'll offer part ownership in the Celtics. Or in a restaurant. Or a hockey team."

"I don't even like hockey," Terrell said.

"Well, then, that's out," Coach Wilcox said. "Almost everything else you can think of isn't."

At the very least, Terrell thought, he'd be curious to hear what anyone had to say to him. He remembered something his mother always said after dinner in a restaurant: "Looking at the dessert menu doesn't mean you *have* to eat dessert."

So the season had come down to this. Boston. The state championship.

The team that had beaten Lexington in the final game the previous year was back again too. Central High's star player, six-foot ten-inch Wilson Walton, had already announced that he was going to Kentucky. Their point guard, Andrew Norton, was a fast-talking, cocky kid who was going to UConn. They'd be taking on Barnstable High School, the Cinderella team in the Final Four, while Lexington's first game would be against Gloucester. Gloucester had a great shooting guard named "Trey" Benson, who had committed to Duke. Benson, as his nickname attested, was a deadly three-point shooter.

As good as Benson was, Terrell thought his team could handle Gloucester. He fully expected a rematch with Central in the final.

Each of the four teams was given an hour on Thursday morning for a shoot-around so they'd have a chance to get on the court at TD Garden and get accustomed to the shooting backgrounds and the massiveness of the building before they played that night.

"Pretty cool, huh?" Danny said to Terrell as they rode

the elevator up to the third floor, which was the building's floor level.

"The freight elevator, you mean?" Terrell said, unable to resist tweaking his friend who, he knew, was almost quaking at the thought of playing on the Celtics' home court.

"Come on," Danny said. "Look at this place! Tell me it's not cool. It's a lot different than last year in Springfield, admit that."

Terrell didn't see anything especially cool in the hallways or even in the locker room, which wasn't that much larger than their locker room at home. But when they walked into the huge, empty building and he looked up and saw all the Celtics' championship banners—Danny had already told him there were seventeen—and all the retired numbers of great Celtics, he had to admit he was impressed.

Coach Wilcox had come prepared for the awestruck look on his players' faces. When they assembled at midcourt, he smiled and asked them if they had seen the movie *Hoosiers*. Of course they'd seen it. Anyone who had ever looked at a basketball had seen *Hoosiers*.

"Okay, then, if you want me to get a tape measure and show you that the baskets are ten feet high, like Gene Hackman did, I'll do it," he said as they all laughed. "You're going to have to trust me that the court is ninety-four feet long. And I'll tell you one other thing: None of the other teams has ever played in here before, either, so it will be just as new for them. Just try to remember, everyone is still just playing basketball."

Terrell was trying hard to remember that. It wasn't so

much the TD Garden that was weighing on his mind as everything else. If this was going to be the weekend of reckoning—off the court—he wanted to be ready for it. His mom was driving into town that evening with Valerie, Laurie, and Coach Stephenson. He figured the super friends were assembling as well.

After practice, Danny asked his father if it would be okay if he and Terrell walked back to the hotel so they could take a detour to eat in the Quincy Market at Faneuil Hall. Danny and his dad came into town to go to Celtics games pretty often, so he knew his way around. Coach Wilcox said it was fine as long as they didn't walk around too much with a game to play that night.

It was a beautiful late-winter day, and the walk from the Garden to Faneuil Hall only took about ten minutes. Terrell loved Quincy Market—anyplace that had that many different kinds of food available in one place was okay by him. They decided on pizza at a place called Regina's and walked outside to sit down and eat.

Terrell was happily devouring his second slice of pizza when he heard Danny say, "Well, look who's here." He looked up and saw Bobby Kelleher walking in their direction. "You set this up?" he asked.

"Of course," Danny said. "I knew my dad wouldn't want us to do this on a game day, but Bobby said it was important."

Bobby didn't exaggerate much, so Terrell figured Danny had made the right call.

"Pizza on game day?" Kelleher said, shaking hands upon arrival. "Danny, what would your coach say?"

"He'd say pizza is okay seven hours before tipoff, but not reporters," Danny said.

Kelleher laughed and sat down on a bench next to them. "I'm sure you're right," he said. "Terrell, you a hundred percent? Your stats certainly are."

"I'm fine, perfect," Terrell said. "Danny said you had something important to tell us."

"Patience, Terrell," Kelleher said. "I have a lot to tell you, so I'm going to need a slice of that pizza too. . . ."

THIRTY-ONE

Bobby came back with two slices of pizza and cut right to the chase. "This is the weekend it all comes to a head," he said. "All the players are going to be in town, are probably here already. Except for the coaches—they can't travel right now and they all have tournament games this weekend anyway. That doesn't mean they don't have people here watching you."

"Like who?" Terrell asked.

"Well, the presidents of both Atlanta and Mass State will be here. They can't contact you directly, but they can buy a ticket and let you know they're here to show you their support."

"Support," Danny said. "Just what Terrell needs."

"Here's the deal," Kelleher continued. "You are not only the biggest star in this class, Terrell, you're the only really big name left. Michael Jordan has committed to Kentucky. He says he wants to follow in the footsteps of Anthony Davis."

"Davis is a center," Danny said.

"True. But he was national player of the year, won a

national title, and was the number one pick in the NBA draft after his freshman year. Jordan's going to announce for Kentucky because Calipari is the best at dealing with one-and-done players."

"Is Coach Calipari paying him?"

Kelleher shook his head. "Absolutely not. No smart coach ever does that. Oh, and your friend Alex Mayer is locked up for Mass State."

"Have you talked to Omar recently?" Terrell asked.

This seemed off-point to Danny, but Kelleher just nodded. "He's at home, still rehabbing. His goal is to walk again someday. He told me he wants to write a book about how quickly your friends disappear when you can't play anymore."

Terrell snorted. "I could add a chapter."

Kelleher nodded. "True enough." Then he plowed on. "Terrell, if my sources have it right—which I'm pretty sure they do—there are two schools putting together deals for you."

"Two?" Terrell said. "I thought it was just Atlanta. . . ."

"Nope," Kelleher said. "It's Mass State too. They just use a different M.O. Coach Todd isn't involved, but Brickley takes care of things for him. That's apparently how they landed Mayer."

"I never met anyone from Brickley when I was there," Terrell said, puzzled. "In fact, I don't remember seeing anyone from Brickley all season."

"Who funds Billy Tommasino's camp? They've had other

guys at your last few games. Because they're more estab-
lished than Athena, they can afford to be more subtle. Plus,
Mass State *tries* to recruit guys on the up-and-up if they can.
Brickley gets involved only when it's absolutely necessary.
That's what happened with Mayer. He was ready to go to
Kentucky until Brickley upped the bid."

Danny shook his head. "If you'd asked me to name one
kid I thought wasn't on the take last summer, it was Alex."

"He wasn't then. But his family got involved. Or, more
accurately, the people recruiting got his family involved.
And his coach. He's going to be an assistant at Mass State
next season."

Danny sat back in his chair and whistled. "Well, bad
news for anyone recruiting Terrell. They're not going to get
to him by offering his coach a job."

"No," Kelleher said. "Not *his* coach."

They both looked at him quizzically.

"Okay, look. The Mass State people know you like
Coach Todd. Plus, it's a good school. They're *calling* themselves Duke North. Anyway, they think they have a good
shot at you. But Brickley wants to be sure. They've already
made an offer for you that's pretty impressive."

"An offer?" Terrell said. "What are you talking about?"

Kelleher held up his hand. "Hang on. Let me finish.

"There's nothing subtle about Atlanta, as you know.
Your friend Maurice has been on the payroll all season just
to keep an eye on you, although they cut him off after you
got hurt."

"Can't imagine why," Danny said.

"Yeah, well. They started paying again when Terrell started playing again. Plus, I hear he began dropping hints about going public if they didn't. In the end, he might be their biggest mistake because he's even less trustworthy than the rest of them.

"Stan Montana and Athena are in the middle of the Atlanta offer, which I know will shock you. But that guy you met on the plane, Glenn Hitchcock? At least as important. Athena has lots of money and increasing clout, but no more than Brickley. Hitchcock can take Athena's money and get you into all sorts of initial public offerings through his company. You can be wealthy before you finish college without any money actually touching your hands.

"That's what they're going to propose to you. Of course, if you turn it down, they'll deny ever knowing you."

"And if I don't turn it down?" Terrell said.

"Then you'll be rich," Kelleher said. "At least for a while."

Danny waited for Terrell to tell Kelleher that none of it mattered because he wasn't going to be bought.

"Okay, but what, exactly, are they going to offer?" Terrell finally said.

"You really want to know?" Kelleher said, a rare look of surprise crossing his face.

"Yes," Terrell said. "I do."

Kelleher looked at Danny and sighed.

"I want to be prepared . . . ," Terrell said, though, in truth, he didn't know what he wanted.

Kelleher took out a notebook and said, "Okay, here's what I've got.

"You go to Mass State, Brickley will give you a five-year contract the day you turn pro, with a million dollars a year guaranteed; a two-million signing bonus up front; and incentive clauses, some while you're in college, like getting to the Final Four, being conference player of the year, national freshman of the year, or player of the year. Then there are more incentives in the pros: all-rookie team, all-star team, points-per-game, rebounds. Plus, you'll 'work' Billy Tommasino's camp this summer, which means you'll go there, play pickup basketball, and get paid about ten thousand a day. They also have a 'working relationship,' as it's called, with Fox. If you want it, you get a reality show as a rookie, and that can be worth *huge* money."

"A reality show?" Danny said. "Seriously?"

Terrell laughed. "That's ridiculous."

"No more ridiculous than the Kardashians . . . I'm just telling you what's there. Want more?"

"Sure."

"The Atlanta deal has more to it because they know you don't really want to go there. The Athena money is probably close to double the Brickley money. What's more, they're going to name a sneaker for you. They want to call it the Terrell Jam shoe. There's also that Hitchcock guy getting you into IPOs and increasing your initial stake. And if you sign something now, committing to Paul Judson being your agent, you'll get another couple million up front from his agency when you turn pro. They're going to have a camp of their own in Atlanta next summer, and you'll work there, just like with the Brickley deal."

Finally, Bobby took a breath. Then he added, "They're also creating a job for Barrett Stephenson."

Danny had been doing his best to listen and not interrupt, but now he couldn't help it. "I *knew* he was in on this. Man. Unbelievable."

Kelleher held up a hand. "There's one other thing that's pretty significant."

"What?" Terrell asked, his mind reeling.

"Your mom gets a house. Nothing outrageous—that would be too obvious. But if she moves to Atlanta with Stephenson, they'll get something nice in Buckhead. If she stays in Lexington, they'll set her up in a small house. Or if she wants to move a little farther out from Boston, something with some land."

Danny had known all along that Terrell's super friends were willing to do a lot to get him on their team, but he was staggered by how much *a lot* turned out to be. "But . . . ," he said finally. "But—no offense, Terrell—is he worth this much? What if he *does* get hurt? Or *doesn't* become a superstar in the NBA?"

"If he gets hurt before all of this kicks in, they pay off a flat fee—I think it's a million for Mass State and Brickley and two million for Atlanta and Athena. In either case, your mom keeps the house. If he turns out to be a lousy player, or not a great player, even . . . well, it's their loss, and they move on to the next guy," Kelleher said. "Danny, for these people, this is pocket change. It's a risk/reward deal, certainly. They all are. But if they get Terrell locked up now and he takes off, he's worth much, much more than what they're paying."

"Why not just wait until I turn pro, when doing all of this isn't against any rules?" Terrell said. "Why risk getting caught?"

Kelleher smiled. "That's a question for you, Terrell. What's *their* risk, really? The NCAA can't void any contracts. There's some risk for Judson, because he could get decertified as an agent by the NBA. But this stuff happens all the time, and agents get around it. Atlanta and Mass State will claim they knew nothing and get off with an NCAA wrist slap. The only one who gets in trouble is you. And then only if you get caught while you're still a student. If it comes out after you've gone pro, it would be a scandal and that could damage your reputation . . . but by how much is hard to know. Still, they'll encourage you to be one-and-done. Sooner you're in the pros, less risk for everyone— except your college coach. The only question for him will be 'Can he play?' It always is."

"What if I don't want to do it?" he said. "What if I say I want to go to Duke or UCLA—or even Mass State— without any money? What if I just say no?"

Kelleher stood up because it was time for all of them to get going. "That's what I hope you'll do, Terrell," Kelleher said. "I honestly think it's the best thing for you in the long term, even if it doesn't look that way right now."

Terrell sighed. "I should talk it over with my mom," he said. "And I'd *like* to talk with Coach Stephenson. . . ."

Danny snorted. "I have a few things I'd like to say to him too." But he wasn't at all sure that they were the same things Terrell had in mind.

Danny and Terrell talked it over on the walk back to the hotel and decided that three o'clock in the afternoon with a state semifinal to play in four hours was not the time to make any decisions.

Danny was concerned that Terrell might not be able to focus on the game that night.

He needn't have worried.

Terrell played as if he was on some kind of a mission, and that wasn't good for Gloucester. He made his first six shots, two of them threes, and had 12 rebounds by halftime. Gloucester managed to hang around for a quarter, trailing just 23–20, but it was 47–37 by halftime, and the lead got to be as much as 20 before the third quarter was over. Lexington cruised to an 81–66 win. Terrell finished with 33 points and 18 rebounds. Danny didn't shoot much, scoring just six points, but he had 14 assists, and James Nix added 23 points.

The state high school association had set up a "family reception area," where the players could go after the game. It was actually a storage area for things like the Zamboni machine, which had been cleared out for the weekend. Blue curtains had been hung to dress up the walls and to section off an area for food, another that had couches and chairs and TV sets, and another where there was a bar.

Naturally, the area was open to a lot more people than just family members. It was also open to sponsors—which meant all the major shoe companies—and their guests. That pretty much meant that anyone with a ticket could get into the "restricted" area.

The place was packed when Danny, Terrell, and James Nix walked in after their win. They found Terrell's mom looking far more dressed up than Danny could ever remember seeing her, standing in the crowded bar area with Coach Stephenson. There was no sign of Valerie or Laurie, but super friends were everywhere.

"Where are Valerie and Laurie?" Terrell said about a half second before Danny could get the question out.

"In the next room, eating," Coach Stephenson answered. "Great playing, you guys. Game was never in doubt." Danny was having serious trouble not glaring at Coach Stephenson, whom he had decided to blame for Terrell's sudden wavering. Terrell's mom gave her son a hug and a kiss and then did the same for Danny.

"I'm so proud of you boys," she said just as Stan Montana, Paul Judson, and Judson's boss, Donald what's-his-name the Third, magically appeared at her elbow.

"We're proud of you too," Judson said, giving Terrell a warm handshake, as did Donald the Third. Montana followed with a hug that clearly made Terrell want to scream.

"Paul, Donald, Stan, you've met Danny, haven't you?" Mrs. Jamerson, always polite, said.

"Of course," Judson said, offering his hand. "Danny's done a nice job of feeding off Terrell the last two years."

Reluctantly, Danny shook hands with all three of them. It was Terrell who couldn't resist a jab. "If you knew anything about basketball, Mr. Judson, you'd know that it's Danny who's been feeding *me,*" he said, his voice ice-cold.

"Terrell!" Mrs. Jamerson said.

"Sorry, Mom, but these two have been putting Danny down since last summer," Terrell said. "I'm kind of tired of it."

"Hey, Terrell, I think it's cool that you stand up for your pal," Montana said. "Your unselfishness is part of what makes you the player you are."

Danny thought he might throw up—preferably *on* Montana.

Clearly, Terrell wasn't going to take a deal from these guys because he liked any of them.

That didn't mean he wouldn't take it.

THIRTY-TWO

As Terrell and Danny were being oozed on by super friends, Central High School was wrapping up their slot in the championship game. Wilson Walton scored 36 points and also grabbed 24 rebounds in Central's win over Barnstable. Like Lexington, Central ended any notion of an upset early, taking a 24–11 lead at the end of the first quarter and never looking back, winning by a final score of 79–47.

Cinderella had been sent home from the ball, and now the two best teams in the state would play for the title for the second year in a row. Terrell was determined to come away the winner this time.

"Walton's going to be a handful," Coach Wilcox said at breakfast the next morning. "The key is going to be stopping the other four guys. He's going to get his."

Terrell, Danny, and Coach Wilcox were sitting in the dining area of the Marriott a few minutes past eight.

"I'll keep him under control, Coach," Terrell said. "I'm a better player now than I was a year ago."

"I know you are, Terrell," Coach Wilcox said. "But you

aren't going to guard him. We're going to play zone, and you're going to work the opposite side of the court from him."

"But—"

Coach Wilcox held his hand up. "I watched Central play last night. You didn't. We need you all thirty-two minutes tomorrow."

"He's right, Terrell," said Danny, who hadn't been at all surprised when his father brought up playing zone. "The only way they beat us last year was because you fouled out. Wilson will score a lot, but we'll outscore him. And if he tries to guard you, then you'll foul *him* out."

Terrell nodded. Periodically throughout the season the team had switched to zone, specifically so they would be familiar with it if they needed to play it. It wasn't as if they would be doing something they were clueless about.

"Okay, I get it," he said. "I guess we'll walk through it when we practice today." They were scheduled to bus to Harvard that afternoon to practice after they had gone sightseeing and eaten lunch.

"That's exactly what we'll do," Coach Wilcox said. "Now, tell me why you guys wanted to have breakfast with me. I figured you'd sleep in until it was time for our walk on the Freedom Trail."

Terrell and Danny looked at each other. "You tell him," Danny said. "It's your story and your life, not mine."

Terrell nodded. He proceeded to walk Coach Wilcox through everything Bobby Kelleher had told them and about the way Stan Montana, Donald Johnston the Third, and Paul Judson had been stuck to his mother like Velcro. Danny filled in a couple of details that he had forgotten.

Coach Wilcox sighed, picked up his coffee mug, and took a long sip. "Boy, I wish I had an easy answer for you," he said. "Those are bigger figures than I imagined. Though I doubt they expected you and your mom to be this tough to convince—especially once they got Barrett on their side."

"It *is* a lot of money," Terrell said. "I know it's easy to say, 'It'll be there after college,' but I can't be *sure*, can I? I could get hurt. Or the next level might be tougher. It happens, right?"

"Yes, it does," Coach Wilcox said, draining his coffee. "If I'm being totally honest with you, Terrell, the only thing I'm really sure of is that if you decide to take the money, you'll always have regrets. You know who these guys are. I know money is nice, and these numbers are almost incomprehensible. But it isn't everything."

"Unless you've never had it."

He nodded. "There's truth in that. Let me ask you: Do you think LeBron James is any happier day to day than you are? I don't. Not really. So maybe think about what will really make you happy."

"I think I need to talk to my mom."

"I think you do, too."

The whole team walked the Freedom Trail around many of Boston's historic sites. Terrell was struck again by how close together all the famous sites were. He and his mom had done the Trail when they first moved to the area the previous year—Boston was a history lover's dream city. Amazingly, Danny hadn't ever done this before. He'd lived near the city all his life but still hadn't seen most of it. They finished at the Old North Church, stopped to eat at the various Quincy Market eateries, and then had an hour to rest before the bus would take them over to Harvard for their two o'clock practice.

Terrell was surprised when the bus didn't cross the Charles River into Cambridge.

"The athletic facilities are actually in Boston," Danny said when Terrell asked him what the deal was. "Everyone walks across the bridge from campus to practice every day."

"Can't that get cold in the winter?"

"Very," Danny said. "But it's still kind of neat."

No question, Terrell thought. *He's sold on Harvard.*

The bus went through a back gate and took them past the ancient football stadium and then wound past various athletic buildings until it parked near the back door of Lavietes Pavilion. Danny had explained on the way over that Lavietes was the second oldest college basketball arena in the country, behind only Fordham's Rose Hill Gym.

As they walked to the front door, a familiar figure was waiting: Harvard Coach Tommy Amaker. Terrell was a little surprised to see Coach Amaker, because he knew this was a recruiting dead period. As if reading his mind, Amaker explained, "I can't come to see you guys, so I thought I'd invite you to come see me," he said, smiling. "If you're on campus and I didn't pay for you to get here, I'm not breaking any rules."

"We really appreciate the invite, Tommy," Coach Wilcox said.

"There are a couple other guys here who want to say hello," Coach Amaker said. Seeing what was probably a terrified look on Terrell's face, Amaker laughed. "Don't panic, Terrell. No agents, no shoe salesmen. Just Frank Sullivan and Tom Konchalski. They got to town today and wanted to swing by and say hello to your coach."

Terrell heard himself breathe a sigh of relief, a sign of how tense he was feeling. They walked inside. The old gym had clearly been spruced up in recent years. The floor gleamed and the bleachers looked like they'd been freshly painted. Harvard had won the Ivy League title for a second straight season and was getting ready to play in a second straight NCAA tournament the following week. Clearly, their success had resulted in an upgrade of the facilities.

Konchalski and Sullivan were sitting on folding chairs under one basket. The two men stood up to greet Coach Wilcox and also warmly welcomed Danny and Terrell, who stopped to say hello while everyone else was directed to the locker room by Amaker.

"Boy, have you two had a ride since last summer," Sullivan said in greeting.

"Yes, but they're right where they want to be right now,"

Konchalski said in his very proper and polite way. "You boys have really played wonderfully this past month."

"Well, we're just glad to be playing this weekend," Coach Wilcox said.

"Spoken like a true coach," Konchalski said. "And in this case, you're absolutely right."

They made small talk for a couple of minutes before Coach Wilcox suggested that Terrell and Danny get changed for practice. Before they left, Terrell made a snap decision. "Coach, before we leave today, do you think it would be okay for me to talk to Mr. Konchalski for a couple of minutes?"

"Absolutely," Coach Wilcox said. "I think that's a good idea, as long as you're okay with it, Tom."

"I'd be delighted," Konchalski said. "Anything I can do to help."

For once, Terrell actually believed that.

They didn't practice very long or very hard. Most of the time was spent going over the offensive sets that Central would be running and working on their zone defense. When Coach Wilcox told the players to spend ten minutes of practice shooting free throws, he motioned Terrell over. "Terrell, you can pass on the free throws. Go spend a couple of minutes with Mr. Konchalski."

Terrell grabbed a towel and walked over to where Konchalski was sitting with Coach Amaker. Frank Sullivan had left a few minutes earlier. Seeing Terrell coming, Coach Amaker stood up. "Take my seat, Terrell," he said.

"You sure, Coach?" Terrell said. "We can go someplace else to talk."

Amaker shook his head. "No, no. I've got to go put together a practice plan. We practice at five today because some of our guys have late labs on Friday."

"Does Danny know about late labs?" Terrell said, grinning.

Amaker looked around as if he'd just been caught at something. "Did I say labs?" he said with a grin. "I meant crabs. Friday is crab day in our cafeteria."

Terrell laughed. "I promise to keep your secret."

"If you come to Harvard," Amaker said, "I'll take your labs for you."

"How about Latin?" Terrell said.

"Can't help you there," Amaker said. "I struggled with English in college. Some people thought I should claim it as part of my foreign language requirement."

He shook Terrell's hand, patted him on the back, and said, "Seriously, Terrell, good luck. You listen to Coach Wilcox and Mr. Konchalski and you'll be just fine."

He waved and headed off. Terrell sat down. "So, Mr. Konchalski, am I going to be fine? Has Coach Wilcox filled you in?"

"The basic story, yes. But I'd like to hear it from you. Tell me what *you* think your choices are. . . ."

Terrell took a deep breath and began.

* * *

Twenty minutes later, as his teammates were heading for the bus, Terrell stood up and shook hands with Konchalski. "Thanks for listening, sir."

"Terrell," Mr. Konchalski said, "I feel confident that you'll make the right choice."

"I just wish I knew for sure what the right choice is. I think I know, but I'm not a hundred percent sure."

"If you were one hundred percent sure," Konchalski said, "you wouldn't be human."

Danny had lingered near the door to wait for him. "So what do you think?" he asked.

"I think he *is* the only honest man in the gym," Terrell said. "I think I know what I need to do now."

"What is it?"

Terrell smiled. "Make sure we win this game."

Danny rolled his eyes. "Okay, Mr. Mysterious. Just promise me one thing."

"What's that?"

"That after we win tomorrow, you won't make any final decision without telling me first."

"Deal," Terrell said. "By the way, I'm also planning to win Sunday against the team from Connecticut."

"Jeez, I almost forgot about the game with Connecticut," Danny said.

"Well, remember it. We could be playing against our old pal Jay Swanson. His team is in the final down there."

"How do you know that?" Danny asked.

"Mr. Konchalski told me. He said he thinks we'll beat Central but that Norwalk will be tough. He thinks they'll win their championship game for sure."

Danny shrugged. "If we beat Central, I don't care that much what happens against Norwalk."

"You want to lose to Jay Swanson?"

"Okay," Danny conceded. "I care."

Central High's Wilson Walton was an excellent player, but his shooting range didn't go much beyond five feet from the basket. Which explained why he hadn't been in the elite group of recruits along with Terrell, Michael Jordan, Alex Mayer, and Jay Swanson.

Coach Wilcox's strategy to play zone defense worked perfectly. Central's guards kept trying three-point shots, and they kept clanging off the rim. As a team, Central shot five-for-twenty-seven for the game from beyond the arc. Danny was five-for-eight by himself. Plus, Walton had no chance to guard Terrell. He picked up two quick fouls before Central decided to collapse on Terrell every chance it got. Lexington's outside shooters, led by Danny and James Nix, made fourteen of twenty-eight from long range, and that was the difference in the game. Alan Inwood even hit two three-pointers. Lexington led by double digits the entire second half, and the final score was 79–64.

It all felt slightly anticlimactic to Terrell. He had waited a year to play this game again, and he was thrilled to win it, especially considering the fact that a month earlier he had wondered if he'd be playing at all. He loved seeing Coach Wilcox being handed the state championship trophy, and he was very happy to be named MVP. But he kept hearing an old song his mother liked by Peggy Lee in his head: "Is That All There Is?"

He found he was happy to have one more game to play the next afternoon. Danny had told him that Norwalk had also won, so they would get to face Swanson one more time. If Tom Konchalski's assessment of Jay's team was right, then the buzz Terrell wanted from a down-to-the-wire final high school game could still happen.

There was just one issue: All the super friends *and* his mom had decided that the state championship game was the big one. They'd planned a party for that night.

"You're coming," he told Danny in the locker room. "You *and* Laurie."

"No way," Danny said. "You do not want me there with those people."

"Come on, man, you have to protect me. They're going to try to convince me to sign."

"*Tonight?*"

"Yes! They didn't all come to Boston for the weekend to cheer me on. And tomorrow after the game, we're all going home. This is it for them. I know it."

Danny sighed. "Okay, we'll come. But I'm bringing one more person with me too."

"Who?"

"Bobby Kelleher. If they want to make some kind of move, let them do it in front of a reporter."

Terrell smiled. "Tell him to bring a notebook," he said.

"I'm going to tell him," Danny said, "to bring a tape recorder."

THIRTY-THREE

Danny and Terrell were both greeted with huge hugs of congratulations from Valerie and Laurie back at the Marriott Long Wharf. Valerie made a big deal about looking at Terrell's MVP trophy. "This is something you'll keep forever," she said. "You should be proud. You should both be proud."

Danny knew she was trying to keep Terrell from worrying too much about what was to come that night. He had pulled Laurie aside to tell her that their plans to go to dinner at Legal Seafood had to be put on hold. "I have to do this for Terrell," he said. "He thinks it's going to be a rough night."

Laurie nodded. "So does Valerie," she said. "I understand."

They settled for a private walk to the end of Long Wharf, where they sat looking out at the harbor for a while. But Terrell's dilemma followed them.

"What do you think Terrell will do?" Laurie asked. "I mean, it's *so* much money, and the way Valerie explains it, the risks are low."

"Yeah, but think what he's risking. If he's caught while he's playing in college, he'd lose his eligibility. If he's caught after that . . . You think having your reputation ruined wouldn't hurt?" Danny said. "Some people wouldn't care, but I think Terrell would." He leaned forward and looked her in the eye. "Valerie doesn't think he should do it, does she?"

Laurie looked straight down at the ground.

"Laurie?"

"No, she *doesn't* think he should do it," she said. "But she wants him to decide for himself. She's afraid that if she tells him not to do it, and then he doesn't because of her and something goes wrong, that it could affect their long-term relationship."

"They're eighteen," Danny said. "No one should be thinking about a long-term relationship at eighteen."

"Really?" she said sharply, and Danny realized he'd made a mistake.

"Well, you know what I mean," he said. "You kind of go one step at a time. See where life takes you. So much will change during college, right?"

She was looking out at the water, and Danny couldn't tell if her eyes were glistening because of the wind or for another reason. "Uh-huh," she said. "Sure. That makes sense. Let's go back inside. I'm getting cold."

So was Danny, and it had nothing to do with the wind. He sighed. It was going to be a long night.

"Terrell, I thought you understood this was . . . well, family only."

Danny wasn't stunned by Barrett Stephenson's greeting when he, Laurie, Terrell, and Valerie walked in the door of the hotel suite that someone—Terrell wasn't sure who—had rented for the evening. Terrell had texted him shortly after he and Laurie had walked back into the hotel and said that he had "issues" and could he *please* hold Bobby Kelleher off—at least for a while. Danny had called Kelleher and suggested he show up closer to eight.

"I was going to come late anyway," Kelleher said. "You guys walk in with me in tow, no one is going to be happy."

Still, even though Danny hadn't expected anyone blowing kisses when he walked in, he was a little bit surprised that Coach Stephenson was so blunt so fast.

Terrell was not only prepared but appeared to be ready to dig in for a fight. "'Family only'?" he said. "I see a lot of people here I don't even like very much. . . . Danny's like a brother to me—you know that. He can leave if you want, but I'll be leaving with him."

"Terrell, take it easy," Valerie said. "We're here to have a good time tonight, remember?"

Stephenson recovered quickly. "Danny, I'm sorry," he said. "We just didn't expect you. Thought you'd be with your dad tonight. Come on in—of course. You too, Laurie. We're thrilled to have you here with us."

Danny resisted the urge to say anything. As Terrell and Valerie headed for Mrs. Jamerson, he took Laurie's arm and steered her in the direction of a bar set up in the corner of the room.

"Danny, we have to go say hello," Laurie hissed.

"I know," he said. "I just need a minute. I have to get the lay of the land—or the people. We'll get drinks for Terrell and Valerie and bring them with us so we don't look rude."

She didn't argue. They ordered three Cokes and a Sprite. While the bartender was pouring, Danny looked around the room. The gang was all here: Stan Montana from Athena and David Forcier the money manager were standing on either side of Mrs. Jamerson, with Paul Judson just off her shoulder. Creepy Donald Johnston the Third was right next to him. Hitchcock, the guy who had "accidentally" run into Danny and Terrell on the flight to Atlanta, was a few feet away, with someone else in a suit. Billy Tommasino was there, and so was Ray Leach—whom they hadn't seen since the summer. Everyone, Danny noticed, was in a suit. The dudes were there too. Maurice had apparently worked his way in this far. He and the others were hanging around the buffet table. Chao, he noticed, was wearing a sports coat but with his "Yao Rules" T-shirt underneath. Danny couldn't help but smile.

There were also a couple of older men whom Danny didn't recognize. One wore a black suit with a garish red tie and a red shirt. When he hugged both Terrell and Valerie, Danny guessed he was the obnoxious university president Terrell had told him about.

"They've brought out all the big guns," Danny whispered as they picked up their drinks.

"They look kind of scary," Laurie said.

Danny nodded. "See the guy in the black and the red? I'm betting that's the president of the University of Atlanta."

"Who's the other old guy?"

"The Mass State president?" Danny said. "Let's go over and find out."

They walked in the direction of the circle of people surrounding Terrell, Valerie, and Terrell's mom. Several of them looked in their direction but said nothing. It was Mrs. Jamerson who finally acknowledged their presence. "Danny!" she said. "Oh, sweetheart, I'm so glad you came."

She put out her arms so Danny could lean down and give her a hug. She did the same for Laurie and then introduced them to the crowd. The guy in black and red was, indeed, Dr. Wayne Haskell, the president of the University of Atlanta. He politely introduced Danny and Laurie to "my competition, the honorable Dr. James McPherson, Mass State University." The two presidents were also the only ones who made any attempt to talk to Danny and Laurie.

"Well, I can see you boys certainly have excellent taste in girls," Haskell said, looking Laurie up and down in a way that made Danny want to slug him. "Young lady, you're so pretty, you'd fit right in on our campus."

"Ours too," McPherson quickly put in.

"Gee, too bad it's too late to apply," said Laurie with a fake smile. "I guess I'll have to go to a school that likes me for my GPA."

Haskell raised an eyebrow. "Beauty *and* brains. Formidable. Good luck, Mr. Wilcox—I suspect you'll need it."

Danny didn't know what to say, but that was fine, Laurie seemed to be on a roll.

"Oh, Danny doesn't need luck. He's got brains and *talent*." Laurie slipped her arm through his. "He's on his way to Harvard."

"Ah, Harvard," Haskell said without missing a beat. "The U of A of the Northeast." He turned his back on them without waiting for a response.

McPherson coughed, smiled, and followed Haskell as if he needed looking after.

Danny looked at Laurie with fresh eyes. "Wow. That was—"

"—rude," finished Laurie. "But really satisfying." She smiled sheepishly and squeezed his arm. "You're a bad influence on me."

Danny laughed. But then he got serious again. "So, you still want Terrell to throw in with these guys?" Danny asked. "You think all the money in the world would make it worth it?"

"He'll never see either of those guys again after tonight," Laurie said.

"I certainly hope you're right about that," Danny said.

He looked around for Terrell, but he was gone. So was his mom. Stan Montana, Judson, and Hitchcock were also missing. Billy Tommasino was talking to Valerie, but Danny thought he had a pained look on his face.

"Where did Terrell go?" Danny asked Valerie, pulling her away from Tommasino.

"Into the bedroom," Valerie said. "Danny, you have to give him some space. He has to figure this out himself."

"Do you think he will?" Danny asked.

"I have faith in him," she said. But she didn't sound as sure as Danny would have liked.

"Well . . . It's time to make some decisions, yes?" Paul Judson said. "We've all been dancing around this for eight months."

It was clear to Terrell that this was Judson's meeting—though *why* wasn't quite so clear. Judson was standing by the window, which had a panoramic view of Boston Harbor. The suite's bedroom was large enough to hold a table and chairs, and there was a comfortable armchair where Barrett Stephenson had guided his mom. Terrell sat at the table. Everyone else—Coach Stephenson, Stan Montana, Glenn Hitchcock, and Donald Johnston the Third—was standing. Apparently, college presidents didn't attend meetings like this one.

"Mrs. Jamerson—and Terrell—the men in this room, along with whichever coach you choose, will be your team for, we hope, a long, long time. You both know I have a working relationship with Billy Tommasino, but right now I'm here just for you—a neutral party to help guide you. You really have two decisions to make here: Which college you want to play for and which sneaker company you would like to represent. I won't come into the picture officially until later."

"So you don't put yourself at risk," Terrell heard his mom say.

Judson smiled at her, said nothing in response, and went on. "We actually did a coin flip before you got here, and it was determined that Atlanta and Athena would have the first shot," he said. "After I present everything to you with Stan and Glenn here, they'll leave and Billy Tommasino and David Forcier will come in. Obviously, if you choose Athena, that will mean Atlanta. If you choose Brickley, it will be Mass State."

"What if I choose neither?" Terrell said, feeling queasy at the thought of going into business with any of the men in the room.

Judson smiled and looked directly at Terrell's mom. "Our job in the next few minutes is to make you understand why you would be making a big mistake by not choosing one or the other. We'll explain how all of us are going to change your life for the better in a lot of ways. Mrs. Jamerson, any questions before I begin?"

"Not at the moment," Mrs. Jamerson said.

Even in four words Terrell could tell by his mother's tone that she was not a big fan of Paul Judson.

Bobby Kelleher's information would prove stunningly accurate—his numbers were almost identical to those that Judson now laid out. He'd been missing only the exact figures for certain performance bonuses. And another thing Bobby hadn't mentioned: an insurance policy that would be taken out for Terrell in case of injury, which, according to

Judson, was actually not against NCAA rules. Terrell could see his mother's eyes widen as Judson, reading from a piece of paper and occasionally pausing to double-check a figure with Montana, Hitchcock, or Johnston the Third, plowed ahead. He finished with a flourish by saying that making a commitment tonight could mean ten million dollars to Terrell within a year. Plus the house for his mom, plus a car, which could be bought, with the insurance policy serving as collateral. Later, both would be paid off by Athena in full.

Terrell took a deep breath. His mom was looking right at Judson.

"Other than the insurance policy, which you made a point of saying isn't against the rules, is anything you've mentioned *within* the rules?" she asked.

"Technically speaking," Judson said. "No."

"Which means, in English, no—right, Mr. Judson?"

"Mrs. Jamerson, we could get into a philosophical discussion here on the validity of NCAA rules," Judson said. "We don't think they are designed to protect the student-athlete."

"Student?" Terrell said. "I haven't heard much about me being a student."

Barrett Stephenson, who had said nothing until that point, jumped in. "Terrell, there's nothing being discussed here that says you *can't* be a student." He was speaking to Terrell but, like Judson, looking mostly at Terrell's mom.

"We should hear the other offer," Mrs. Jamerson said.

Hitchcock and Montana, who was far less cocky than he

had been in the past, quietly left the room. A moment later, Billy Tommasino and David Forcier entered.

Judson ran through all the specifics of the second offer. There were two key differences in the Brickley/Mass State offer: Mike Todd did not, at that moment anyway, have a coaching spot open for Barrett Stephenson. And, because of Brickley policy, a lot more of the money being offered was tied to performance.

"This is what we call an offer that's on the come, Terrell," Judson explained. "If you play as well as we think you can, you'll make more money ultimately with Brickley. On the other hand, there's more up-front money and more guaranteed money with Athena."

"Either way, you'll be involved in the deal, though—right?" Terrell asked.

Judson smiled his smarmy smile. "Yes, Terrell, that's right."

There was an awkward silence.

"Okay, then," Melinda Jamerson said. "Gentlemen, could we please have the room for a few minutes?"

"Of course," Judson said.

"And leave us those papers, if you would."

Everyone headed for the door—except for Barrett Stephenson. Terrell's mom looked at him. "Barrett, excuse us, please."

"But, Melinda . . ."

"My son and I will talk about this alone," she said firmly.

Seeing the look on her face, Coach Stephenson turned and left.

When the door closed, Terrell's mom looked at him and said, "So . . . door number one, door number two, or door number three?"

When Danny saw the last of the super friends finally come out of the bedroom, he breathed a sigh of relief. He was standing with Laurie and Valerie, and the glares from all of the various super friends' minions were beginning to make him wonder if he had forgotten to zip his fly. At one point, just to be sure, he checked. Maybe it was his imagination. . . .

"Why are they all looking at you like that?" Laurie asked—which was a relief, since it meant he wasn't being paranoid, they all really *did* hate him.

"I don't know," he said. "But where are Terrell and Mrs. Jamerson?"

Neither had emerged.

"You need to be patient. Do *not* go in there."

But Danny couldn't stand still. He ducked out into the hallway to call Kelleher. Where the hell was he? He wasn't answering his phone, and Danny ended up leaving a rambling message about the closed-door meetings and the glaring presidents and how Kelleher had to get here soon or it was all going to be over.

But really Danny knew—it was over already.

THIRTY-FOUR

Danny walked back into the room and saw that Terrell and his mom were standing in the corner talking to Laurie and Valerie.

"I was coming to find you, man," Terrell said. "I need to talk to you."

"Terrell, can't this wait?" said Montana, who had followed Danny back into the room.

"No," Terrell said coldly. "It can't." He spun on his heel and walked back in the direction of the bedroom.

Danny followed. He shut the door behind him and looked at Terrell, who sat in a chair next to the bed as if someone had put a 200-pound weight on top of him. Danny's heart sank.

"Listen, before I go back out there, I owe you this," Terrell said.

"Terrell, you don't owe me anything," Danny said. "You don't owe *anyone* anything."

Terrell shook his head. "You're wrong," he said. "I owe my mom. She's sacrificed a lot to get me to this point. She worked two jobs and put herself through school to become a teacher, so that we could have a better life. Now I have a chance to give *her* a better life. Even if something goes wrong—if I get hurt or even if I get caught by the NCAA or someone—she'll have a house and a lot of money. We've never owned a house."

"But what about you?"

"If I get hurt, there's insurance," he said. "Kelleher missed that—they're going to take out *insurance* on me. If I stay healthy, even if the NCAA comes after me, I'll end up in the NBA if I'm good enough."

For a moment, Danny couldn't think of anything to say. "So your mom wants you to do this?" he asked finally. "Did Stephenson convince her?"

Terrell shook his head. "No, he didn't. I talked her into it. She's against it." He smiled. "She said I should go to Harvard with you."

Danny wanted to smile but couldn't. "But she's going to go along?"

"I told her I was doing it. That I knew what I was doing and knew all the reasons not to, but that I still wanted to go ahead. Danny, the concussion scared the hell out of me. And you know as well as I do this isn't a good versus evil decision. It's a dirty game. . . ."

"But *you* get dirty this way. You don't have to."

There was a knock at the door.

"I'll be out in a few minutes," Terrell called.

Danny heard Coach Stephenson's voice. "Terrell, everyone's waiting for you."

"*Yeah, I know,*" Terrell said.

They stared out the window for a moment. The view was spectacular, but neither saw it at all.

"Listen, Danny, I know what you think of all those guys," Terrell said. "I pretty much agree."

"No, you don't," Danny interrupted. "If you did, you couldn't possibly do this. Terrell, you're nothing but a human ATM to those guys."

"You can see it that way. Or you could say they're *my* ATM. Millions, Danny. We're talking *many* millions."

"I know," Danny said softly. "But you're worth more."

Terrell just snorted.

After a pause, Danny said, "So? Atlanta or Mass State?"

"Atlanta. They offered more. If I'm gonna do this, might as well get the most guaranteed money out of it." He looked at Danny. "You gonna stick around?"

Danny shook his head. "You've made your decision," he said. "I can't stop you, but I'm not going to stand there and pretend I support it."

Terrell nodded and stood up. "Understood," he said. "I hope we're still friends."

Danny paused. He actually wasn't sure. But he knew one thing. "I gotta go."

Watching Danny leave, Terrell felt sick to his stomach. He took a deep breath, gathered himself, and walked back into the big room.

Barrett Stephenson was standing by the door. If Danny's

exit had bothered him, he didn't show it. "You ready, Terrell?" he asked.

Terrell looked at Valerie and his mom. Danny was gone, and so was Laurie. His mom had agreed to fill Valerie in while he was talking to Danny. He wondered if she would say something, but she didn't. Neither did his mom. "I guess so," he said. "Ready as I'm ever going to be."

Coach Stephenson led him to the center of the room. "Everyone, can I have your attention, please?" he said, raising his voice.

The room quieted.

"Thank you all for coming tonight. I want to thank Stan Montana and the folks at Athena for being our sponsors for this celebration." He nodded at Montana and held his glass up while everyone clapped. "I know we all want to congratulate Terrell and the rest of the Minutemen for winning Lexington's first state title in boys' basketball!"

More applause.

"But now"—he paused—"for the moment you've all been waiting for . . ."

Everyone laughed.

He put his arm around Terrell. "Terrell and his mom and everyone who cares about him—and I think it's fair to say that includes everyone in this room—have been through quite a process in the last year. He's had to make some very difficult decisions, and he's very lucky to have had the support group around him that he's had. Terrell, I'm very proud of you. And, Melinda, I'm very proud of you too. I know the most important thing to you is taking care of your family, and you've done that tonight."

Lots of applause now from all the "friends."

Terrell's knees were feeling weak.

"Now I'll let Terrell tell you all where he's going to college next year. . . . Terrell, the floor, just like when you play basketball, is all yours."

Terrell would have been a lot happier if he'd been on a basketball floor at that moment. Everyone was clapping. He actually felt a little bit light-headed. "Thanks, Coach," he said. "Thank you, everyone. Thank you for this party." He paused and took a deep breath. "I'd like to tell you where I'm going to go to college."

He saw Dr. Haskell starting to move to the front of the room. He noticed he was carrying something in his hands. He knew almost instantly what it was: a University of Atlanta basketball jersey. He would bet a million dollars it had his name on it. For a split second, he almost laughed. *Heck,* he thought, *I don't need to bet a million dollars, I've got a million dollars—and a lot more.*

He looked at his mom, and he looked at Valerie.

They were both staring at the floor.

"I'd like to tell you where I'm going . . . ," he repeated. He stopped, took one more look around the room, and shut his eyes.

"But I can't."

When he opened his eyes again, everyone was staring at him, jaws dangling.

He went over to his mom and kissed her on the cheek. Then he kissed Valerie. "I'm sorry," he said to the two of them. "I've gotta go."

Then he fled.

Danny was sitting at the end of Long Wharf in the rain, barely noticing that he was slowly getting soaked.

He had his phone in his hand, so he almost jumped when it started vibrating. It was Bobby Kelleher. He knew he should answer, but he wasn't ready to tell him what had happened. After all, if he told Kelleher, he could jeopardize Terrell's future. Then again, it was *Terrell* who was jeopardizing his future.

The phone buzzed again. He sighed and started to turn it off, but when he glanced at the number, he saw it wasn't Kelleher—it was Terrell. For a split second, he thought about not picking up. He didn't want to deal with a plea to come back to the party. But his curiosity was greater than his anger. So he answered. "What's up?" he asked, trying to sound cool.

"Where are you?" Terrell sounded breathless.

"What do you mean? Why?"

"Just tell me where you are, damn it!"

That got Danny's attention.

"I'm at the end of the wharf by our hotel." After leaving the party, Danny had told Laurie he wanted some time alone. She argued briefly, but he insisted, pointing out she would get her dress and her hair wet in the rain.

"Stay there," Terrell said now. "I'll be there in about two minutes."

Danny didn't know what to think. The rain slackened, but it didn't matter because he was already drenched. A moment later he saw a lone figure coming in his direction, half walking, half running. Clearly, it was Terrell—no one else was that tall.

"What are you doing here?" Danny asked as Terrell pulled up, just a little bit winded. "Where are your mom and Valerie?"

Terrell waved a hand. "I couldn't do it," he said. "I looked at all those people—that horrible president and all those sleazy guys, who, it suddenly struck me, I would be so happy never to see again. I don't want to be owned and operated by anyone. I just ran. . . ."

"Oh my god! That's great! Beyond great! But . . . oh—what about your mom and Valerie?"

"Told them I'd see them later," he said. "I doubt either one of them will be upset with me—except for leaving them with those creeps."

"Huh," said Danny. "I might be pretty mad about that."

"Yeah." Terrell shook his head, but he looked happy.

"Why are you smiling?"

Terrell pulled a sheaf of papers from his pocket. "Valerie might be irked that I left without her, but Bobby Kelleher is going to love me for what I *didn't* leave behind. . . ."

* * *

The state champs from Connecticut and Massachusetts were on the court warming up the next morning. The interstate matchup had a noon start because the Celtics were playing at six that evening.

Danny noticed Terrell and Jay Swanson talking intently at midcourt. He had no idea what they were talking about but figured it had something to do with college. Swanson hadn't announced his college choice, either.

Danny and Swanson had actually exchanged hugs when they spotted each other on the court a few minutes earlier. They'd come a long way since Danny had thrown the ball in Swanson's face in New Jersey.

Now he went over to join them. "I guess we should try to get fired up for this game. But the idea of being New England champions . . ."

"I know." Swanson laughed. "And let's not forget, it's the 'Brickley New England Championship.'"

"They can call it whatever they want," Terrell said. "It's our last high school game. We should enjoy it."

Enjoy it they did. The game was played for three quarters almost like an all-star game. No one played much defense, and everyone shot the ball when they felt like it. In the huddles, Danny's dad was as detailed as ever, but the intensity wasn't there. The trophy he wanted was already sitting on the bus for the trip home to Lexington.

It wasn't until the last few minutes that everyone's competitive juices kicked in. Terrell and Swanson had both been putting on a show all day, and in the last two minutes they each drilled a pair of threes. Swanson made the last one with fourteen seconds left to give Norwalk a 95–94 lead. The score alone told you how much defense had been played.

Coach Wilcox called time to set up a last play.

"Let's run our four-down play and let Terrell go one-on-one with Swanson," he said. "I promise you, Terrell, they won't double you unless you go into the lane. I'd just run the clock down and make your move." He looked up at the scoreboard, which showed point totals for each player in the game. "You've got thirty-nine already," he said. "Finish with forty-one or forty-two and let's go home."

Danny liked that idea. He was relieved the teams were only one point apart, because he didn't want overtime. He was exhausted, drained physically and mentally. He was ready to go home. He was more than happy to take his chances with Terrell going one-on-one with Swanson.

They came out of the huddle, and Terrell gave everyone a pat on the back. "I've got it, pal," he said to Danny. Then he walked over to James Nix and whispered something to him—no doubt the same thing.

Terrell inbounded the ball to Danny at midcourt, and Danny immediately flipped it back to him and ran to the baseline. The clock was at ten seconds as Terrell dribbled outside the key, with Swanson giving him a little bit of space to keep him from driving. Everyone else was below the free throw line, so the two superstars could face each other alone.

With five seconds left, Terrell started his move. He

dribbled hard to his left, crossed over to his right, and began to leave his feet with Swanson scrambling to get back to get a hand up. Danny was transfixed, not moving, when he noticed James Nix sprinting to the far corner. The clock was at two seconds as Terrell left his feet. Danny could feel the crowd noise ratchet up as he went into the air, leaping so high that there was no way Swanson had any chance to get near the shot.

Only he didn't shoot. Instead, without even looking in that direction, he flicked a pass to Nix, who was wide open on the baseline. No one on the court—or in the building, for that matter—had been paying any attention to him. Nix caught the pass in full flight, heading directly at the basket. He took one dribble for balance and was in the air as Danny saw the clock go to :01. He hung up there, way above every-one else for a split second, before slamming the ball through the hoop. The ball hit the floor just as the buzzer sounded.

James had his arms in the air and leaped into Terrell's waiting hug as the building, which was about half full with a crowd of roughly ten thousand, exploded. Stunned but thrilled, Danny joined the celebration along with the rest of the Lexington players. "What happened?" he said when he got to Terrell.

"I knew James would be wide open," Terrell said. "I told him to run base-decoy—with me as the decoy—and be ready." He grinned. "Time to pass the torch, old man. We're moving on."

Danny barely heard the last words because they were sur-rounded by revelers. He found his dad for a hug.

"Couldn't be more proud of all of you," his dad said. "I'll never top this season."

"You never know, Dad," Danny said. "But this *was* fun."

"Are you ready to announce where you're going to college?" his dad asked, surprising him. "Terrell wants to do it right now—in the postgame press conference."

"Really?" Danny said.

"Really," his father answered.

"Sure," Danny said. "I thought we were going to wait. But that's fine."

"You haven't changed your mind, have you?" his dad said.

"Absolutely not."

"Good. Then let's go do it."

Terrell, James, and Coach Wilcox all had to do postgame TV interviews. So did Jay Swanson, who had scored 47 points in a losing effort. Then the Brickley Cup had to be presented to Lexington as New England basketball champions. As a result, it was a good twenty-five minutes after the game had ended before Terrell, Danny, James, and Coach Wilcox walked onto the podium in the curtained-off area under the stands that had been used as the interview area all weekend.

Danny noticed the place was packed. He knew that Connecticut had a lot of small and mid-size newspapers that covered high school basketball, but he was surprised by the number of TV cameras in the room. They were everywhere. As if reading his mind, his dad leaned over and said, "Terrell told me before the game he wanted to announce his decision today. I had some of our people from school make calls to the media while the game was going on. I figured they should hear this."

That was very unlike his father. He'd never been a publicity seeker. Maybe he thought that was what Terrell would want? To make a really public statement, so there'd be no going back? Terrell hadn't told Danny what he'd decided, but he assumed it would be Duke—the place Terrell had wanted to go before everything went crazy.

They were asked some questions about the game and about the last play. James handled it beautifully. "Any one of the four of us out there with Terrell could have made the play," he said. "Terrell just chose me, I guess, because I'm the tallest. Or the youngest. I'm not sure which, but I'm happy either way. It won't be easy next year without him and without Danny. I'm going to miss them."

"Not as much as I will," Coach Wilcox said, drawing a laugh.

He then asked if there were any more questions about the game. There was silence.

"Okay, then," he said. "James, thanks. Go get a hot shower."

James departed the podium, but instead of leaving, he went and stood in the back of the room. Much to Danny's surprise, Jay Swanson stepped up and took James's seat on the podium. He was already in his street clothes for the ride back to Norwalk.

"Folks, I asked Jay if he'd like to join us because I know there are a lot of people who want to know where all three of these young men are going to college, and they're all ready to make their decisions public," Danny's dad was saying. "Let me just say that I'm really proud of my son, Danny, for becoming the player he's become, and I'm proud of all three of these guys for being the people that they are. I was lucky to get to coach Danny all his life; Terrell, the last two years; and Jay, last summer. Now, I'll shut up so the boys can tell you what they're going to do. . . . Danny, why don't you go first?"

Danny looked at his dad and nodded. He suddenly felt very nervous though he wasn't sure why. "Dad," he said. "I want you to know I've made this decision because this is where *I* want to go to college. I'm just very glad it's also where *you* want me to go to college. With Coach Amaker's approval, I'm going to enroll in the fall at Harvard."

Applause broke out in the back of the room. Friends and family had apparently been let in, and there was a lot of whooping. Danny could now see all of his teammates were standing in the back along with James Nix. He looked at his dad and saw that he was tearing up a little bit, and his voice was just a tad quavery when he said, "Thank you, Danny. . . . Jay, your turn."

"Thanks, Coach," Jay said. "And let me say it was an honor to play for you this summer. We all got off to a rocky start, but I've learned a lot the last few months about good people and bad people and who your real friends are in life.

I'm very fortunate that, because I'm a decent ballplayer and a decent student, I had a lot of choices. I can't think of anything I'd enjoy more than being Danny's teammate again. So I'm going to Harvard too."

This time the response was applause and gasps. One of those gasping was Danny. He looked down the podium at Swanson. "Are you serious?" he said, leaning back from the mike.

"As a Terrell Jamerson dunk," Jay said, grinning.

"Somewhere Tommy Amaker is picking himself off the floor right now," Danny's dad said. He had a bright-as-the-sun smile on his face. So did Jay.

"Finally," Coach Wilcox said, "the announcement the entire country has been waiting for all winter . . . Terrell?"

Terrell was laughing. "Easiest decision I've ever made," he said.

Danny could sense a hush fall over the room.

"I'm not leaving my point guard," he said. "Harvard."

The place exploded. People were shouting questions all at once. Terrell sat back with his arms folded, looking happier than Danny had ever seen him. Danny jumped from his seat and ran to Terrell. "Seriously?" he said. "You're not joking?"

"I called Coach Amaker this morning to make sure it was okay and that I could still apply this late. He said it was *very* okay."

"And that's what you were talking to Jay about before the game?"

Jay was now standing too. "Yup," he said. "Didn't take much convincing to tell you the truth. I mean, Harvard with you two guys? We'll make history!"

They answered questions for another fifteen minutes. Terrell explained that after everything he'd gone through in recruiting he knew he wanted to go to college for four years—the NBA and all those pressures could wait. He wanted to stay close to home. He loved the idea of playing with Danny, and adding Jay was a huge bonus. He thought Coach Amaker would be great to play for. Plus, he added with a blush, his girlfriend was going to Harvard. . . . He didn't want to let a smart girl like that get away.

At that, all the photographers turned around and found Valerie in the crowd. Flashguns went off. She wasn't someone who liked attention, but she looked so thrilled with Terrell's decision that Danny figured she'd forgive him.

When they were finally finished, they walked outside the curtains and Mrs. Jamerson, Valerie, and Laurie were all there, laughing and wiping away tears.

"Terrell," Mrs. Jamerson said as she hugged her son. "I'm so proud of you. I'm *so* glad you changed your mind."

"Thank Danny and Coach Wilcox," Terrell said. "It couldn't have happened without them."

"Don't forget him," Coach Wilcox said, nodding at Tom Konchalski, who was standing a few feet away.

"There's one other person to thank," Danny said, nodding

in the direction of Bobby Kelleher, who was standing a few feet away from everyone else. "I guess you're going to need to talk to us, aren't you, Bobby?"

"At length," Kelleher said. "But not right now. I've worked on this story for eight months. I can wait another day or two to finish it up."

"There's a lot more to tell," Terrell said. He had called Kelleher the previous night to say he had some documents that might help him out.

"So I've gathered," Kelleher said. "We'll go to Nettie's. I'll buy."

Terrell laughed. "Yeah, you'd better. I'm just a poor student, you know."

Everyone cracked up.

But as Terrell looked around at the friends—true friends—surrounding him, he knew he had everything he needed . . . and then some.

-

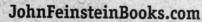